Year's Best Weird Fiction

Volume Two

Year's Best
Weird Fiction

VOLUME TWO

Guest Editor

KATHE KOJA

Series Editor

MICHAEL KELLY

UNDERTOW
PUBLICATIONS

Year's Best Weird Fiction, Vol. 2
copyright © 2015 by Kathe Koja & Michael Kelly

Foreword © 2015 Michael Kelly

Introduction © 2015 Kathe Koja

Cover Art copyright © 2015 Tomasz Alen Kopera

Cover Design copyright © 2015 Vince Haig

Interior design and layout Alligator Tree Graphics

Story credits appear at the end of the volume.

First Edition

All Rights Reserved

ISBN: 978-0-9938951-1-1

Undertow Publications
Pickering, ON Canada

undertowbooks@gmail.com / www.undertowbooks.com

CONTENTS

MICHAEL KELLY

Foreword

Welcome to the second volume of the *Year's Best Weird Fiction*.

Ah, weird fiction. What is weird fiction? It's a question I am still asked. And if you asked a dozen proponents of The Weird that same question, you'd likely get a dozen different responses. I'll not rehash what I said in my Foreword to last year's inaugural volume—I implore you to seek out the book—but I'll just note that to me weird fiction is speculative and often (but not always) works to subvert the Laws of Nature. More than any other mode or stream or genre of fiction, The Weird is a feeling. A kind of continuous distortion of ambient space. So, weird tales can be comprised of elements of science fiction, fantasy, and horror, but can also occupy those more sensate liminal areas. Hence, it is a diverse mode of literature that can claim work by Sheridan Le Fanu, Julio Cortázar (who is represented in this volume), Shirley Jackson, Kelly Link, and many more. In fact, this second volume of the Year's Best Weird Fiction is proof of the diversity and breadth of the weird tale. Expertly curated by Kathe Koja, this volume is vastly different than Laird Barron's excellent inaugural edition. Both volumes are, in my estimation, brilliant. Each has a unique flavour; a distinct voice. That, of course, is the idea.

The worldwide literary antecedents of the weird tale date as far back as 8th Century BC Greece (*The Iliad*), 1st Century AD Roman Empire (*The Golden Ass*), 3rd Century India (*Panchtantra*) through 10th Century Japan (*The Tale of the Bamboo Cutter*), to modern United Kingdom (*The Cicerones*).

Recently, Faber & Faber have reissued the work of Robert Aickman, and Tartarus Press has released *The Strangers and Other Writings*, featuring new short stories by Aickman. As well, my own imprint, Undertow Publications, published *Aickman's Heirs*, a tribute anthology to the master of the strange, weird tale. These publications, along with publication of the *Year's Best Weird Fiction*, *The New Weird*, and others, has rekindled interest in the strange tale and weird fiction. Some are calling it a Weird Renaissance. But, truthfully, the Weird tale didn't go anywhere. So, call it that if you must, but I won't. I find that once you name something and compartmentalize and categorize it, you rob it of its influence. And you make it exclusionary. Remember the New Wave? We want to be inclusive. It's weird fiction. It's here to stay.

I read a lot of fiction for this year's volume—about 2,800 stories. In what I thought was a unique opportunity, I sent out a call for submissions and invited writers to personally submit to the project. About half the submissions came in this way. Some of those writers then accused me of not reading their submissions, which is patently false. I read everything. Why wouldn't I? I did not want to leave a stone unturned. Then I heard grumblings about how our selections were too SF, as if weird fiction is consigned to one narrow genre. It amounts to sour grapes. And I address it hear to make the point that this volume, with a policy of rotating guest editors, is going to feel refreshingly different each year. Part of the excitement comes from comparing and contrasting each year's volume.

And we have a great volume for you this year. There is an impressive, eclectic, and diverse range of authors, voices, themes, style, etc. When I conceived the idea of rotating guest editors, Kathe Koja was at the forefront of my list. I love Kathe's fiction. It's sharp, incisive, and intense—just like Kathe. I knew she'd make a terrific guest editor, and I wasn't wrong. She has put together a simply stunning collection of weird works. I am very grateful to her. She is the epitome of a professional. Herewith, my sincere thanks to Kathe for agreeing to edit this volume. Thank you for your patience.

The stories that make up this volume were culled from submissions directly from writers, anthologies, and magazines (both print and online). In fact, 60 percent of our choices were from online venues. Thank you to all the writers, editors, and publishers who sent in material.

Having put together the first two volumes in this series, and currently working on the third, I am disappointed that the European publishers mostly ignore my queries for material. It's a particularly time-consuming and maddening endeavour. There is undoubtedly much good fiction that I am not seeing. It may be that it is just a by-product of being the new kid on the block; that we haven't yet established ourselves. I do hope that these publishers will come around.

Volume 3 of the *Year's Best Weird Fiction* will be guest edited by Simon Strantzas. We are both busily assembling that volume. It'll no doubt be another fresh take on the state of weird fiction

As always, I am happy to listen to your recommendations, questions, complaints, and even the odd word of encouragement. We cannot do this without you.

Stay weird!

—Michael Kelly
Pickering, Canada
August 16, 2015

KATHE KOJA

At Home With the Weird

THE TOWN OF RIDDLE HAS LIVED IN MY MIND EVER SINCE I glimpsed it, an outskirt utopia conjured by Todd Haynes' Dylan (Dylanish? Dylanesque?) film *I'm Not There*: sepia streets of stilt-walkers and costumed townsfolk, where a giraffe grazes like a horse; and in reference to which (is it?) another version of Dylan opines: "All these songs about roses growing out of people's brains and lovers who are really geese and swans that turn into angels...mystery is a traditional fact...it's too unreal to die."

The first time I saw Riddle, I thought: *That's where I'm from.*

But you and I and all of us—we're all from Riddle, really. We all know that there's more to this world than what our senses combined can convey, though we use those hard-working senses (including the less-documented but no less real "sixth" sense, proprioception) to daily investigate our outer and inner geographies, and decide from the information we take in whether a thing is actual or not, able to give pleasure or cause danger, something to welcome, to flee or to watch.

So let's call the sense of the strange our seventh sense: that deep compass of the mysterious and "unreal," of, yes, the weird, formidably deployed by some of us—like the writers collected in this book—and by others as a corner-of-the-eye sense, a swift breathing-in, a light from nowhere that startles and sparks. Still others are too afraid ever to acknowledge, let alone directly exercise, that sense, because to do so would be to admit, what? That nothing is weird because everything—the sum total of all that inhabits space and all we think we see—already is? And we are, too?

Because if Riddle is where we really live and who we really are, then—What would *you* do, if you were weird? How would it cause you to act, what would you want, who would you run to, or from? If the past is not the past, if the ground beneath your feet were to turn suddenly to yellow velvet, if you peeled back the skin of your own throat and found inside a clean plastic mechanism, if, if, if...You could fall, and keep falling, having lost control (a control you never had to begin with); you could drift on the waves of what the universe really is.

And then what?

Religions have been founded on less. Wars, too.

Editing this book, I read the manuscripts Mike Kelly sent with my own lens of that seventh sense: it was how I made my choices, picked which of the stories were "best." Recognizing the weird, and being able to share that recognition with economy and power, create a living fictive world, requires a complement of skills, so presume those skills as the cost of entry. The stories I received were all well-written; the stories I chose were the ones that spoke most surely and strongly of the truth of the weird, its presence, its power when revealed to unsettle or make an end; or a beginning. An egg, a grenade, a wet, articulate monster—these and others spoke to me in the language of Riddle, and I believed them; I was held in the telling until the telling was through—and afterwards, too.

And what all these stories share, at bedrock, is delight. Even if the news they bring is dark, even if the characters within them struggle or know pain—and lots of them do—still the delight, for this reader certainly, is the same I felt when I saw that meandering giraffe, those grease-painted townsfolk: it's the shock of truth, the confirmation that yes, *this* is the world, this *is* the world, this is *our* world, to be navigated with both eyes open, with hands ready to give and to accept what gifts are offered, to work with the monsters and go where the silence is, to meet ourselves coming and going: to plunge into the strange and find it stranger than we can imagine[†], and find ourselves at home in Riddle, as natives of the weird.

For those to whom this news is emphatically not a delight, all I can say is, Read this book. Not every story all at once; perhaps not even every story. But read it, with one hand on the doorknob if you must, ready to bug out if a mask falls from the ceiling or something winks at you from inside your mirror: read, and let the disquiet you feel be a beautiful symptom of something more beautifully disquieting in process: the way you see has now been altered, and nothing will ever look the same.

For the rest of you, plunge into and enjoy the varied scenarios created by each writer's seventh sense—the participatory energy required of a reader (as opposed to a viewer) makes this method of meeting the weird maybe the most ideal. And if Mike Kelly's and my own process of selection has introduced you to a writer whose voice you'll begin to follow, whose byline you'll seek, then we're well rewarded for all the effort it took (and there was a fearful lot of it, nearly all of it Mike's) to make this book come alive in your hands. Herewith my own thanks to Mike, for inviting me to be part of the process, and to all the writers whose work I met with pleasure, these mapped moments of that shared terrain, its boundaries and contours forever in flux and spin: welcome to Riddle. Welcome home.

[†] "My own suspicion is that the universe is not only queerer than we suppose, but queerer than we *can* suppose."—J.B.S. Haldane

Year's Best
Weird Fiction

Volume Two

NATHAN
BALLINGRUD

The Atlas of Hell

"HE DIDN'T EVEN KNOW HE WAS DEAD. I HAD JUST SHOT this guy in the head and he's still standing there giving me shit. Telling me what a big badass he works for, telling me I'm going to be sorry I was born. You know. Blood pouring down his face. He can't even see anymore, it's in his goddamn eyes. So I look down at the gun in my hand and I'm like, what the fuck, you know? Is this thing working or what? And I'm starting to think maybe this asshole is right, maybe I just stepped into something over my head. I mean, I feel a twinge of real fear. My hair is standing up like a cartoon. So I look at the dude and I say, 'Lay down! You're dead! I shot you!'"

There's a bourbon and ice sitting on the end-table next to him. He takes a sip from it and puts it back down, placing it in its own wet ring. He's very precise about it.

"I guess he just had to be told, because a soon as I say it? Boom. Drops like a fucking tree."

I don't know what he's expecting from me here. My leg is jumping up and down with nerves. I can't make it stop. I open my mouth to say something but a nervous laughs spills out instead.

He looks at me incredulously, and cocks his head. Patrick is a big guy; but not doughy, like me. There's muscle packed beneath all that flesh. He looks like fists of meat sewn together and given a suit of clothes. "Why are you laughing?"

"I don't know, man. I don't know. I thought it was supposed to be a funny story."

"No, you demented fuck. That's not a funny story. What's the matter with you?"

It's pushing midnight, and we're sitting on a coffee-stained couch in a darkened corner of the grubby little bookstore I own in New Orleans, about a block off Magazine Street. My name is Jack Oleander. I keep a small studio apartment overhead, but when Patrick started banging on my door half an hour ago I took him down here instead. I don't want him in my home. That he's here at all is a very bad sign.

The bookstore is called Oleander. I sell used books, for the most part, and I serve a very sparse clientele: mostly students and disaffected youth, their little hearts love-drunk on Kierkegaard or Salinger. That suits me just fine. Most of the books have been sitting on their shelves for years, and I feel like I've fostered a kind of relationship with them. A part of me is sorry whenever one of them leaves the nest.

The bookstore doesn't pay the bills, of course. The books and documents I sell in the back room take care of that. Few people know about the back room, but those that do pay very well indeed. Patrick's boss is one of those people. We parted under strained circumstances a year or so ago. I was never supposed to see him again. His presence here makes me afraid, and fear makes me reckless.

"Well if it's not a funny story, then what kind of story is it? Because we've been drinking here for twenty minutes and you haven't mentioned business even once. If you want to trade war stories it's going to have to wait for another time."

He gives me a sour look and picks up his glass, peering into it as he swirls the ice around. He'd always hated me, and I knew that his presence here pleased him no more than it did me.

"You don't make it easy to be your friend," he says.

"I didn't know we were friends."

The muscles in his jaw clench.

"You're wasting my time, Patrick. I know you're just the muscle, so maybe you don't understand this, but the work I do in the back room takes up a lot of energy. So sleep is valuable to me. You've sat on my couch and drunk my whiskey and burned away almost half an hour beating around the bush. I don't know how much more of this I can take."

He looks at me. He has his work face on now, the one a lot of guys see just before the lights go out. That's good; I want him in work mode. It makes him focus. The trick now, though, is to keep him on the shy side of violence. You have to play these guys like marionettes. I got pretty good at it back in the day.

"You want to watch that," he says. "You want to watch that attitude."

I put my hands out, palms forward. "Hey," I say.

"I come to you in friendship. I come to you in respect."

This is bullshit, but whatever. It's time to settle him down. These guys are such fragile little flowers. "Hey. I'm sorry. Really. I haven't been sleeping much. I'm tired, and it makes me stupid."

"That's a bad trait. So wake up and listen to me. I told you that story for two reasons. One, to stop you from saying dumb shit like you just did. Make you remember who you're dealing with. I can see it didn't work. I can see maybe I was being too subtle."

"Patrick, really. I—"

"If you interrupt me again I will break your right hand. The second reason I told you that story is to let you know that I've seen some crazy things in my life, so when I tell you this new thing scares the shit out of me, maybe you'll listen to what the fuck I'm saying."

He stops there, staring hard at me. After a couple seconds of this, I figure it's okay to talk.

"You have my full attention. This is from Eugene?"

"You know this is from Eugene. Why else would I drag myself over here?"

"Patrick, I wish you'd relax. I'm sorry I mad you mad. You want another drink? Let me pour you another drink."

I can see the rage still coiling in his eyes, and I'm starting to think I pushed him too hard. I'm starting to wonder how fast I can run. But then he settles back onto the couch and a smile settles over his face. It doesn't look natural there. "Jesus, you have a mouth. How does a guy like you get away with having a mouth like that?" He shakes the ice in his glass. "Yeah, go ahead. Pour me another one. Let's smoke a peace pipe."

I pour us both some more. He slugs it back in one deep swallow and holds his glass out for more. I give it to him. He seems to be relaxing.

"All right, okay. There's this guy. Creepy little grifter named Tobias

George. He's one of those little vermin always crawling through the city, getting into shit, fucking up his own life, you don't even notice these guys. You know how it is."

"I do." I also know the name, but I don't tell him that.

"Only reason we know about him at all is because sometimes he'll run a little scheme of his own, kick a percentage back to Eugene, it's all good. Well one day this prick catches a case of ambition. He robs one of Eugene's poker games, makes off with a lot of money. Suicidal. Who knows what got into the guy. Some big dream climbed up his butt and opened him like an umbrella. We go hunting for him but he disappears. We get word he went further south, disappeared into the bayou. Like, not to Port Fourchon or some shit, but literally on a goddamn boat into the swamp. Eugene is pissed, and you know how he is, he jumps and shouts for a few days, but eventually he says fuck it. We're not gonna go wrestle alligators for him. After a while we just figured he died out there. You know."

"But he didn't."

"That he did not. We catch wind of him a few months later. He's in a whole new ballgame. He's selling artifacts pulled from Hell. And he's making a lot of money doing it."

"It's another scam," I say, knowing full well it isn't.

"It's not."

"How do you know?"

"Don't worry about it. We know."

"A guy owes money and won't pay. That sounds more like your thing than mine, Patrick."

"Yeah, don't worry about that either. I got it covered when the time comes. I won't go into the details, 'cause they don't matter, but what it comes down to is Eugene wants his own way into the game. Once this punk is put in the ground, he wants to keep this market alive. We happen to know Tobias has a book that he uses for this set-up. An atlas that tells him how to access this shit. We want it, and we want to know how it works. And that's *your* thing, Jack."

I feel something cold spill through my guts. "That's not the deal we had."

"What can I tell you."

"No. I told…" My throat is dry. My leg is bouncing again. "Eugene told me we were through. He told me that. He's breaking his promise."

"That mouth again." Patrick finishes his drink and stands. "Come on. You can tell him that yourself, see how it goes over."

"Now? It's the middle of the night!"

"Don't worry, you won't be disturbing him. He don't sleep too well lately either."

I've lived here my whole life. Grew up just a regular fat-white-kid schlub, decent parents, a ready-made path to the gray fields of middle-class servitude. But I went off the rails at some point. I was seduced by old books. I wanted to live out my life in a fog of parchment dust and old glue. I apprenticed myself to a bookbinder, a gnarled old Cajun named Rene Aucoin, who turned out to be a fading necromancer with a nice side business refurbishing old grimoires. He found in me an eager student, which eventually led to my tenure as a librarian at the Camouflaged Library at the Ursulines Academy. It was when Eugene and his crew got involved, leading to a bloody confrontation with a death cult obsessed with the Damocles Scroll, that I left the Academy and began my career as a book thief. I worked for Eugene for five years before we had our falling out. When I left, we both knew it was for good.

Eugene has a bar up in Midcity, far away from the t-shirt shops, the fetish dens and goth hangouts of the French Quarter, far away too from the more respectable veneer of the Central Business and the Garden Districts. Midcity is a place where you can do what you want. Patrick drives me up Canal and parks out front. He leads me up the stairs and inside, where the blast of cold air is a relief from a heat which does not relent even at night. A jukebox is playing something stale, and four or five ghostlike figures nest at the bar. They do not turn around as we pass through. Patrick guides me downstairs, to Eugene's office.

Before I even reach the bottom of the stairs, Eugene starts talking to me.

"Hey fat boy! Here comes the fat boy!"

No cover model himself, he comes around his desk with his arms outstretched, what's left of his gray hair combed in long, spindly fingers over the expanse of his scalp. Drink has made a red, doughy wreckage of his face. His chest is sunken in, like something inside has collapsed and he's falling inward. He puts his hands on me in greeting, and I try not to flinch.

"Look at you. Look at you. You look good, Jack."

"So do you, Eugene."

The office is clean, uncluttered. There's a desk and a few padded chairs, a couch on the far wall underneath a huge Michalopoulos painting. Across from the desk is a minibar and a door which leads to the back alley. Mardi Gras masks are arranged behind his desk like a congress of spirits. Eugene is a New Orleans boy right down to his tapping toes, and he buys into every shabby lie the city ever told about itself.

"I hear you got a girl now. What's her name, Locky? Lick-me?"

"Lakshmi." This is already going badly. "Come on, Eugene. Let's not go there."

"Listen to him now. Calling the shots. All independent, all grown up now. Patrick give you any trouble? Sometimes he gets carried away."

Patrick doesn't blink. His role fulfilled, he's become a tree.

"No. No trouble at all. It was like old times."

"Hopefully not too much like old times, huh?" He sits behind his desk, gestures for me to take a seat. Patrick pours a couple of drinks and hands one to each of us, then retreats behind me.

"I guess I'm just trying to figure out what I'm doing here, Eugene. Someone's not paying you. Isn't that what you have guys like him for?"

Eugene settles back, sips from his drink, and studies me. "Let's not play coy, Jack. Okay? Don't pretend you don't already know about Tobias. Don't insult my intelligence."

"I know about Tobias," I say.

"Tell me what you know."

I can't get comfortable in my chair. I feel like there are chains around my chest. I make one last effort. "Eugene. We had a deal."

"Are you having trouble hearing me? Should I raise my voice?"

"He started selling two months ago. He had a rock. It was about the size of a tennis ball but it was heavy as a television set. Everybody thought he was full of shit. They were laughing at him. It sold for a little bit of money. Not much. But somebody out there liked what they saw. Word got around. He sold a two-inch piece of charred bone next. That went for a lot more."

"I bought that bone."

"Oh," I say. "Shit."

"Do you know why?"

"No, Eugene, of course I don't."

"Don't 'of course' me. I don't know what you know and what you don't. You're a slimy piece of filth, Jack. You're a human cockroach. I can't trust you. So don't get smart."

"I'm sorry. I didn't mean it like that."

"He had the nerve to contact me directly. He wanted me to know what he was offering before he put it on the market. Give me first chance. Jack, it's from my son. It's part of a thigh bone from my son."

I can't seem to see straight. The blood has rushed to my head, and I feel dizzy. I clamp my hands on the armrests of the chair so I can feel something solid. "How... how do you know?"

"There's people for that. Don't ask dumb questions. I am very much not in the mood for dumb questions."

"Okay."

"Your thing is books, so that's why you're here. We tracked him to this old shack in the bayou. You're going to get the book."

I feel panic skitter through me. "You want me to go there?"

"Patrick's going with you."

"That's not what I do, Eugene!"

"Bullshit! You're a thief. You do this all the time. Patrick there can barely read a People Magazine without breaking a sweat. You're going."

"Just have Patrick bring it back! You don't need me for this."

Eugene stares at me.

"Come on," I say. "You gave me your word."

I don't even see Patrick coming. His hand is on the back of my neck and he slams my face onto the desk hard enough to crack an ashtray underneath my cheekbone. My glass falls out of my hand and I hear the ice thump onto the carpet. He keeps me pinned to the desk. He wraps his free hand around my throat. I can't catch my breath.

Eugene leans in, his hands behind his back, like he's examining something curious and mildly revolting. "Would you like to see him? Would you like to see my son?"

I pat Patrick's hand; it's weirdly intimate. I shake my head. I try to make words. My vision is starting to fry around the edges. Dark loops spool into the world.

Finally, Eugene says, "Let him go."

Patrick releases me. I slide off the desk and land hard, dragging the broken ashtray with me, covering myself in ash and spent cigarette butts. I roll onto my side, choking.

Eugene puts his hand on my shoulder. "Hey, Jack, you okay? You all right down there? Get up. God damn you're a drama queen. Get the fuck up already."

It takes a few minutes. When I'm sitting up again, Patrick hands me a napkin to clean the blood off my face. I don't look at him. There's nothing I can do. No point in feeling a goddamn thing about it.

"When do I leave?" I say.

"What the hell," Eugene says. "How about right now?"

We experience dawn as a rising heat and a slow bleed of light through the cypress and the Spanish moss, riding in an airboat through the swamp a good thirty miles south of New Orleans. Patrick and I are riding up front while an old man more leather than flesh guides along some unseeable path. Our progress stirs movement from the local fauna—snakes, turtles, muskrats—and I'm constantly jumping at some heavy splash. I imagine a score of alligators gliding through the water beneath us, tracking our movement with yellow, saurian eyes. The airboat wheels around a copse of trees into a watery clearing, and I half expect to see a brontosaurus wading in the shallows.

Instead I see a row of huge, bobbing purple flowers, each with a bleached human face in the center, mouths gaping and eyes palely blind. The sight of them shocks me into silence; our guide fixes his stare on the horizon, refusing even to acknowledge anything out of the ordinary. Eyes perch along the tops of reeds; great kites of flesh stretch between tree limbs; one catches a mild breeze from our passage and skates serenely through the air, coming at last to a gentle landing on the water, where it folds in on itself and sinks into the murk.

Our guide points, and I see shack: a small, single-room architectural catastrophe, perched on the dubious shore and extending over the water on short stilts. A skiff is tied to a front porch which doubles as a small dock. It seems to be the only method of travel to or from the place. A filthy Rebel flag hangs over the entrance in lieu of a door. At the moment, it's pulled to the side and a man I assume is Tobias George is standing there, naked but for a pair of shorts that hang precariously from his narrow hips. He's all bone and gristle. His face tells me nothing as we glide in toward the dock.

Patrick stands before we connect, despite a word of caution from our guide. He has some tough-guy greeting halfway out of his mouth when the airboat's edge lightly taps the dock, nearly spilling him into the swamp, arms pinwheeling.

Tobias is unaffected by the display, but our guide is easy with a laugh and chooses not to hold back.

Patrick recovers himself and puts both hands on the dock, proceeding to crawl out of the boat like a child learning to walk. I'm grateful to God for the sight of it.

Tobias makes no move to help.

I take my time climbing out. "You wait right here," I tell the guide.

"Oh, *wye*," he says, shutting down the engine and fishing a pack of smokes from his shirt.

"What're you guys doing here?" Tobias says. He hasn't looked at me once but he can't peel his gaze from Patrick. He knows what Patrick's all about.

"Tobias, you crazy bastard. What the hell do you think you're doing?"

Tobias turns around and goes back inside, the rebel flag falling closed behind him. "Come on in I guess."

We follow him inside, where it's even hotter. The air doesn't move in here, probably hasn't moved in twenty years, and it carries the sharp tang of marijuana. Dust motes hang suspended in spears of light, coming in through a window covered over in ratty, bug-smeared plastic. The room is barely furnished: there's a single mattress pushed against the wall to our left, a cheap collapsible table with a plastic folding chair, and a chest of drawers. Next to the bed is a camping cooker with a little sauce pot and some cans of Sterno. On the table is a small pile of dull green buds, with some rolling papers and a Zippo.

There's a door flush against the back wall. I take a few steps in the direction and I can tell right away that there's some bad news behind it. The air spoils when I get close, coating the back of my throat with a greasy, evil film that feels like it seeps right into the meat. Violent fantasies sprout along my cortex like a little vine of tumors. I try to keep my face still, as I imagine coring the eyeballs out of both these guys with a grapefruit spoon.

"Stay on that side of the room, Patrick," I say. I don't need him feeling this.

"What? Why?"

"Trust me. This is why you brought me."

Tobias casts a glance at me now, finally sensing some purpose behind my presence. He's good, though: I still can't figure his reaction.

"Y'all here to kill me?" he says.

Patrick already has his gun in hand. It's pointed at the floor. His eyes are fixed on Tobias and he seems to be weighing something in his mind. I can tell that whatever is behind that door is already working its influence on him. It has its grubby little fingers in his brain and it's pulling dark things out of it. "That depends on you," he says. "Eugene wants to talk to you."

"Yeah, that's not going to happen."

The violence in this room is alive and crawling. I realize, suddenly, why he stays stoned. I figure it's time we get to the point. "We want the book, Tobias."

"What? Who are you?" He looks at Patrick. "What's he talking about?"

"You know what he's talking about. Go get the book."

"There is no book!"

He looks genuinely bewildered, and that worries me. I don't know if I can go back to Eugene without a book. I'm about to ask him what's in the back room when I hear a creak in the wood beyond the hanging flag and someone pulls it aside, flooding the shack with light. I spin around and Patrick already has his gun raised, looking spooked.

The man standing in the doorway is framed by the sun: a black shape against the sun, a negative space. He's tall and slender, his hair like a spray of light around his head. I think for a moment that I can smell it burning. He steps into the shack and you can tell there's something wrong with him, though it's hard to figure just what. Some malformation of the aura, telegraphing a warning blast straight to the root of my brain. To look at him, as he steps into the shack and trades direct sunlight for the filtered illumination shared by the rest of us, he seems tired and gaunt but ultimately not unlike any other poverty-wracked country boy, and yet my skin ripples at his approach. I feel my lip curl and I have to concentrate to keep the revulsion from my face.

"Toby?" he says. His voice is young and uninflected. Normal. "I think my brother's on his way back. Who are these guys?"

"Hey, Johnny," Tobias says, looking at him over my shoulder. He's plainly nervous now, and although his focus stays on Johnny, his attention seems to radiate in all directions, like a man wondering where the next hit is coming from.

I could have told him that.

Fear turns to meanness in a guy like Patrick, and he reacts according to the dictates of his kind: he shoots.

It's one shot, quick and clean. Patrick is a professional. The sound of the gun concusses the air in the little shack and the bullet passes through Johnny's skull before I even have time to wince at the noise.

I blink. I can't hear anything beyond a high-pitched whine. I see Patrick standing still, looking down the length of his raised arm with a flat, dead expression. It's his true face. I see Tobias drop to one knee, his hands over his ears and his mouth working as though he's shouting something; and I see Johnny, too, still standing in the doorway, as unmoved by the bullet's passage through his skull as though it had been nothing more than a disappointing argument. Dark clots of brain meat are splashed across the flag behind him.

He looks from Patrick to Tobias and when he speaks I can barely hear him above the ringing in my head. "What should I do?" he says.

I step forward and gently push Patrick's arm down.

"Are you shitting me?" he says, staring at Johnny.

"Patrick," I say.

"Am I fucking cursed? Is that it? I shot you in the face!"

The bullet-hole is a dime-sized wound in Johnny's right cheekbone. It leaks a single thread of blood. "Asshole," he says.

Tobias gets back to his feet, his arms stretched out to either side like he's trying to separate two imaginary boxers. "Will you just relax? Jesus Christ!" He guides Johnny to the little bed and sits him down, where he brushes the blond hair out of his face and inspects the bullet hole. Then he cranes his head around to examine the damage of the exit wound. "God damn it!" he says.

Johnny puts his own hand back there. "Oh man," he says.

I take a look. The whole back of his head is gone; now it's just a red bowl of spilled gore. What look like little blowing cinders are embedded in the mess, sending up coils of smoke. Most of Johnny's brains are splashed across the wall behind him.

"Patrick," I say. "Just be cool."

He's still in a fog. You can see him trying to arrange things in his head. "I need to kill them, Jack. I need to. I never felt it like this before. What's happening here?"

Tobias pipes up. "I had a job for this guy all lined up at The Fry Pit! Now what!"

"Tobias, I need you to shut up," I say, keeping my eyes on Patrick. "Patrick, are you hearing me?" It's taking a huge effort to maintain my own composure. I have an image of wresting the gun from his hand and hitting him with it until his skull breaks. Only the absolute impossibility of it keeps me from trying.

My question causes the shutters to close in his eyes. Whatever tatter of human impulse stirred him to try to explain himself to me, to grope for reason amidst the bloody carnage boiling in his head, is subsumed again in a dull professional menace. "Don't talk to me like that. I'm not a goddamn kid."

I turn to the others. The bed is now awash in blood. Tobias is working earnestly to mitigate the damage back there, but I can't imagine what it is he thinks he can do. Brain matter is gathered in a clump behind them; he seems to be scooping everything out. Johnny sits there forlornly, shoulders slumped. "I thought it would be better out here," he said. "Shit never ends."

"The atlas," I say.

"Fuck yourself," Tobias says.

I stride toward the closed door. If there's anything I need to know before I open it, I guess I'll just find out the hard way. A hot pulse of emotion blasts out at me as I touch the handle: fear, rage, a lust for carnage. It's overriding any sense of self-preservation I might have had. I wonder if a fire will pour through the door when it's opened, a furnace exhalation, and engulf us all. I find myself hoping for it.

Tobias shouts at me: "Don't!"

I pull it open.

A charred skull, oily smoke coiling from its fissures, is propped on a stool in an otherwise bare room no bigger than a closet. Black mold has grown over the stool, and is creeping up the walls. A live current jolts my brain. Time dislocates, jumping seconds like an old record, and the world moves in jerky, stop=motion lurches. A language is seeping from the skull—a viscous, cracked sound like breaking bones and molten rock. My eyes sting and I squeeze them shut. The skin on my face blisters.

"*Shut it! Shut the door!*"

Tobias is screaming, but whatever he's saying has no relation to me. It's as though I'm watching a play. Blood is leaking from his eyes. Patrick is grinning widely, his own eyes like bloody headlamps. He's violently twisting his right ear, working it like an apple stem. Johnny is sitting quietly, holding his gathered brains in his hands, rocking back and forth like an unhappy child. My upper arms are hurting, and it takes me a minute to realize that I'm gouging them with my own fingernails. I can't make myself stop.

Outside a sound rolls across the swamp like a foghorn: a deep, answering bellow to the language of Hell spilling from the closet.

Tobias lunges past me and slams the door shut, immediately muffling the skull's effect. I stagger toward the chair but fall down hard before I make it, banging my shoulder against the table and knocking Tobias's drug paraphernalia all over the floor. Patrick makes a sound, half gasp and half sob, and leans back against the wall, cradling his savaged ear. The left side of his face is painted in blood. He's digging the heel of his hand into his right eye, like he's trying to rub something out of it.

"What the fuck was that!"

I think it's me who says that. Right now I can't be sure.

"That's your goddamn 'atlas,' you prick," Tobias says. He comes over to where I am and drops to the floor, scooping up the scattered buds and some papers. He begins to assemble a joint; his hands are shaking badly, so this takes some doing.

"A skull? The book is a skull?"

"No. It's a tongue inside the skull. Technically."

"What the Christ?"

"Just shut up a minute." He finishes the joint, lights it, and takes a long, deep pull. He passes it over to me.

For one surreal moment I feel like we're college buddies sitting in a dorm. It's like there's not a scorched, muttering skull in the next room, corroding the air around it. It's like there's not a man with a blown-out skull moping quietly on the bed. I start to laugh, and I haven't even had a toke.

He exhales explosively, the sweet smoke filling the air between us. "Take it, man. I'm serious. Trust me."

So I do. Almost immediately I feel an easing of the pressure in the room. The crackle of violent impulse, which I had ceased to even recognize, abated to a low thrum. My internal gauge ticked back down to highly frightened, which, in comparison to a moment before, felt like a monastic peace.

I gesture for Patrick to do the same.

"No. I don't pollute my body with that shit." He's touching his ear gingerly, trying to assess the damage.

"Patrick, last night you single-handedly killed half a bottle of ninety-proof burden. Let's have some perspective here."

He snatches it from me and drags hard on it, coughing it all back out so violently I think he might throw up.

Johnny laughs from his position on the bed. It's the first bright note he's sounded since his head came apart. "Amateur!"

I notice that Johnny's head seems to be changing shape. The shattered bone around the exit wound has smoothed over and extended upward an inch or so, like something growing. A tiny twig of bone has likewise extended from the bullet wound beneath his eye.

"We need to get out of here," I say. "That thing is pretty much a live feed to Hell. We can't handle it. It's time to go."

"We're taking it with us," Patrick says.

"No. No we're not."

"Not up for debate, Jack."

"I'm not riding with that thing. If you take it you're going back alone."

Patrick nods and takes another pull from the joint, handling it much better this time. He passes it back to me. "Okay, but you gotta know that I'm leaving this place empty. You understand me, right?"

I don't, at first. It takes me a second. "You can't be serious. You're going to kill me?"

"Make up your mind."

For the first time since his arrival at my shop last night, I feel genuine despair. Everything to this point has had some precedence in my life. Even this brush with Hell isn't my first, though it's the most direct so far. But I've never seen my own death staring back at me quite so frankly. I always thought I'd confront this moment with a little poise, or at least a kind of stoic resignation. But I'm angry, and I'm afraid, and I feel tears gathering in my eyes.

"God damn it, Patrick. That doesn't make any sense."

"Look, Jack. I like you. You're weak and you're a coward, but you can't help those things. I would rather you come with me. We take this skull back to Eugene, like he wanted. We deliver Tobias to his just reward. You go back to your little bookstore and all is right with the world. But I can't leave this place with anybody in it."

Tobias doesn't seem to be paying attention. He's leaning back against the bed, a new joint rolled up and kept all to himself. I can't tell if he's resigned to his own death or if he's so far away he doesn't even know it's being discussed.

I can't think of anything to say. Maybe there isn't anything more to be said. Maybe language is over. Maybe everything is, at last, emptied out. I still feel the skull's muted influence crawling through my brain. It craves the bullet. I anticipate the explosion of the gun with a terrible relish. I wonder, idly, if I'll hold onto myself long enough to feel myself flying.

The bellow from the swamp sounds again. It's huge and deep, like the ululating call of a mountain. It just keeps on going.

Johnny smiles. "Brother's home," he says.

Patrick looks toward the flag-covered doorway. "What?"

Tobias holds his hand aloft, finger extended, announcing his intention to orate. His eyelids are heavy. The joint he'd made for himself is spent. "There's a hell monster. Did I forget to tell you?"

I start to laugh. I can't stop myself. It doesn't feel good.

Johnny smiles at me, mistaking my laughter for something else. "It appeared the same time I did. Toby calls it my brother." He sounds wistful.

Patrick uses the gun barrel to open the flag a few inches. He peers outside for a few moments, then lets it fall closed again. He looks at me. "We're stuck. The boat's gone."

"What? He left us?"

"Well... it's mostly gone."

I take a look for myself.

The airboat is a listing heap of bent scrap metal, the cage around its huge propeller a tangled bird's nest. Our guide's arm, still connected to a hunk of his torso, rests on the deck in a black puddle. The thing that did this is swimming in a lazy arc some distance away, trackable by the rolling surge of water it creates as it trawls along. Judging by the size of its wake, it's at least as big as a city bus. It breaches the surface once, exposing a mottled gray hide and an anemone-like thistle of eye stalks lifting skyward. The thing barrel-rolls until a deep black fissure emerges, and from this suppurated tear comes that stone-cracking bellow, the language of deep earth that curdles something inside me, springs tears to my eyes, brings me hard to my knees.

I scramble weakly away from the door. Patrick is watching me with a sad, desperate hope, his intent to murder momentarily forgotten, as though by some trick known only to me this thing might be banished back to its home, as though I might fix this scar that Tobias George, that mewling, incompetent little thief, has cut into the world.

I cannot fix this. There is no fixing this.

Behind us both, locked in its little room, the skull cooks the air.

It's the language that hurts. The awful speech. While that thing languishes in the waters out front, we're trapped inside. It seems to stay quiet unless it's provoked by some outrage to its senses: an appearance by one of us, or—we believe, since none of us heard the attack on the airboat and our guide—the effects of the skull in the room. As long as we're quiet and hidden, we seem to be safe.

"Why would you do that to a man?" Patrick says. We're all sitting in a little huddled circle, passing the joint around. We might have been friends, to someone who didn't know us. "Why would you send him a piece of his own dead son?"

"Are you serious? No one deserves it more than Eugene. He humiliated me. He made me feel small. All those years sending him a cut from money I earned, or doing errands for him, or tipping him off when I hear shit I think he should know. Never a 'thank you.' Never a 'good job.' Just grief. Just mockery. And his son was even worse. He would lay hands on me. Slap the back of my head. Slap my face, even. What am I going to do, challenge Eugene's son? So I became everybody's bitch. The laughing stock."

Patrick shakes his head. "You didn't, though. Truth is we barely ever thought about you. I didn't even know your name until you knocked over that poker game. Eugene had to remind me."

This is hard for Tobias to hear. He stares hard at the floor, the muscles in his jaw working. He looks at me. "See what I mean? Nothing. You just have to take it from these guys, you know? Just take it and take it and take it. It was one of the happiest days of my life when that kid finally got wasted."

He goes on. We have nothing but time. He robbed the poker game in a fit of deranged anger and then fled south, hoping to disappear into the bayou. The reality of what he'd just done was starting to sink in. He's of the vermin class in criminal society, and vermin come in multitudes. One of his vermin friends told him about this shack where his old granddaddy used to live. He gets a boat and comes out here, only to find s surprise waiting for him.

"The skull was in a black, iron box," he says, "sitting on its side in the corner. There's a hole in the bottom the box, like the whole thing was meant to fit around someone's head. It had a big gouge in the side of it, like someone had chopped it with something. I don't know what cuts through metal like that though. And inside, this skull...talking."

"It's one of the astronauts," Johnny says.

I rub my fingers in my eyes. "Astronauts? What?"

Johnny leans in, grateful for his moment. He tells us that there are occasionally men and women who wander through Hell in thin processions, wearing heavy gray robes and bearing lanterns to light their way. They are invariably chained together, and led through the burning canyons by a loping demon: some malformed, tooth-spangled pinwheel of limbs and claws. They tour safely because they are shuttered against the sights and sounds of Hell by the iron boxes around their heads, which gives them the appearance of strange, prison-skulled astronauts on a pilgrimage through fire.

"I recognized the box," Johnny says. "This is one of those guys. The box was broken, so I guess something bad happened to him."

"Where is it?"

Tobias shrugs. "I threw it out in the bayou. What do I need a broken box for? I started asking for things, and it sent them. The rock, the shard of bone."

"Hold on. How did you know to ask it for things? You're leaving something out."

Tobias and Johnny exchange a look. The burning embers in the back of Johnny's head seem to have gathered more life: little tongues of flame spit into the air from time to time, as though a small fire has kindled. The extending bone around his head has grown further, opening out as though a careful hand has begun to fashion a wide, smooth bowl. The bone growing from his face has grown little offshoots, like a delicate branch.

Patrick picks up on their glance, and retrieves his gun from the floor, holding it casually in his lap.

"Everything that's brought here has a courier," Tobias says. "That's how Johnny got here. He brought the bone. And there was one already here when I found the skull. It told me."

"It?"

"Well…it was a person at first. Then it changed. They change over time. Evolve."

Patrick gets it before I do. "The thing in the water."

"Holy Christ. You mean Johnny's going to turn into something like *that?*" I look again at the fiery bowl his head is turning into.

"No no no!" Tobias holds out his hands, as if he could ward off the very idea of it. "I mean, I don't know. I'm pretty sure that's only because the other one never went away. I think it's the proximity of the skull that does it. There was one other courier, the girl who brought me the rock. I sent her away."

"Jesus. Where?"

"Just…" He waves, vaguely. "Away. Into the bayou."

"You're a real sweetheart, Tobias."

"Well come on, I didn't know what to do! She was just—there! I didn't know anybody was going to be coming with it! I freaked out and told her to get out! But the important thing is I never saw any sign that she changed into anything. I haven't seen or heard anything from her since. You notice how the plants get weird as you get close to this place? It's gotta be the skull's influence."

"That's not exactly airtight logic, Tobias," I say. "What if it's not just from the skull? What if it comes from them too? I could tell something was fucked up about Johnny as soon as I saw him."

"Well I'm taking the fucking chance! If there are going to be people coming out, they need to have a chance at a better life. That's why I got Johnny here a job. He'll be far away from that skull, so maybe he won't change into anything." He looks at his friend and at the lively fire that's crackling inside his head. "Well, he wouldn't have if you guys hadn't fucked it all up. I've got this all worked out. I'm going to find them jobs in little places, in little towns. I got money now, so I can afford to get them set up. Buy them some clothes, rent them out a place until they can start earning some money of their own. A second chance, you know? They deserve a second chance."

He's getting all worked up again, like he's going to break down into tears, and I'm struck with a revelation: Tobias is using this skull as a chance to redeem himself. He's going to funnel of people out of Hell and back into the world of sunlight and cheeseburgers.

Tobias George may be the only good man in a fifty mile radius. Too bad it's the most doomed idea I've ever heard in a life rich with them. But there are several possibilities for salvaging this situation. One thing is clear: Eugene cannot have the atlas. The level of catastrophe he might cause is incalculable. I need to get it back to my bookstore and to the back room. There are books there that will provide protections; at least I hope so.

All I need is something to carry it in.

I know just where to get it.

"Patrick. You still want to bring this thing to Eugene?"

"He's the boss. You change your mind about coming?"

"I think so, yeah. Tobias, we're going into the room." He goes in gratefully. I think he feels in control in this room in way that he doesn't out there with Patrick. It's almost funny.

The skull sits on the moss-blackened stool, greasy smoke seeping from its fissures and polluting the air. The broken language of Hell is a physical pressure. A blood vessel ruptures in my right eye and my vision goes cloudy and pink. Time fractures again. Tobias moves next to me, approaching the skull, but I can't tell what it's doing to him: he skips in time like I'm watching him through strobe lights, even though the light in here remains a constant, sizzling glare. I try not to vomit. Things are moving around in my brain like maggots in old meat.

The air seems to bend into the skull. I see it on the stool, blackening the world around it, and I try to imagine who it once belonged to: the chained Black Iron Monk, shielded by a metal box from the burning horrors of the world he moved through. Until something came along and opened the box like a tin can, and Hell poured inside.

Who was it? What order would undertake such a pilgrimage? And to what end?

Tobias is saying something to me. I have to study him to figure out what.

The poor scrawny bastard is blistering all over his body. His lips peel back from his bloody teeth.

"Tell it what you want," he says.

So I do.

The boy is streaked with mud and gore. He is twelve, maybe thirteen. Steam rises from his body like wind-struck flags. I don't know where he appears from, or how; he's just there, two iron boxes dangling like huge lanterns from a chain in his hand. I wonder, briefly, what a child his age had done to be consigned to Hell. But then, it doesn't really matter.

I open one of the boxes and tell the boy to put the skull inside. He does. The skin bubbles on his hands where he touches it, but he makes no sign of pain.

I close the door on it, and it's like a light going out. Time slips back into it groove. The light recedes to a natural level. My skin stops burning, the desire to commit violence dissipates like smoke. I can feel where I've been scratching my own arms again. My eye is gummed shut with blood.

When we stumble back into the main room, Patrick is on his feet with the gun in his hand. Johnny is sitting on the bed, the bony rim of his open skull grown further upward, elongating his head and giving him a alien grace. The fire in the bowl of his head burned briskly, crackling and shedding a warm light. Patrick looks at me, then at the boy with the iron boxes. "You got them," he says. "Where's the skull?"

I take the chain from the boy. The boxes are heavy together; the boy must be stronger than he looks. Something to remember. "In one of these. If it can keep that shit out, I'm betting it can keep it locked in, too. I think it's safe to move."

"And those'll get us past the thing outside?"

"If what Johnny said is true."

"It is," Johnny says. "But now there's only one extra box."

"That's right," I say, and swing them with every vestige of my failing strength at Patrick's head, where they land with a wet crunch. He staggers to his right a few steps, the left side of his face broken like crockery, and he puts a hand into the rancid scramble of his own brain. "I'll go get it," he says, "I'll go."

"You're dead," I tell him gently. "You stupid bastard."

He accepts this gracefully and collapses to his knees, and then onto his face. Dark blood pours from his head as though from a spilled glass. I scoop up the gun, which feels clumsy in my hand. I never got the hang of guns.

Tobias stands in shock. "I can't believe you did that," he says.

"Shut up. Are there any clothes in that dresser? Put something on the kid. We're going back to the city." While he's doing that, I look at Johnny. "I'm not going to be able to see. Will you be able to guide me out?"

"Yes."

"Good," I say, and shoot Tobias in the back of the head.

For once, somebody dies without an argument.

———

I don't know much about the trip back. I open a slot on the base of the box and fit it over my head. I am consumed in darkness. I'm led out to the skiff by Johnny and the boy. The boy rides with me, and Johnny gets into the water, dragging us behind him. Fire unfurls from his head, the sides of which are developing baroque flourishes. His personality is diminished, and I can't tell if it's because he mourns Tobias, or because that is changing too, developing into something cold and barren.

The journey takes several hours. I know we pass the corpse flowers, the staring eyes and bloodless faces pressing from the foliage. I am sure that the creature unleashes its earth-breaking cry, and that any living thing that hears it hemorrhages its life away, into the still waters. I know that night falls. I know the flame of our new guide lights the undersides of the cypress, runs out before us across the water, fills the dark like the final lantern in a fallen world.

I make a quiet and steady passage there.

Eugene is in his office. The bar is closed upstairs and the man at the door lets us in without a word. He makes no comment about my companions, or the iron boxes hanging from a chain. The world he lives in is already breaking from its old shape. The new one has space for wonders.

Eugene is sitting behind his desk in his dark. I can tell he's drunk. It smells like he's been here since we left, almost twenty-four hours ago now. The only light comes from the fire rising from Johnny's empty skull. It illuminates a pale structure on Eugene's desk: a huge antler, or a tree made of bone. There are human teeth protruding along some of its tines, and a long crack near the wider base of it reveals a raw, red meat, where a mouth opens and closes.

"Where's Patrick?" he says.

"Dead," I say. "Tobias, too."

"And the atlas?"

"I burned it."

He nods, as though he'd been expecting that very thing. After a moment he gestures at the bone tree. "This is my son," he says. "Say hi, Max."

The mouth shrieks. It stops to draw in a gasping breath, then repeats the sound. The cry is sustained for several seconds before stuttering into a sob, and then going silent again.

"He keeps growing. He's going to be a big boy before it's all over."

"Yeah. I can see that."

"Who're your friends, Jack?"

I have to think about that before I answer. "I really don't know," I say, finally.

"So what do you want? You want me to tell you you're off the hook? You want me to tell you you're free to go?"

"You told me that before. It turned out to be bullshit."

"Yeah, well. That's the world we live in, right?"

"You're on notice, Eugene. Leave me alone. Don't come to my door anymore. I'm sorry things didn't work out here. I'm sorry about your son. But you have to stay away. I'm only going to say it once."

He smiles at me. He must have to summon it from far away, but he smiles at me. "I'll take that under advisement, Jack. Now get the fuck out of here."

We turn and walk back up the stairs. It's a long walk back to my bookstore, where I'm anxious to get to work on the atlas. But I have a light to guide me, and I know this place well.

SIOBHAN CARROLL

Wendigo Nights

Day Eleven

LATELY I'VE BEEN THINKING ABOUT EATING MY children.

When Olivia tugs at her glossy curls, I think about her hair in my mouth. Paper-dry, tasting of smoke and strawberry shampoo. The strands would break between my teeth. The sound they'd make—a tiny crunch, like a foot falling through snow—that sound would fill me. I would not be so hungry after that.

I allow myself the hair. It is better than the other things I imagine eating.

Macleay says, "I'm going to try again this afternoon. I think today's the day." We nod as though we believe him.

I study Macleay's hands. They're large and dirt-streaked. I imagine crunching through his knuckles and rolling the tattered joint on my tongue like a marble.

"What about you, Hui?" Sanderson's tone is a bit too casual. "Any news on that canister?"

I shrug. I don't want to open my mouth. I'm afraid of what might happen.

The arctic wind howls through our silence. It's blizzarding outside the research station,

−36 Celsius by the thermometer, god-knows-what once you factor in wind chill. The kind of weather even the locals complain about.

"They'll send a plane as soon as the weather clears," Bannerjee mutters. She's been saying the same thing for a week now.

"Yeah." Macleay doesn't look at her. "I'll try again this afternoon."

"You okay, Hui?" I can feel Sanderson's eyes on me. He knows something's off.

31

Carefully, very carefully, I part my lips. Not much. Just enough to reply. And I know this is my chance—maybe my last chance—to warn them.

Olivia giggles in the corner. The thought darts into my head: *If not Macleay, then her.*

"Fine," I mutter. "I'm fine."

After a moment, Sanderson nods.

That was on day eleven.

Day Nine

They say people who've received a terminal diagnosis brood over history. They go looking for mistakes: theirs or someone else's. They try to identify the moment things started to go wrong.

I can think of two possibilities. In my mind, I flip them like a coin.

The first possibility: eleven days ago.

Bannerjee set something dull and gray on my work bench. "Check this out." She looked flushed, proud as an angler who's caught his first salmon. "It was in the ice, about a meter down."

I picked it up. A gray canister, about the size of a paint can, weighing about two kilos. It was made out of a clouded, dull metal, striated with rings.

"What is it?" I wasn't interested, just being polite. Nothing about the canister suggested danger.

"No idea." Bannerjee leaned forward. "But I saw another can down there. And clothing." She was practically squirming with excitement.

"Clothing?"

"A wool coat." She grinned. "I stopped drilling. Shifted the borehole. We need to call this in." Seeing my confusion, she added: "Could be old."

Now something connected. "How old?"

"Dunno. But....it could be old."

I turned the canister over. Once, maybe, we'd have shrugged our shoulders over a frozen coat. But not these days. The scramble for the melting Arctic is on, and governments look to history to strengthen their territorial claims. Canada has resumed the nineteenth century's search for Franklin. Hell, a few years ago, Russia planted a flag on the sea-bed beneath the North Pole. A *flag*. Like in the Eddie Izzard skit. Everything old is new again.

"Franklin et al.," I said. "They wore wool coats, didn't they?" Like me, Bannerjee wore Canada Goose, the unofficial uniform of the frigid zone. Her coat was blazing red; a slot for the Arctic Rescue tag gaped emptily on her back.

"Yeah." Bannerjee's eyes glittered with what I assumed was excitement.

Now, looking back, I wonder if I was wrong about the look in Bannerjee's eyes. If, like the slow crack of lake-ice underfoot, things were already getting out of hand.

Day Twelve

"We need to talk about Bannerjee," Sanderson says in a low voice.

I grunt. So far I have managed to get through the morning without opening my mouth. I am thirsty, but the hunger is much, much worse. It claws at my insides like a wild animal stuffed in a cage. If I open my mouth, I fear it will get out.

"I can't find her anywhere," says Macleay of the edible fingers. "I thought….I thought she might have tried for the mine. But when I checked the snowmobiles I found this." He opens his dirty hands to reveal a tangle of black wires.

"She butchered the machines." Sanderson's voice sounds wet and heavy, like warm-weather snow.

It takes me a moment to register what they're saying. I raise my eyebrows at Macleay.

"I can't repair this," Macleay says in disgust. His eyes are frightened. "We're stuck here until the plane comes. Or until the satellite phone starts working again." He makes no mention of trying the phone again this afternoon.

The blizzard moans through our walls. Out of the corner of my eye, I see Ethan and Olivia watching us. *Dohng, Suug Yee,* I would say, were I to call them by their Cantonese names. Unlucky names. I try to smile at the children reassuringly, but my heart is sinking.

We are in more trouble than I can bear to think about. Some facts I can face head-on: the damaged snowmobiles, the missing plane. Others I can only sneak glances at.

Fact: *I was the first person to touch the canister after Bannerjee.*

Fact: *Something is wrong.*

Fact: *I do not, and never have, had any children.*

"Well," Sanderson says eventually. "Keep an eye out for her." He looks deflated, as though he has finally realized what I have suspected for eleven days now.

Escape is no longer an option.

Day Nine

The second possibility: five years ago.

My then-girlfriend, Anna, wanted to see the Anthropology museum. One of her college friends was in Vancouver for a conference. So I drove her and the other folklorists to the weird borderland-city of UBC.

I circled the Bill Reid sculpture while Anna and Joel reminisced about grad school. I've always loved wood, and the honey-glow of the giant raven appealed to me. Not so the rest of the museum. A bunch of masks with distorted faces and stringy grass hair.

"The last murder was in the 1960s," Joel said.

That jerked my attention back to their conversation. "What?"

"Creepy," Anna agreed. Her skin was almost the same color as the yellow cedar. Ethereal.

She turned to me. "They left the uncle to babysit their kids." Her words were aimed in my general direction, but her eyes drifted past mine. Another one of the disconnections that had become common between us. "When they came back, he'd built a fire on the lawn. He was roasting his nephew's body. And crying about it."

The mask that reared up behind them was ugly. Lips peeled back from red-lined teeth. Black eyes staring nowhere.

"Did you hear about that bus murder in Winnipeg?" Joel said, out of nowhere.

Anna grimaced. The news was full of the Greyhound murder, which fascinated and repelled us. It was the sort of thing our Vancouver friends avoided talking about.

But Joel was from New York. "Beheading and cannibalism," he continued, staring at the mask. "I'm just saying. Maybe wendigo psychosis is still with us."

"Wendigo?" I could feel the conversation rushing past me, the way they usually did when Anna and her grad-school comrades got together.

"Yeah." Joel's face got the bright, careful look I imagined he must wear when teaching. "You've heard of the wendigo?"

And that was it. The moment of infection.

Day ???

I am finding it difficult to keep track of time.

This is a common complaint in the Arctic. The land of the midnight sun. It disorders everything.

Still. Time is becoming difficult. I watch the old plastic clock on the wall to make sure the seconds are still advancing.

I hear sounds from the kitchenette. But I will not get up. I will not investigate.

Things must be kept in order. Or else.

Day Twelve

My children are playing with leftover office paper. Olivia is showing Ethan how to fold the green-and-white sheets into dolls. They decorate their creations with pencil: people don't bring pens to our latitude.

Ethan batters the dolls against each other, making them fight. It disturbs me, but I don't know why.

Outside the wind is raging. I try not to think about Anna's description of a deranged uncle roasting kids on the lawn. I don't even know the whole story. The gaps in my knowledge make it worse, somehow.

"Hui."

I hear Ethan drop his pencil. Olivia's eyes widen and I follow her gaze to where Bannerjee stands, dripping and wide-eyed. Dried blood cakes the side of her head.

The sudden, frozen silence of my children's fear gives me the strength to take Bannerjee gently by the arm. I steer her out of the small dorm room.

"*What are you doing?*" I spit through clenched teeth. I want to rip her throat out. "*What have you done?*"

Bannerjee shakes her head. She's always been a small, anxious woman. Now she's trembling like someone's running a current through her.

"Macleay," Bannerjee manages. There's something wrong with her eyes. "I found him by the snowmobiles. He....was tearing them apart. He tried to *kill* me, Hui."

I feel the same way I did in the museum all those years ago. Things are rushing past me faster than I can handle.

"Macleay?"

Bannerjee nods. She's crying now, big, fat tears that track mascara and blood down her face. "You have to help me. He's looking for me."

I feel dizzy. I can't remember the last time I ate. I feel my mouth move—"How can I help?"—although I'm not sure I trust Bannerjee. I'm not sure I trust Macleay either. Something about the way he held those wires.

Here's a question I never thought about when I flew up here: *If the world goes haywire, is there anyone in this station you can trust?*

"It's the canister," Bannerjee says hoarsely. That look in her eyes. "We need to get it out of here. We need to give it back."

I nod as though this makes sense. Part of me—a part I can barely keep track of right now—agrees, but wants to warn her. Because here's the thing about extracting resources. It's always easier to take something out of the land than it is to put it back.

But suddenly I am too tired to say anything.

"Sure," my mouth says. And I watch myself follow Bannerjee down the hallway. She keeps glancing back at the way we came. She's dragging her left leg a little.

As we enter the field lab, Bannerjee whispers something that gives me pause. "We've angered the *vetala*."

"The what?" I hear myself say. An echo of a museum long ago.

Bannerjee looks at me strangely. "The air is full of ghosts." She delivers this information as though it were an ozone reading: a fact, visible to us all.

Later I wish that Bannerjee had explained herself. If I could have heard her version of the last twelve days—maybe I could have altered something.

But maybe not. "Come on," Bannerjee says and pushes the door open.

I don't like to think about what happens next.

Day One

"Is that it?"

Sanderson is framed by the doorway, a big, burly man who likes to wear his beard long and curly. He's typical of a certain kind of Arctic visitor: the geologist who thinks of himself as a frontier throwback. And like a lot of geologists, he's a bit odd.

Automatically I've thrown a cloth over the canister. For some reason I don't want people to see it. Now, reluctantly, I remove the cloth.

Sanderson snorts. "Doesn't look like much. Thought it might be the holy grail the way Bannerjee's been carrying on."

My stomach grumbles, and I am suddenly, painfully hungry. But I've already eaten three meals today. It isn't even noon yet.

"Has she got through?"

Sanderson shakes his head. "All the com's down. Murphy's law. Bannerjee makes a find and she can't tell anyone. It's driving her nuts." His shoulders shake as he laughs. Sanderson prides himself on being laid back. He finds the high-strung Bannerjee amusing.

"Do you think the plane will come through?"

Our station gets a bi-monthly supply drop. The pond-hopper that visits us and the southern Inuit villages is a tough little bird. It might be able to get through in this weather. But I'm not surprised to see Sanderson shrug.

"Maybe." He sounds bored. "Wind's bad. Don't blame them if they postpone the drop. It'll drive Bannerjee extra-nuts though." He chuckles.

I wonder now if Sanderson remembers this moment. I wonder if he appreciates the irony.

The pond-hopper never arrives. Normally I mark a missed drop with a minus symbol in my diary: -1 day of supplies. But that evening, I write "Day One" at the top of the page. Because that is what it feels like. Like something has begun.

Day Twelve

The day she left, Anna and I argued in the parking lot. She said I was incapable of love. Worse, she said it sadly, as though it was something we both knew and had just been too polite to mention until now.

I protested, but words have never been my strong point.

If I could talk to Anna right now—if we could get a line out, if I could feel confident about baring my teeth to the air—I'd tell her that she was wrong. That what I find difficult isn't love, but expressing it.

If she could see me now—the way I'm trying to shelter the children from danger, the way I'm trying to protect them from myself—I think she'd think differently.

At least, I hope she would.

"Tell us a story," Olivia begs. I look away from her dark curls and

Ethan's bright, plump cheeks. The only stories in my head are awful ones. Franklin and his men staggering in the dark. Starving men cutting up their comrades for cooking pots. And the story Joel told me all those years ago.

"No," I mumble. "No story tonight." Olivia wails. Ethan bounces up and down.

"Fine," I say. "Once upon a time there was...."

"A canithter," Ethan lisps.

It takes me a moment to respond. I am tired. So very tired of fighting. And I really can't think of anything else to say.

"A canister." My voice sounds dull, even to my ears. "Buried in ice."

"And then one day...." Ethan prompts. They look at me expectantly, with glittering eyes.

"One day," I agree.

"One day," Olivia says, her voice rising with excitement, "it gets *out!*"

Five Years Ago

Joel turns to me and says, "You've heard of the wendigo?"

I shake my head. Out of habit I want to stop him; I tend to be bored by Anna's descriptions of legends and tale-types. But she is watching me closely.

"'*This is the blue hour / The ravenous night...*'" Joel quotes. He pauses, looking at me. When I show no sign of recognition, he moves on. "It's a Native American legend." (Anna winces at his word choice.) "A cannibal spirit that possesses a person and makes him want to feed on human flesh. Particularly friends and family members."

"We always hurt the ones we love." Anna is smiling sadly to herself.

"Vampire and werewolf stories are similar that way," Joel reflects. "But I think the wendigo's scarier."

"Why?"

"Because of the way it's transmitted."

Joel smirks and preens a little. I know he wants me to ask him about the transmission. I don't want to ask him. I try to catch Anna's eye, but she isn't looking at me. And I can't figure out a way to exit this conversation. So I turn back to Joel, and ask him, "How?"

This, ultimately, is my tragedy. I go along with things.

"Anyone can become a wendigo," Joel says. "It's a culturally-transmitted madness. That's actually documented, by the way. Wendigo psychosis."

"Which means?"

"As soon as you learn about the wendigo, you can turn into a wendigo." He grins triumphantly, haloed by the amber light of the museum. "Just by listening to this, you've been infected."

I feel a flash of anger. Even now, all these years later, I still want to punch him.

I think I could forgive Joel for telling me about the wendigo. But I can't forgive him for that grin.

Me, I apologize. I don't know if that makes it any easier. I was just trying to make sense of things. And it was easier for me to do that on paper.

Even in reading these words, you have been infected.

Day ???

This is the blue hour. The ravenous night.

I find Macleay in the kitchenette. His body is bent like a broken straw. He looks dead. But I can hear his breath, even above the sound of the wind. The slow pump of blood in his veins.

His eyes slide open as I approach. Puppet's eyes.

"Still alive, Hui?" He gives a mad, wet giggle.

I sink down in a crouch before him. I'm salivating at the metallic taint of blood in the air. This disgusts me. I wish I didn't know what was going to happen next.

"It's the canister," Macleay says and smiles. His face slides into the same holy-fool expression that Bannerjee's wore at the end. "Not from this planet after all."

His smugness irritates me. Like Bannerjee, he thinks he has found an explanation. Bannerjee blamed ghosts. Macleay wants aliens. I suppose it does no harm to let them believe they figured it out at the end. That there was an answer."

"What happened?" I rasp, trying to delay the inevitable.

"Sanderson," Macleay whispers. He smiles a red smile. "I thought he was all right. But he fooled me. The son-of-a-bitch."

"Where is he?"

Macleay rolls his eyes towards the door. *Outside. In the death-storm.*

I hear a gasp behind me and know that Olivia has trailed me into the kitchen. I motion her back with my free arm. I don't want her to see my face.

"Get him for me, will you?" The shred that remains of Macleay wants vengeance. I nod, to keep him happy.

The crunch of bone fills my mouth and I try to think about other things. About the line I once came across in an old explorer narrative that Bannerjee had picked up in Anchorage. "The North has induced some degree of insanity in the men."

The North has induced some degree of insanity in the men. It's untrue, of course. One of those annoying stories that southerners like to tell about the Arctic. But we bring those stories with us when we come up here.

My opinion? I don't think there was anything in that canister. There didn't need to be. All it needed was our stories.

"Sanderson's putting gasoline around the building," Olivia announces in a detached voice. I nod. I can smell it, an ugly, thick stench that corrupts the taste of blood in my mouth. I clamber to my feet, ignoring the stickiness on my hands and face.

I've always been good at ignoring uncomfortable truths. The wariness in Anna's eyes. Macleay's corpse at my feet. The children.

The only excuse I can make is that, when things descend into nightmare, you cling to the parts of the story you want to believe in.

"Hui!" Somewhere, Sanderson is screaming my name. He wants to test his story against mine. I grin a death-mask grin and click my nails together. I can feel my body stretching to accommodate the life it has devoured.

"Don't worry," I tell my silent, ghost-faced children. "I'll protect you."

I put my hand on the howling door. I pull it open.

This is the blue hour. The ravenous night.

JULIO CORTÁZAR

Headache

Translated by Michael Cisco

We owe the most beautiful images in this story to Dr. Margaret L. Tyler. Her admirable poem, "A Guide to the Most Common Remedies for Symptoms of Vertigo and Headaches" appeared in the review *Homeopathy* (published by the Argentinian Association of Homeopathic Medicine), vol. XIV, no. 32, April 1946, page 33 passim.

Likewise, we thank Ireneo Fernando Cruz, who first imparted to us, during a trip to San Juan, his knowledge of the mancuspias.

W E LOOK AFTER THE MANCUSPIAS UNTIL PRETTY LATE in the afternoon. Now that the summer heat has come they have become changeable and full of caprices, the latecomers require special nourishment and we bring them malted oats in big china bowls; the largest ones are shedding the fur on their backs, so we have to keep them separated, tying a blanket around them and taking care they do not socialize at night with the other mancuspias that sleep in cages and receive food every eight hours.

We aren't feeling well. It's been coming on since the morning, maybe caused by the hot wind that blows every day at dawn, before the rising of a sun that pours down on the house all day like a rain of hot pitch. It is hard for us to attend to the sick animals—this at around eleven—and check up on the young ones taking their naps. Walking is getting to be more difficult, keeping up the routine; we suspect that one solitary night of neglect could spell doom for the mancuspias, and irreparably ruin our lives. So we proceed without a thought, completing tasks one after the other alternating according to routine, pausing only for food (there are bits of bread on the table and on top of the mantelpiece in the living room) or to stare at ourselves in the mirror that duplicates the bedroom. At night we fall abruptly into bed, and the inclination to brush the teeth before sleeping yields to our fatigue, so that we can only manage a wave of the hand toward the lamp or the medicine bottles. Outside is the sound of the adult mancuspias walking and walking in circles.

We aren't feeling well. One of us has to take *Aconitum*, a name derived from drugs containing large amounts of aconite in solution, which are used if, for example, fear induces an attack of vertigo. *Aconitum is a violent thunderstorm, that passes quickly.* How else would you describe the counterattack of an anxiety that is triggered by any insignificant thing, by nothing. A woman is abruptly confronted with a dog and begins to feel wildly dizzy. Then aconitum, and after a little while the fit becomes a sweet giddiness, with a tendency to move in reverse (this happened to us, but it was a case of *Bryonia*, which caused us to collapse just the same, with a feeling as if we were sinking into bed).

The other one of us, in marked contrast, is thoroughly *Nux Vomica*. After bringing the mancuspias their malted oats, maybe after doing too much bending down to fill the bowl, one experiences a rush as if the brains were suddenly spinning, not that everything around one spins—as is the case with vertigo—rather it is the vision itself that spins, such that the inner consciousness rotates like a gyroscope in its hoop, while the exterior is all tremendously immobile, it is only that which is fleeing, and impossible to grasp. We have wondered if it might not be a case of *Phosphorus*, because one is terrified by the perfume of flowers (or of the little mancuspias, that smell weakly of lilacs) and it physically resembles the phosphorus box: tall, thin, craving cold drinks, ice cream and salt.

At night it is not so bad, the fatigue and the silence come to our aid—because the mancuspias keep watch sweetly over the silence of the pampa—and at times we sleep until dawn and awake with a hopeful feeling that things will improve. If one of us jumps out of bed before the other, that one may be smitten with trepidation at the prospect of a repetition of the phenomenon *Camphora monobromata*, which causes one to believe one is going in one direction when in reality one is going the opposite way. It's terrible, we go with complete assurance toward the bathroom, and suddenly we are pressing up against the naked skin of the tall mirror. We always laugh off such things, because you have to keep your mind on the work and we would gain nothing by getting disheartened so early on. We look for the capsules, to follow the instructions of Dr. Harbin scrupulously without comment or discouragement. (Maybe we're secretly a touch *Natrum muriaticum*. Typically, a natrum cries, but nobody can be permitted to see that. One is sad, one is reserved; one likes salt).

Who can lose time contemplating such vanities when there's work waiting for us in the corral, in the greenhouse and in the dairy? Chango and Leonor are already stirring up a racket outside, and when we go out with the thermometers and drive them toward the bath, those two precipitate themselves into the work as if they wanted to become tired quickly, to look busy for us and postpone their goofing off for later. We know what's what, and thankfully we are still fit enough to handle the daily work ourselves. As long as we're not too busy, or suffering headaches, we can keep it up. Now it's February, in May the mancuspias will be sold and we will be secure through the wintertime. We can hold out.

The mancuspias are very entertaining, in part because they are clever and full of wickedness, in part because raising their young is a tricky business, which requires exacting oversight, incessant and thorough. There isn't much to say about it, but here's an example of how it works: one of us releases the mother mancuspias from their greenhouses—that would be at 6:30 AM—and they are gathered in the corral, which is lined with dry grass. They are left to frolic for twenty minutes, while the others check the young left in their numbered pigeonholes where each one undergoes a quick physical and rectal temperature exam. Those who exceed 37 C are returned to their pigeonholes while the rest are placed in a chute of sheet metal to nurse their mothers. This might be the most beautiful time of morning, as we are touched by the joy of the little mancuspias and their mothers, their noisy, nonstop chatter. Leaning on the railing of the corral we forget the phantom of midday that approaches us, the hard afternoon that will not be postponed. For a moment we are a little afraid to look toward the ground of the corral—a very distinct case of *Onosmodium*—but the episode passes and the light saves us from the complementary symptom, the headache that is aggravated by darkness.

Eight o'clock is bathtime, one of us goes and throws handfuls of Krüschen salts and bran into the basins, the other tells Chango to bring buckets of tepid water. The mother mancuspias don't like the bath, so they have to be handled carefully by the ears and legs, held firmly like rabbits, and dunked and redunked in the water over and over. The mancuspias bristle in desperation, and that is what we want, as it allows the salt to penetrate to their very delicate skin.

The task of feeding the mothers falls to Leonor, who does it very well; we have never known there to be an error in the distrubtion of portions. They are given malted oats, and twice a week they get milk with white wine. We don't entirely trust Chango, it seems to us that he drinks the wine himself, so it would be better to keep the Bordelaise inside, but the house is small and the sweet smell would leak out when the sun is high anyway.

Maybe what we're saying would be monotonous and useless if things did not gradually alter as they repeat; the last few days—now that we are entering into the critical weaning period—one of us must acknowledge, with bitter feelings, that a *Silica* phase is coming on. It begins the moment one goes to sleep, a loss of stability, an inner leap, a vertigo that scales the spinal chord and into the head; just like the creepy crawling (it can be described in no other terms) of the little mancuspias up the posts of the corrals. Then, suddenly, above the black hole of sleep we'd fallen deliciously into, we sense just what hard and caustic post the playful mancuspias are climbing on. And closing the eyes makes it worse. So much for sleeping, no one sleeps with open eyes; we're dying of fatigue but a little nod-off is enough to make us feel vertigo crawling, swinging in the skull, as if the head were full of living things spinning around and around inside. Like mancuspias do.

And it is pretty ridiculous, since it's well-known that the illness proceeds from a lack of *silica*, which is to say, sand. And we are surrounded by sand dunes here, we live in a little valley threatened by immense dunes of sand, and yet we have none when we go to sleep.

Notwithstanding the likelihood that encroachment will continue, we prefer to spend a bit of time severely doped up; by noon we have noticed the medications taking effect, and the afternoon of work that follows comes off seemingly without a hitch, except maybe for a few minor derangements of things, so that, after a little while, the objects seem to stand motionless before us; a sensation at the very edge of life in every way. We suspect things are becoming more *Dulcamara*, but it is not easy to be sure.

In the air the down of the adult mancuspias floats gently, after our naps we go with scissors, rubber bags, and Chango out to the corral where they are gathered for shearing. The nights in February are cooling already, the mancuspias needed their coats to sleep in, because they sleep stretched out and so are more vulnerable than animals that curl up to sleep with their legs crossed. However, the fur on the back sheds, sloughing off bit by bit and floating in the air, eventually filling the corral with a floury haze of lint that tickles the nostrils and chases us back into the house. So we gather them together and trim their backs only halfway, being careful not to leave them too much exposed to the cold. When the clippings are too short to billow in the air, they fall in a yellowish residue of dust that Leonor wets down with the hose and rolls up into the daily wad of paste, which is then tossed down the well.

One of us has his hands full matching up the males to the young mancuspias, weighing these chicks while Chango reads aloud the results of the previous day's weight checks, verifying the development of each mancuspia and separating out the more slow-developing ones for extra feed. We keep this up until nightfall; until finally Leonor distributes the oats of the second meal in a flash, and then we lock up the mother mancuspias while the little ones squeal and obstinately try to follow alongside them. It's Chango's job to take them off separately, while we inspect the veranda. At eight we close the doors and windows; at eight we are inside, alone.

This was once a sweet moment, when we would recount incidents and hopes. But now that we are not feeling well it seems as if this hour only extends the tedium. Vainly do we beguile ourselves with the arrangement of our little pharmacy—the alphabetical order is constantly being upset by oversight—; on and on we linger silently at the table, reading the manual of Alvarez de Toledo ("Educate Yourself") or of the Humphreys ("Homeopathic Mentor"). One of us has been experiencing an intermittent *Pulsatilla* phase, that is to say, exhibiting symptoms of volubility, moroseness, exactingness, and irritability. This comes on at dusk, and coincides with the *Petroleum* stage that affects the other, a state in which everything—things, voices, memories—roll over one, as the sufferer becomes tumescent and stiff. There is no conflict between them, it's hardly comparable to the other, and tolerable enough. Afterwards, sometimes, sleep will come.

We would not wish to insert an artificially sequential scheme into these notes, one which will increase in articulation until it bursts with all the pathos of a great orchestra, after which the voices subside and droop into the tranquility of satiety. Sometimes we write of things that have already happened to us (like the great *Glonoinum* headache the day that the second litter of mancuspias was born), and sometimes we write of what happens now or just this morning. We believe it necessary to document these phases for Dr. Harbin to add to his new medical history when we go back to Buenos Aires. We are not clever, we know that we lose the thread pretty fast, but Dr. Harbin prefers to understand the details surrounding the case. This rubbing against the bathroom window that we hear at night might be significant. It might be a symptom of *Cannibis indica*; already it is known that a *Cannibis indica* has exalted sensations, with exaggerations of time and distance. It could be a mancuspia who has gotten loose and come to the light.

We started out optimists, and we have not lost hope of gaining a good sum with the sale of the young ones. We rise early, since time is of the essence during the final phase, and, at least to begin with, we are almost unaffected by the flight of Chango and Leonor. Without advance notice, without fulfilling any of their statutory obligations, last night those sons of bitches made off with our horse and the sulky [translator's note: a kind of cart], one of our rugs, the carbide lantern, and the latest issue of *Mundo Argentino*. The silence in the corrals made us suspect their absence, we have to rush to release the young and get them nursing, preparing the baths, the malted oats. We keep telling ourselves not to brood over this occurrence, we work without admitting that now we are alone, without a horse to cover the six leagues to Puan, with provisions for a week, now being used by useless bums making the rounds of towns, now that the stupid rumor has spread that we breed mancuspias and everybody should keep clear of us for fear of infection. Only with healthy exertion can we tolerate the conspiracy of forces that oppresses us at midday, at the height of the lunch hour (one of us throws together a plate of tongue and a can of peas, fried ham and eggs), that rejects the idea of going without our siesta, locks us up within the shade of the bedroom more implacably than the double bolted doors. It's only now that we clearly remember last night's bad sleep, that weird vertigo, transparent, if one may be permitted such an expression. Waking, starting up, looking straight ahead at some object—the wardrobe, for example—which is seen spinning at variable velocity and deviating inconsistently on one edge (the right side); while at the same time, through the vortex, the same wardrobe can be seen standing firmly in place and not moving. One doesn't have to think too hard to recognize it as a *Cyclamen* stage, of the kind that responds to treatment in only a few minutes and braces us to get up and back to work again. Far worse to be jolted out of the depths of a siesta (when things are so very much themselves, when the sun brusquely draws its edges around things) by agitation and jabber from the corral of the adult mancuspias, when one of them abruptly and with disquiet renounces their fattening repose. We don't want to go out, the high sun would mean a headache, how can we chance the possibility of headaches now, when everything depends on our work. But what else can we do, the disquiet of the mancuspias is growing, now it is possible to hear from the house the unprecedented racket spreading over the corrals, so then we throw on our protective pith helmets, and divide up after a hasty consultation. One of us hustles out to the mothers in their crates while the other verifies that all the gates are locked, and the water level in the Australian tank is all right, and checks for the possible invasion of a fox or a mountain lion. We had only just arrived at the entrance to the corral when we were blinded by the sun. Like albinos we waver between the white flashes, we would like to continue the work but it is late, the *Belladona* stage harrasses us and flings us down exhausted in the somber recesses of the barn. Congested, face red and hot; pupils dilated. Violent pulsation in the head and carotid. Violent twinges and lancings. Headache like shaking. Pressing down with each step like a weight on the occipital. Cleavings and impalements. Exploding pain; as if it were driving into the brain; worse when bending forward, as if the brain were dribbling outward, as if it were shoving its way out the front, or the eyes were being forced out. (*Like* this, *like* that; but the truth is never like anything.) Worse with the noises, the shaking, motion, light. And then just like that it stops, the shadow and the coolness banish it all in an instant, leaving us to a marvellous gratitude, a wish to run, shaking our heads, amazed that just a moment before...But there is work to do, and now we suspect that the disquiet of the mancuspias results from a lack of fresh water, thanks to the absence of Leonor and Chango—they are so sensitive that they must be feeling that absence in some way—, and this morning's work was a little different from usual, owing to our blunders, our difficulties.

Since it is not a shearing day, one of us is occupied with arrangements for breeding and with weight control; it is obvious that the young ones have suddenly gotten worse since yesterday. The mothers eat poorly, sniffing languidly at the malted oats before deigning to nibble the tepid porridge. In silence, we attend to the last tasks, now the coming of the night has a different feeling that we do not wish to examine, and we do not deviate, as we did before, from the established and functional order, with Leonor and Chango and the mancuspias in their proper places. To close the doors of the house is to shut out an unlegislated world, in which night and dawn do as they please. We enter fearfully and overcautiously, demurring for a while, incapable of putting it off and this makes us furtive and evasive, with all the night waiting like a watching eye.

Luckily we are drowsy. The sun and work can dispense with more than one of our worries. We're straying off into sleep over our cold leftovers, pitifully masticating shrivelled bits of fried egg and bread soggy with milk. Something scratches once again at the bathroom window, and what seems like furtive slithering can be heard on the roof; the wind isn't blowing, it is the night of the full moon and the roosters would be crowing before midnight, if we had roosters. We go to bed without a word, doling out the last doses of the medication groping blindly with our fingers. With the light out—but those aren't the right words, the light is not put out, the light is simply gone, the house is a tenebrous well and outside everything is lit by the full moon—we want to say something to ourselves and we're barely able to ask ourselves about tomorrow, about how we will get the feed from town. And we slept. One hour, no more, the ashen thread the window throws has barely edged toward the bed. All of a sudden we are alert in the dark, listening in the dark so that we may listen better. There's something going on among the mancuspias, the noise is now a rabid or terrified clamor, in which we can make out the keen howling of the females and the more bronchial ululations of the males, suddenly interrupted, like a volley of silence moving over the house, then once again the clamor mounts against the night and the distance. We do not think of going out there, just listening is already too much, one of us wonders if the shrieks are coming from outside or in here because sometimes they seem to be coming from the inside, and over the course of this vigil we enter into an *Aconitum* stage, where all is confused and nothing is less certain than its opposite. Yes, the headaches come on with a violence that can hardly be described. Sensation of ripping, of burning in the brain, in the scalp, with fear, with fever, with anguish. Fullness and heaviness in the forehead, as if there were a weight inside that is pushing outward: as if everything were being torn out through the forehead. *Aconitum* is abrupt; savage; worse in cold winds; with anxiety, anguish, fear. The mancuspias surround the house, it is useless to repeat that they are in the corrals, that the locks are holding.

We do not notice the dawn, toward five o'clock we tumble from rest- less dreams as our hands stir to life at the usual hour, lifting capsules to our mouths. There has been a knocking at the living room door for some time now, the blows increase with fury until the sneakers put one of us on and go creeping up to the keyhole. It's the police, come to tell us that Chango has been arrested; they are bringing the sulky back, which they suspected had been stolen and abandoned. There's a report to sign, all is well, the high sun and the great silence of the corrals. The police inspect the corrals, one covers his nose with a handkerchief, making like he is coughing. We tell them what they want to hear, we sign, and they take their leave almost at a run, they go far back from the corrals and look at them, and at us too, stealing a glance into the interior (which emits a stagnant odor from the open doorway), and they almost hurry off. It is very strange that these brutes didn't want to poke around a bit more. They fled this place like the plague, scurrying along the side road.

One of us seems to decide personally that the other will take the sulky and hunt up some feed, while the morning chores are attended to. We get going without enthusiasm, the horse is worn out because it has been driven relentlessly already, consequently we go along little by little and lingeringly. All is in order, so that means the mancuspias were not the ones that are making noises in the house, the roof tiles will have to be fumigated for rats, amazing the racket that one solitary rat can make in the night. We open the corrals, gather the mothers together but there's barely any malted oats left and the mancuspias are fighting ferociously, ripping pieces from the back and neck. The blood sprays from them, and it takes the whip and shouts to separate them. In the aftermath, the little ones nurse with difficulty and imperfectly, we can tell the chicks are famished, yet some of them wobble over to us or support themselves leaning against the barbed wire. There is a male lying dead in the entrance to his crate, inexplicably. And the horse doesn't want to trot, we're already ten lots from the house with further to go, and his head is nodding and snorting. Dejected, we undertake the tour, seeing how the last remnants of feed are lost in one convulsion of violence.

We're not all that determined to go through with it, and so we come back to the veranda. There is a dying mancuspia chick on the first step. We lift it, we put it in the basket with straw, we want to know what it is dying of but it dies the obscure death of an animal. And the locks are intact, there is no way to know how this mancuspia got out, if its death was its escape or if its escape was its death. We put ten capsules of *Nux Vomica* in its beak. They remain there like little pearls, which it is unable to swallow. From where we are we can see a male fallen on its forefeet; trying to raise itself with a shudder, letting itself fall again as if praying.

We seem to hear cries, so near to us that we look under the straw chairs on the veranda; Dr. Harbin has prepared us for brute assaults in the morning, but we didn't imagine it could have taken the form of a headache like this. Occipital pain, so much that there is, now and again, an explosion of crying: *Apis*, pains like bee stings. We throw our heads back, or press them against the pillow (somehow we've managed to get into bed). Without thirst, but sweating; scanty urine, piercing cries. As if bruised, sensitive to the touch; once we shook hands, and it was terrible. Until that fades, little by little, and we are left with the fear of a repetition with a different animal, since we have already had the bee, maybe next time it will be the serpent's image. It's two thirty.

We prefer to complete these reports while the light lasts and we are still all right. One of us should go into town now. If we wait until after the siesta, it will be too late to make the trip, and we will remain alone all night in the house, perhaps without the means to medicate ourselves... The siesta stagnates in silence, the rooms are getting hot, if we go into the veranda the gleam of the chalky ground, the barns, the tiled roofs, drives us back. Other mancuspias have died but the remainder are keeping quiet, one must draw near to hear them panting in their boxes. One of us thinks that we can sell them, that we must go to town. The other is getting together these notes and he doesn't think much about anything. No going anywhere until the heat breaks, and that won't be 'til night. We go out just before seven, there are still a few handfulls of feed left in the barn, a fine oaten dust sifts from shaking bags, we gather it up like treasure. They get a whiff of it, and the agitation in the crates is violent. We do not dare to release them, it is better to drop a spoonful of porridge into each crate, in this way it seems that more of them are satisfied, that the distribution is more even. Nor do we dare to remove the dead mancuspias, nor is there an explanation for ten empty crates, or for how some of the young ones came to be mixed in with the males in the corral. It can barely be seen, now that night is falling all at once and Chango has robbed us of the carbide lamp.

It seems as if, in the road, there against the mountainous willows, there were people. If we are going to send someone to town, this is the moment; there is still time. Sometimes we wonder if they aren't spying on us, the people are so ignorant and they don't have much between their eyes. We prefer not to think and we close the door happily, retreating to the house where everything is more our own. We would like to consult the manuals so as to avoid a new *Apis*, or some other, still worse beast; we leave supper and read aloud, almost without hearing. Some phrases climb over the others, and outside it is the same, some mancuspias howl louder than the rest, keeping it up and repeating a piercing ululation. "*Crotalus cascavella* causes peculiar hallucinations..." One of us repeats the line, we're glad we know Latin so well, crotalo cascabel, rattlesnake rattle, but it is redundant because cascabel, rattle, is equivalent to crotalo, rattlesnake. Maybe the manual does not want to alarm the ailing layman by naming the animal directly. Nevertheless it does present this name, this terrible serpent..."whose venom acts with horrible intensity." We have to yell to make ourselves heard over the clamor of the mancuspias, once again we can feel them surrounding the house, on the roof, scratching at the windows, against the lintels. In a way it isn't so strange, for lately we've seen so many open crates, but the house is closed and the light in the dining room enwraps us in its chill protection while we shout over the scratching. Everything is clear in the manual, direct unprejudiced language for invalids, the description of the symptoms: headache and great excitement, caused by the onset of sleep. (Good thing we won't be doing any sleeping.) The cranium squeezes the brain like a steel helmet—well said. Something living roams in circles within the head. (In that case, the house is our head, we feel the roaming, each window is an ear shut against the howls of the mancuspias right outside.) Head and chest burdened by iron armor. A red hot iron driven into the vertex. We are not sure about that word vertex, a moment ago the lights flickered, dwindling little by little, we must have forgotten to start the mill this afternoon. When reading is no longer possible, we light a candle right next to the manual so we can familiarize ourselves completely with the symptoms, it is better to know in case, later on—Stabbing pains sharp in the right temple, it is a terrible serpent whose venom acts with horrible intensity (we just read this, it is difficult to make out by candlelight), something living roams in circles within the head, we read that too, it's just like that, something living that roams in circles. We are not worried, it is worse outside, if there is an outside. We look at each other across the manual, and if one of us gestures at the howling that keeps getting louder and louder, we just go on reading as if we were sure all of this was in there, something living that roams in circles howling at the windows, at the ears, the mancuspias, dying of hunger, howling.

Amanda C. Davis

Loving Armageddon

SHE PRESSES HER CHEEK TO THE CENTER OF HIS CHEST, listening to the beat of his hand-grenade heart.

It ticks like a time bomb, but no, he insists it's a grenade, pin forever almost-pulled, and through the skin at his sternum she can feel the telltale ridges, precise metal squares, sharper than bone. She strokes the shallow indents. He shudders.

"It might go off at any time," he says. A bit warning. A bit bragging.

She raises her head, and he shrugs so that his shirt falls closed again—most of the way, anyway.

She says, "Do you want to go out again tomorrow?"

His core may be metal, but the flesh around it flushes delightfully warm.

Every time he tells her how it happened, he has a different story.

He was born with no heart and the obstetrician grabbed the nearest replacement. He was in a car crash and died when he was young; the mortician filled his empty chest with something of the same size and heft but it quickened and beat, and he was returned to his puzzled parents alive, almost whole. He went to war and the grenade lodged there in a desert firefight. (Isn't it the same type his unit carries? He won't speculate.) He never dared remove it.

(The war story can't be true, can it? He's so young. Too young to both go to war and return from it.)

She accepts any story he tells. Then she files the stories in her mind so she can call on any of them when she needs them. He's a lucky accident, a medical miracle, a war hero. Whichever story she needs right then, so she can love him.

Some days—most days—she doesn't think of it at all. There's so much more to think about. Meals, chores, television. Jokes and laundry. Bedroom, bathroom, smiling, sharing the car, sharing the bed.

But when they make love, his heart pounds like cannonfire, and she draws him as close as she can, so the metal throbs against her own chest, urging its rhythm into her own heart. The threat of explosion excites her.

She can't ask how it's doing. She can't ask how it feels. That invited uncomfortable evasion first, then snappishness. It's a ticklish thing. She doesn't always enjoy the threat.

The week before Valentine's Day they have a volcanic fight. It's the kind that sparks from nothing and ranges around the world, the kind of fight that grows so ferocious that it becomes masochistically fun, like poking bruises or picking scabs. There's vile satisfaction in making an Ouroboros out of a fight: jamming a snake's tail down its throat.

They are on the cusp of wringing out their past gripes, ready to shatter their future, when without warning he takes her by both arms and shoves her away from him, into the hallway.

"Run," he says. "It's happening."

They only need lock eyes for her to understand. She flees to the bedroom, the farthest room from the front door, and she hears both doors, hers and his, slam at once. She crouches on the far side of the room (his side) with her back against the bedside table. She clutches her knees, first shuddering, then shivering, and all of her past and future with him scream through her head like bullets.

She waits minutes. More minutes.

She hears no explosion.

He's leaning against the brick wall by the front door with a lit cigarette between his fingers. He's paying it no attention. She's not sure where he got it. He never smokes.

He says, "It's really going to happen someday." He throws the cigarette into a snowbank and it dies with an angry, impotent hiss.

She knows this is true. She's imagined it a hundred times. In her fantasy, she recognizes it's happening, and she has enough time to clutch him as tight as she can, so they're almost one—jumping on the grenade—and she imagines the burst of metal racking their bodies, the shrapnel cutting escape paths through their muscles and minds, their flesh singed, their blood mingling.

But she has just spent minutes crouching behind the bed.

He says, "I put it in myself, you know. Replaced my heart. So I wouldn't have to use it."

She files away his story. Whatever it takes to love him. She slides her hand into his. His fingers smell like smoke, and in the February breeze, they are as cold as metal, every one.

K. M. FEREBEE

The Earth and Everything Under

Peter had been in the ground for six months when the birds began pushing up out of the earth. Small ones, at first, with brown feathers: sparrows, spitting out topsoil, their black eyes alert. They shook and stretched their wings in the sunlight. Soon they were pecking the juniper berries and perching on rooftops, just like other birds. They were small, fat, and soft; Elyse wanted to hold them. But they were not tame and they would not come to her.

The next birds were larger: larks and grackles. They crawled their way not just out of the dirt round Elyse's own house, the old Devereaux homestead, but farther out west, towards the town of St. Auburn. When Elyse drove down for her week's worth of groceries, she could see the holes by the sides of the fields, the raw earth scuffed up and still teeming with worm-life. The birds picked at the worms for their meals, pulling them like long threads from a sweater, unweaving their bodies' hard wet work. Sometimes the corn had died in patterns close to the holes, like it had been burned.

Elyse thought the town's new sheriff would notice, and he turned up just as the grackles gave way to magpies. His old police cruiser ground in the driveway, wheels spinning on rock, a sound she knew, and she went out on the front porch to meet him. She was barefoot. She did not like to wear shoes. An old superstition; she had not outgrown it.

"Sheriff," she said.

He squinted through sunlight. Did not approach her. "Miss Mayhew."

"Is there something I can help you with?"

She was aware of the way she must look to his eye: her black hair tangled, autumn skin sunburned, the backs of her hands and her wrists cross-hatched where she'd scraped them rooting through cedar and yew. She would have put on a whiter dress, she thought, something less hedge-witching than wine-colored cotton—but no, let him see it, the darker stains on it.

"Some strange reports," he said. "What you might call violations."

A magpie took flight over his head: black-and-white plumage precise and foreign. The sheriff raised his hand in a gesture to ward off ill luck—then caught himself. Still, he tracked the bird on the skyline.

"One for sorrow," Elyse said.

"Hell of a lot more than one in town. If you'll excuse my saying."

She held his gaze, thought about staring him down. She couldn't, though, summon up the anger. She toed the peeling paint of the porch. "It's not my work," she said. "You know that. And *he's* under the dirt."

"Still," he said. He had keen eyes, blue eyes. Hair the sandy color of birch when you'd stripped all of the pale skin off it. And he gave her that same kind of stripped-plain look. "It'd be best if you scared the birds off."

They both looked up, to the gabled rooftop. The brown slates of it were covered in birds, a shifting mass of dappled feathers. The house looked alive. Elyse heard a burst of song—a lark, she thought—and then another bird singing, and another bird, but none of the songs seemed quite complete. They quit mid-pitch, fell off too soon, as though the birds had not learned the notes yet; as though no one, in the places they had come from, had ever been able to teach them the tune.

"They're birds," Elyse said. She crossed her arms: final. "They're not my creatures. They'll do what birds do."

But larger birds began to surface: a turkey vulture, a hawk or two. There was talk in St. Auburn about a condor. A farmer in Woodbine shot a goose, and turned up on Elyse's doorstep.

"Cut it open," he said, "to clean out the soft parts. For cooking. Found a letter addressed to you." He held out the letter: blood-stained and wrinkled. It hadn't been opened.

Elyse looked down and knew what spindly hand had written that address. She touched the paper, dry as the rue she kept hanging over her kitchen counters. It was a special kind of lacewing dryness. It made her think of insects that moved in the summer night, all wings and shadows. They might have been ten thousand years in the tomb by the time she found them, all lifeless. Just tinder. She swept them off of the porch with a broom, thinking how they had been wet with life once.

The farmer said, "Do you want the feathers?"

Startled, she looked up.

"The bones and feathers. I saved the most of the bird for you."

He was a shy man, with that shut country look to his face, and she took the bones and feathers because she didn't know what else to do. All of it fit in one plastic bag: a mass of down and sinew, so light now that the meat was not on it.

She waved goodbye to the farmer's truck. It bounced down towards the two-line blacktop. She could see black birds circle over the cornfields. The bright of the sun turned their wings to fishhooks. She could not say if they were crows or vultures. The wind sighed; dust stirred, and the corn moved.

Later she sat and read the letter. The lamp in the kitchen wrote a curve on the whitewood top of the breakfast table. The letter, when she held it up to the light, was marked with blood through and through. She could still read the writing, crooked and narrow.

My dear Elyse,

I write from the ocean. I cannot know what messages have reached you. Perhaps you do not know there is an ocean. I mean the ocean that is here, not the Atlantic or the Pacific or any such body. The body here is not seawater. It is dark in your hand, and the double moons cast no kind of reflection on it. Sometimes I can see fish in the water, or some things that look like fish, the color of fish if you peeled the skin off them, but they move so fast they drop from view.

I am never hungry here, and I don't drink the water. I lie in the well of the boat to sleep, but it seems sleep is not of this country. I watch the stars. They still turn in a wheel, the strange stars I wrote you about. And sometimes I sail past the shapes of islands and see lanterns on them—are they lanterns? is that the word?—and I hear voices, but not any human voices. The lanterns scatter when I come near.

I think about you, the stroke of an eyebrow, the shell of an ear, the map of your hairline. That long uncharted archipelago you make with all the parts of your spine. There is nothing I forget about you.

    Peter

When she was done, she folded the page back in segments. She poured herself a finger of whiskey and drank it just out of the lamp-light. Dusk had gone and darkness was settled. Insects were pocking their bodies on glass, trying to come in out of the night. Peter's work boots were still in the corner. She had not moved them in his absence. The mud on them had long since dried. Flakes had cracked off of the leather like skin. Tomorrow, she thought, she would put them out-side; out on the porch, maybe clean the soles. Prise the mud off with a pocketknife.

She slept sitting up in the velvet armchair. Her mother had told her that when witches died in the old days, no one who'd seen or known them would sleep in a straight-bed for a fort-night, for fear that the witch would sit on their chest and steal the breath from them. Elyse had tried to picture this: the witch pressing his ghost against a body, trying to get what was inside. She had thought, I just want to press my body against another body, when I'm a witch and I die. But she knew bodies did not work like this; had known it already when she was a child.

In the morning, the sheriff was on her porch step. His hat was in his hands. He stood up fast when he heard the door open. "Miss Mayhew," he said.

She was wearing a gray cotton dress with flowers. The weight of her long black hair was wet. She still felt scrubbed-clean, unshelled by the shower. She didn't want to face a man like that. She put Peter's boots down on the porch boards, rested a hand on her hip. "Sheriff," she said. "Have you come to arrest me?"

"No, ma'am." He put his hat back on his head; went around to his car and opened the trunk. He came back with a white swan in his hands. It was dead: there was blood still on its chest-feathers, gone dark now, not that living red. She could see the place where the bullet was in it. Its wings and its lithe neck drooped in death.

She reached out and put one hand on a wing. Lightly, only: the brush of her fingers. She didn't want to trouble it.

"Fellow out in Marsdale brought it down. I figured you'd know what to do with it." The sheriff fixed her with his gaze. His face was very patient.

"It's not mine."

"Never said it was. A letter, though, once it's sent…"

Elyse said, "You spend too much time talking to farmers." But she took the swan from him. It felt like a child, the weight in her arms. Cradling was what you called the motion. There was no other way to carry it.

She didn't want the law in her house. There was lead and gunpowder lining the threshold, cloves over the door to guard against it. But she asked the sheriff, "Have you got a name?"

He paused halfway to turning. "Linden."

"You'll bring the birds?"

"When I find them."

"Did you shoot this one down?" She hefted the swan a little.

He looked at her with those August sky eyes, like she was confusing to him. "No, ma'am. I never had much time for hunting birds."

Elyse said, "Only men."

Later she watched him drive off, the lone car on the road. It was early, still, and the air was cold. Autumn had started moving in: setting the first of its furniture up in the room that summer had not vacated.

There was no point to putting off unpleasant tasks. She set the swan on a broad cutting board and went to work dismantling it. The feathers went first, in matted handfuls, because she could make some use of them. Then she took the butchering knife and carved a space between the ribs. She had to snap the breastbone first. It was hard, the bone slippery in her grip. Even birds had such tough bones, bodies built for survival. She marveled at it. But when she got into the soft meat of organs, she found the letter almost at once, feeling for it with her fingertips. The same envelope, sealed and dirty; the same precise and crooked address.

She opened it and read it with the blood still on her hands.

Elyse,

I worry that time doesn't pass for you the way it does here. I worry that I'll get out of sync before I find you, before I find my way back. I told you about the birds in the forest, how they seemed to migrate so fast, so that one moment there were summer birds, then just starlings. And moss seemed to cover the bark of trees as I walked past. Like everything was living in motion. I saw a flower open and close. A fox get carried apart by ants, till all that was left was the bones of it. I want to date these letters somehow, but don't think I can.

I am following the railroad out towards the ocean. There are no trains ever, only tracks. I see animals, but no other people. Sometimes lights very far in the distance, lights that look like cars in the dusk, driving on highways, out to the west. If there are train tracks, why not cars? But it makes me so sad to see them.

I miss our own quiet country road. I miss the unmarked settler graves you found along it, that summer that we went bone-hunting. You were the one who could find the dead where the ground hid them under its skin. You are a better witch than I was. I admit it. I miss the way you smelled of witchcraft. Soot on your fingertips, sage and hyssop, sweet dock and cedar tips. Even in the thick of the forest, nothing here has a scent.

Be safe and know I am trying to reach you.

Peter

Elyse put the letter beside its cousin, in a box she had once kept recipes in. She finished stripping the swan of feathers and set them aside. The meat and bones and skin she took outside and laid in the garden, hoping wolves would come to eat at it—the skinny wolves that haunted the fields, gray interlopers. Being a witch, Elyse had nothing to fear from their presence. The townsfolk objected, were frightened of them. But Peter had had the gift of wolf-speaking, and when Elyse saw their black shapes in the night, the glint of their eyes, she thought of him.

Out in the yard, she saw new hollows, places where birds were still breaking the surface. The roof of her house was thick and busy. A crane landed for a moment, ghostly white legs crooked and graceful, then flourished its wings and was flying again. Elyse could not think why the sheriff had spared her. By rights, she should have been taken in; the birds were evidence of witching, and this was the place they had marked as their home. Men had been put in the ground for less; she would know. She would know.

She cleaned off the cutting board in the kitchen; made a sandwich, cut it in two. The whole house smelled of blood and magic. She could hear the birds on the roof. For a long time, when Peter went into the ground, she had not eaten. It had been hard to swallow, hard to chew; hard even to take the knives from their drawers, to knead the bread, measure coffee to brew. This was not a widow's grief, or not all of it; green onions, when she touched them, sprouted anew, and eggs cracked, and the yolks crawled out on the counter. Potatoes sent out new roots. A leg of lamb once pulsed with blood. She feared what her hands might do, while something in her reached for resurrection. It was easier not to touch food.

The wolves left rabbits out on her doorstep. A whole deer once, its eyes still dark, its dun skin soft and smooth. Wolves, she thought, had simple thoughts. Hunger, not-hunger, and sometimes the moon.

The sheriff—newly appointed—had brought a casserole. From the ladies down at Mission Valley, he said. Then another day: from the ladies at St. Jude's. Elyse had thought they came from the same kitchen.

"Charity," she'd said: scornful in her anger.

He'd shrugged: awkward in the new uniform. "It's just food."

Now she ate in hard little bites. A hummingbird floated at the window, all dark green chest and nose like a needle. It was too small to carry a letter, she thought. Maybe just the tiniest rune, written down on a thin strip of paper, wrapped round its heart. Or the very same rune, cut into the fluttering muscle. Carved in one motion: a word, a wound.

She drove into town. The neighbors were watching. She wore her best dress: bright red, with a plume of flowers that spread up across her chest. Her hair was unbrushed; it frayed like a spume of water just breaking off the ocean. She'd thought for a moment of going barefoot; instead, wore Peter's old work boots. She shopped through the aisles of the little co-op, ignoring the whispers. Her feet were heavy, and she liked it; felt knobbly and wild, substantial, good.

In frozen foods, a woman stared: somebody's mother or grandmother, in a lime-green-colored cardigan and laced white tennis shoes. The cashier, through heavy eyelashes, kept sneaking furtive looks. She didn't want to touch Elyse's money, not at first; then grabbed it in one rushed fistful and shoved it under the register's hooks, breathing out in one heavy exhale.

Outside, Elyse leant against the store and ate an apple. Scattered birds came and sat at her feet. The wind, when it blew, had a charred spark to it: the scent of autumn or witching or both, embers blossoming, ashy and new. She licked her lips. The apple was still green, sour.

A car pulled up, dust-covered: the sheriff. He rolled down his window. "Miss Mayhew."

"Linden," she said.

"You have an audience." He nodded at the birds.

"Everywhere."

He rummaged in the passenger seat for a moment; came back with a bundle of letters that he held out in the air. "Got something for you."

She stepped forward to take it. There were five or six letters, she thought. Hard to tell. Her fingers were sticky from the apple. Her hand brushed the sheriff's. She glanced at him.

"Told folks to bring in what they find. They ought to pay me for delivering your mail," he said.

Elyse didn't know what to say. She said, "I appreciate the gesture."

The sheriff shrugged. "Any idea when this might end?"

"The letters?"

"The birds. The whole damn uncanny."

She moved back, minding her feet round the birds. Some rose in a rush; one perched on her shoulder. "I'm not doing it," she said.

"I know that. Just hunting around for some insight." He started to roll up his window, then paused. "Got a cider tree in my backyard, been giving up apples early. If you like them. I don't have much use for so many."

Elyse looked down at the core in her hand. She could see her own teethmarks in the white flesh. "I'd like that," she said.

"I'll bring some around with the next batch of letters."

He left. Elyse watched. The bird on her shoulder toyed with an uncoiled strand of her hair. She brushed it aside, harsh and impatient. Witches had to be careful with hair, with toenails and blood, with bones and eyelashes; leave any part of yourself, unaware, and someone, somewhere, would set it against you. Burn what you shed: that was the lesson. She combed her thick hair back with her fingers, feeling its mass, its thousand snares.

At dusk, she lit a lamp with witch-fire and sat on the porch. Moths came crawling through still air, and clicking junebugs with hard little bodies. A few fireflies made themselves signal flares. Elyse sipped wine from a solid glass jam jar; unfolded the letters.

Beloved Elyse,

There is a road that leads down to the sea. I have to believe that it's the way out, the one. I have to believe.

Seagulls keep circling as I walk. It's winter here already. But things keep pushing up through the snow; not plants, exactly. I can't ever seem to get warmer or colder, but I feel it in objects: the ice, the heat. I never thought I would miss the chill, but I do; I think of when I would run alongside the wolves, in December or January, and come home to find the house full of warmth. You at the kitchen sink: peeling rosemary leaves from the stalk, slicing ginger, the smell prickling.

I never see another person. I wonder where they all must be? No ferrymen, even; no toll-takers. Only me. I write these letters to keep words alive. It gets strange when I don't speak. I forgot the name for an arum lily the other day; couldn't think of it, just couldn't—think. Then I worried I'd get like the wolves. There'd be a wilderness that I couldn't come in from. You'd be inside a warm scented house. I'd come to the window; I'd press my cheek just there, against the pane of glass. But you wouldn't ever let me inside. By then I'd be just claws and teeth.

Don't lock me out, O arum lily. O rose of Sharon, don't forget me.

    Peter

She put that letter to one side. She didn't want to go on with the rest. She didn't know if she had the strength. A moth batted up against her hand. She nudged it away gently. The witch-fire burned with a red-moon light inside its lamp, wavering. Out in the dark, a nightingale called. There was no answer. The silence waited; went on waiting.

At last she stood and gathered the letters. She would read them, she thought, when she was in bed. She doused the lamp and went indoors. The air was sticky: the end of summer. It promised no easy sleep.

Elyse,

I cannot remember the names of colors. I put my ear to the railroad tracks and hear a rumbling. Something moves under the earth, a light or a dark thing. Do you think that if I die in this place, I'll go in the ground and find another country, just a little bit dimmer and stranger than this one? I don't want to die again, Elyse.

At night here the stars are very thick, and I think that none of the animals sleep. I hear them moving out in the forest. Pacing, clawing; the stir of air when they breathe…

Distant, silent, surly, beautiful, so-dream-like Elyse,

Sometimes I think I could walk on this water. The world here is flat and like a dream. I walked on water once before—you remember—the old mill pond—handspan insects—Spanish moss drooping—soaking our socks right up to the ankles. It smelled like a color. Cut vegetables. Herb beds. Dowsing rods. Grave digging. But how could I make the spell last so long here? You're far from me; I see how far. It just stretches on, the sea. Sea, is what we used to call it.

I see catamarans out on the horizon. Catamarans: is that the word I mean? Something floating, something with sails. It looked like a cut lily. Then I was homesick, crying for you, but I can't cry in this country. I make the motion but no tears come. What is the name for that kind of motion? It isn't a color. It tastes of salt. It's like and not like breathing. I know you'll remember the word for it…

Elyse,

I woke in the dark green wild of a forest, filled with birds, all migrating…

It rained for a week, and the birds started dying. The sky up over the fields was blue—not the cloudless blue of an arid August, but a peat-smoke color. Peter's blue. His eyes had once been almost that color. Elyse waited to feel melancholy.

The rain was a steady, scouring fall. It turned dirt to muck and washed out seeds that Elyse had planted in the herb garden. She went out to eye the ongoing damage. Her blouse and skirt plastered flat under siege; her hair stuck to her face and shoulders. She wiped the water out of her eyes and saw two dead birds: a crow and a starling. They were lying feet-up by the lemon verbena. Rain had distorted the shape of their wings.

Elyse scraped them into a cardboard shoebox and brought them inside. They did not smell like anything: not particularly of death, nor even of herb beds. No worms or beetle-marks could be seen. When she touched them, Elyse could feel the echo of witchcraft under their feathers, very faintly. She resisted the urge to cut them open, to check for letters. If every bird had a letter, she thought—all the sparrows and larks, the nightingales, all the geese, every bird that had crawled its way up…She imagined the envelopes moldering in boxes, more than she could ever read.

The next day she found three more birds in the front yard: three grackles, dead, with storm-battered wings. She picked them up, carried them to the porch by the hooks of their little clawed feet. Over yonder the crust of the earth was upset, by the root of a live oak tree, where another bird was scrabbling to surface. Its curved beak poked up. A kestrel, she thought, or some kind of hawk.

It was still raining.

The sheriff came by one morning, early, when Elyse was still asleep. Later she woke and went out on the porch. A milk crate of apples was waiting, and a grocery sack filled with water-stained letters. The apples were small and hard, but sweet-smelling. She rolled one in the palm of her hand. Broke its skin with her teeth. It tasted like autumn, red and familiar. A note on the crate said:

Hope didn't wake you. Harvest good. Need to talk re: plague of birds. Will swing by later this wk.

She smiled, and was mystified by the motion. She touched her hand to her lips, her cheek. The smile remained. She finished the apple, bemused, watching the branches of wide trees bow in the rain. She could see on them the tips of autumn, leaves beginning to shine like copper. Soon the whole would be ablaze.

She carried the apples indoors to the kitchen, thought of pie-making. The letters she left in their bag on the porch. They could hardly get more battered or wet. She left the door open to smell the rain. Clouds shifted on the far horizon. The light got darker, then lighter again. She went barefoot all day, enjoying the feeling, the thrill of the first cold starting to set.

Nineteen birds died in the garden that week. She picked them up and stowed them in boxes; set them on the porch with the rest.

———

It was dusk when the sheriff drove up the gravel. The clouds had cleared, but the twilight was heavy: damp and filled with swollen scents. Elyse sat on the edge of the porch. There was mud on the narrow crests of her ankles. She drank cider cold from a jar in her hand.

The sheriff approached. He said, "Storm's broken."

"Not much of a storm."

"You say that, and yet I got a river over in Woodbine's been flooding. Water up all the way to the town line. Carrying off houses. Power's down."

"Is it." She'd never had much use for that kind of power.

"Funny thing: lot of dead birds in that flood. Not just river birds. Eagles. Cactus wrens. Your fair number of sparrows, seeing as lately we're overrun." His eyes strayed to the back of the porch, where the bodies of all the dead birds sat. Elyse had not bothered to cover them over. She had found that the wolves and the foxes and vultures were not interested in them, not unless she took out the heart, took the witch-craft and made them just birds again. They took up a lot of room on the porch. She'd stopped counting them.

"Seems you have a problem yourself," the sheriff said.

Elyse took a sip of murky cider. "Why don't you sit down," she said.

He did: settling long legs on the porch stoop. She offered him the mason jar. He drank from it and grimaced. "Are those my apples?"

"Put to good use."

"I remember them having less of a kick."

They sat in silence for a while. Moths moved in the early darkness. A mourning dove uttered a short sad cry and plunged to its death, pale gray and not particularly graceful. Neither Elyse nor the sheriff paid much mind to it.

"They'll all die eventually," Elyse said. "It's in their nature."

"And then? They die, but they don't go away. Can't seem to burn or bury 'em."

She didn't know how to answer that statement.

He sighed. "I was real sorry about what happened to your husband."

"It's the law. He knew the risk he ran."

"And you?"

"The witch woman of Auburn County?" She laughed. The sound rasped her throat. "If you've come for repenting—"

"No." He drank again from the jar. "I was there that day at the station. You know."

"I knew you might have been."

"I should have done something. I wanted to."

Elyse pushed one bare toe down in the dirt. The rain had left it rich and wet. "They planted quick-tree—witchbane—all around his grave so witches can't come near. Standard procedure. Can't even visit."

"They don't want him coming back."

"He's not coming back," Elyse said. She covered her mouth.

"No," the sheriff said.

She felt his hand on her hand in the dark. Just a touch, nothing more or less.

She asked, "So what the hell do I do with all these birds?"

He laughed: a low and gentle sound. "Have you considered witchcraft?"

"It's against the law."

"I promise not to look."

He stood up and turned his back, placing his broad hands over his eyes. A joke.

"No," Elyse said. "Look. I want you to look."

It was almost night by then, but she could still see his face. He leveled his curious eyes on her. She walked out in the yard and picked up the dove. It was still slightly warm, like a stone in summer, ghosting with heat when the sun has gone down. She could feel the magic inside it, inert.

"I can't bring them to life," she said. "Not in a way you would want. The witchcraft doesn't work like that. I don't think they were real birds to start with, you know. Just other things made into flesh."

"Sure seem real enough when they're eating the sweet corn. They've got bones and blood, don't they?"

"Lots of things have that." She thought of Peter, lost somewhere on his ocean, long underground. For a moment she felt his lips on her neck, his breath against her collarbone. But he was not really Peter anymore. He was speaking a language, a kind of wolf-language, that she had not learned yet.

She held the dove up close to her heart. A white glow started between her hands. There was no heat to it, no smell and no texture. Still, it made her flinch. She forced herself to hold very steady. She felt the dove fold up like paper. The weight of it lessened. When she opened her hands, there was nothing in them up pale gray ashes. Fistfuls of ashes, and bits of burned paper. She could see the ink on some of them. She let the wind take them out towards the cornfields. She wiped her hands against the skirt. The air smelled of witching, a mournful scent.

"There," she said. "Just wishes and paper. Nothing to it."

She looked at the sheriff. She thought he'd been crying. The magic sometimes took them like that. She affected not to see his expression. Men got odd. She leaned against the porch railing.

"I'll have to do all of them, one by one. Better to get it done fast," she said.

"You want to make a night of it?" His look was not very readable.

Elyse tilted her head. "You won't be needed."

"I know," he said.

After a moment's pause, she said, "It'll be a *long* night, so you'd better come in, then. Have something to eat, find a place to set down."

The doorway was still guarded by gunpowder. She broke the line of it as she passed. Later she could take down the cloves, unmark the lead; redo the witching, to keep out what needed keeping out, and keep in what needed keeping in.

Elyse,

It stretches so far, this scentless water. Every day I forget and forget. I wave to the flowers that drift in the distance. What is their name again? There was something I promised not to lose. I locked it in the cage of my chest. I can feel it there, like a bright-winged bird. But the bird is restless…

Elyse
　Elyse. Elyse I. Everyday I think. Elyse. Elyse, Elyse: forget.

Sometimes a bird still struggles through to the surface, breath coming in unsteady gasps—even in the dead of winter. Elyse finds and carries them in her bare hands to the reed birdcage at the back of the house. They don't live long. But she feeds raw seed to them, coaxing the life in them while she can. At night they sing (they are all songbirds) and when she wakes, she feels she can almost finish it: the last line of the song they are singing. She feels it in her bones, that coming warmth, the completeness.

KAREN JOY FOWLER

Nanny Anne
and the Christmas Story

Rain lashed the house. Fiona heard it, drumming on the roof and rushing through the gutters. A handful of drops hit the window so hard the glass shook. A sudden sheet of light, and there were the black trees at the end of the yard, their branches bare and tossing wildly about. Underneath the window, in the other bed, Dacey was crying, great gulps of agony because the thunder was scaring her and she couldn't find Moe Bear. Could there be any two twins so different from each other? Fiona's knees were bent, the covers tented, so that no one would see the lump that was Moe Bear under her legs.

She wasn't the only one taking things that didn't belong to her. Nanny Anne was wearing their mother's locket. The pendant was hidden under her bulky sweater, but she was kneeling now, looking under Dacey's bed, and Fiona could see the distinctive chain around the white back of her neck. When the time was right, Fiona would return Moe Bear, pretending to have just found him, saving the day. Fiona loved to save the day. She did it a lot. What was Nanny Anne's plan? No one was looking for her mother's locket.

"Nanny Anne is what makes it all work," Fiona's mother often said. Fiona and Dacey's parents were very particular about who took care of their children. "There's an old soul in that young body. I never worry for a minute. And she's got a playful nature. The girls adore her."

"We never planned on twins!" Fiona's father always said.

But sometimes women asked Fiona's mother if she didn't worry just a bit to have such a beautiful, young woman in the house. At eight years old, Fiona was already very good at hearing what she wasn't supposed to hear.

Fiona's mother and father had both gone off to a conference to give a paper they had written together and they were both supposed to be home in plenty of time for Christmas. But yesterday their flight had been canceled and they hadn't been able to book another. Yesterday they'd called and they'd still promised to be home for Christmas, but now Fiona had her doubts. "Let me talk to Nanny Anne," Fiona's mother had said, and Fiona wanted to tell them that she didn't adore Nanny Anne any more, that something was going on with Nanny Anne, but Nanny Anne took the phone away, so she couldn't.

Now Nanny Anne sat in the big chair between the beds. The light from the lamp fell on one side of her face, turning her hair from black to gold, making her eyes shine. She was giving up on finding Moe Bear and Dacey was slowly giving up on sobbing about it.

"Once upon a time," said Nanny Anne.

Fiona's mother and father read to them at night, *Frog and Toad* and *Mary Poppins* and *Amelia Bedelia*, but Nanny Anne said she was tired of those same old stories and would tell them some new ones. Thunder made the lights all flicker and Nanny Anne's voice was a little flickery, too. She was using the voice she used when she talked to Dacey.

"Make it a true story," Dacey said gamely. She was still sniffling and gulping.

"Once upon a time, in this very house."

"With no rain," said Dacey.

"Once upon a winter's day, it snowed and snowed and snowed," said Nanny Anne. "The cats they huddled by the fire, the wind it fiercesome blowed."

"No wind either," said Dacey. "No storms."

"But this was just a little storm. A strange and little storm. It didn't snow in the town or the school you go to or the park you play in. The only place it snowed was right here, on this house and the yard right here and the little stand of woods behind. The rest of the town didn't even know it was snowing.

"But right here," said Nanny Anne, "the snow came all the way up to the nursery sill." She pointed to the window by Dacey's bed and the shadow of her hand swept across the wall.

"This isn't a nursery," said Fiona.

"Once upon a time it was.

"With a cradle gently rocking and a baby soundly sleeping and the snow it softly falling and the woods a silence keeping."

"Was the baby a boy or a girl?" Dacey asked.

"A girl. With a little wisp of brownish hair and long, dark eyelashes and tiny fingers. Her mother and father had waited a long time to have a baby, waited and wished and wished and waited."

One day a man in a knitted cap with a point like an acorn came out of the woods with a cradle to sell. He'd said he'd carved it himself, all from one block of oak, and it looked like a leaf and it rocked like a boat and he said that if they bought it, it would fill itself. It was a magic cradle. He asked for a lot of money for that cradle.

The mother told him to go away, her heart was that broken, she'd given up. Anyway, she knew they didn't have so much money. But the father followed the man into the woods and offered him the money they did have. And the man took that money and gave him the cradle. The father took it home and he didn't tell the mother what the man had said, that because the money was short, there'd be an owing later.

Soon even he forgot about it, because all the wishing came true and one day there was a baby. They had never been so happy.

"The end," Dacey suggested. Sometimes even *Frog and Toad* was too much for Dacey. There were lots and lots of parts of *Mary Poppins* that had to be cut. Fiona imagined that she herself would like those parts best of all if she ever got to hear them.

Nanny Anne paused.

"Keep going," Fiona told her and when Dacey didn't protest, Nanny Anne continued. But she switched over to the voice she used for Fiona, which was not so flickery. Before Fiona's mother and father had left for their conference, she'd had the same voice for both of them.

———

The baby was only six days old, when the mother and the father woke in the morning, surprised to have slept so long. They hurried to the nursery where the bedroom window was open with the wind whipping the curtains and the cradle full of snow. And then the father remembered the owing.

They fell to their knees and they dug with their hands, finding each other's fingers so they kept thinking the baby was buried there. But she wasn't. And their first thought was to be relieved.

And their second thought was to be afraid. They looked outside and they could see a shallow indent of footprints leading up to the window and away again into the woods.

They ran outside in their nightclothes. The snow fell on their hair and their faces and into their slippers; it came down fast and it filled in all the footprints, including their own, erased them as if they had never been. They never saw trace of the baby or the person who took her.

Deer and squirrel, fox and crow, left their prints atop the snow. Drifts came down, wind did blow, gone the prints atop the snow."

Dacey drew in a long, shuddering breath and Nanny Anne paused again. But Dacey didn't speak and Nanny Anne went on. "The police came and they looked, too, and never saw trace, so they didn't believe in this person who had come and taken the baby. They thought that someone in the house, either the mother or the father, had killed the baby and hidden her body."

"I don't want this story!" Dacey's voice was filled with panic. She was the one with the bed by the window.

"The baby isn't dead," Fiona told her impatiently. "The police just think that."

Dacey was crying again, even louder this time. "I want Moe Bear."

"Is this the end of the story?" Nanny Anne asked.

"No," said Fiona.

"Yes," said Dacey. "Please."

And because Dacey said please and Fiona didn't, Nanny Anne stopped telling it. She stood and came and kissed them, first Dacey and then Fiona, on the forehead. She smelled of their mother's perfume, lily of the valley.

"Sleep tight, Dacey. Sweet dreams, Fifi," she told them. Fiona's mother was the only one who called her Fifi. Fiona's father hated it. He said it was a name for a dog and a poodly-sort of dog at that. They both called Dacey 'Dacey' or rarely 'Oopsa' for Oopsa Dacey. Nobody called his dog Oopsa.

Nanny Anne had gone, shutting the door. Fiona could still feel the mark of her lips. The door always made a shushing sound as it scraped the rug, but the rain was too loud for Fiona to hear it. Right away, Dacey came and got in bed with her. Her feet were cold and her toenails scratchy. Fiona gave her Moe Bear since she was about to find him anyway. "I won't tell," she said. Dacey was the sort of girl who never told. Fiona was a different sort of girl.

It was still raining at breakfast the next morning. The herb garden under the window, the one with the dead rosemary in it, was a pudding of mud and water. Fiona and Dacey went into the kitchen and Nanny Anne was already up, had already eaten.

"Today is a let's-pretend day," Nanny Anne told them. "Today, let's pretend I'm your mommy. I'll make you French toast just the way she does."

"I don't want to pretend that," Fiona told her.

Nanny Anne was pinning up her hair the way Fiona's mother did when she was going out. Fiona would have thought Nanny Anne's hair was too short to be pinned up like that. "Don't be silly, Fifi," Nanny Anne said. "It's just a game. It's not like you won't know the difference."

"I'll play," said Dacey. And sometimes, as the day went on, she remembered and called Nanny Anne Mommy and sometimes she forgot. They finished breakfast and got dressed and brushed their teeth. Nanny Anne played cards with them, Spit and Fish and Slap Down, which took five decks. Dacey sat in Nanny Anne's lap while they watched "Come-Again Mulligan" on television.

Their real mother called in the afternoon, but Fiona had her earbuds in, listening to music, and she didn't hear it. Nanny Anne didn't tell Fiona until later. "No plane yet," Nanny Anne said.

Fiona went upstairs and hid in her mother's closet, way in the back where the laundry hamper was. She cried a little because she hadn't gotten to talk with her mother and she was more and more sure they would be spending Christmas with only Nanny Anne. She found two sticker books under her mother's sweaters, sticker books that were probably presents for her and Dacey. She picked the one with jungle animals, and began to do it. The tiger went in the grasses. The giraffe in the trees. She fell asleep.

She woke up when Nanny Anne opened the closet door. Fiona had a strange feeling, as if she were doing something wrong and didn't want to get caught at it. She held as still as she could while Nanny Anne took a pair of her mother's shoes from the shoe rack and put them on her own feet. She put them back and tried another pair. She settled finally on Mother's silver ballet flats. Nanny Anne put her own shoes in their place on the shoe rack, closed the door and went away. Fiona's mother's feet were larger than Nanny Anne's. Fiona had walked around the house in both their shoes on many occasions, so she knew this.

She waited until the room was quiet and then she pushed open the door to her mother's closet. She saw Nanny Anne's shoes on the shoe rack and she took them down, hid them behind the little yellow curtain on her mother's vanity table. She went back downstairs, into the kitchen where Dacey and Nanny Anne were making cookies shaped like stars, decorating them with colored balls and sprinkles of sugar. "What have you been up to?" Nanny Anne asked her.

"Nothing." Fiona climbed up on a chair beside Dacey. It was very easy to tell which cookies Dacey had decorated and which ones were Nanny Anne's. She looked down at Nanny Anne's feet. "You shouldn't be wearing Mommy's shoes," she said.

"It's just to help with the game," said Nanny Anne.

"We won't tell," said Dacey.

The kitchen was warm and smelled of the baking. The sound of the rain was soft, windless. For just a moment, Fiona could see how it was almost like having her mother home. Only not. She climbed down and went to her room to finish her sticker book. As soon as her mother came back, she was absolutely telling on Nanny Anne.

That night they decorated the tree without Mommy and Daddy, but Nanny Anne said they'd told her to go ahead without them. Dacey fell asleep on the couch and Nanny Anne covered her with the knitted afghan. The Christmas lights bubbled and blinked and turned one wall and the photo on that wall, the photo of Dacey and Fiona when they were littler girls, red and then green and then white. Fiona sat on the floor and watched this. She had a horrible, abandoned feeling inside. Mostly sad, but a bit of outrage, too, that she should be made to be sad at Christmas time. "I'm afraid Mommy won't be home for Christmas," she said. She'd lost track of how many days were left. She'd lost track of how many times she'd said this. Rain on the roof. Wind in the trees.

"Don't be silly. She wouldn't miss it." Nanny Anne smiled and Fiona saw the tips of her teeth. She had come downstairs wearing their mother's party dress, the black one with leg slits and a heart-shaped bodice. The pendant to their mother's locket was now settled in the crease between Nanny Anne's breasts. The dress was just a little large for Nanny Anne so the straps kept falling off her shoulders.

"I could tell you the end of the story," Nanny Anne offered. "The part Dacey didn't want to hear," and Fiona knew she should say no, but Nanny Anne looked so pretty now she was all dressed up, so much like a princess in a movie, that no words came out of Fiona's mouth. The colored lights continued to stroke sleepily across the wall, across the faces of little Fiona and little Dacey.

"For two days after the baby had gone, the police kept coming back," said Nanny Anne, "and they tore the house apart, looking for the baby's body.

They emptied out the closets and they pulled the wood from the walls in the basement. And all the while, the cradle sat empty in the nursery.

The father felt so guilty over the owing—that he'd agreed to it, that he'd concealed it from the mother. The police saw that guilt and it made them think he was the one had killed the baby.

But on the third day, a policeman was dusting for the prints on the nursery windowsill when he noticed that the cradle was rocking. He leaned over it and there was the baby, just waking up, stretching and yawning and looking at him with her infant-blue eyes.

He took her to the parent's bedroom where the father was weeping and the mother was wondering if it was possible she had married a man who would kill his own child. But when the policeman tried to hand her the baby, she screamed. She said that it wasn't her baby. Everyone wondered at that, because the baby looked exactly like her baby.

Eyes the same, same the hair, child of flesh, and child of air.

They all thought that grief and doubt had made her a little crazy. The father told her to nurse the baby, thinking that would bring her back to her right mind. Her breasts were so painful it wasn't hard to convince her. She opened her soggy blouse and gave the baby her breast. And all the while she said, this isn't my baby, this isn't my baby. This baby didn't smell right, didn't suck right. But she went on nursing and it did seem to calm her down.

When she had finished with one breast and was about to offer the other, a second policeman came into the room, carrying a second baby. He said he'd heard her crying in the nursery and gone in. The magic cradle had filled again. And this time the mother reached out, weeping with joy, because this one, she said, this one was her own little girl. The two girls were identical, one a perfect copy of the other.

Only the father said he couldn't be sure which was which and so the police went away and left them both babies. They couldn't figure out what to charge the parents with; there was no law against producing two babies where there should only have been one. And so they went away.

And the father and mother raised the two girls as if they were sisters.

That was the owing the father had agreed to, though he didn't know it at the time. The owing was to raise the second child as if she were their own.

And they lived happily ever after," said Nanny Anne, switching suddenly to her Dacey voice. Dacey had woken, was sitting up.

"And they lived happily ever after," she repeated sleepily.

"Let's get you to bed," said Nanny Anne. She picked Dacey up and took her to the bedroom, Dacey's arms and legs loose and flopping, as she was only half awake and almost too big for Nanny Anne to carry. Fiona followed behind, because Nanny Anne had Dacey. Fiona's feelings were all an unhappy blur, except for this sharp one—that she didn't want to be alone with Nanny Anne and she didn't want Dacey to be alone with Nanny Anne either.

"You *said* a true story," Fiona reminded her. It was her last hope, that Nanny Anne would admit she'd made the whole thing up.

"I did say that," Nanny Anne agreed. "Under the covers now, Fifi, and straight to dreamland." She leaned down, kissed Fiona on the forehead the way she always did at bedtime.

"Which one was the real child?" Fiona asked, knowing she wouldn't like the answer, whatever it was.

Nanny Anne turned the light off so Fiona couldn't see her face. "The real child was the one her mother has always loved best, of course." She moved in the dark like a shadow, back to Dacey's bed where she kissed her, too.

Dacey wasn't awake, but she wasn't asleep either. "Good night, Mommy," Dacey said.

Fiona woke up sometime later and it seemed to her that she could hear Nanny Anne singing even though Nanny Anne wasn't in the room. The rain came hard and the singing was soft. Fiona had to strain to hear it and even so words were lost. It was something about dreaming and something about the woods. It was something about a mother's love and a cradle and the snow. It was a lullaby that woke Fiona up. Or else it was another of those things Fiona wasn't supposed to hear.

Or else Fiona didn't wake up. Maybe she only dreamed this part. She had another dream that the window was open. It rained on Dacey and then grass grew under her on her bed and she was lying in a meadow with a cat curled under her arm. And then the grass grew over Dacey and Fiona couldn't see her anymore and she was frightened and calling for Dacey to come back.

When she woke up next, her head was in her mother's lap on the living room couch and it was early morning. The lights on the tree had all been turned off. "I told you I'd be home for Christmas," her mother said and Fiona felt a rush of relief. She smelled her mother's lily of the valley perfume.

"When did you get here?"

"A few hours ago. You don't remember, but I went in and kissed you. And then you had a bad dream," her mother said. "You were so frightened. So we came down here to see the tree and you fell asleep again. Do you remember that part?"

Fiona didn't. She rested her cheek on her mother's terry-cloth bathrobe. She felt the nubs of the fabric, bumpy against her face. She started to tell on Nanny Anne. But before she spoke, something twisted the words back inside her. "Where's Daddy?"

"He'll be home later, maybe tonight, maybe tomorrow. I couldn't wait to see you so I took the only seat." I couldn't wait to see you and Dacey, is what her mother should have said, but didn't.

Fiona had a horrible feeling that if she lifted the hem of her mother's bathrobe, the black party dress would be underneath.

She was too frightened to do it. Instead she got up, carefully, and slower than she wanted. "I didn't hear you come home."

"No. You were a-roaming dreamland. Are you ready for breakfast? I'll make French toast."

Fiona followed her into the kitchen, and then, when her back was turned, went on through the kitchen and into the mudroom. She took Dacey's coat and Dacey's boots because they were the closest and put them on as quietly as she could, listening to the sounds of the skillet coming out of the cupboard, the eggs and milk from the refrigerator, the knife from the butcher's block.

When she was dressed, she ran out into the rain, which came in slanted under Dacey's hood and pelted her face and her hair. The door banged behind her.

"What are you doing?" her mother shouted. "Where are you going?" She stood on the porch under the eaves, her bathrobe tightly wrapped around her. "Fifi! Come back inside! You'll catch your death!"

Fiona turned back to look at her. She wiped the rain from her eyes with her dripping hands. Her mother looked exactly like her mother.

And then she ran for the trees, each step making its own squelching sound, some of the puddles so deep they splashed into Dacey's boots, turned Fiona's toes to ice. It was less wet, but more treacherous underfoot once she made the woods. She kept running, but she wasn't running away exactly. She wasn't thinking that she would never go back, that she would leave Dacey or miss Christmas. She just needed to see if it was a little storm, a strange and little storm. She needed to know if she could run to where it wasn't raining.

CAT HELLISEN

The Girls Who Go Below

WE PRACTICE DROWNING EACH OTHER. IT'S THE BEST WAY to spend summer, by Vera's lake (not *Aunt* Vera, she said. It made her feel old and she didn't like to be reminded, thank you, girls) where the sun slants between the pale clouds like Zeus's own fingers to stroke the ripplewaves and stir them up.

We love the way water lies to us. From Vera's house it will look pewter-flat but as we tumble toward it, the water will shrug off its mirror face and turn amber and gold and brown and blue and filled with clouds and trees like a gateway to another world.

Here at the edges with our bare feet oozing into black and squishy cow-pat mud, the water will change again, grow red as sloe gin and suck at the roots of trees. It will be bottomless and filled with little fish-tremors, flicks of silver sides in the dark.

"This is the worst part," says Millicent. "The getting in." We sink, waiting for the right moment to slap forward into the froggy water, to where the big things live, all smooth and mysterious as monsters from the Jurassic oceans.

Vera says there are no monsters here, that the lake isn't big enough to support one, herbivorous or carnivorous. That we are safe.

We find that sadly boring. We want monsters. That's the fun of lakes and hollow black hills and forests deep and old as the bones of the Earth. They're supposed to be the homes of things we can't explain, otherwise what's the use of them?

Our feet are growing cold, mud oozing between our toes. Millicent steps forward first, splashing black slime in a perfect arc across the front of my knees. I bound after her, shoving and catching hands, and we screech and crow, our voices the only things to break the fat, summer-sweaty silence of the lazy morning.

The water is best once we are far out, floating on our backs. We hold hands so we don't drift apart. The lake is warm in patches, sun-heated, and every now and again we slip into a cold section, so surprisingly cold that it makes us believe we are not in a lake on a hillside farm under the looming Tsitsikamma mountains, but floating over nothingness, over an endless wellspring from which all things come. The damselflies skim past us, catching midges, oblivious to the monsters waiting yellow-eyed at our backs.

We drown in turns, holding each other under for longer and longer, counting out the seconds, waiting to see what will come first—the end of the countdown, or the manic flail that is our signal to stop drowning.

I'm gasping, head in the brightness, my eyes streaming with brackish tears, when Millicent stills next to me. Our legs and arms are entangled. We are as close as we've always been, but in that moment before she opens her mouth, I feel the snap that breaks us apart.

"Lucienne," she whispers, hot in my ear, making me shiver. "Who's that?"

We turn together, feet gently swirling, our bodies in layers of cold and warm and dark and amber, our hair serpenting around our throats, diamonds and rainbows in our eyelashes.

There is an invader on our bank, cross-legged calm, watching us from under the white milkwood. He raises one hand.

We do not.

"We don't like him," I say.

"Yes we do, Lucy," Milly tells me. "He might be interesting."

"Oh." Milly lies on her bed, knees up, the pillow clutched in her arms like a lover. "We should invite him next time we go swimming."

I scowl. Vera says that he is the son of one of the neighboring farmers, that he has been away at Rhodes University, studying "some arty rubbish." He has a name. Mallery. I think it is a foolish name, reminding me too much of Great Uncle Milo, but Millicent adores it. "Millicent and Mallery, isn't that hilarious?" she says.

The years between us never felt big, but Mallery is like a wooden peg driven into a split pine. We are being pushed apart.

I wait for Milly to fall asleep before I creep out of the house and tumble like a blackguard through carrot ferns and Cape ivy, down the moonlit paths where the stones are bright as plucked-out eyes reflecting the stars.

The farm is not far, though no self-respecting *English* girl would travel there alone in the dark. Vera pointed it out to us when we— *when Millicent*—asked, and even in the dark the way is easy, my feet leading me sure as can be. Only when I reach the farmhouse door and see between the curtains that blue ghostly flicker of the television, hear the laughter, and taste sour peat in the air, do I think perhaps I am the one being foolish.

After all, Mallery is just a boy. Millicent has seen boys before, has drawn their initials in her diary and trapped them in closed-circuit hearts. I know all these things. I don't need to keep a diary. Milly's is enough for me.

So why am I upset by Mallery's coffee-ground eyes and the curling snare of his hair? Do I think that perhaps this time it is Millicent in danger of being caught, and not the other way around? Milly always lets them go, after all.

I wait on the wide farm stoop, wondering. Night has fallen with a cold wind, and I am dressed only in my nightdress and summer gown, my feet bare. Just as I'm about to turn and go back to my sister and to sleep, the door opens, and the boy intruder is staring at me, frowning.

"Hi," he says, confusion all slow and sweet on his tongue. "You're one of the Stephenson girls."

I stare at him.

"From the lake. Vera Notley's nieces, am I right?"

"No." I hold my head straight and high. "You're wrong. And stay away from our lake. And from us."

He calls out after me as I leave. "Wait." His feet thud soft, like a hunting dog, and then he is beside me. I pretend to ignore him. "It's not your lake," he says, huffing as he walks. I have long legs, a quick stride, I am sure-footed in the dark. "It's public land."

"I don't care what you think," I tell him. "You are invading our privacy."

He stops, and I turn to look back at him against my better judgment. "Ah, is that it."

"Is what it?"

"Nothing." He smiles at me, white fangs under the fat moon, and he raises his hand again. It's not a greeting, or a good-bye. He is saluting me. "Challenge accepted."

"There's no challenge—" But he is gone. I blink, and after a moment, go back to Vera's grand old wooden house, to my bed and my dreams. But it's impossible to fall asleep. My feet are burning as though I walked through a field of crushed glass, and the feeling works its way up my legs and my belly and the hollow space meant for my heart, and the dreams I do have are hot and sharp like bottles broken at the edge of a fire.

It rains for three days and we use the time to practice our music. Mother has always pointed out that we are English ladies, and we shall have a Classical education and know our Heras from our Aphrodites, and play an instrument, and walk very prettily. I think she plans for us to go back to England, though I do not know how we can return to a place we have never been. Milly sings, trilling up and down scales, holding her position just so, while I play a dutiful piano accompaniment. My technique is very good, very precise. Our old teacher used to tell us that I was all slick perfection with no heart, which we thought was a terribly stupid thing to say. A piano is wires and wood and dull teeth. There's no place in machines for wet lumps of meat.

Milly bounces through our song, every crotchet and quaver, while the rain veils the hills, makes a thick curtain of moving dark and light across the glass. We perform for Vera, who drinks a port like watered blood and claps in delight when we are done. Milly smiles small, acknowledging her talent, and presses one hand to her neck, her fingertips just touching her earlobe. She's wound her golden hair up like an adult, but there are still streaks of sun-bleached white and those are not grown-up at all. Grown-ups do not play in the sun and pretend to drown their sisters.

We neither of us mention Mallery. Instead, we sing along to old swing records that buzz and crackle and jump on Vera's turntable, we take over the front parlor with a world map puzzle that is longer and wider than both of us. There are whales spouting in the oceans, and tigers prowling through India. It is lovely. It smells of cardboard. A sweet nutty smell like something might grow from it if we were to water the world.

But soon the sun is back, scattering butterfly-white wings across the rolling greens, and everything is perfumed damp and sweet and clean and when Milly kicks my feet and says, "We can't stay inside all day," I know that we are going back to the sloe gin lake.

There's no sign of Mallery by the shore, and perhaps this is good, he has understood he cannot take my sister from me. It's only when we are waist-deep in the water and spinning each other in circles, hands clasped, fingers tight and white, that we hear the sobbing.

Sweet and high, it throbs across the water and we still, the water hushing around us, pushing and lapping. We rock in place.

"What's that?"

I twist my mouth in annoyance. It's not as though we have never heard a violin before.

The music rises out of the tree line that stands a little distant from the lake. From the milkwood and yellowwood forest that crawls up the slopes, draping them in rustling shivery green.

"We should ignore it," I say. "Or go home."

Milly pulls her hands out of mine and wades to shore.

After a moment, I unstick my feet from the grabbing mud and follow her, the silt from her steps clouding around me, swirling like underwater storms. Something slides underfoot, eel-fast, and is gone.

Mallery is standing in the shadows of the ancient trees, his violin tucked under his chin. He doesn't even look at us until he has finished playing, then he lowers his instrument and stares at us like he has called us here, little water beasts entranced by Orpheus's lyre.

Millicent hasn't bothered to throw a towel around herself, and the breeze has teased her cold. She stands, dripping and smiling, her sun-white streaks as bright as her teeth, her skin pale gold, like a palomino kelpie. I tuck my borrowed olive-green towel over my swimsuit and keep my distance. My skin has also been sun-dusted, but I am like our mother, and like her, a shadow behind the sun.

"Mallery!" Milly smiles for him, waves. "That was beautiful. Aunt Vera—"

"Just Vera," I say.

"—Vera says you're from—" She pauses to shake topaz from her hair. "Delchik Farm." She unleashes her first weapon and smiles quickly, just once.

I sigh and roll my eyes.

"And that you're at Rhodes—is that what you're studying—music?"

"It's a hobby," he says. "Are you enjoying the lake?"

"Oh, yes. It's lovely, simply beautiful here." She turns to look back at me, wriggles her fingers, beckoning. "This is my sister Lucy—"

"Lucienne."

Her smile doesn't falter. "And I'm *Millicent*, but god, that is such a dreadful name, so I insist you call me Mill."

"Mill." He nods in greeting, and then to me, because we have never met. One time in the dark doesn't count. "Lucienne." Mallery holds his violin before him like a lovely breakable shield, and the fragile javelin of his bow dangles from his fingers. "I'm actually here to deliver a message."

Millicent—*Mill*—lets herself frown just the slightest. "A message. For us?"

"You're invited to dinner," he says. "Tonight, if that suits. You and your aunt."

We make plans—Millicent makes plans while I watch, and Mallery gets caught on the hooks of her fingers, tangled in the bleached-white web of her drying hair. Even though there is a space between them, I can already see the ghost of it happening.

"It's not really suitable, dears," says Vera when we tell her about the invitation. Her eyes are cloudy, worried.

"Oh, but why, it's perfectly respectable—you're going with us, after all," Milly says, a pout waiting to form. I know the tiniest twitches of her mouth, what each one means.

"It's not about that." Vera frowns. "The Delchiks are a strange lot." She means unsuitable. Mother wants us to marry well, or not at all, like *Dearest Aunty Vera*.

"Isn't everyone out in the country?" Milly waves her insult away almost as soon as she says it. "Not you, of course, Vera dearest, but most of them."

"They are not—" She sighs. "Fine. It's all just rumor, anyway."

I'm intrigued now, for the first time. I look up from the terrible sampler I've been mangling. "What rumors?"

"Oh, nonsense stuff, that the Delchiks have fairy blood, witch blood. That they can trick a person out of their money and land and mind—it's supposedly why they have the nicest bit of farmland in the whole area. Nonsense, of course. You're right. Utter country rubbish, fueled no doubt by jealousy." She smiles too brightly. "We'll need to find you something to wear, Millicent. Those dresses of yours are getting outgrown."

Dinner is dark, filled with meat and wine. I am allowed a glass; Vera says sixteen is a perfectly acceptable age to begin the path to alcoholism, and Mallery fills my glass with tarry red wine from Franschhoek that I have to sip at and pretend to like. Millicent drinks as though she was born to it, and for the first time I wonder how much of my sister I don't know. Her thin fingers are tight around the stem of the glass, waiting to break it, like it's a rose she wants to take home and press between family Bibles.

Vera insists Milly sing after dinner and Mallery's parents, who look as normal and unwitchy as is possible, are eager to hear my sister's famous voice. We are settled before the piano, Milly resting one hand on my shoulder so that we strike the perfect tableau: her in a burgundy dress I have never seen before, myself in my forest-green Sunday velvet, my brown hair pulled back into a child's ponytail. We are only a few measures into the piece when the violin sweeps in soft and slow, and

Milly's voice soars with it. I strike an off note, and the sound of it reverberates in my head, drowning out the rest of the music.

Milly's fingers dig into my shoulder.

"You were off tonight," she says afterwards.

"I need fresh air. The wine." I leave her alone with the Delchiks and Vera, and step out onto the wide stoop, trying to breathe deep and catch again the feel of Milly and me perfectly in time and in tune. It's fading. A dream. Unreal.

The air here is pine-tinged, sharp as shards of falling mirrors, and I take in lungfuls of it, wondering why it feels like I can't remember how to breathe. The front door clicks, and I hang on to the stoop rail and wish I could grow into the smooth dead wood. I do not want to talk to anyone now.

"She's very good," says Mallery.

"Go away."

"So are you."

"But I have no heart," I finish for him.

He moves behind me, shadow-slipping over the wood boards. From the forests, the bushpigs squeal. "I wouldn't say that."

That makes me turn. "I have always been told I have no heart."

Mallery shrugs. He's lit a hand-rolled white cigarette and the bright cherry of it sweeps through the dark, a little fire fairy. "Maybe you hid it so it could never be broken."

I laugh. "No."

But he carries on, and I might as well not have spoken. "You cut out your heart and hid it inside a...inside a little girl's music box—the type that plays a terrible plinking tune and spins a pink ballerina when it opens."

Milly has a box like that. I do not. But I listen.

"Then you took the box and hid it inside a shoebox filled with the love letters of people long dead, and placed that inside a lead-lined chest, and locked it with thirty locks, before rowing out to the middle of the lake and dropping it overboard, where it sank to a place no one could ever reach." He sucks on his flat cigarette and blows out snaky smoke, then grins. "How did I do?"

"Awfully," I tell him. "There were thirty-one locks." I leave him, run back to my sister.

"Mallery makes his own violins," Milly tells me. "Can you believe that?"

"I don't care." I put a missing piece into Siberia and pick up another. I have been saving all the palest puzzle pieces for last, like icing on a cake.

It is not raining, but we are not swimming. Milly is waiting for Mallery to come fetch her—he's driving her into town so she can do some shopping. She wants a new dress. I'm invited but I do not want to go. "Go drive with idiot Mallery and the two of you can shop all day. I don't care."

Milly flicks the piece out of my hand. "You are in a beastly mood, Lucy. Beastly. I don't know what's gotten into you." She uncurls, stands, smooths her beautiful skirt down. "Well, I'm going. Don't say I didn't ask you."

After she's gone, I take my towel down to the lake and practice drowning myself. It's not as much fun. I let out slow, silvery streams of bubbles and try to tell my future in their constellations. Nothing. I dive for my heart, fingers combing through years of settled mud, but all I do is cloud the water and scare the frogs and leave the water filthier than when I got in. I have to shower twice to get the stickiness off my skin.

Vera has gone with Milly and Mallery, and I drift through her empty, lonely house, peering under the claw-footed furniture.

It is full of places to hide a heart, but I cannot find mine anywhere.

The first night Mallery visits me, Milly is asleep, snoring softly against the pillow she holds as close to her as she used to hold me. He comes to my window and I open it against my better judgment. He sits on the ledge and grins, legs swinging.

"What do you want?" I ask him. We are on the second floor. I could shove him off and listen for the crack and the snap. And the screaming, I suppose, if he didn't die clean.

"Why didn't you want to come with us?"

"Us?" There is no us. There was once, but Mallery was never part of my Us. "Go away," I say. "Before you wake my sister."

He kisses me before he goes, and it tastes like the bloody red heart I cannot find. It tastes small and lonely.

Milly twirls for me, dancing on demi-pointe, the wings of her new dress curling about her thighs. In the long mirror, her reflection dances and the ivory dress drapes her like liquid bones.

"So." She flops next to me on my bed.

I stop chewing on the end of my pencil and close the little diary I have begun. "So what?"

"What do you think?"

"Of?"

She pokes my shoulder. "The dress, stupid." She leans over and I can smell the wine and mint chewing gum on her breath, sour and sharp. "What's this then you're writing then?"

"Nothing."

"So do you think Mallery will like the dress?"

"I suppose."

She hums to herself as she holds earrings against her cheeks, discarding this one and that one. I frown. She's off-key. Milly knows this piece as well as she knows the angles and planes of her own face—she would usually correct herself immediately if she went even the slightest bit flat.

It digs into my eardrums like the morning screeching of the hadeda ibis flocks and I will my sister to go, to take her tuneless happiness away from me.

When she leaves I erase all the words I have written until they are just faint scratches on the paper, ghost writing, ghost dreams. I write a new diary over the old; inconsequential nonsense and I like that, because I can remember the bones of what I wrote underneath, like fossils. I smile and obliterate my dreams of Mallery, of finding my heart in the lake mud and playing a perfect piano, singing a song better and brighter than anything Milly can do. Could do.

This is how the summer holiday passes. I learn to keep secrets from my sister, and she grows a new life that doesn't include me. At night, when she is dreaming, I slip through the house and meet Mallery by the peaty beach, and we stand barefoot in the cold black water and count the ripples of moonbreath on the skin of Vera's lake, listen to the screaming things. He tells me he has seen the elephants in the forest pass by like ghosts, and I tell him he is a liar, that they are all dead.

"The forest is full of things that people say don't exist."

We kiss until I learn what a heart tastes like.

"You're not like your sister," Mallery says, but I cannot tell if that is meant to be a compliment or a critique.

I straighten, turn away from him, my arms folded across my chest, cradling the things I feel and keeping them safe.

Mallery touches the back of my neck. "I would like to hear you sing."

"So you can see which of us is better?" I shift away from him, shrug off his touch.

"Maybe," he says, but he laughs as he does and I know he has already chosen.

"Milly thinks that you're in love with her." I tell him, though he already knows this. "And that she's in love with you."

"*Millicent* is capable of thinking many things, not all of which I agree with."

Finally, I turn to look at him. He's thoughtful, brow crinkled softly. I think of forests, of wild things, of ghost animals. Of the gleam of moonlight and kisses until the shadow of my sister slides between us. I frown.

"Would you like to see how I make a violin?" Mallery asks.

———

The perfect violin needs the right material, and even then, the luthier needs to work with that material, shape it so that it can sing the song inside itself, its heart. Mallery tells me this, and explains what he needs.

"She'll be beautiful, you'll see," he says. "But it takes time, preparation."

I nod. My fingers itch, my throat is dry with want. I cannot speak. My lungs have filled with a strange fluid, like drowning in sloe-gin and honeyed wine. When Mallery smiles at me, I think of witch blood, of fairy blood.

"She's not what she used to be, is she?" Mallery whispers to me as he holds me closer. His whispers curl around me, tight as threads.

She's not my sister anymore, that much is true. But Mallery made her that way. Didn't he?

Didn't he?

She was supposed to trap his name in an ink heart and then forget about him. Like she always does. It's Milly who changed. Not me. Not anyone else. She broke the rules.

"I can make her like she was again," Mallery says. "Give her back her voice."

On the last day of summer I drown the thing that used to be my sister. I count out the seconds in silvery bubbles, past her flailing hands.

When she is still and quiet, Mallery cuts a lock of her sun-bleached hair with a pair of my embroidery scissors. He curls Milly's hair up into a tight little noose, wraps it in his handkerchief, then tucks it back into his shirt pocket. I am a little jealous of that intimacy; her palomino hair embraced in monogrammed cotton, pressed close to his heartbeat.

We weight the body with stones before we push the corpse deep. The lake bed is a sludgy mess of drowned trees and silt so deep Millicent's body will be swaddled away, waiting for us to return. I mark where the body goes below, or I'll never find her. Then I wipe the shallow grazes on my arms clean, and stare at them. She didn't fight us very much. The thing that was my sister knew it had to drown.

Although I know I lost her when summer started, I find myself sobbing. Mallery says nothing to my grief, just watches me crouch at the edge of the lake, my legs black with mud, my tears salting the water.

Next summer I go back to Vera's lake alone, one half of Us. I have cried myself out, emptied the space inside, ready to find my heart in the dark. I told my story over and over, that I did not see her go into the lake, that she was meant to meet me, and never turned up. Divers came all the way from George to search the lake, but found nothing, and the police soon turned their attention to the forests, and to the workers who lived on the neighboring farms.

Vera is sombre-faced, older than she likes to pretend she isn't. "Oh, darling," she says. "Are you sure?"

I'm wearing my bathing togs, a borrowed towel slung over one shoulder. "I have to," I tell her. "Do you understand?" And then in a whisper. "I have to."

She doesn't tell me to be careful, just cries silent tears that fall down her cheeks like slow worms. But she nods, because I suppose she thinks she understands.

I meet Mallery by the water's edge and we dive in the place where we sank Milly, holding our breath until it feels like we are drowning, our fingers carding through the mud.

I'm the one who finds her, cushioned and pillowed and blanketed in her lake-bed, and we pull up the clumps of her that we can use and afterward I sit on the bench in Mallery's workshop and watch him as he whittles and carves her breastbone into a violin neck, makes tuning pegs from her knuckle bones. He strings her hair on the bow, rosins it ready, and it is perfect, so beautiful, just like my sister.

When she's ready, Mallery plays for me, and the strings weep under the white-bleach hair of the bow. I listen to my sister sing, sweet and filled with her sobbing. Then he lowers his bow, tucks the golden violin into the crook of his arm, and waits for my reaction.

"Oh," I say. "Bow and balance me." I take the violin from him and set it on my shoulder, tuck it under my chin. Mallery comes to stand behind me, correcting my grip on the bow, and when I slide my sister's taut-pulled hair across the gut strings, the first long, sweeping note throbs in my chest.

KIMA JONES

Nine

Friday

TANNER NAMED THE MOTEL STAR MOTEL BECAUSE calling the place North Star Motel would've been asking for it. Colored folks recognized that "star" and the little lights Jessie insisted they burn in the windows. Most of their customers were hungry, travel-weary young men who did not believe the VACANCY sign as they approached the motel and did not believe that Tanner, round as a dishpan, wide as the door, was its owner. None of them had the nerve to ask her if she was a man or a woman, but she saw their longways looks anytime she entered a room. They never stayed more than a night or two and spent most of that time asleep. Tanner checked them in at $1.25 a night on weekdays and $2.00 on weekends. She never shamed anyone for not having the full fee and would accept three quarters and a "thank you kindly."

"Get up, Tanner, sounds like the iceman is here. Last time he didn't ring the bell and most of the ice melted all over the porch. We don't have money to waste, and I can't stretch half a block of ice for a whole week." Jessie was sitting up in bed, her breasts and collarbone soaking in the day's first light. "I said go on and get the ice. The Campbells are checking out this morning, and Flo needs to get breakfast out to them by nine."

"If you run me out this bed one more time, woman, you're going to know it."

"Ain't nobody running you, just go get the ice. You can come back to bed after. Oh, and feed Rinny!"

Tanner knew Jessie was lying, but she got out of the bed anyway. By the time Tanner got the ice into the icebox and came back to their bedroom, Jessie would be halfway dressed, talking about the ledgers and dividing the day's work between them. Best to go get the ice and start the day.

The ice was melting by the time Tanner reached the porch, but not enough to make Jessie have a fit. The iceman slipped everybody's blocks into their iceboxes. Except for colored people. He left their ice sitting outside, anywhere, in dirt or sand or on a dusty porch. Tanner poured hot water down the block and quickly lifted it inside of the wooden box. Didn't make no sense to tip the iceman but Jessie tipped him every delivery. "He don't have to come out here, Tanner. Ain't like we can leave to go into town and get it," she would say.

Tanner headed back into the house and to the bedroom she shared with Jessie. "Mr. Campbell say what time they'd be heading out?" Jessie stood wearing a white blouse and ankle length skirt, her brown leather ankle booties tied tightly. "He wants an early start on the road. Almost fifteen hundred miles between here and Seattle. He thinks they could be there by this time tomorrow."

Tanner grunted. Could be. She tried to talk more sense into Mr. Campbell the night before, but he was determined to make it his way. Tanner thought it would be better for them to stop somewhere in California for a few days and then head back to the road. Maybe leave his wife and newborn in San Francisco for a week or two and then send for them later. But Campbell wouldn't hear of it. Said he was driving straight through, driving even if his eyeballs went bloodshot and burst through his head. "Give me the rundown, baby," Tanner said to Jessie as she pulled her work trousers over her belly and bent to cuff them.

"Did you feed Rinny?"

"Yes, I fed Rinny, now give me the rundown."

"Well, Campbell's checking out this morning. That'll leave us empty for the weekend, which is good because we're sure to fill up the singles." Tanner nodded. Single people always ran off the job on Fridays, soon as the boss paid them. By Monday morning they were long gone and so far on their way north or west it didn't make sense to send Klan after their families. They were just gone. "Flo is getting started on the weekend menu, and I'm waiting for a cigarette delivery and the bread delivery. Me and Flo will get the parlor ready for this evening. I'll air out the singles and Newt will sweep them. All you need to do is change the oil on the Campbells' car and check the tires and whatnot. Maybe wash down the sides of the house."

The house was peach-colored with a brown roof and sat a quarter of a mile from the highway. Travellers could see the Star's marquee from the road whether on foot or automobile. The marquee was its own detached, two-pronged structure painted in mint green and white and lit up every night at 9:00 p.m. The house's front room served as the motel's lobby, stripped of all furniture save an upright and uncomfortable sofa, two wing chairs, a wall clock, and a small lobby desk with a silver bell. Tanner kept a wide black leather barstool behind the desk to sit on when her knee acted up. All other times, she preferred to greet her guests standing. The single rooms stood in a row of six to the left of the house. The doubles, another six, off to the right. The only formal place for colored folks to stay headed west on the lonely, desert highway.

It was Flo who came up with the idea of having jook nights on Fridays for the locals and travellers alike. Black folks were starting to stay in Phoenix to make a home and needed a place to go on the weekends. Friday nights at the Star Motel were for card playing, thigh slapping, and smoky mingling. Tanner hated the idea at first. She needed to keep her family safe and didn't want all of colored Phoenix in their parlor room on Friday nights, but the women were lonely. Flo complained of never having company and Jessie didn't have to open her mouth for Tanner to know she was cross about it all.

Flo was one of Tanner's first guests. Flo arrived with a belly brimming over its due date. Tanner knew the kinds of things that would make a woman run, pregnant and all, out of the swamps of Florida. They never spoke about it or how Flo found the place. She was flat out with her intentions when she checked in that night. "I can cook. If you let me stay on until my baby big enough, I'll be your cook. I used to cook lunches for the orange pickers and deliver them in my truck. I can cook anything, and I can kill anything." After Flora went into labor, she named the boy Newt, half because Tanner slipped on birth water running over trying to catch him out of the birth canal and half because he kind of looked like one.

Jook night at Star Motel started at nine o'clock, but folks trickled in around ten thirty. It gave Flora and Jessie time to change, time to tuck Newt in, time to perfume behind the neck, time to cast their muscled legs in nylon. The women always wore all black, including Tanner. That was the rule, everybody in something bright. Other rule was no outside food and no outside liquor. Tanner played the doorman and Jessie worked the bar. Flo managed the kitchen, bringing plates out to the cards players and collecting tips in her bosom. Flo wore a deep, matte red lipstick but kept her fingernails short and bare. "Can't cook with that shit on my hands," she'd say and wink at whatever woman was questioning her manicure. The manicure-questioning woman always knew Flo's reputation: she could outlast a man, she took her time, she could cook, and she didn't lie. Flo was thickset, with an impressively square jaw and roundish eyes. She openly bedded other women; the few nights a month she spent with Tanner were in one of the single rooms.

Tanner stood at the front door of the house, on the porch, collecting the dollar fee it cost to get in. "Order your plates with Flo," she said, "All plates from Miss Flora. All booze from Jessie." The parlor was lit just enough to see a card hand but barely enough to see if you were putting your fork in meat or vegetables. As soon as the brass band started up, Jessie rattled her tambourine. She bounced it off of her hip and then smacked it into her open hand. Her feet moved in time, and her hair wagged back and forth on her head with every tambourine slap. They would bring in an easy three or four hundred dollars between the food and hootch and card games. They split the income evenly and saved for their future plans. Jessie was going to Los Angeles, Miss Flora was sending Newt to Howard, and Tanner would open another motel.

Hours of dancing passed on top of hours of drinking and the night winded down. Couples were filing out on foot, holding each other up. Tanner walked over to each spades and craps table and announced that it was closing time in ten minutes. "Last bets for the night. Make them count." A hand reached out for Tanner's and caught her at the wrist. Tanner looked down at her hand and over to the arm holding hers. "Can I help you with something, sir?" She was used to the belligerent drunk from time to time and escorted them to the front yard to sober up. Come morning, they'd be gone and ashamed. This man's front tooth was as gold as his watch, and he smiled big as payday, not a whiff of alcohol on him. His suit was a butter yellow and his white shoes were unscuffed. There was no dust on them either. He was a good foot and a half taller than Tanner and his reach, she estimated, twice that of hers. "I think maybe you can help me, ma'am. I'm looking for a missing person. Any information you could fetch me would sure be a nice gesture on the part of you and yours. Name is Tanner Harris, wanted dead or alive. Ring any bells for you ma'am?" The man's grin faded as he whispered through his teeth, "Maybe you want to be clearing the party on out of here so we can settle this. You got a debt to pay, girl."

Flora, never missing a thing, hit the lights. "All right now, y'all heard Tanner. Jook's closed. Next week, same time, same place." She moved from table to table pointing folks to the way out. Some of the drunk ones begged a dance from her, and she chided them, "Go on, now. Go on, I said." The last patrons bid farewell to Jessie and promised to be back. Jessie thanked them for coming and walked them to the front porch. Tanner stayed in the parlor with the gold-toothed man.

When Jessie returned to the parlor, Flora headed in a quick scramble for the kitchen door. "Come on over here and take a seat," the gold-toothed man said. He kept his hand wrapped tightly around Tanner's wrist and had a smile on his face as she sat. Flora returned to the parlor with a gun pointed at the back of her head. The man had not come alone. His companion was thin, with a face slender as toilet plumbing. He wiped his mouth with the back of his hand and nudged Flora forward with the gun. "This one here was reaching for this gun, boss." The gold-toothed man looked over at Flora and smiled at Tanner. "Tanner love a talented woman, don't you Tanner? I'll be damned. I come to talk to you and your girlfriend here want to shoot me down."

The gold-toothed man let go of Tanner's wrist and draped an arm around her shoulders. Tanner looked over to Flo, but she ignored the gaze. Flo pushed back on the mouth of the gun, putting weight on her captor's arm. Jessie was still sitting at a table, weaponless and remote.

Jessie was good at disappearing inside of herself. The gold-toothed man cleared his throat, making a show of himself. "Seems to me like we have us a problem here. See, I only need Tanner, but it don't seem like you girls gonna let me leave here with what I need. Second problem is I know either one or two of you bitches helped this fat nigger kill off all my brothers. I'm no adding man, but that's simple enough math to me." Droplets of sweat populated his upper lip as he talked. "Except Maud can count and do. Eight dead boys divided by three living niggers ain't enough change at all."

"Speak plain, if you come to speak. Kill if you come to kill," Jessie blurted at the man.

"I'll be damned, Tanner. I thought that other one was a robust woman, but this one here, this one got some nerve, don't she?" The man turned his full attention to Jessie. "You want it plain, country girl? I'll give it to you plain, baby. Name's Glenn, Maud's baby boy, and I come to collect this here debt. You see, girl, dead don't scare Maud because Maud been dead, but she lonely something awful. Now Tanner here, and you bitches, the two of you, end up killing every messenger she sends. That ain't right. Maud took her time when she made her sons. Took her time when she found Tanner, too. You know what taking time is, country girl? Let me spell it out for you. Eight niggers minus three niggers is five and you going to pay that five out in lifetimes. With Maud. Maud'll like you. She'll like your big girlfriend over there, too."

"I never did nothing to Maud," Jessie said.

"You call killing eight grown children nothing? If that's nothing, I sure would like to see what you call something," Glenn said.

"Maud's the one doing it. She already done cursed us. Why she keep sending her sons to kill us?"

"That don't have much to do with me. I come for Tanner, and I come for Tanner's women keep helping Tanner. That's all."

Peanuts shot into the air like fireworks following a parade. Flora had picked up a tray full of them and smashed it against the head of her captor. His face burned down to the bone and revealed rat's teeth. Jessie ran toward Flora, and Tanner booted Maud's boy with the flat of her shoe. "Salt, Jessie, Salt!" Tanner screamed out. Jessie hit Flora's captor with another tray of bar nuts. Flora held the man's head and snapping jaw in the crook of her arm as Jessie threw every salty thing she could find. The man's arms and legs flailed about. He snapped his jaw at Jessie's torso until he melted into the creases of Flora's black dress, blue and red clumps of him exploding down her front, into her patent heels. The women were so busy they didn't hear the shot. Didn't see Glenn's body slumped at Tanner's feet or see the blood trickling from his nose and into the wood floor.

"Flora, how'd you know that wasn't no real man?"

"When I went into the kitchen to get the gun, he was eating Rinny."

"Eating him?"

"That's what I said."

"The dog?"

"Only one, unless you know another."

Saturday

Tanner looked at the dead man on the floor, turning the bottle opener over in her hands. She listened to Jessie opening then slamming drawers for a sheet to wrap the body in and knew that, even in distress, Jessie would not waste a good sheet on a dead man. Tanner listened to the sound of the whiskey cabinet's old latch and heard the shuffle of glasses sliding onto the bar. Jessie poured faster than usual and Tanner half-smiled when she gulped. Tanner liked to see Jessie throw her head back and down a drink. Jessie was no wine woman. "Want one?" Jessie asked. Tanner looked at the dead man again, figuring out how long it would take to strip him down, bleed him and bury him. "Set me up," she whispered back, letting the back of her shaved head cool on the wall behind her.

Jessie came from behind the bar holding Tanner's drink in her right hand and a ragged sheet draped across her left arm. Her hair, usually mussed about her shoulders, was braided into a single rope, doubled over itself and secured with a rubber band. "You can't keep killing these boys and expecting they won't come back bigger and badder," Jessie said. His was the ninth body on the floor in almost five years.

"You'd think they'd stop coming after me by now, Jessie. I'm trying to live good on this place here. I didn't send for them, they come for me. You'd think Maud'd be tired of sending her boys to slaughter by now." Tanner held the drink in hand but didn't sip from it. Maud only had nine boys, just nine of them. If she could get this one buried by nightfall, she would be rid of Maud for good. "We need to get a move on it, baby. You know sundown comes quicker than a fly to shit."

Jessie fixed the sheet around the dead man's body, tucking its ends beneath him. She stood up to get salt and licorice root for his ears and mouth and backside. "He's stinking already. We got to plug him up."

"Can't plug him until he's bled through and through," Tanner said, "this ain't a time to be skipping steps. You know the way it's got to be done."

Jessie stared at Tanner as if to cut her down. "I didn't leave Georgia to get caught up in this mess you got yourself into with Maud. And now I'm trapped, just like Flo and just like Newt. You got me here plugging up dead bodies because you couldn't tell your last woman goodbye the right way. Now I'll never get to California. It ain't no more safe for me here in Phoenix burying Maud's sons than it was in Georgia. At least in Georgia I could walk off the land when I wanted to."

Tanner didn't shush her. Didn't make sense to. It was all true. Tanner left Maud one morning without so much as packing a bag. She left on foot, the weight of travel and her body at times too much for her knee. She stopped every few days in a field or under a tree to wash herself and rest up. Sometimes she found a rabbit, other times she ate nothing. She laid her suit out in the sun to dry and napped, naked, through afternoons too hot to travel. She chewed leaves of mint and packed them under her arms to keep her dry. When she could hop a train car she did and shared liquor with the men aboard. Men with names like Willie and Richard and Bartholomew and with pasts as unspeakable as her own. Most of them were going north or west. Most of them had left women behind, too. And kids to send back for. No one was lucky enough to ride one train all the way out, but no one was willing to hop off before getting into Arkansas. Some piled out in northern Texas and others in New Mexico. None of the men bothered her because none of them knew she was a woman. Her breasts were no larger than the chest of a very stout man. She wore her hair shaved close to her scalp and carried a handkerchief to wipe sweat from it. She kept a pair of socks stuffed down her shorts and listened as the other men chortled through stories of close encounters with another man's wife. She told her own stories of being ran out of a house and marked for death. When she spoke, the gap between her two front teeth seemed to grow and swallow her audience. The soft flap of gum that hung there was the most delicate thing about her. By the time she walked from New Mexico to Phoenix, her knee had doubled in size and her cane was about ready to give up the ghost. She settled on a little abandoned ranch and in a year converted it into a motel for colored people traveling west. Out of the south, Lord knows.

It took Maud almost as long to find her and send the first boy. That first one wasn't sent over to kill Tanner so much as he was sent to tie her there. Maud's juju kept Tanner bound to the place. She could go anywhere on the property, but she could not leave. The first time Tanner tried to leave the motel, she learned what it was to die and come back. The juju allowed her to walk off but every step took a little bit of her life force from her. Walking off the motel property meant dying. She couldn't leave if she wanted to and, by extension, anyone she loved couldn't leave either. That meant Jessie. It meant Flora. It meant Newt. Maud was holding them hostage until she was ready for them all. Most Tanner could do, the most she asked her family to do, was make the best life they could. "Ain't no such thing as life with both feet tied," Jessie would say, "no such thing."

Flo came down the stairs with Newt in hand, not bothering to shield the child's eyes in any way. "The two of you can keep the hollering down because some of us need to sleep before folks start ringing on the bell tonight," Flo said, stepping over the dead man. "What's taking y'all so long to get this one in the ground? He the last one, ain't he?" Jessie waited for Tanner to answer and continued to work on the body.

"Well Miss Flora, we need to get him outside and my knee is in no good condition today. Can't bleed him in here, on the wood floor, but Jessie done washed him down with turpentine soap. If you could help get the body out back, I'd be mighty obliged, ma'am." Tanner's grin spread across her face when she said ma'am and tipped her head toward Flo.

Flora kicked up at Tanner, "Just shut the hell up and get the hell on before I change my damn mind. Least you could do is grab the stretcher out the back for me and Jessie, or we got to do that too?"

Newt ran from his mother's side to follow behind Tanner and held the screen door open as Tanner came up the back steps with the canvas and wooden pole contraption. Tanner held out her hand to the boy, and he slapped her five. "Thought I told you not to come out on this back porch without any shoes on, boy. I gotta start repeating myself around here?"

"No, Uncle Tanner," Newt said, running through the parlor, over the dead body and into the coat closet for his shoes.

Flo rolled the dead man on his side and slipped a new ragged sheet halfway under his body, then turned him back toward her so Jessie could get to the other side. With the sheet in place, they slid the body onto the stretcher and out into the yard. They left him atop a butcher block table like they had with his brothers. Tanner walked over with her knife in hand and made incisions in his neck, groin, and armpits. Newt placed buckets around the table where Tanner had made the cuts. They sat around the dead man and said nothing, Jessie sometimes looking at Tanner, Tanner sometimes looking at Jessie. "Maybe the bottom of his feet too. This is taking too long," Jessie said and Tanner walked over, knife and cane in hand, and bored a hole through the dead man's arch.

"Ain't nobody had breakfast yet," Flo said, "no more courting the dead until we all eat. C'mon, Newt."

Newt looked over to Tanner and waited for her to get up. "Mama said let's eat, Uncle Tanner."

Tanner smiled at the boy, "Tell Auntie Jessie that your mama said come and eat. I don't think Auntie Jessie wants to come in the house. What you think, Newt?"

Newt shrugged his shoulders and smiled at Jessie. "Better come and eat before Mama gets mad at you, Aunt Jessie." Newt pulled Jessie up off the ground playfully, making a show of his little muscles until Jessie laughed.

The three of them walked into the house as Flo set the table. "About time. Thought the dead man got up and walked away with all of you."

Sunday

They got on good together, but Tanner never wanted any juju, not even for her knee. Most Maud could do was offer a poultice of steamed herbs or strong tea. Wasn't church that kept Tanner away from juju. Maud thought maybe she was raised in the Christian way, but that wasn't it, wasn't it at all. It scared her. Tanner was plain scared of juju. Scared of going to bed with a locked knee and waking up to throw out her cane. Scared of having split teeth then the next minute all the spaces gone. Scared to know the hair on her head didn't gray as long as she was with Maud, and her skin didn't grow slack. Because Maud told Tanner that the only reason why her knee still hurt was so she wouldn't have to hear no mess about juju, because she told Tanner that as long as she lived so would Tanner, Tanner walked down the road. Because Tanner wanted a natural death, she kept walking. Carried a little salt with her for all she learned and kept on walking.

"I think the best thing to do is send Newt on up the road," Tanner said to the women. "If he drops, one of us can go fetch him. If the juju is broke for sure, he'll make it past the general store. Then we'll know for sure." All four of them were up early. "If one of you go out, I'm not sure I could get you back to the house before the juju took your soul altogether. If I go out, the two of you can't drag me back, and I'm dead for sure. Best thing is to send our boy because he's light enough to run with. Plus somebody has to perform the rights over Glenn." Jessie looked at Flora and so did Tanner. Newt was everybody's child, but he was Flo's boy. She would have to make the say. "Newt big enough to walk down the highway by himself. He's been wanting to since he started walking," Flo said, not trying to conceal her smile. "This going to be the first time he walked down the road. Four years old and the boy never walked down the road leading to his own house."

Newt made it a quarter of a mile off the grounds before his calves lost their way and he slipped into the couch grass. Tanner stood watching, the NO VACANCY sign alit behind her like a solitary headlight. Tanner, leading her body with her left foot and then stepping with her right foot, walked out toward the boy. Every step was lighter than the last, the marrow in her bones being pulled away from her heart and out of her skin. It did not hurt, this dying, it was more like wrestling a witch off your back—involuntary paralysis of body but total control of mind. When she reached Newt he was supine, tufts of couch grass in his hands. He was holding on. Tanner dragged Newt back to the motel by his left leg, her cane eating through the soil. She left his body at the bottom of the porch steps, having dragged it as far as she could before collapsing just steps away.

"Why didn't Newt make it, Flo?" Jessie asked. Her eyes were tired but no water fell from them. "This was supposed to be all over, but it ain't. We going to die here and Maud coming to collect our souls." The two women were crouched over the bodies of Newt and Tanner, pressing cold rags against their foreheads.

"I don't know what's doing, Jessie, but we need to get to that grave and move that man on to where he got to go next." Flo looked down at her child, his loose pants and plaid buttoned shirt, his eyes flickering every few minutes. The blood running from his nose. He was fighting it. Soon his heart would start beating again and his color would return. Harder for children to come back from the dead after their soul's been snatched from them. First time Miss Flora tried to leave the grounds, it felt like a pebble found its way into her shoe, snaked up her leg, and then went straight through her lungs. Wasn't so much pain as it was surprise. Like someone snatched a piece of fruit from a tree inside her and kept snatching and snatching and instead of taking the last piece of fruit or letting it drop to the ground for harvest, they stood on their tiptoes, opened their mouth to the branch and ate her seed and stem and all. Even after she came out of it and understood she couldn't leave the grounds, Flo would still try every now and again, checking her shoe for the elusive pebble when she came to.

"I don't understand why we have to ask a dead man to move on," Jessie said. "Every time Maud sends one of her boys out here I end up standing up for them in her place. Don't make no kind of sense."

"What don't make sense is that they can come back. That don't make sense. Feels like sense to make sure a dead man is really dead to me."

Jessie thought on it. "Well what if somebody pulls up for a room and sees the two of them spread out here like this?"

"Nobody stopping for a room with two dead-looking niggers out front. Let's go." Flo and Jessie walked around to the back of the motel where hours before they threw a warm body into a new grave. They held hands and repeated the same words at the same time again and again. *Leave from here. It's safe to go. Leave from here. It's safe to go. Leave from here. It's safe to go.* Their clasped hands looked like prayer, but their heads weren't bowed and neither dared to close their eyes.

Tanner ascended the porch steps as the women returned. She opened her mouth to greet them, but her voice had not returned from the other side of life. Miss Flora bent down to scoop up Newt's body, his bare feet dirtying the front of her trousers. She cradled his neck with her right hand and kissed his small face. "I better get you washed and put to bed, little baby," she said into her son's neck. Jessie rubbed Newt's back as soon as Miss Flora got him close enough to touch. Tanner watched the boy's dangling feet and thought of him as an infant, before he could walk. "We thought we lost you, boy, out there in that couch grass like that. C'mon back and come see us. We waiting for you, hear me Newt? Mama here. Auntie Jessie here. Uncle Tanner right here. We'll be right here when you wake up."

Tanner stuck her free hand into Jessie's hair, her other hand gripped around the porch railing. She massaged Jessie's scalp while looking out to the road at passing cars. "Nobody dying just yet. We gotta get this place ready for guests. No bookings since the Campbells left." The three of them had scrubbed the parlor shortly after they took Gleen out to bleed him, so that was one less thing to be done, but there was still food to be made, linens to take out, the porch needed mopping with boiled water and salt.

Miss Flora headed upstairs with Newt, while Tanner went to the backyard after the mop bucket and Jessie moved pots and pans around in the kitchen. Today was the largest supper day of the week. Folks expected a family meal on a Sunday evening. Even the man who grew up eating nothing except corn mush and butter expected a decent Sunday dinner on a Sunday afternoon. Jessie stacked her ingredients all over the countertop, opening a cabinet door and reaching for everything by memory; Flora kept a well-run kitchen with everything in its place. Jessie rubbed birds down with salt, paprika, sage, and black pepper and stuck white onions, garlic, and several carrots into the hole where their hearts used to beat.

Flo came downstairs and washed her hands so she could help Jessie. "Where's Tanner?"

Jessie kept her hands and eyes on the dough she was kneading, "Tanner mopping the front down with saltwater. How's Newt? Sleep yet?"

"Newt's fine. I rubbed him all over with rum and laid him on his side until his nose stops bleeding."

"What nose-bleeding you talking about, Miss Flora?" Tanner asked, coming into the kitchen for more water. "Newt ain't been having nosebleeds."

"I thought it might be peculiar but then I figured he was having a tough time getting back from the other side. No fever, no sweats, but his nose is bleeding."

"Out the nose, hunh?"

"Where else you bleed from, Tanner? Yes, out his nose."

"Let's all go check him. Jessie wash your hands good and grab the salt."

Jessie and Flo turned to Tanner with widened eyes but nothing to say. Flo retraced the morning in her head: the four of them up early, deciding to send Newt down the road, feeling happy, Newt laid out in the couch grass, Tanner gone to get him, Tanner's cane tip covered in dust, Newt's skinny feet, Newt in the bathtub cradled in her arm the way she used to nurse him. His heartbeat returned, shallow. Nothing was different about the boy except the blood coming from his nose. And who doesn't bleed a little coming back to life?

Tanner wiped her brow with the back of her hand and wiped the sweat from it on her pant leg. "I used to know a boy whose nose bled all the time. Boy was bumped up and bruised up all over his body. Lost a tooth and bled for two gotdamn weeks. Couldn't go to school, couldn't go out to play. Those kids with it bad like that don't live past eleven, twelve."

"With what, Tanner?" Jessie asked.

"Doctors called it hemophilia. I known it to be called bleeding. Just bleeding."

"Bleeding? I never heard of no children bleeding, Tanner, where you get this mess from?" Jessie demanded.

Miss Flora interrupted Jessie's question, her arms folded. "But what happened to the boy? What happened to the little boy you knew?"

"He died, Miss Flora, he died and every time he died, his mama brought him right back." Tanner didn't wait for her women to piece the puzzle of it together. "Glenn was Maud's favorite boy. And her last."

Jessie grabbed onto Tanner and Flo just stared. "You trying to tell me there's a haint in my boy, Tanner? You trying to tell me the boy upstairs ain't my own? Like I didn't spend the last half hour washing his ass, you going to tell me that ain't Newt up there?"

"Miss Flora, I'm not saying you wrong, I'm saying we should go check. Can we go check on the boy?"

"You want to go check on my boy with salt in your hands? That's what you want to do?"

"I'm afraid so, Miss Flora."

"Jess, you hear this woman? This woman climb in your bed and mines the same and now she talking about killing my son."

"I ain't talking about killing, Flo, I said let's check him."

"Checking sounding a lot like killing. Ain't nobody killing my child but me. You got that? Only shot'll be fired is mine."

Tanner opened Newt's bedroom door and found the boy sitting up in bed putting on his shoes, trickles of blood hanging from his nostrils.

Jessie and Flo flanked Tanner's sides, Jessie with a fistful of salt, Flo carrying a musket.

"Glenn, you got to leave this place," Tanner said. The boy did not look up from lacing his shoes. "I said Glenn you got to leave this place now."

The boy looked at the trio, stood and walked toward them. "That's exactly what I intend to do, Uncle Tanner. I'm going to bring this body back to Maud like she told me."

"What you say, haint?" Flora screamed at the boy, aiming the gun off-center.

Newt began to laugh. "So it is in life, so it is in death. Heard something you didn't like, woman? I can't call her Uncle Tanner no more? You didn't like that?" The boy put one hand on his hip and continued, "Maud found a way to settle this here debt of Tanner's. Nine sons for one. Nine boys for one boy. That's the new math. All my brothers and me for Newt."

Miss Flora let off a shot over the child's shoulder. "You ain't leaving here with my boy, haint."

"I don't think you got much of a choice, Flora, seeing as though your boy is dead. He died out there in the couch grass this morning. I'm just wearing him. He died a *natural death*. Tanner is a fan of that, those natural deaths. Your boy gone on, girl. You and your friend sent his soul off mighty right this morning. He dancing right now with the little colored niggers on the colored side of heaven. How you like that?"

The man-boy passed between Jessie and Tanner. Neither of them moved to stop him. The man-boy called out over his shoulder as he marched down the steps, "Your debt is clear. Nine sons and one son paid in full." Then he twisted the door handle, walked off the porch, made it past the quarter of a mile mark where Newt had dropped dead that very morning and kept on going.

Miss Flora remained laid out on the floor like a pile of dirty clothes. Tanner sat on Newt's bed. Jessie went downstairs first, salt in fist. The sun was high. She closed the front door hard, turned the VACANCY sign on and stood at the lobby desk, waiting.

Caitlín R. Kiernan

Bus Fare

SHE KNOWS THERE WAS A TOWN HERE ONCE, BECAUSE THE deserted streets are lined with deserted, boarded-up buildings. The roofs of some have sagged and collapsed in on themselves, and one has burned almost to the ground. If there was a town here once, there must have been people, too. So, she thinks, maybe only their ghosts live here now. She's seen plenty of ghosts, and they usually prefer places living people have forsaken. These are the things the albino girl named Dancy Flammarion is thinking, these things and a few more, while the black-haired, olive-skinned girl talks. The girl is sitting on the wooden bench with Dancy. She's barefoot, and her clothes are threadbare. She might be fourteen, and she could pass for Dancy's shadow. Dancy glances from her duffel bag to the faded bus sign, but she doesn't look into the talking girl's eyes. She doesn't like what she's seen there.

"Are you sure the bus still stops here?" she asks, interrupting the girl, who said her name was Maisie. Maybe, Dancy thinks, people named Maisie look different in South Carolina than they do in Florida and Georgia, because the girl doesn't look much like a Maisie.

"Last anyone bothered telling me," the girl replies. She doesn't have any luggage, not even a duffel bag, and Dancy is pretty sure she isn't waiting on a bus that may or may not come. "I still don't understand why you gave up a perfectly good ride and decided to Hound it instead."

"Hound it?" Dancy asks, and the girl who might be named Maisie jabs a thumb at the faded Greyhound sign. The thumbnail, like all her other fingernails, is thick and chocolate colored.

"The sun was setting," she says. "That's why I didn't stay in the car. The dead boy and girl in the trunk were waking up, and the Bailiff said they'd be hungry, and how it would be best if I walked a while."

"The Bailiff," Maisie says and smiles. "Yeah, I heard of him. Man ain't got no right name, you know." And then she stares silently at Dancy for a while. Dancy watches the empty streets of the empty town. She sees a huge black dog cross the street.

"You sure seem to know an awful lot of things," Dancy says to the girl.

"That I do," Maisie admits. "That I do. You're getting a reputation, Dancy."

That's what the monster in Waycross told her, and the crazy women in the big house in Savannah, and the Bailiff, he seemed to know, too.

"You're like Joan of Arc, right?" the girl asks.

"No," Dancy tells her. "I'm not like Joan of Arc."

"How's that?" Maisie wants to know. "You got yourself an angel who tells you where to find the monsters, and then you kill them. You're just a crazy girl doing the righteous work of the Lord. Sounds like Joan of Arc to me."

"I'm not like Joan of Arc," Dancy says again. "And I'm not crazy."

"Have it your way," Maisie sighs and lights a cigarette. She offers one to Dancy, but Dancy's never smoked a cigarette in her life, and she doesn't mean to start tonight. "How old are you, anyway? Fifteen?"

"Sixteen," Dancy tells her. "Seventeen soon now."

"You ain't got no folks?"

"Not anymore."

Of course, Dancy suspects Maisie already knows the answers to all the questions she's asking, and this is just going through the motions. She knew about Bainbridge, and the old man with the caged panther, the cat who was really a woman, and Maisie knew about the Bailiff and the vampire children, the monster in Waycross who wore other people's skin because it didn't have one of its own. She knew about the nine women in Savannah who were cannibals and dug up corpses and…did other things she'd rather not wonder about. She knew how many of them Dancy's killed. So, she knows all that, surely she knows how old Dancy is, and that her mother and grandmother are both dead.

Dancy sits back down on the wooden bench near the Greyhound sign, trying not to dwell on how thirsty she is, or whether or not a bus will ever show up, or what it means that the girl calling herself Maisie knows so much. The night is almost as hot as the day was, though at least there's no sun. No sun, so she doesn't need the raggedy black umbrella leaning against the bench. The air smells like cooling asphalt, kudzu, and pine trees. And it also smells like dog, which is the way that Maisie smells.

"Why do you smell like dog?" Dancy asks, gazing at the street, trying to catch another glimpse of the big black mutt she spotted a few minutes before.

"That's not a very polite thing to ask a stranger," Maisie says, pretending to be offended.

"The way you keep asking *me* questions, didn't think you'd much mind. You ask a lot of questions."

"And you don't smell so sweet your own self, Dancy Flammarion."

It rained a few days ago, and that's the closest Dancy's come to a bath since the night she stripped down and bathed in a muddy stream. And that bath, it was before the Bailiff and the dead children found her hitchhiking along Route 76, but she's having trouble recalling exactly how many days have passed since then.

"It's just sweat," Dancy says. "Just dirt and sweat. I don't smell like a dog." There's an old Coke machine outside an abandoned gas station across the road, and she wishes the gas station weren't abandoned and she had change for a cold drink.

Maisie sighs, very loudly, and she asks, "So, you just wanna cut to the chase, then? Stop dancing round the truth of the matter?"

"You ask a lot of questions," Dancy tells the girl for the second time. And finally, she makes herself turn and look directly at the dark-haired girl. In the moonlight, the girl's eyes glint iridescent red, like the eyeshine of alligators and possums.

"The night's young," the girl tells her. "And I like some sport before dinner. Didn't think you'd mind all that much. Didn't think you'd care one way or the other." The girl who says her name is Maisie smiles and shows off a lot more teeth than she ought to have. Maisie takes a last draw off her cigarette and flicks it away.

"I ain't scared of you," Dancy says, trying hard to sound like she means it. She looks at the duffel bag, but tries not to *look* like she's looking. The handle of the big carving knife is sticking out of the bag. Maisie, she's one of the one's the seraphim didn't bother to tell her was coming. That happens sometimes.

"Hardly thought you would be, not after all you done and seen, little Miss Joan of Arc cutting a swath across the countryside, laying all the bad folk low. Figure you ain't smart enough to be scared of nothing."

"Someone sent you?" Dancy wants to know. "The women in Savannah, did they send you after me?"

"No one *sent* me. We got curious, when we heard you'd be passing our way. Then this bitch made a bet. I drew the short straw, that's all."

"Sometimes I don't know they're coming." Dancy says it out loud, though she hadn't meant to, had only meant to think those words to herself.

"Well, that makes it a tiny bit more fair, don't you think, not getting the drop on people."

"You ain't people. I don't kill people."

"Strictly speaking, Snow White, that's not exactly factual. Not Gospel truth, I mean."

Dancy gives up on the duffel bag, because there's no way she'd ever have time to reach it and get hold of the knife before the olive-skinned girl who smells like a dog will be on her. She turns back to Maisie.

"You ain't the first ever called me that, you know. Snow White, I mean."

"I expect not. That mop of cornsilk hair, those pink rabbity eyes, that skin like you been playing in the flour bin. Figure you hear it a lot."

"Ain't never met one quite like you before," Dancy says, which isn't true, but she's stalling for time. If she has another minute or two, maybe she can think of a way to reach her knife or some other way to stop Maisie from eating her. "I never really believed in werewolves. Didn't know they were real."

Maisie furrows her brow and leans a little nearer Dancy. Her breath stinks of raw meat. "You're kidding me. You hitch rides with vampires, but you don't believe in werewolves?"

"Oh, now I do," Dancy says. "Sure. Just not before."

A warm wind stirs the underbrush at the edge of the road and the beard of Spanish moss in a nearby stand of live oaks. Dancy smells herself sweating—fresh sweat, not stale—and Maisie wrinkles her nose and flares her wide nostrils (which didn't seem quite so wide only a few seconds before).

"Oh, I almost forgot," Maisie says, and she produces something from…well, Dancy isn't sure where she was hiding it, but now there's an old cardboard cigar box in the girl's hand.

"That's mine," Dancy tells her. "I lost it—"

"—when you murdered them poor folks down in Waycross."

"Weren't folks, neither of them."

"Kinda depends on your point of view," says the olive-skinned girl who claims her name is Maisie.

"Well, it's mine. So you should give it back."

"I should?" the girl asks, and looks inside. "Mostly just a bunch of junk," she says.

And maybe it looks that way to her, or to anyone who isn't Dancy. In her head, Dancy counts off the contents of the cigar box, all that's left of her life before all that was left to her was the road and her knife, the seraphim and the parade of horrors it expects her to kill. She glances over her shoulder, and she's not at all surprised to find the angel looming behind the bench, looking over her and Maisie. The seraphim's tattered muslin and silk robes are even blacker than the night, than the dark inside the deserted shop fronts. They flutter and flap in a fierce and holy wind that touches nothing else. The angel's four ebony wings are spread wide, and it holds a burning sword high above its four shimmering kaleidoscope faces, both skeletal hands gripped tightly around the weapon's silver hilt. It stares down at her, and makes a sound like thunder that surely isn't thunder.

Just this once, she thinks, while Maisie paws through the cigar box. *Just this once, you could do the deed your own self. Seems like I earned that much.*

The angel doesn't answer her, but Dancy knows its moods well enough to know it's not about to intercede. Those aren't the rules, and it never breaks the rules. She looks at Maisie again, who's taking stuff out of the box and lining it up on the bench between them. So far, there are two plastic checkers (one black, one red), a tiny, battered copy of the New Testament that had been her mother's, and her grandmother's rosary, a spent shot gun shell she found at the edge of the road, two buttons, a green crayon, and a little statue of the Virgin Mary.

"It's mine, and you should give it back," she says to Maisie.

"You know better. Ain't nothing ever that easy." Maisie takes out a Patsy Cline cassette and a rubber band, then lines them up with all the rest.

"Maybe I could win it back," Dancy suggests, not taking her eyes off all the meager treasures she'd never hoped to see again. "Maybe we could have some sort of contest, and if I win, you gotta give it back."

Maisie looks up from the box. Her red eyes glimmer, and Dancy sees that her eyebrows meet in the middle, though they hadn't before. Maisie is holding a matchbox between those dark nails that have become claws. Inside the matchbox is thirty-five cents in pennies, dimes, and nickels that Dancy found along the highways.

"What do you have in mind? And what's in it for me? I had in mind I'd just eat you and be done with it. Why go complicating the situation?"

"Thought you wanted some sport?"

Maisie stars at her, and Dancy wonders how her eyes can have eyeshine, when there's no light shining on them. *There's the moon,* she thinks, then pushes the thought away.

"What you got in mind," the girl asks her.

"You any good at riddles?"

The girl, who is very slowly becoming not so much a girl, but something else, replies, "Not too shabby. Is that what you propose, a riddle game?"

"Yeah, and if I win, I get my box back, and you let me go. You win, I won't put up a struggle."

The girl thing scratches at her chin and seems to consider the offer. "Just three riddles," she says, "so there can't be no tie."

"Fine, just three riddles."

"And I go first."

"Fine, you go first."

"But how do I know you ain't gonna up and renege if you lose?"

"Everything you heard about me, ever heard of me telling lies?" Dancy asks.

"No, but still and all. I'd like some insurance."

Dancy Flammarion glances at the angel again, and it stares back at her with all its eight eyes. *Maybe you're gonna help after all*, she thinks directly at it. "Yeah, okay," she says to the werewolf. "I swear on the name of my angel I won't go back on my word."

Maisie looks surprised and chews her coal-colored lips. "That's a lot more than I expected. You'll say its name aloud and swear on it? You do that, you can't lie."

"That's what I just said, ain't it?"

Maisie stops taking Dancy's treasures out of the cigar box and nods her head. "Deal," she smiles, flashing all those sharp teeth. Her ears have grown to points, and each one has a small tuft of hair at the tip. Behind Dancy, the seraphim makes an awful, ugly noise and beats its wings, but she ignores it. The angel had its chance to help, but it was willing to stand by and let her be eaten and not even raise a finger to help, after all she's done just because it told her to.

"I get two riddles," Maisie says. "You just get the one," which hardly seems fair. The game's rigged in the werewolf's favor.

Dancy almost doesn't protest, but then says, "We could have five, instead. Five riddles, and I get two, and you get three. Still, no chance of a tie. Like you said, night's still young."

"Ain't *that* young," the werewolf says, and licks at its lips with a mottled tongue that's too long for a fourteen-year-old girl named Maisie. "You don't like the terms, I can always keep the box and eat you right here and now, get it over with."

"Fine," Dancy sighs. "Three riddles, you first," and then she swears on the name of the seraphim. She says its name aloud, which she's never done before. This time, she can tell Maisie also hears the thunder, and a trickle of blood leaks from the werewolf's nose. She wipes it away and grins.

"God's own fucking magic," she says. "And here I thought all I'd won was a free meal and a notch on the bedpost."

"You ain't won nothing yet," Dancy tells her. Then she reaches out and picks up the red checker. Maisie doesn't try to stop her. "Your move," she says to the crimson-eyed girl.

"I don't have to tell you, Dancy Flammarion, you lose this first one, and I get the second one right, that's all she wrote. Won't be need of a third riddle, it goes that way, will there."

"No," Dancy scowls. "You *don't* have to tell me that. Being an albino doesn't make me stupid."

"Just let me think a second."

Dancy shrugs and says, "the night's not *that* young, Maisie." She rubs the checker between her thumb and index finger. She smiles, wishing her smile was half so unnerving as the werewolf's.

"Then you answer me this, Joan of Arc," says Maisie, and she recites:

> "Although it never asked a thing
> Of any mortal man,
> Everybody answers it
> As quickly as he can."

Dancy shuts her eyes, because sometimes she thinks better that way. She closes her eyes, though maybe that's not the best thing to do when you're sitting on a bench with a werewolf who wants and fully intends to eat you. She lets the four lines run over and over again in her head.

"You don't know, do you?"

Dancy opens her eyes and sets the checker back down between them. "A knock at a door," she says, and the words come out more triumphantly than she'd meant them to come out. Maisie glowers and stares at the gravel and weeds between her bare feet.

"My turn," Dancy says, and she already knows the riddle she's going to ask. She's known it since she was a little girl:

> "Green as grass, but grass it ain't.
> White as snow, but snow it ain't.

Red as blood, but blood it ain't.
Black as ink, but ink it ain't."

"Your grammar's atrocious," the werewolf grunts and continues staring at the space between its feet. It repeats the riddle aloud several times. Dancy reaches into the cigar box and takes out her old St. Christopher's medal. The silver's tarnished, but she feels better just holding it, because St. Christopher's the patron saint of travelers, and she's been traveling for what feels like a very long time. It feels like she's been traveling her whole life.

"Don't know, do you," she whispers hopefully.

But Maisie snaps her fingers, her claws snicking together like a pair of scissors. "A blackberry," Maisie says and raises her head. Her hair's a lot longer than it was, shaggy and almost not like hair at all. Almost like a mane. "A ripening blackberry. That's it, right?"

"Yeah," Dancy says, then opens her hand and glares at the medal in her palm. First the angel, now a saint that's supposed to be watching over her, but clearly isn't. *Tonight*, she thinks, *all Heaven's gone and turned its back on me.*

"So, this one, she's the bitch of the litter. She's all do or die. You better stew on it long and hard." And then Maisie says:

"Red in the valley,
Red on the hill.
Feed it, live it will.
Water it, it will die.
This is true, and not a lie."

This time, Dancy doesn't shut her eyes. Maisie's a lot more wolf than girl now, her face become a muzzle, her legs the long, powerful hindquarters of a beast. There's only deeper shades of night waiting in back of Dancy's eyelids, and it's bad enough sitting across from the monster as it is, with only moonlight. The sun's hard on her skin, and she's rarely wished for sunrise. But she wishes for it now, even though it's still hours away.

"How do I know you're gonna keep your promise," she says. "I gave you insurance, but you didn't give me nothing but your word."

"Then my word's all you got, Snow White. You know the answer or don't you?"

"You didn't set a time limit," Dancy replies, then repeats the riddle aloud. "Red in the valley, red on the hill…"

"That's what I said," Maisie says, only she sounds more like she's growling now than talking.

Dancy ignores her. She knows the wolf is a deceitful, wicked demon, that it's only trying to distract her, trip her up, make it harder for her to concentrate. "Feed it," she continues, "live it will. Water it, it will die."

"This is true, and not a lie," the werewolf growls, then makes a noise that Dancy supposes is meant to be a laugh, if wolves could laugh.

A minute more comes and goes. Then five, and ten. Then Maisie (if she still is or ever was a Maisie) growls, "Times up."

"No," Dancy says. "We didn't set a time limit."

"We didn't *not* set a time limit, and I'm bored and hungry, and I say time's up. You *don't* know the answer, and sitting here all damn night long ain't gonna help you conjure up the right answer." There's finality and a faint hint of exasperation in the creature's gruff voice, and Dancy knows there's absolutely no point trying to reason with it. Maisie never intended to let her live. The riddles were nothing but a game of cat and mouse.

"Yeah," Dancy says, sparing another quick glimpse at the angel. "You win the game." She's pretty sure she's never seen the seraphim half so angry before. When she looks back at the werewolf, it's gotten up off the bench and is standing on its hind feet. It towers over her, grown at least a yard taller while they traded riddles. The girl's clothes hang in shreds from the lean, ribsy body.

"Looks like you don't get enough to eat," Dancy tells the wolf and points at its ribs.

"Tonight I will," it sneers, and saliva drips from its mouth and spatters on Dancy's duffel bag. "Tonight, I get a feast."

Dancy nods, gripping the St. Christopher's medal as tightly as she can. "What big eyes you have," she says, then flips the medal like it was a quarter, and it strikes the werewolf squarely in its right eye. There's a sizzling sound, and the smell of burning pork. A second later, there's a soft pop when the monster's eye boils and bursts. It howls, a howl that's nothing but pain and anger, and it clutches at its face, trying to brush away the smoldering talisman seared into its flesh.

"Wasn't even halfway sure that was gonna work," Dancy mutters, and she leans over and draws the carving knife from the green canvas bag. The blade shines dully in under the moon. "Thought maybe that was just in books."

Maisie lunges for her then, its steaming jaws open wide as the gates of any hell, its left eye blazing and nothing but a scorched black pit where its right had been. Dancy swings the knife, *her* sword, opening the werewolf's throat from ear to ear, slicing through jugular and carotid arteries, through muscle and larynx, cutting all the way to the bone. The blade lodges firmly in a vertebra, and as Maisie, gurgling, stumbles backwards, the knife's yanked from Dancy's hand with enough force that she loses her balance and falls hard on her hands and knees.

"It's a fire, puppy," she says, not caring whether or not the beast can hear her. "The answer's a fire."

An hour later, and Dancy's dragged Maisie's naked body into the woods behind the bus stop. Dead, she became nothing but a fourteen-year-old girl again, so she wasn't all that heavy. Dancy covered her decently with magnolia and sycamore leaves and with branches torn from bushes. She figured the coyotes and wild dogs, maybe coons and feral pigs and whatever else sniffed out the corpse, would do the rest. Now, she's back at the bench, wiping the blood from her knife and she holds the cigar box tucked under one arm. All her treasures are safe inside it again, everything but the St. Christopher's medal, which melted away to nothing. The seraphim has gone, took its leave the moment she killed the werewolf that meant to kill her, and Dancy knows it won't ever be back. It said not one word as it departed in a veil of flame and smoke, but there wasn't anything it might have said she didn't already know. It plays by the rules, laws older than the universe, and she's sure there's always someone else willing to do its bidding.

"That's only fair and right," she says, and slips the knife back into the duffel bag. "I was scared. I didn't want to die, not here. Not tonight. So, I went and took your name in vain. I spoke your name, *used* your name, then cheated. I'm not gonna say it ain't fair. I knew better."

But Dancy Flammarion's never been on her own before, and that part frightens her almost as much as Maisie did. On the road alone and no shelter in a storm, and no angelic host to tell her where to go and what to expect when she gets there. She's already done so much damage that every speck of evil, every fiend for hundreds of miles around, knows her name. They whisper it in their hiding places, and make plans for her undoing. And if she needed proof that the hunter has become the hunted, the werewolf was precisely that. She doesn't need to be told twice.

There's a rumble, and for just half a second, there's hope it might be the seraphim. That maybe her sin wasn't so unforgivable, after all. But then she sees the headlights of the Greyhound bus moving towards her through the deserted town. Dancy stares up at the night sky for a moment, all the stars, the empty space between the stars, and the moon that must have been the girl's goddess, but couldn't be bothered to save her. Any more than the angel could be bothered to save Dancy. As the bus pulls to a stop, raising clouds of dust and grit, she shoulders her heavy duffel bag and waits for the door to swing open.

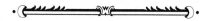

RICH LARSON

The Air We Breathe is Stormy, Stormy

In Baltic waters, gnashed by dark waves, there stood an old oil platform on rusted legs. It was populated as rigs always are, by coarse men young and strong whose faces soon overgrew with bristle and bloat. Cedric was one of these.

He'd fled his father in New Zealand, then a pregnant girlfriend in Perth, arriving on the rig with insomniac eyes and an inchoate smile and a bank account in need of filling. In the pocket of his dull blue coverall, he carried an old Kindle with a spider-webbed screen and a Polaroid photograph of Violet when she was still slim and still laughed.

His days were filled by the slow geometry of pipefitting, the bone-deep clank of machinery, the shrieks and swoops of soot-stained gulls. At night, when the running lights cast wavery orange on the black water and a sea-breeze scoured at the omnipresent stench of oil, Cedric thought the rig was not so bad. At night he read Moby Dick and anything else vaguely nautical. At night, Violet was blurred beautiful by the webcam window, distended curve of her stomach cropped neatly away, and he nearly loved her again.

Some nights, Cedric stayed up top for hours to watch the starless sky and the ink-black sea. Dregs from this or that leak shimmered around the derrick's legs. Scabs of tangled plastic bobbed between them. Some nights, Cedric thought he saw a shape moving in the water, but he knew all fish had fled long ago.

Long months stacked on months, and the weekend before the fresh crew was brought in, everyone shattered themselves on whiskey hidden under bunks and coke stashed in jacket linings. Cedric copped a dime-bag of weed from Biggs, who wore Arsenal gear religiously but was otherwise sound, and sawed himself a bong from an empty 2-litre.

Biggs stayed for a few hoots, then it was only Cedric and the gurgle of bong-water, the gasp-catch of a held lungful, the electronic melody of a Skype dial tone. *Any day now, love,* Violet said, when she appeared. Cedric nodded blearily, leaking smoke from chapped lips. She showed him, then, and it was impossibly pale and round and sized like the moon.

Cedric cut the line, because that was more merciful, wasn't it, than telling her he would go anywhere but back to her in Perth. He clumped up top, through drinking songs and flitting cards and eruptions of laughter. He went to the rail with his head full of helium. The icy pitch was thick, thick below him.

And there: a gleaming face, ivory-white. Cedric thought to call for help, thought the drifting body was crew drunk and toppled overboard, but the face made no sound, only blinked oil-black eyes, and so he knew he was imagining it. He went back below with his feet heavy as stones.

In the morning, Cedric found the operations coordinator and told him he needed an extension on his contract. The OC listened through a hard liquor hangover as Cedric badgered, Cedric argued, and in the end he agreed so he'd be left to his silence and Tylenol. The old crew pushed off. Fresh crew came in. Cedric had an empty bunk in his room, and he found a new dealer for weed—none of Biggs' laced shit, either.

Skype slipped off into angry emails, then nothing at all. Cedric worked hard during the day, building aches into every part of his body, and stayed up most of the night. He read Auden and then anything else vaguely elegiac. It made the dark sea friendlier.

Then, one night, he saw her. She was adrift, flotsam, pale limbs splayed like a starfish, hair ebbing tendrils around her head. Cedric had never seen a corpse, only dreamed one, and he found the sight paralyzed him. Then she revolved in the water and began pulling languid strokes towards the rig.

Cedric watched with needles up his neck, wondered dimly if he should try to fish her out with a lifebuoy. Her face was angled towards his now and he recognized her wide liquid eyes. Cedric eased himself over the barrier and onto the rungs of a maintenance ladder, swearing when his palms stung against the cold metal. He climbed lower; she swam closer, smooth strokes, no drowning man's flail.

Are you alright, he croaked to her. He scuttled down until the dark water licked his waders and realized he'd left the lifebuoy. She was right below him now, treading in place and staring at him with eyes deep as the well. *Are you alright,* he said again, because he had nothing else to say.

Cold was the word that tumbled off her lips. She reached; he reached, to her hand of slick rubber. She was impossibly light as he lifted her up the ladder, as if every one of her bones was hollow, but she clung to his back with fierce fingers. Her naked weight shivered against him.

On deck, Cedric shrugged out of his thermal and handed it over. She watched the bunched fabric for a moment, then slipped it slowly, clumsily, over her head. As she pulled her wet black hair from this side of her neck to the other, Cedric realized she was beautiful. Bee-stung lips, immaculate skin, that bone structure that begged him to touch her.

There was no doctor on the rig. Cedric knew there was a former EMT, and a half-dozen men with First Response, but there was no doctor and he felt, deeply, that if he passed her on to anybody else he would never see her again. He almost didn't hear her when she said, *I need some sleep.*

I would, too, Christ. Cedric helped her to the door and dragged his card through the mag-lock. The iron stairwell was empty. Her feet slapped wetly on the way down to his cabin; Cedric hoped nobody was up to hear it. *Sleep here,* he told her, clearing his Acer and a tangle of laundry off the bottom bunk. *Sleep here and I'll call for someone.*

She plunged into the mattress, strings cut. Cedric watched the slack line of her spine, the curve of her ass, and thought thoughts. His porn bored him lately and Violet's last webcam teasing was months removed. In his head he slipped into the bunk with her and she grabbed at him with those fierce fingers, with her lips and teeth.

Her breathing evened. Cedric reached for the handset, thinking maybe the company man, maybe his OC, but stopped when he saw the webbing stretched taut between her long fingers. He knelt close, studying a tracery of blue veins like canals.

When her dark eyes flicked open, he jumped. She smiled with gray needle teeth. Then Cedric blinked, and her teeth were Crest-commercial white again, and when he looked at her hand the slim fingers were unbound. *Piss off*, she whispered, closing her eyes.

Three hours on, in a raw red dawn, she had not vanished and Cedric had not much moved. It wasn't until his phone rattled out 5:45 AM on the dresser that he roused. His body dressed on automatic; his mind was still numbed.

Stay here, Cedric said to her snores, and he went to work. The new crew knew Cedric as the quiet type; today he was dead silent in thought. He'd seen her before, he was sure of that now. Faded on Biggs' weed, sick from a strange sort of fear, he'd seen her face peering up from the black water.

When they breaked for food, Cedric half-walked, half-jogged back down to his cabin. The hallucination was lounging on his bottom bunk, brushing crumbs of granola bar off the sleeve of his thermal. She looked up as he entered.

Where did you come from, he asked. She balled the wrapper in her fist and dropped it onto the floor. *From the sea*, she said. *Like everybody does.*

I mean, before you were in the water.

Imagine I was in a uterus, before, she said. *Can I wash now?*

Cedric's eyes caught on the pristine edge of her collarbone. *Not unless you want to shower with a dozen blokes.* She raised one dark eyebrow and shook her head. *Tonight, then*, Cedric said. He stumped towards the door, then paused. *I'm Cedric, by the way.* She rolled her eyes up as if debating. *Volkova.* Cedric nodded, and let the door clank shut behind him.

That evening he brought her spaghetti Bolognese reheated in the kitchenette microwave, not chancing the stove, and two cans of Coke. When she opened the door he found she'd dressed herself more thoroughly, which squirmed him with relief and disappointment. The trousers were oversized but held by shoelace.

She ate slowly and grimly, like someone preparing for a long march, and Cedric asked no more questions, skimming Hans Christian

Andersen instead. By eleven, he knew the showers were empty. *I haven't told anyone,* he said, not sure if it mattered. *But I don't think you should be here, either.*

Do you think I'm a mermaid, she asked, and gave a soft scornful laugh. Cedric draped two towels over his shoulder and led her quietly to the showers. Fluorescents flickered on over cold fractured puddles. Cedric pointed her to the furthest nozzle, difficult to see from the doorway, and felt a distant embarrassment about the grout creeping between the bathroom tiles.

He turned on his own shower, listening despite himself for the telltale slither of her borrowed clothes coming away. When steam started to billow, he stripped but kept his briefs, as he did in the presence of company, and stepped into the hot spray. *Leaving those on, are you.* Cedric didn't turn his head to look at her, but he put a deliberate finger up to his lips. She was silent then, and for a moment he imagined she wasn't there at all, that it was only him and the sweat and grime sliding off his skin in dirty tendrils.

Then she started to retch. Cedric stared straight ahead as long as possible, but the ragged sound was impossible to ignore. He turned and saw her jackknifed over, shivering, heaving, and the gleaming black vomit she'd left on the floor was unmistakeable. *I live under the platform,* she rasped, as if to explain. *You need a hospital,* Cedric said, blindly thrusting a towel towards her.

She insisted she didn't, and a few minutes later they stole quickly and quietly back to the cabin. Cedric waited for a roughneck to slouch into the corridor with cigarette and lighter, but their path was empty, completely empty. *I saw you one night,* he said when they were back in the room. *Didn't I?*

That's why I decided to come up the ladder, she said. *You looked so damn lonely.* She trailed soft fingers along Cedric's wrist; he felt his cock thicken against his thigh.

Not because you're sick?

Maybe a bit of that, too. Tired of eating garbage. She peeled off the towel and slipped into the bottom bunk without another word, making herself a cocoon of his staled sheets. *You're not a mermaid,* Cedric decided aloud, thumbing the light-switch, clambering past her. *Something else.* He tugged off silently as he could in the upper bunk.

She stayed. During the day she was holed up in the cabin—there wasn't much in the way of diversion, since she didn't seem to understand the laptop, but she did devour the thick dusty stack of maintenance manuals and guidebooks that had gone months untouched. Cedric, for his part, wolfed down wikis of Irish mythology. It led to one speed-fueled night spent gutting the cabin, searching high and low for an oil-slicked pelt, while she watched and laughed her soft contemptuous laugh that tingled like morphine.

Most nights they snuck to the showers, or up to the deck. She was happiest near water, where her eyes seemed blacker and her hands more like bony fins, though when Cedric brought her microwaved mahi-mahi she preferred the lasagne.

Every so often she would heave up the black vomit, and sometimes Cedric was there to hold back her hair and mutter small nothings the way he had back when Violet first had the morning sickness. Afterwards they would sit together, sometimes with a cloud of vapor between them, sometimes only words.

She asked him about the work, about the faulty water injector, the company man's blow habit, and then one night about where he'd grown up, about New Zealand and about his family. *I hated my father,* he said around a hit, and she said, *that's original.* He laughed, eyes pink and glassy, then showed her the Maori tattoos down his back. She showed him the no tattoos down her front, leaned in, kissed hard.

As they see-saw stumbled towards the bunk, her hand found the spiral ridge of scar tissue under his briefs. *Oh.* And then Cedric had to explain, as he had to Violet so long ago, about the boiling coffee he hadn't watched, being glued to Action Man on the telly instead, and how when his father found the mess he turned the electric range back on and shucked off Cedric's trousers.

He explained about standing there, wailing and snuffling, watching the rusty element turn slowly bright orange. He explained about the sizzle and the gut-sick smell. She still fucked him, fiercely, urgently. Their writhing shadow was aquatic.

Later, in the bruised hours of the night, Cedric's heavy eyes opened on her rooting through his coverall. She had the Polaroid of Violet held between two fingers like a cigarette. *She's pretty.* Cedric nodded. Still warm with post-coital chemicals, he told her about the move to Perth and the pregnancy and the way Violet sang to herself if she thought he was still asleep.

And that's why you live here? To earn enough money for three, I mean.

Yeah, said Cedric, then, to change subjects: *Why did you live under the rig for all those years?* She gave that morphine-yellow laugh. *Stubborn, I imagine,* she said. *Figured to find nothing better.* His eyes were closed again when she draped herself over him like a long-coat, breathed secrets into the skin of his neck.

Things became different. She was always restless now, jittery. She'd worked out how to use the cracked Kindle and Cedric found Kierkegaard and Ibsen on its screen. In the night she took his card and slipped out of the cabin; he knew by the wet footprints and damp kisses. He dreamed of her slicing through the black water, diving and turning somersaults through metal struts. She smiled less often and too widely.

One night, with her head against his ribcage, she told him she was leaving. Cedric was unsurprised in a hollow way, reminded of another night, of Violet's cigarette-scorched table and rolls of gauze.

It wasn't because I was stubborn, she said. *I lived down there in the muck because I knew it well, and I was scared of cleaner things.*

Cedric clenched and unclenched his teeth. *I'm not here because of the money,* he said. *Not anymore.* He told her, then, about the night before he left. Six, seven bottles of Swan deep, and Violet had been looking for an argument, needing one last one, but instead of arguing how he usually did he shoved her and her scalp split on the edge of the table. *A baby's head is soft for months,* he said. *Because of the brain growing.*

She put her hand down to his hidden scar. *You'll be nothing like him,* she said. *Oh, Cedric. The air we breathe is stormy, stormy. Isn't it?*

He tried and tried but couldn't remember her name. At 1:53 AM she kissed his chin, and at 1:55 AM she was leading the way up the iron stairs one last time. The starless sky was sea-colored, the inky sea was sky-colored. She stripped naked before she descended the ladder. *Come for a swim,* she suggested through chattering teeth, raising one webbed hand. Cedric raised a brow and shook his head.

She laughed, first soft and low, then shrill and barking. At the support strut Cedric watched her untie a floating garbage bag and pull something slick and heavy over her head. There was a rending sound of flesh and bone finding new places, or maybe old ones, and then she was a dark shape cutting through dark water, away from the rig, away from the running lights. And then, she was nothing at all. Cedric calculated the time difference. He went back to his cabin and called, called, called.

The next day, the water injector quit working completely. Cedric wrote and rewrote his emails. The day after that, compressor problems. Cedric tried her number until the Skype dial-tone was ricocheting through his skull. Pumps stalled, electronics bugged; everyone agreed it was suspect. Cedric's key-card had been many places it shouldn't have, but so had a dozen others that had gone mysteriously missing.

The day Violet answered was the day the rig evacuated, mutters of permanent shutdown following the second electrical fire. She picked up furious, how couldn't she be furious, but by the time the boats were loading she promised to let Cedric call again, and before the line cut he heard the small voice that would carry him over the Baltic waves.

CARMEN MARIA MACHADO

The Husband Stitch

(If you read this story out loud, please use the following voices:

Me: as a child, high-pitched, forgettable; as a woman, the same.

The boy who will grow into a man, and be my spouse: robust with his own good fortune.

My father: Like your father, or the man you wish was your father.

My son: as a small child, gentle, rounded with the faintest of lisps; as a man, like my husband.

All other women: interchangeable with my own.)

In the beginning, I know I want him before he does. This isn't how things are done, but this is how I am going to do them. I am at a neighbour's party with my parents, and I am seventeen. Though my father didn't notice, I drank half a glass of white wine in the kitchen a few minutes ago, with the neighbour's teenage daughter. Everything is soft, like a fresh oil painting.

The boy is not facing me. I see the muscles of his neck and upper back, how he fairly strains out of his button-down shirts. I run slick. It isn't that I don't have choices. I am beautiful. I have a pretty mouth. I have a breast that heaves out of my dresses in a way that seems inno-cent and perverse all at the same time. I am a good girl, from a good family. But he is a little craggy, in that way that men sometimes are, and I want.

I once heard a story about a girl who requested something so vile from her paramour that he told her family and they had her hauled off to a sanitarium. I don't know what deviant pleasure she asked for, though I desperately wish I did. What magical thing could you want so badly that they take you away from the known world for wanting it?

The boy notices me. He seems sweet, flustered. He says, hello. He asks my name.

I have always wanted to choose my moment, and this is the moment I choose.

On the deck, I kiss him. He kisses me back, gently at first, but then harder, and even pushes open my mouth a little with his tongue. When he pulls away, he seems startled. His eyes dart around for a moment, and then settles on my throat.

—What's that? he asks.

—Oh, this? I touch my ribbon at the back of my neck. It's just my ribbon. I run my fingers halfway around its green and glossy length, and bring them to rest on the tight bow that sits in the front. He reaches out his hand, and I seize it and push it away.

—You shouldn't touch it, I say. You can't touch it.

Before we go inside, he asks if he can see me again. I tell him I would like that. That night, before I sleep, I imagine him again, his tongue pushing open my mouth, and my fingers slide over myself and I imagine him there, all muscle and desire to please, and I know that we are going to marry.

We do. I mean, we will. But first, he takes me in his car, in the dark, to a lake with a marshy edge. He kisses me and clasps his hand around my breast, my nipple knotting beneath his fingers.

I am not truly sure what he is going to do before he does it. He is hard and hot and dry and smells like bread, and when he breaks me I scream and cling to him like I am lost at sea. His body locks onto mine and he is pushing, pushing, and before the end he pulls himself out and finishes with my blood slicking him down. I am fascinated and aroused by the rhythm, the concrete sense of his need, the clarity of his release. Afterwards, he slumps in the seat, and I can hear the sounds of the pond: loons and crickets, and something that sounds like a banjo being plucked. The wind picks up off the water and cools my body down.

I don't know what to do now. I can feel my heart beating between my legs. It hurts, but I imagine it could feel good. I run my hand over myself and feel strains of pleasure from somewhere far off. His breathing becomes quieter and I realize that he is watching me. My skin is glowing beneath the moonlight coming through the window. When I see him looking, I know I can seize that pleasure like my fingertips tickling the end of a balloon's string that has almost drifted out of reach. I pull and moan and ride out the crest of sensation slowly and evenly, biting my tongue all the while.

—I need more, he says, but he does not rise to do anything.

He looks out the window, and so do I. Anything could move out there in the darkness, I think. A hook-handed man. A ghostly hitchhiker repeating her journey. An old woman summoned from the rest of her mirror by the chants of children. Everyone knows these stories—that is, everyone tells them—but no one ever believes them.

His eyes drift over the water, and then land on my neck.

—Tell me about your ribbon, he says.

—There is nothing to tell. It's my ribbon.

—May I touch it?

—I want to touch it, he says.

—No.

Something in the lake muscles and writhes out of the water, and then lands with a splash. He turns at the sound.

—A fish, he says.

—Sometime, I tell him, I will tell you the stories about this lake and her creatures.

He smiles at me, and rubs his jaw. A little of my blood smears across his skin, but he doesn't notice, and I don't say anything.

—I would like that very much, he says.

—Take me home, I tell him.

And like a gentleman, he does.

That night, I wash myself. The silky suds between my legs are the color and scent of rust, but I am newer than I have ever been.

———

My parents are very fond of him. He is a nice boy, they say. He will be a good man. They ask him about his occupation, his hobbies, his family. He comes around twice a week, sometimes thrice. My mother invites him in for supper, and while we eat I dig my nails into the meat of his leg. After the ice cream puddles in the bowl, I tell my parents that I am going to walk with him down the lane. We strike off through the night, holding hands sweetly until we are out of sight of the house. I pull him through the trees, and when we find a patch of clear ground I shimmy off my pantyhose, and on my hands and knees offer myself up to him.

I have heard all of the stories about girls like me, and I am unafraid to make more of them. There are two rules: he cannot finish inside of me, and he cannot touch my green ribbon. He spends into the dirt, *pat-pat-patting* like the beginning of rain. I go to touch myself, but my fingers, which had been curling in the dirt beneath me, are filthy. I pull up my underwear and stockings. He makes a sound and points, and I realize that beneath the nylon, my knees are also caked in dirt. I pull them down and brush, and then up again. I smooth my skirt and repin my hair. A single lock has escaped his slicked-back curls, and I tuck it up with the others. We walk down to the stream and I run my hands in the current until they are clean again.

We stroll back to the house, arms linked chastely. Inside, my mother has made coffee, and we all sit around while my father asks him about business.

(If you read this story out loud, the sounds of the clearing can be best reproduced by taking a deep breath and holding it for a long moment. Then release the air all at once, permitting your chest to collapse like a block tower knocked to the ground. Do this again, and again, shortening the time between the held breath and the release.)

I have always been a teller of stories. When I was a young girl, my mother carried me out of a grocery store as I screamed about toes in the produce aisle. Concerned women turned and watched as I kicked the air and pounded my mother's slender back.

—Potatoes! she corrected when we got back to the house. Not toes!

She told me to sit in my chair—a child-sized thing, only built for me—until my father returned. But no, I had seen the toes, pale and bloody stumps, mixed in among those russet tubers. One of them, the one that I had poked with the tip of my index finger, was cold as ice, and yielded beneath my touch the way a blister did. When I repeated this detail to my mother, the liquid of her eyes shifted quick as a startled cat.

—You stay right there, she said.

My father returned from work that evening and listened to my story, each detail.

—You've met Mr Barns, have you not? he asked me, referring to the elderly man who ran this particular market.

I had met him once, and I said so. He had hair white as a sky before snow, and a wife who drew the signs for the store windows.

—Why would Mr Barns sell toes? my father asked. Where would he get them?

Being young, and having no understanding of graveyards or mortuaries, I could not answer.

—And even if he got them somewhere, my father continued, what would he have to gain by selling them among the potatoes?

They had been there. I had seen them with my own eyes. But beneath the sunbeams of my father's logic, I felt my doubt unfurling.

—Most importantly, my father said, arriving triumphantly at his final piece of evidence, why did no one notice the toes except for you?

As a grown woman, I would have said to my father that there are true things in this world only observed by a single set of eyes. As a girl, I consented to his account of the story, and laughed when he scooped me from the chair to kiss me and send me on my way.

It is not normal that a girl teaches her boy, but I am only showing him what I want, what plays on the insides of my eyelids as I fall asleep. He comes to know the flicker of my expression as a desire passes through me, and I hold nothing back from him. When he tells me that he wants my mouth, the length of my throat, I teach myself not to gag and take all of him into me, moaning around the saltiness. When he asks me my worst secret, I tell him about the teacher who hid me in the closet until the others were gone and made me hold him there, and how afterwards I went home and scrubbed my hands with a steel wool pad until they bled, even though after I share this I have nightmares for a month. And when he asks me to marry him, days shy of my eighteenth birthday, I say yes, yes, please, and then on that park bench I sit on his lap and fan my skirt around us so that a passerby would not realize what was happening beneath it.

—I feel like I know so many parts of you, he says to me, trying not to pant. And now, I will know all of them.

There is a story they tell, about a girl dared by her peers to venture to a local graveyard after dark. This was her folly: when they told her that standing on someone's grave at night would cause the inhabitant to reach up and pull her under, she scoffed. Scoffing is the first mistake a woman can make.

I will show you, she said.

Pride is the second mistake.

They gave her a knife to stick into the frosty earth, as a way of proving her presence and her theory.

She went to that graveyard. Some storytellers say that she picked the grave at random. I believe she selected a very old one, her choice tinged by self-doubt and the latent belief that if she were wrong, the intact muscle and flesh of a newly dead corpse would be more dangerous than one centuries gone.

She knelt on the grave and plunged the blade deep. As she stood to run she found she couldn't escape. Something was clutching at her clothes. She cried out and fell down.

When morning came, her friends arrived at the cemetery. They found her dead on the grave, the blade pinning the sturdy wool of her skirt to the ground. Dead of fright or exposure, would it matter when the parents arrived? She was not wrong, but it didn't matter any more. Afterwards, everyone believed that she had wished to die, even though she had died proving that she could live.

As it turns out, being right was the third, and worst, mistake.

My parents are pleased about the marriage. My mother says that even though girls nowadays are starting to marry late, she married father when she was nineteen, and was glad that she did.

When I select my wedding gown, I am reminded of the story of the young woman who wished to go to a dance with her lover, but could not afford a dress. She purchased a lovely white frock from a secondhand shop, and then later fell ill and passed from this earth. The coroner who performed her autopsy discovered she had died from exposure to embalming fluid. It turned out that an unscrupulous undertaker's assistant had stolen the dress from the corpse of a bride.

The moral of that story, I think, is that being poor will kill you. Or perhaps the moral is that brides never fare well in stories, and one should avoid either being a bride, or being in a story. After all, stories can sense happiness and snuff it out like a candle.

We marry in April, on an unseasonably cold afternoon. He sees me before the wedding, in my dress, and insists on kissing me deeply and reaching inside of my bodice. He becomes hard, and I tell him that I want him to use my body as he sees fit. I rescind my first rule, given the occasion. He pushes me against the wall and puts his hand against the tile near my throat, to steady himself. His thumb brushes my ribbon. He does not move his hand, and as he works himself in me he says I love you, I love you, I love you. I do not know if I am the first woman to walk up the aisle of St George's with semen leaking down her leg, but I like to imagine that I am.

For our honeymoon, we go on a trip I have long desired: a tour of Europe. We are not rich but we make it work. We go from bustling, ancient metropolises to sleepy villages to alpine retreats and back again, sipping spirits and pulling roasted meat from bones with our teeth, eating spaetzle and olives and ravioli and a creamy grain I do not recognize but come to crave each morning. We cannot afford a sleeper car on the train, but my husband bribes an attendant to permit us one hour in an empty room, and in that way we couple over the Rhine.

(If you are reading this story out loud, make the sound of the bed under the tension of train travel and lovemaking by straining a metal folding chair against its hinges. When you are exhausted with that, sing the half remembered lyrics of old songs to the person closest to you, thinking of lullabies for children.)

My cycle stops soon after we return from our trip. I tell my husband one night, after we are spent and sprawled across our bed. He glows with delight.

—A child, he says. He lies back with his hands beneath his head. A child. He is quiet for so long that I think that he's fallen asleep, but when I look over his eyes are open and fixed on the ceiling. He rolls on his side and gazes at me.

—Will the child have a ribbon?

I feel my jaw tighten. My mind skips between many answers, and I settle on the one that brings me the least amount of anger.

—There is no saying, now, I tell him finally.

He startles me, then, by running his hand around my throat. I put up my hands to stop him but he uses his strength, grabbing my wrists with one hand as he touches the ribbon with the other. He presses the silky length with his thumb. He touches the bow delicately, as if he is massaging my sex.

—Please, I say. Please don't.

He does not seem to hear. Please, I say again, my voice louder, but cracking in the middle.

He could have done it then, untied the bow, if he'd chosen to. But he releases me and rolls back on his back. My wrists ache, and I rub them.

—I need a glass of water, I say. I get up and go to the bathroom. I run the tap and then frantically check my ribbon, tears caught in my lashes. The bow is still tight.

There is a story I love about a pioneer husband and wife killed by wolves. Neighbours found their bodies torn open and strewn around their tiny cabin, but never located their infant daughter, alive or dead. People claimed they saw the girl running with a wolf pack, loping over the terrain as wild and feral as any of her companions.

News of her would ripple through the local settlements. She menaced a hunter in a winter forest—though perhaps he was less menaced than startled at a tiny naked girl baring her teeth and howling. A young woman trying to take down a horse. People even saw her ripping open a chicken in an explosion of feathers.

Many years later, she was said to be seen resting in the rushes along a riverbank, suckling two wolf cubs. I like to imagine that they came from her body, the lineage of wolves tainted human just the once. They certainly bloodied her breasts, but she did not mind because they were hers and only hers.

My stomach swells. Inside of me, our child is swimming fiercely, kicking and pushing and clawing. On a walk in the park, the same park where my husband had proposed to me the year before, I gasp and stagger to the side, clutching my belly and hissing through my teeth to Little One, as I call it, to stop. I go to my knees, breathing heavily and near weeping. A woman passing by helps me to sit up and gives me some water, telling me that the first pregnancy is always the worst.

My body changes in ways I do not expect—my breasts are large, swollen and hot, my stomach lined with pale marks, the inverse of a tiger's. I feel monstrous, but my husband seems renewed with desire, as if my novel shape has refreshed our list of perversities. And my body responds: in the line at the supermarket, receiving communion in church, I am marked by a new and ferocious want, leaving me slippery and swollen at the slightest provocation. When he comes home each day, my husband has a list in his mind of things he desires from me, and I am willing to provide them and more.

—I am the luckiest man alive, he says, running his hands across my stomach.

In the mornings, he kisses me and fondles me and sometimes takes me before his coffee and toast. He goes to work with a spring in his step. He comes home with one promotion, and then another. More money for my family, he says. More money for our happiness.

I am in labour for twenty hours. I nearly wrench off my husband's hand, howling obscenities that do not seem to shock the nurse. I am certain I will crush my own teeth to powder. The doctor peers down between my legs, his white eyebrows making unreadable Morse code across his forehead.

—What's happening? I ask.

—I'm not satisfied this will be a natural birth, the doctor says. Surgery may be necessary.

—No, please, I say. I don't want that, please.

—If there's no movement soon, we're going to do it, the doctor says. It might be best for everyone. He looks up and I am almost certain he winks at my husband, but pain makes the mind see things differently than they are.

I make a deal with Little One, in my mind. *Little One*, I think, *this is the last time that we are going to be just you and me. Please don't make them cut you out of me.*

Little One is born twenty minutes later. They do have to make a cut, but not across my stomach as I had feared. The doctor cuts down, and I feel little, just tugging, though perhaps it is what they have given me. When the baby is placed in my arms, I examine the wrinkled body from head to toe, the colour of a sunset sky, and streaked in red.

No ribbon. A boy. I begin to weep, and curl the unmarked baby into my chest.

(If you are reading this story out loud, give a paring knife to the listener and ask them to cut the tender flap of skin between your index finger and thumb. Afterwards, thank them.)

There is a story about a woman who goes into labour when the attending physician is tired. There is a story about a woman who herself was born too early. There is a story about a woman whose body clung to her child so hard they cut her to retrieve him. There is a story about a woman who heard a story about a woman who birthed wolf cubs in secret. Stories have this way of running together like raindrops in a pond. They are each borne from the clouds separately, but once they have come together, there is no way to tell them apart.

(If you are reading this story out loud, move aside the curtain to illustrate this final point to your listeners. It'll be raining, I promise.)

They take the baby so that they may fix me where they cut. They give me something that makes me sleepy, delivered through a mask pressed gently to my mouth and nose. My husband jokes around with the doctor as he holds my hand.

—How much to get that extra stitch? he asks. You offer that, right?— Please, I say to him. But it comes out slurred and twisted and possibly no more than a small moan. Neither man turns his head toward me.

The doctor chuckles. You aren't the first—

I slide down a long tunnel, and then surface again, but covered in something heavy and dark, like oil. I feel like I am going to vomit.

—the rumor is something like—

—like a vir—

And then I am awake, wide awake, and my husband is gone and the doctor is gone. And the baby, where is—

The nurse sticks her head in the door.

—Your husband just went to get a coffee, she says, and the baby is asleep in the bassinet.

The doctor walks in behind her, wiping his hands on a cloth.

—You're all sewn up, don't you worry, he said. Nice and tight, everyone's happy. The nurse will speak with you about recovery. You're going to need to rest for a while.

The baby wakes up. The nurse scoops him from his swaddle and places him in my arms again. He is so beautiful I have to remind myself to breathe.

My son is a good baby. He grows and grows. We never have another child, though not for lack of trying. I suspect that Little One did so much ruinous damage inside of me that my body couldn't house another.

—You were a poor tenant, Little One, I say to him, rubbing shampoo into his fine brown hair, and I shall revoke your deposit.

He splashes around in the sink, cackling with happiness.

My son touches my ribbon, but never in a way that makes me afraid. He thinks of it as a part of me, and he treats it no differently than he would an ear or finger.

Back from work, my husband plays games in the yard with our son, games of chase and run. He is too young to catch a ball, still, but my husband patiently rolls it to him in the grass, and our son picks it up and drops it again, and my husband gestures to me and cries Look, look! Did you see? He is going to throw it soon enough.

Of all the stories I know about mothers, this one is the most real. A young American girl is visiting Paris with her mother when the woman begins to feel ill. They decide to check into a hotel for a few days so the mother can rest, and the daughter calls for a doctor to assess her.

After a brief examination, the doctor tells the daughter that all her mother needs is some medicine. He takes the daughter to a taxi, gives the driver directions in French, and explains to the girl that, at his home, his wife will give her the appropriate remedy. They drive and drive for a very long time, and when the girl arrives, she is frustrated by the unbearable slowness of this doctor's wife, who meticulously assembles the pills from powder. When she gets back into the taxi, the driver meanders down the streets, sometimes doubling back on the same avenue. The girl gets out of the taxi to return to the hotel on foot. When she finally arrives, the hotel clerk tells her that he has never seen her before. When she runs up to the room where her mother had been resting, she finds the walls a different colour, the furnishings different than her memory, and her mother nowhere in sight.

There are many endings to the story. In one of them, the girl is gloriously persistent and certain, renting a room nearby and staking out the hotel, eventually seducing a young man who works in the laundry and discovering the truth: that her mother had died of a contagious and fatal disease, departing this plane shortly after the daughter was sent from the hotel by the doctor. To avoid a citywide panic, the staff removed and buried her body, repainted and furnished the room, and bribed all involved to deny that they had ever met the pair.

In another version of this story, the girl wanders the streets of Paris for years, believing that she is mad, that she invented her mother and her life with her mother in her own diseased mind. The daughter stumbles from hotel to hotel, confused and grieving, though for whom she cannot say.

I don't need to tell you the moral of this story. I think you already know what it is.

Our son enters school when he is five, and I remember his teacher from that day in the park, when she had crouched to help me. She remembers me as well. I tell her that we have had no more children since our son, and now that he has started school, my days will be altered toward sloth and boredom. She is kind. She tells me that if I am looking for a way to occupy my time, there is a wonderful women's art class at a local college.

That night, after my son is in bed, my husband reaches his hand across the couch and slides it up my leg.

—Come to me, he says, and I twinge with pleasure. I slide off the couch, smoothing my skirt very prettily as I walk over to him on my knees. I kiss his leg, running my hand up to his belt, tugging him from his bonds before swallowing him whole. He runs his hands through my hair, stroking my head, groaning and pressing into me. And I don't realize that his hand is sliding down the back of my neck until he is trying to loop his fingers through the ribbon. I gasp and pull away quickly, falling back and frantically checking my bow. He is still sitting there, slick with my spit.

—Come back here, he says.

—No, I say.

He stands up and tucks himself into his pants, zipping them up.

—A wife, he says, should have no secrets from her husband.

—I don't have any secrets, I tell him.

—The *ribbon*.

—The ribbon is not a secret, it's just mine.

—Were you born with it? Why your throat? Why is it green?

I do not answer.

He is silent for a long minute. Then,

—A wife should have no secrets.

My nose grows hot. I do not want to cry.

—I have given you everything you have ever asked for, I say. Am I not allowed this one thing?

—I want to know.

—You think you want to know, I say, but you do not.

—Why do you want to hide it from me?

—I am not hiding it. It is not yours.

He gets down very close to me, and I pull back from the smell of bourbon. I hear a creak, and we both look up to see our son's feet vanishing up the staircase.

When my husband goes to sleep that night, he does so with a hot and burning anger that falls away only when he starts dreaming. I sense its release, and only then can I sleep, too.

The next day, our son touches my throat and asks about my ribbon. He tries to pull at it. And though it pains me, I have to make it forbidden to him. When he reaches for it, I shake a can full of pennies. It crashes discordantly, and he withdraws and weeps. Something is lost between us, and I never find it again.

(If you are reading this story out loud, prepare a soda can full of pennies. When you arrive at this moment, shake it loudly in the face of the person closest to you. Observe their expression of startled fear, and then betrayal. Notice how they never look at you in exactly the same way for the rest of your days.)

I enroll in the art class for women. When my husband is at work and my son is in school, I drive to the sprawling green campus and the squat grey building where the art classes are held.

Presumably, the male nudes are kept from our eyes in some deference to propriety, but the class has its own energy—there is plenty to see on a strange woman's naked form, plenty to contemplate as you roll charcoal and mix paints. I see more than one woman shifting forwards and back in her seat to redistribute blood flow.

One woman in particular returns over and over. Her ribbon is red, and is knotted around her slender ankle. Her skin is the colour of olives, and a trail of dark hair runs from her belly button to her mons. I know that I should not want her, not because she is a woman and not because she is a stranger, but because it is her job to disrobe, and I feel shame taking advantage of such a state. But as my pencil traces her contours so does my hand in the secret recesses of my mind. I am not even certain how such a thing would happen, but the possibilities incense me to near madness.

One afternoon after class, I turn a hallway corner and she is there, the woman. Clothed, wrapped in a raincoat. Her gaze transfixes me, and this close I can see a band of gold around each of her pupils, as though her eyes are twin solar eclipses. She greets me, and I her.

We sit down together in a booth at a nearby diner, our knees occasionally bushing up against each other beneath the Formica. She drinks a cup of black coffee. I ask her if she has any children. She does, she says, a daughter, a beautiful little girl of eleven.

—Eleven is a terrifying age, she says. I remember nothing before I was eleven, but then there it was, all colour and horror. What a number, she says, what a show. Then her face slips somewhere else for a moment, as if she has dipped beneath the surface of a lake.

We do not discuss the specific fears of raising a girl-child. Truthfully, I am afraid to ask. I also do not ask her if she's married, and she does not volunteer the information, though she does not wear a ring. We talk about my son, about the art class. I desperately want to know what state of need has sent her to disrobe before us, but perhaps I do not ask because the answer would be, like adolescence, too frightening to forget.

I am captivated by her, there is no other way to put it. There is something easy about her, but not easy the way I was—the way I am. She's like dough, how the give of it beneath kneading hands disguises its sturdiness, its potential. When I look away from her and then look back, she seems twice as large as before.

Perhaps we can talk again sometime, I say to her. This has been a very pleasant afternoon.

She nods to me. I pay for her coffee.

I do not want to tell my husband about her, but he can sense some untapped desire. One night, he asks what roils inside of me and I confess it to him. I even describe the details of her ribbon, releasing an extra flood of shame.

He is so glad of this development he begins to mutter a long and exhaustive fantasy as he removes his pants and enters me. I feel as if I have betrayed her somehow, and I never return to the class.

(If you are reading this story out loud, force a listener to reveal a secret, then open the nearest window to the street and scream it as loudly as you are able.)

One of my favourite stories is about an old woman and her husband—a man mean as Mondays, who scared her with the violence of his temper and the shifting nature of his whims. She was only able to keep him satisfied with her unparalleled cooking, to which he was a complete captive. One day, he bought her a fat liver to cook for him, and she did, using herbs and broth. But the smell of her own artistry overtook her, and a few nibbles became a few bites, and soon the liver was gone. She had no money with which to purchase a second one, and she was terrified of her husband's reaction should he discover that his meal was gone. So she crept to the church next door, where a woman had been recently laid to rest. She approached the shrouded figure, then cut into it with a pair of kitchen shears and stole the liver from her corpse.

That night, the woman's husband dabbed his lips with a napkin and declared the meal the finest he'd ever eaten. When they went to sleep, the old woman heard the front door open, and a thin wail wafted through the rooms. *Who has my liver? Whooooo has my liver?*

The old woman could hear the voice coming closer and closer to the bedroom. There was a hush as the door swung open. The dead woman posed her query again.

The old woman flung the blanket off her husband.

—*He* has it! She declared triumphantly.

Then she saw the face of the dead woman, and recognized her own mouth and eyes. She looked down at her abdomen, remembering, now, how she carved into her own belly. Next to her, as the blood seeped into the very heart of the mattress, her husband slumbered on.

That may not be the version of the story you're familiar with. But I assure you, it's the one you need to know.

My husband is strangely excited for Halloween. Our son is old enough that he can walk and carry a basket for treats. I take one of my husband's old tweed coats and fashion one for our son, so that he might be a tiny professor, or some other stuffy academic. My husband even gives him a pipe on which to gnaw. Our son clicks it between his teeth in a way I find unsettlingly adult.

—Mama, my son says, what are you?

I am not in costume, so I tell him I am his mother.

The pipe falls from his little mouth onto the floor, and he screams. My husband swoops in and picks him up, talking to him in a low voice, repeating his name between his sobs.

It is only as his breathing returns to normal that I am able to identify my mistake. He is not old enough to know the story of the naughty girls who wanted the toy drum, and were wicked toward their mother until she went away and was replaced with a new mother—one with glass eyes and thumping wooden tail. But I have inadvertently told him another one—the story of the little boy who only discovered on Halloween that his mother was not his mother, except on the day when everyone wore a mask. Regret sluices hot up my throat. I try to hold him and kiss him, but he only wishes to go out onto the street, where the sun has dipped below the horizon and a hazy chill is bruising the shadows.

He comes home laughing, gnawing on a piece of candy that has turned his mouth the color of a plum. I am angry at my husband. I wish he had waited to come home before permitting the consumption of the cache. Has he never heard the stories? The pins pressed into the chocolates, the razor blades sunk in the apples? I examine my son's mouth, but there is no sharp metal plunged into his palate. He laughs and spins around the house, dizzy and electrified from the treats and excitement. He wraps his arms around my legs, the earlier incident forgotten. The forgiveness tastes sweeter than any candy that can be given at any door. When he climbs into my lap, I sing to him until he falls asleep.

Our son is eight, ten. First, I tell him fairy tales—the very oldest ones, with the pain and death and forced marriage pared away like dead foliage. Mermaids grow feet and it feels like laughter. Naughty pigs trot away from grand feasts, reformed and uneaten. Evil witches leave the castle and move into small cottages and live out their days painting portraits of woodland creatures.

As he grows, though, he asks questions. Why would they not eat the pig, hungry as they were and wicked as he had been? Why was the witch permitted to go free after her terrible deeds? And the sensation of fins splitting to feet being anything less than agonizing he rejects outright after cutting his hand with a pair of scissors.

—It would huight, he says, for he is struggling with his r's.

I agree with him. It would. So then I tell him stories closer to true:

children who go missing along a particular stretch of railroad track, lured by the sound of a phantom train to parts unknown; a black dog that appears at a person's doorstep three days before their passing; a trio of frogs that corner you in the marshlands and tell your fortune for a price.

The school puts on a performance of *Little Buckle Boy*, and he is the lead, the buckle boy, and I join a committee of mothers making costumes for the children. I am lead costume maker in a room full of women, all of us sewing together little silk petals for the flower children and making tiny white pantaloons for the pirates. One of the mothers has a pale yellow ribbon on her finger, and it constantly tangles in her thread. She swears and cries. One day I have to use the sewing shears to pick at the offending threads. I try to be delicate. She shakes her head as I free her from the peony.

—It's such a bother, isn't it? she says.

I nod. Outside the window, the children play—knocking each other off the playground equipment, popping the heads off dandelions. The play goes beautifully. Opening night, our son blazes through his monologue. Perfect pitch and cadence. No one has ever done better.

Our son is twelve. He asks me about the ribbon, point-blank. I tell him that we are all different, and sometimes you should not ask questions. I assure him that he'll understand when he is grown. I distract him with stories that have no ribbons: angels who desire to be human and ghosts who don't realize they're dead and children who turn to ash. He stops smelling like a child—milky sweetness replaced with something sharp and burning, like a hair sizzling on the stove.

Our son is thirteen, fourteen. He waits for the neighbour boy on his way to school, who walks more slowly than the others. He exhibits the subtlest compassion, my son. No instinct for cruelty, like some.

—The world has enough bullies, I've told him over and over.

This is the year he stops asking for my stories.

Our son is fifteen, sixteen, seventeen. He begins to court a beautiful girl from his high school, who has a bright smile and a warm presence. I am happy to meet her, but never insist that we should wait up for their return, remembering my own youth.

When he tells us that he has been accepted at a university to study engineering, I am overjoyed. We march through the house, singing songs and laughing. When my husband comes home, he joins in the jubilee, and we drive to a local seafood restaurant. Over halibut, his father tells him, we are so proud of you. Our son laughs and says that he also wishes to marry his girl. We clasp hands and are even happier. Such a good boy. Such a wonderful life to look forward to.

Even the luckiest woman alive has not seen joy like this.

There's a classic, a real classic, that I haven't told you yet.

A girlfriend and a boyfriend went parking. Some people say that means kissing in a car, but I know the story. I was there. They were parked on the edge of a lake. They were turning around in the back seat as if the world was moments from ending. Maybe it was. She offered herself and he took it, and after it was over, they turned on the radio.

The voice on the radio announced that a mad, hook-handed murderer had escaped from a local insane asylum. The boyfriend chuckled as he flipped to a music station. As the song ended, the girlfriend heard a thin scratching sound, like a paperclip over glass. She looked at her boyfriend and then pulled her cardigan over her bare shoulders, wrapping one arm around her breasts.

—We should go, she said.

—No, baby, the boyfriend said. Let's go again.

—What if the killer comes here? The girl asked. The insane asylum is very close.

—We'll be fine, baby, the boyfriend said. Don't you trust me?

The girlfriend nodded reluctantly.

—Well then, he said, his voice trailing off in that way she would come to know so well. He took her hand off her chest and placed it onto himself. She finally looked away from the lakeside.

Outside, the moonlight glinted off the shiny steel hook. The killer waved at her, grinning.

I'm sorry. I've forgotten the rest of the story.

The house is so silent without our son. I walk through it, touching all the surfaces. I am happy but something inside of me is shifting into a strange new place.

That night, my husband asks if I wish to christen the newly empty rooms. We have not coupled so fiercely since before our son was born. Bent over the kitchen table, something old is lit within me, and I remember the way we had desired before, how we had left love streaked on all of the surfaces. I could have met anyone at that party when I was seventeen—prudish boys or violent boys. Religious boys who would have made me move to some distant country to convert its denizens. I could have experienced untold numbers of sorrows or dissatisfactions. But as I straddle him on the floor, riding him and crying out, I know that I made the right choice.

We fall asleep exhausted, sprawled naked in our bed. When I wake up, my husband is kissing the back of my neck, probing the ribbon with his tongue. My body rebels wildly, still throbbing with the memories of pleasure but bucking hard against betrayal. I say his name, and he does not respond. I say it again, and he holds me against him and continues. I wedge my elbows in his side, and when he loosens from me in surprise, I sit up and face him. He looks confused and hurt, like my son the day I shook the can of pennies.

Resolve runs out of me. I touch the ribbon. I look at the face of my husband, the beginning and end of his desires all etched there. He is not a bad man, and that, I realize suddenly, is the root of my hurt. He is not a bad man at all. And yet—

—Do you want to untie the ribbon? I ask him. After these many years, is that what you want of me?

His face flashes gaily, and then greedily, and he runs his hand up my bare breast and to my bow.

—Yes, he says. Yes.

—Then, I say, do what you want.

With trembling fingers, he takes one of the ends. The bow undoes, slowly, the long-bound ends crimped with habit. My husband groans, but I do not think he realizes it. He loops his finger through the final twist and pulls. The ribbon falls away. It floats down and curls at my feet, or so I imagine, because I cannot look down to follow its descent.

My husband frowns, and then his face begins to open with some other expression—sorrow, or maybe pre-emptive loss. My hand flies up in front of me—an involuntary motion, for balance or some other futility—and beyond it his image is gone.

—I love you, I assure him, more than you can possibly know.—No, he says, but I don't know to what he's responding.

If you are reading this story out loud, you may be wondering if that place my ribbon protected was wet with blood and openings, or smooth and neutered like the nexus between the legs of a doll. I'm afraid I can't tell you, because I don't know. For these questions and others, and their lack of resolution, I am sorry.

My weight shifts, and with it, gravity seizes me. My husband's face falls away, and then I see the ceiling, and the wall behind me. As my lopped head tips backwards off my neck and rolls off the bed, I feel as lonely as I have ever been.

CARMEN MARIA MACHADO

Observations About Eggs From the Man Sitting Next to Me on a Flight from Chicago, Illinois to Cedar Rapids, Iowa

1. Lord, it's hot in this cabin. I could hard-boil an egg inside my mouth. What's your name?

2. Have you ever poached an egg? The trick is white vinegar. Everyone forgets the white vinegar, and the blasted thing falls apart, and then they miss one of the greatest wonders of the world. Here's what you do: Add it to the boiling water. The vinegar, I mean. Break the egg into a bowl, not directly into the pot. Next, spin a spoon in the vinegar water and make a vortex. Drop the egg inside of it. If you look down, you can see the dense heart of the yolk through the clear atmosphere of white, and it is not entirely unlike looking at the Earth from space. The heat will make the egg go opaque. If the water is the right temperature, you can see it happening in slow motion—the yolk developing a skin, then the white going, well, white. It's like watching the egg being formed inside the looped guts of a warm and bleating hen. Bleating, not bleeding.

Anyway, when you watch the egg like this, you are seeing what only a god might see. This might seem like just a quaint observation, but what if I told you that by imagining yourself a god while watching an egg being formed, you *become* that god, for just a second or two? Of course, now that I've said it, now that I've told you about this little quirk of the natural world, you'll never be able to actually do it. That's the rule, and I didn't make it. But if, before I told you of these temporary god-powers, you had been watching that egg poaching, and at that precise moment wished to create an entirely new world, somewhere in all of existence, it would have popped into being, and though you wouldn't have known it, it would have been there, and you would have been its deity. And periodically you would find scraps of paper in your pocket with words scrawled on them or you'd mishear a fragment of a

sentence spoken by a coworker or you'd discover Word documents you
didn't remember creating, and the truth is those would have been the
prayers of your created people, calling out to you because they feel lost
and alone and afraid. It is a very terrible thing to be a god and I don't
really recommend it.

3. Have you ever seen a frozen egg? No? I'm sorry for you. You have
not been so fortunately careless as to leave the carton too close to the
top shelf of the fridge, as I have. The shell pops off like a bottle cap,
and if you pull out the contents, the whole inside of the egg sits in
your hand like a stone. If you pinch the white, it comes apart like snow.
Beneath running water, the white falls away and the yolk is gold, hard.
It sits in your hand like an oversized marble. It's the most perfect shade
of yellow. In some countries, none of them accessible by a plane like
this one, four of these yolks can be exchanged for the basic necessities:
seeds, a sack of potatoes, one shoe—though for the other, you'll need
four more yolks. If you plant them in the ground, there are rumors that
better things than potatoes might grow. But these are just rumors, and
you might end up hungrier than before.

4. Have you ever opened an egg and seen the inside of another egg?
No? Are you sure? Here is how you can tell: Crack open an egg. Look
inside. Sometimes, in another place entirely, another person has also
cracked open an egg and is also looking inside, and you are both, in fact,
looking at the innards of the exact same egg. If you examine the egg
carefully enough, you will find that the scene being reflected back at you
in the gelatinous curve of the yolk is not, in fact, your own kitchen, with
its fluorescent light bulb, dirty counter, Matisse print, and collection of
empty wine bottles, but rather a different kitchen, possibly in Brooklyn,
possibly in Big Sur, possibly in an alternate universe to your own, with
an entirely different face peering back at you. You cannot crawl through
the common egg into that other place, though, so don't try. Greater
women than you have tried and failed.

5. I once dated a woman who thought that you had to cut a cow open

to get the milk inside. What a silly thing—the idea and the woman. And what a mess to try. All that blood, curling into the milk, spoiling it. What a waste.

The egg, now. Eggs are more practical. They can be cut out of hens, though this is rarely necessary. And if that happens, and the eggs are covered in down feathers and blood, they can be washed clean, and nothing is ruined—all is perfectly usable. Well, except for the hen, ha-ha!

6. An egg is the most dangerous thing in the universe.

7. Have you ever gone to the farmer's market and paid a little extra for those brown eggs that look so healthful, the kind that you know were warming under hens that very morning, and carry the carton home, and crack open one, and a fetal dragon flops out into the pan? No? If this ever happens to you, know that the dragons will all be dead. They were taken away from their mothers; they never had a chance to survive. If you put the unbroken ones beneath a heat lamp, they'll just spoil. These are not Schrödinger's eggs. There was never a chance you could have hatched a dragon army, and anyway, it would have been foolish to try. Dragons always eventually turn on you, and in a way that makes you regret all of your decisions. Anyway, if you return to the market for edible eggs, the stand will most likely be vacant. Dragon eggshells are a powerful aphrodisiac, though, so don't throw them away.

8. Hermann Hesse wrote, "The bird fights its way out of the egg. The egg is the world. Who would be born must first destroy a world." I know a few truths about Hermann Hesse that aren't exactly common knowledge, but I can assure you that he is using fewer metaphors in that sentence than you might think. Also, Hermann Hesse was a bastard and I don't want to talk about him anymore.

9. You look like a person who has eaten a few eggs in her lifetime. How many would you estimate? Five hundred? A thousand? The trouble is

that eggs are in everything, so even if you are able to think about your self-prepared and ordered breakfasts, and church potluck deviled egg trays with their easily quantifiable eggs, it's hard to add up all of the baked goods and cream sauces and mayonnaise on your sandwiches, and anything else that might have contained an egg. But let's say you've eaten one thousand eggs in your lifetime. One thousand eggs, each of which was full of potential life.

Now, don't look at me like that, I'm not talking vegan-talk, I'm just saying that sometimes food is full of wonder and you really should think about it. Imagine that one thousand chickens could have possibly been born, and they would have gone about pecking and watching and thinking chicken thoughts and dreaming chicken dreams and nibbling and fighting other chickens, and eventually would have fallen beneath the blade or gone to chicken-sleep and never woken up. You are now full of those chickens, their potential wishes and dreams and—don't laugh!—their experiences. Their lives, and their deaths. Somewhere inside of you, you are contentedly strutting about the dirt, in the sun. Somewhere inside of you, your head is missing and you are chasing a farmer's terrified child across the yard. I think, in a way, we are all one thousand chickens.

10. It is a really good thing to smash an egg, very satisfying. I don't just mean just to drop one, but take it in your hand and splat it with all of your might against a hard surface. I once visited a village between two great mountains where this was a common pastime. It could get competitive! The winner was measured by the distance the egg innards were strewn. If the yolk got on the judges, well, that was a bonus. It was a very strange little village with some very strange people, but they had been through a lot of hardships in their lifetimes, so they can be forgiven some eccentricities.

11. I'm pretty sure that the stewardess—my apologies, the flight attendant, you can only say so much nowadays—*does* have some eggs in the back, with the meal-trays, but perhaps not enough for everyone, and

so she doesn't want to make anybody jealous. Plus, I'm sure first class would take all the eggs if given the chance, and then there wouldn't be enough eggs for all of us cattle back here, ha-ha! You were probably smart to bring your own eggs in that little lunchbox, even if it does count as your carry-on.

12. People forgot about Patsy Cline's parallel universe theories because they were so busy singing her songs. Can you imagine a fate worse than that? I'll never record a ballad as long as I live. Anyway, she believed that all of the parallel universes touched each other in the wet places of the world. Puddles and spilled milk and even bits of the body, all creating little puckers in time and space and touching realities together. She was right, of course. Sometimes, before shows, they would find her in her dressing room pushing her fingers through eggs, calling in a singsongy voice to that child she lost. You know, Patsy herself died in a plane crash. Not a plane like this, mind you, a small one. Not like this. Don't look so worried.

13. Here is the embarrassing truth: I know you. We've met before. We shared an egg, once. Don't you remember? Of course not, it was your first time egg-side, and I'd done it many times before. Just because I'm an old man and you're some young thing does not mean that we have not shared experiences. You didn't have a name yet, but I'd recognize that pretty mouth anywhere. I remember seeing you and thinking, she knows so little, but so much of the world is ahead of her. She is so beautiful; maybe one day I will run into her again and see her shining face. So of course, you can imagine my disappointment when I saw you here, familiar, but looking so sullen, so angry. Smile! You survived. We were one of a dozen double-yolks, cracked open and born into this world—well, I was *reborn*, but it all amounts to the same—and you look pretty good, if I say so myself. So be grateful to live in a world with eggs, which give us life and have so many uses besides.

14. Miss, I don't think she meant to throw the egg at me per se, she's

just a little worn out from the flight. I am certain that it was an accident. No, I can stay here. It was just an accident. Isn't that right? Ha-ha!

15. That hardboiled egg looks delicious, and I think I should like a bite.

USMAN T. MALIK

Resurrection Points

I WAS THIRTEEN WHEN I DISSECTED MY FIRST CORPSE. IT was a fetid, soggy teenager Baba dragged home from Clifton Beach and threw in the shed. The ceiling leaked in places, so he told me to drape the dead boy with tarpaulin so the monsoon water wouldn't get at him.

When I went to the shed, DeadBoy had stunk the place up. I pinched my nostrils, gently removed the sea-blackened aluminum crucifix from around his neck, pulled the tarp across his chest. The tarp was a bit short—Ma had cut some for the chicken coop after heavy rainfall killed a hen—and I had to tuck it beneath DeadBoy's chin so it seemed he were sleeping. Then I saw that the fish had eaten most of his lips and part of his nose and my stomach heaved and I began to retch.

After a while I felt better and went inside the house.

"How's he look?" said Baba.

"Fine, I guess," I said.

Baba looked at me curiously. "You alright?"

"Yes." I looked at Ma rolling dough peras in the kitchen for dinner, her face red and sweaty from heat, and leaned into the smell of mint leaves and chopped onions. "Half his face is gone, Baba."

He nodded. "Yes. Water and flesh don't go well together and the fish get the rest. You see his teeth?"

"No."

"Go look at his teeth and tell me what you see."

I went back to the shed and peeled the pale raw lip-flesh back with my fingers. His front teeth were almost entirely gone, sockets blackened with blood, and the snaillike uvula at the back of the throat was half-missing. I peered into his gaping mouth, tried to feel the uvula's edge with my finger. It was smooth and covered with clots, and I knew what had happened to this boy.

"So?" Baba said when I got back.

"Someone tortured him," I said. Behind Baba Mama sucked breath in and fanned the manure oven urgently, billowing the smoke away from us toward the open door.

"How do you know?" Baba said.

"They slashed his uvula with a razor while he was alive, and when he tried to bite down they knocked out his teeth with a hammer."

Baba nodded. "How can you tell?"

"Clean cut. It was sliced with a blade. And there are no teeth chips at the back of the throat or stuck to the palate to indicate bullet trauma."

"Good." Baba looked pleased. He tapped his chin with a spoon and glanced at Mama. "You think he's ready?"

Mama tried to lift the steaming pot, hissed with pain, let it go and grabbed a roughcotton rag to hold the edges. "Now?"

"Sure. I was his age when I did my first." He looked at me. "You're old enough. Eat your dinner. Later tonight I'll show you how to work them."

We sat on the floor and Ma brought lentil soup, vegetable curry, raw onion rings, and cornflour roti. We ate in silence on the meal mat. When we were done we thanked Allah for his blessings. Ma began to clear the dinner remains, her bony elbows jutting out as she scraped crumbs and wiped the mat. She looked unhappy and didn't look up when Baba and I went out to work the DeadBoy.

DeadBoy's armpits reeked. I asked Baba if I could stuff my nostrils with scented cotton. He said no.

We put on plastic gloves made from shopping bags. Baba lay the boy on the tools table, situating his palms upward in the traditional anatomical position. I turned on the shed's naked bulb and it swung from its chain above the cadaver, like a hanged animal.

"Now," Baba said, handing me the scalpel, "locate the following structures." He named superficial landmarks: jugular notch, sternal body, xiphoid process, others familiar to me from my study of his work and his textbooks. Once I had located them, he handed me the scalpel and said: "Cut."

I made a midline horizontal and two parallel incisions in DeadBoy's chest. Baba watched me, shaking his head and frowning, as I fumbled my way through the dissection. "No. More laterally" and "Yes, that's the one. Now reflect the skin back, peel it slowly. Remove the superficial fascia" and "Repeat on the other side."

DeadBoy's skin was wet and slippery from water damage and much of the fat was putrefied. His pectoral and abdominal musculature was dark and soft. I scraped the congealed blood away and removed the fascia, and as I worked muscles and tendons slowly emerged and glistened in the yellow light, displaying neurovascular bundles weaving between their edges. It took me three hours but finally I was done. I stood, surrounded by DeadBoy's odor, trembling with excitement, peering at my handiwork.

Baba nodded. "Not bad. Now show me where the resurrection points are." When I hesitated, he raised his eyebrows. "Don't be scared. You know what to do."

I took a glove off and placed it on DeadBoy's thigh. I tentatively touched the right pec major, groping around its edges. The sternal head was firm and spongy. When I felt a small cord in the medial corner with my fingers, I tapped it lightly. The pec didn't twitch.

I looked at Baba. He smiled but his eyes were black and serious. I licked my lips, took the nerve cord between my fingers, closed my eyes, and discharged.

The jolt thrummed up my fingers into my shoulder. Instantly the pec contracted and DeadBoy's right arm jerked. I shot the biocurrent again, feeling the recoil tear through my flesh, and this time DeadBoy's arm jumped and flopped onto his chest.

"Something, isn't it," Baba said. "Well done."

I didn't reply. My heart raced, my skin was feverish and crawling. My nostrils were filled with the smell of electricity.

"First time's hard, no denying it. But it's gotta be done. Only way you'll learn to control it."

I was on fire. We had talked about it before, but this wasn't anything like I had expected. When Baba did it, he could smile and make conversation as the deadboys spasmed and danced on his fingertips. Their flesh turned into calligraphy in his hands.

"That felt like something exploded inside me, Baba," I said, hearing the tremble in my voice. "What happens if I can't control it?"

He shrugged. "You will. It just takes time and practice, that's all. Our elders have done it for generations." He leaned forward, lifted Dead-Boy's hand, and returned it to supine position. "Want to try the smaller muscles? They need finer control and the nerves are thinner. Would be wise to use your fingertips."

And thus we practiced my first danse macabre. Sought out the nerve bundles, made them pop and sizzle, watched the cadaver spider its way across the table. With each discharge, the pain lessened, but soon my fingers began to go numb and Baba made me halt. Carefully he draped DeadBoy.

"Baba, are there others?" I asked as we walked back to the house.

"Like us?" He nodded. "The Prophet Isa is said to have returned men to life. When Martha of Bethany asked him how he would bring her brother Lazarus back to life, Hazrat Isa said, 'I am the Resurrection and the life. He who believes in me will live, even though he dies.'"

We were in the backyard; the light of our home shone out bright and comforting. Baba turned and smiled at me. "But he was a healer first. Like our beloved Prophet Muhammad Peace-Be-Upon-Him. Do you understand?"

"I guess," I said. DeadBoy's face swam in front of my eyes. "Baba, who do you think killed him?"

His smile disappeared. "Animals." He didn't look at me when he said, "How's your friend Sadiq these days? I haven't seen him in a while." His tone was casual, and he tilted his jaw and stared into the distance as if looking for something.

"Fine," I said. "He's just been busy, I think."

Baba rubbed his cheek with a hairy knuckle and we began walking again. "Decent start," he said. "Tomorrow will be harder, though." I looked at him; he spread his arms and smiled, and I realized what he meant.

"So soon?" I said, horrified. "But I need more practice."

"Sure, you do, but it's not that different. You did well back there."

"But—"

"You will do fine, Daoud," he said gently, and would say no more.

Ma watched us approach the front door, her face silvered by moonlight. Baba didn't meet her eyes as we entered, but his hand rose and rubbed against his khaddar shirt, as if wiping dirt away.

Ma said nothing, but later, huddled in the charpoy, staring through the skylight window at the expansive darkness, I heard them arguing. At one point, I thought she said, "Worry about the damn house," and he tried to shush her, but she said something hot and angry and Baba got up and left. There was silence and then there was sobbing, and I lay there, filled with sorrow and excitement, listening to her grief, thinking if only there was a way to reconcile the two.

The dead foot leaped when I touched the resurrection point. Mr. Kurmully yelped.

"Sorry," I said, jerking my fingers away. "Did that hurt?"

"No." He massaged the foot with his hand. "I was…surprised. I haven't had any feeling in this for years. Just a dry burning around the shin. But when you touched it there," he gestured at the inner part of his left ankle, "I *felt* it. I felt you touching me."

He looked at me with awe, then at Baba, who stood by the door, hands laced behind his back, looking pleased. "He's good," Mr. Kurmully said.

"Yes," Baba said.

"So when are you retiring, Jamshed?"

Baba laughed. "Not for a while, I hope. Anyway, let's get on with it. Daoud," he said to me, "can you find the pain point in his ankle?"

I spent the next thirty minutes probing and prodding Mr. Kurmully's diabetic foot, feeling between his tendons for nerves. It wasn't easy. Over the years, Mr. Kurmully had lost two toes and the stumps had shriveled, distorting the anatomy. Eventually I found two points, braced myself, and gently shot them.

"Feel better?" I said, as Mr. Kurmully withdrew his foot and stepped on it tentatively.

"He won't know until tomorrow," Baba said. "Sometimes instant effect may occur, but our true goal is nocturnal relief when the neuropathy is worst. Am I right, Habib?"

"Yes." Mr. Kurmully nodded and flexed his foot this way and that. "The boy's gifted. I had some burning when I came. It's gone now. His first time?"

"Yes."

"Good God." Mr. Kurmully shook his head wonderingly. "He will go far." He came toward me and patted me on the head. "Your father's been a boon to our community for twenty years, boy. Always be gentle, like him, you hear me? Be humble. It's the branch laden with fruit that bends the most." He smiled at me and turned to Baba. "Let me pay you this once, Jamshed."

Baba waved a hand. "Just tip the Edhi driver when he takes the cadaver. One of their volunteers has agreed to bury it for free."

"They are good to you, aren't they."

Baba beamed. He opened his mouth to speak, but there was sudden commotion at the front of the clinic and a tall, gangly man with a squirrel tail mustache strode in, followed by the sulky-faced Edhi driver looking angry and unhappy.

Baba's gaze went from one to another and settled on the gangly stranger. "Salam, brother," Baba said pleasantly. "How can I help you?"

The gangly man pulled out a sheath of papers and handed it to Baba. He had gleaming rat eyes that narrowed like cracks in cement when he spoke. He sounded as if he had a cold. "Doctor Sahib, you know why I'm here."

"I'm not sure I do. Why don't you tell me? Would you like to take a seat?"

"Just read the papers, sahib," he said in his soft, nasal voice.

"Oh?" Baba looked at the Edhi driver. He was a gloomy, chubby boy fond of charas and ganja and often rolled joints one-handed on his fat belly when waiting at red lights. I had ridden with him a couple of times and once he showed me his weird jutting navel. Everted since birth, he told me proudly.

"Zamir, what's going on?" Baba said.

"Sahib, they're giving us trouble with the burial," Zamir said. "This man is from the local Defend The Sharia office. They have a written fatwa stating that since the dead boy was Christian he cannot be buried in a Muslim cemetery."

Baba turned back to the gangly man. "Is that true, brother?"

Gangly Man thrust the papers into Baba's hands. "This is from Imam Barani. Take a look."

Baba took the roll, but didn't open it. "This boy," Baba said, "was tortured by someone."

Gangly Man's shoulders stiffened.

"He was beaten badly. His teeth knocked out with a hammer. Someone took a razor to his mouth. When he was near dead, they threw him in the river."

Gangly Man's lips pressed into a thin, white line.

"He was sixteen. He had a scar on his stomach from a childhood surgery, probably appendectomy. He wore a tawiz charm on his forearm his mother likely got from a Muslim saint. You know how illiterate these poor Christians are. Can't tell the difference between one holy man and another, and—"

"Doctor Sahib." Gangly Man leaned forward and whispered conspiratorially, "He and his filthy religion can ride my dick. My orders are simple. He will not be buried in the Muslim cemetery, and if I were you I wouldn't push it." He grinned and shook his head as if talking to a child.

Baba's face changed color. He looked around and for the first time I saw how angry and tired he was. He looked like he hadn't slept in days. Maybe he hadn't. It was hard to know. He and Ma were talking less to each other lately.

"If you make it difficult for us, well, things could go many ways, couldn't they? Sometimes clinics run by quacks can be shut down by provincial governments until NOCs are obtained. I don't even see a diploma on your wall. Surely, you went to medical school?" Still smiling, he toed the foot of the threadbare couch, the only piece of furniture in the room. "Besides, you might be Muslim but blasphemy is blasphemy, brother, and punishable under the Hadood Ordinance. The boy is Christian. That cemetery is not."

The Edhi driver took Baba's arm and led him aside. They talked. Zamir gestured furiously. Baba's shoulders rose and sagged. They came back.

"We will take the body to Aga Khan Medical College and donate it to their anatomy lab," cried Zamir.

"But he has already been—" Baba began

"I'm sure they will find more to do with it," Zamir said, nodding and smiling.

Gangly Man took the front of his own shirt with a tarantula-like hand and began to shake it, fanning his chest. "Very wise. How they will appreciate you!"

Baba remained silent, but a heavy ice block appeared in my belly and settled there. I turned and ran from the clinic, ran all the way to our house three streets down. I burst into the shed and went to DeadBoy and wrenched away the tarp. His insides were tucked in with thin stitches. I yanked the stitches out, peeled back his skin, and pressed my gloveless fingers into his muscles. I discharged the biocurrent again and again until his limbs twirled and snapped, a lifeless dervish whirling around his own axis. I let the electricity flow through my fingertips like a raging torrent, until the room sizzled with charge and my nostrils filled with the odor of burnt flesh.

After a while I stepped back. My cheeks burned and the corners of my eyes tickled. Even though it was close to noon, the shed was dark from a low-hanging monsoon ceiling. Interstices of sunlight fell on DeadBoy's half-face, revealing the blackness of his absent teeth and his mutilated lips.

"Sorry, DeadBoy," I said.

He twitched his shoulder.

The movement was so unexpected that I jerked and fell over the toolbox on the floor. I sat on the sodden ground, gazing at DeadBoy, my heart pounding in my chest. He was still. Had I imagined it? That movement—it was impossible. The deadboys couldn't move without stimulus.

I got up and went to him. His disfigured flesh was placid and motionless.

"Hey," I whispered, feeling foolish and nervous. "Can you hear me?" The shadows in the room deepened. Somewhere outside a swallow cheeped.

DeadBoy never said a word.

After the Edhi driver hauled DeadBoy away, I walked around for a while. Soon it began to drizzle, the kind of sprinkle that makes you feel hot and damp but never really cool, so I took off my shirt, tucked it into my armpit, and ran bare-chested to Sadiq's house.

He lived in the Christian muhallah near Kala Pul, a couple kilometers away. His two-room tin-and-timber house was next to a dirty canal swollen with rainwater, plastic bags, and lifeless rodents, and the rotten smell filled the street.

His mother opened the door. Khala Apee was a young-old woman. Her cheeks were often bruised. Her right eye was swollen shut today.

"He's at the Master sahib's," she told me in a hoarse voice. She smoked cigarettes when her husband was not home, Sadiq had told me. "He'll be back in an hour. Want a soda?"

They couldn't afford sodas. It was probably leftover sherbat from last Ramadan. But what was Sadiq doing at Master sahib's? Summer vacation wouldn't be over for another month. "Thank you, but no, Khala Apee. I'll wait under the elm outside."

She nodded and tried to smile. "Let me know if you want something. And if you can, do stay for dinner."

Plain roti with sliced onions. No gravy. "I'll try, Khala Apee. May I borrow a plastic bag?"

She brought me one. I went to the charpoy under the elm where we sometimes sat and made fun of our families. Rain pattered on the elm leaves and hissed on the ground, and as I sat there with my plastic-draped head on the steeple of my fingers I thought about Baba and Ma and how they had been arguing for months. Ma was worried about the house, she wanted Baba to start charging patients. Baba refused. His father and grandfather had never charged a fee, he said. They lived on food and gifts people gave them.

Ma laughed bitterly. Those were different times, you fool. So different. And the house, what about the house, Jamshed? We are in debt. So much debt. What will you do when they come to take our home? If you cared as much about your family as you do about your goddamn corpse-learning, we could live like normal people, like normal human beings.

But we're *not* normal, Baba protested. This is a good way to blend in, to be part of this world. Be part of the community—

Blend in? Mama said. We will never blend in if you keep antagonizing them. What was the point of arguing with that mullah? You know they are dangerous people. You keep going like this, we will never be part of the community. How could we be? We are ...

Sadiq was shaking me awake. "Hey, Daoud, hey. Wake up."

I opened my eyes. "Hey, how was ... *what?*" I said when I saw his face. Sadiq was a small boy with mousy features and at the moment they were chiseled with worry.

"You've got to leave, Daoud," said Sadiq, glancing around. "Now."

"What's going on? Everything okay?"

"Yes. Master sahib had heard some rumors and he wanted to warn us. He ..." Sadiq gnawed at his lip, his fingers still tugging at my arm. "Go home. We'll talk tomorrow."

"Why?" But he was already leading me away from the elm and toward the canal. The drizzle had stopped and the canal water eddied gently. I put on my shirt and watched as Sadiq took a tin box from his pocket and tied a brick around it with jute twine and twice-doubled rubber band. He waded into the shallow canal and deposited the box at a spot two feet from the bank.

"What are you doing?" I said when he climbed back up the embankment.

"Nothing," he said, but his voice was strange. "Run back home now. I'll come by in a couple days if I can."

I went up the canal road, occasionally looking back, trying to make sense of what had just happened. Sadiq stood there, hands in the pockets of his shorts, a skinny, brown boy with a sad face and a fake-silver cross gleaming around his neck. Sometimes even now I see that cross in my dreams, throwing silver shadows across my path as I trudge down alleys filled with heartache and rotting bodies.

As I glanced back one last time, Sadiq took off the cross and slipped it into his pocket.

Baba was waiting for me.

"Where were you?" he said, his eyes hard and red. "I was worried sick."

"At Sadiq's. I wanted to—"

"Foolish boy," he said. "Don't you know how dangerous that was? Don't you realize?" I stared at him, feeling my head throb. He saw my incomprehension and his voice softened. "Someone vandalized a church in Lahore yesterday. Someone else found feces strewn in a mosque in Quetta. As a result, two people are dead and tens more injured in riots around the country. These tensions have been building for a while. You saw what that *Defend The Sharia* asshole did this morning. This will only get worse. You cannot visit Sadiq until things settle down."

"But what does Sadiq have to do with that?"

Baba gazed at me with pity. "Everything."

I met his eyes and whatever was in them frightened me so much that my hands began to shake. I couldn't stand facing him anymore. Quickly I walked past him and went to my room, where I sat on my rickety charpoy and watched the dusk through the skylight. In the other room, Ma prayed loudly on the *musallah*. She might have been crying, I couldn't tell. I tried to read a medical textbook Baba gave me for my last birthday, but my mind was too restless, so I gave up and went to the kitchen where Ma had arranged unwashed raw chicken breasts on a chopping board.

I lay my hands on the meat. I thought about Sadiq and his tinbox, and softly let the current flow. The chicken breast jumped and thudded on the wood. I discharged again, this time with more force, removed my hands, stepped back, and watched as for a whole minute the meat slapped up and down, squirting blood that puddled on the wooden board, making curious dark shapes.

That should have been impossible but clearly wasn't.

In school during physics class our teacher had explained capacitors to us. Strange ideas came to me now. Words that Baba taught me from his textbooks: cell membranes, calcium-gates, egg-shaped mitochondria and polarized ionic channels. Could *they* act as capacitors at times and hold charge so the flesh would stay alive even after I removed my fingertips?

The boy is gifted, someone said in my head.

I should have felt better. Instead I felt angry and miserable. I went to Ma's room and opened the door.

She was sitting on her haunches in front of the only pretty piece of furniture in the room, a mahogany dresser Baba's mother gave her as a wedding present. Ma had been fiddling with a half-open drawer, a jewelry box glittering in her hand. When I entered, she plunged the drawer into place. "Are you so ill-mannered now that you won't knock?"

"Sorry, Ma. I wasn't thinking."

"Idiot boy," she said quietly. Her gaze drifted back down to the box she held, fingers sliding up and down its metallic edges. The space beneath her eyes was dark and wet. "Next time mind your manners."

I thought it prudent to remain silent. Ma lifted the lid and gazed within and her eyes turned inward. The effect was so intense that for a moment she looked dead, her lifeless eyes watching something in the box, or behind it. Uneasy, I took a step forward and glanced inside. A picture of a naked man nailed to a cross, surrounded by wailing people; then Ma was snapping the lid back into place so violently that I jerked and fell back.

Ma's hands shook and she said something that didn't make sense, "Never wanted to come here. Your father made me. I never wanted to leave my people," and she glared at me hatefully. It was a brief moment, but nothing in my life since has made me feel so ashamed. So lonely and self-loathing; a mutant child broken and hated forever.

I turned and ran from the room, blinded by anger or tears or both, while my mother watched me from the darkness of her room, the jewelry box still in her callused hands.

Later they told us it was an accident, that a wooden shanty caught fire and set the muhallah ablaze, but we all knew better.

It was the tail end of monsoon season and the rains had petered out which worsened the conflagration. Fifty Christian houses burned down that night; the flames and smoke ceiling could be seen from as far as Gulshan Iqbal, we were told. Twenty people died; Sadiq's father, (who survived Tuberculosis and, later, the 1999 Kargil War) was among them. Their corpses were pulled out from the wreckage, burnt and twisted. Sadiq's mother recognized him only by the hare-shaped mole on his left foot.

When I went to see Sadiq, he sobbed on my shoulder.

"They took everything," he wept. "My house, our belongings. My father," he added as an afterthought. "They burnt the house down. My cousin saw them, I swear to God."

"Which God?" I said. My right arm was around him. My left hand dug so hard into the flesh of my thigh I popped the blood blister a biocurrent discharge had raised on my finger. "Which God?"

He stared at me with bloodshot eyes, threw his head back, and cried some more; while his mother sat stone-like in the charpoy under the elm, rocking back and forth, her face blank. One hand tapped the bruises on her cheek. The other hid her lips.

I held Sadiq for as long as I could, then I went home, where Ma sat knitting a cotton sweater. Winter would come in two months, and we couldn't afford to buy new clothes. Baba was out—he'd been delayed at the clinic—so I sat at Ma's feet and counted her toes. Ten.

She watched me through the emptiness between her needles and said, "I'm sorry."

"Yes."

"It was horrible, wasn't it?"

"Yes."

"Tell you what. Why don't we take Sadiq and his mother some naans and beef korma tomorrow? I'm sure his mother is too upset to cook right now."

I recalled Khala Apee's vacuous stare, the hand covering her mouth, and nodded.

Ma placed her knitting needles aside, lowered herself to the floor, and hugged me.

"The world is a bad place," she whispered. "We're in danger all the time. People who are different like you, like us…can sometimes seem like a threat to others."

I listened. Outside, thunder cracked. The skylight window rippled with water as the night opened.

"You use your gift to heal others, you hear me?" she said. "Don't get involved with anger or hatred or sides. There are no sides. Only love and hate."

Behind me the door banged open. My left eye twitched, the vision in it dimmed transiently, and cleared. Ma sprang to her feet.

"Zamir?" she said. "What is it?"

"Your husband," someone said. I turned. It was the Edhi driver. His hair was dark from rain. His cotton shirt was soaked and I could see his abnormal navel protrude through it like a hernia.

"What about him?" Ma's voice was full of fear. "What happened?"

Zamir had a look on his face I had never seen before. His lips trembled. "There was an incident at the clinic."

Ma stared at him, eyes wide and unbelieving, then comprehension dawned in them and she screamed. It was a sudden noise, sharp and unfamiliar, and it wrenched the air out of me. I shrank back and clutched the end of Ma's love couch, and the knitting needles slipped and fell to the floor, forming a steel cross.

"No, God, no," Ma said. Her hair was in her eyes. She clawed it away, looked at the ends, screamed again. "Please don't let it be true. I told him to be careful. I *told* him."

Zamir's face was ashen. He said nothing.

I scrabbled blindly on the dirty floor. The steel cross glinted at me. Pinching the skin of my thighs, I hauled myself up, feeling the world flicker and recede. Zamir was holding Ma's hand and speaking gently. Your husband went to the Police, he was saying. He reported the Christian boy's mutilated body. The mullahs didn't like that. Then someone somewhere discovered an old marriage certificate with *your* maiden name on it.

Ma yanked her hand away from Zamir's. "I killed him," she whispered. Her fists flew to her chest and beat it once, then again and again. She rushed to the door, she shrieked at the rain, but the night was moonless.

Bewildered and crying, I thought about the tin box Sadiq hid in the canal when he realized they would be attacked. I thought about dead bodies and festering secrets; of limbs thrashing on a healer's fingertips; of the young Christian boy who was tortured to death. I thought of how "Daoud" could have been "David" in a different world, such a strange idea, that. Most of all I thought about the way the chicken breast thrummed under the influence of my will, how it kept jerking long after I took my hands away. Would Baba whirl if I touched him, would he dance a final dance for me?

I wiped my tears. From the crevasse of the night rain blood-black gushed and pawed at my eyes. Then we went in Zamir's rickshaw to pick up my father's corpse.

Someone once told me dust has no religion.

Perhaps it was the maulvi sahib who taught me my first Arabic words; a balding kind, quiet man with a voice meant to chant godly secrets and a white beard that flowed like a river of Allah's nur. The gravedigger who was now shoveling and turning the soil five feet away looked a bit like him, except when he panted. His string vest was drenched with sweat, even though the ground was soft and muddy from downpour.

Perhaps it was Ma. She stood next to me before this widening hole, leaning on Khala Apee as if she were an axed tree about to fall. Her lips moved silently all the time. Whether she prayed or talked to Baba's ghost, I don't know.

Or perhaps it was Baba who lay draped in white on the charpoy bier under the pipal tree. The best cotton shroud we could afford rippled when the graveyard wind gusted. It was still wet from his last bath. Before they log-rolled him onto his back, the men of our neighborhood had asked me if I wanted to help wash him.

I said no. My eyes never brimmed.

Now I let a fistful of this forgiving dust exhaust itself between my fingers. It whispered through, a gentle earthskin shedding off me and upon Baba's face. It would carry the scent of my flesh, let him inhale my presence. I leaned down and touched my father's lips, so white, so cold, and a ghastly image came to me: Baba juddering on my fingertips as I reach inside his mouth, shock his tongue, and watch it jump and thrash like a bloodied carp. Tell me who murdered you, I tell my father's tongue. Talk to me, speak to me. For I am Resurrection and whoso believes in me will live again.

But his tongue doesn't quiver. It says nothing.

Someone touched my shoulder and drew me back. It was Ma. Her mouth was a pale scar in her face. She gripped my fingers tightly. I looked down, saw that she had colored her hand with henna, and dropped it.

A shiny flaming orange heart, lanced in the middle, glistened on her palm.

It was dark enough to feel invisible. I left Ma praying in her room and went to Kala Pul.

Lights flickered in the streets and on chowrangis. Sad-faced vendors sold fake perfumes and plastic toys at traffic signals. Women with hollow eyes offered jasmine motia bracelets and necklaces and the flower's scent filled my nose, removing Baba's smell in death. Children fished for paan leaves and cigarette stubs in puddles, and I walked past them all.

Something dark lay in the middle of the road under a bright fluorescent median light. I raised a hand to block the glare and bent to look at it. An alley cat, a starved, mangy creature with a crushed back. Tread marks were imprinted on its fur; clots glistened between them. A chipped fang hung from one of whiskers.

I didn't know my right hand was on it until I saw my fingertips curve. They pressed into the carcass like metal probes seeking, seeking. I didn't even need to feel for a point. In death, the creature's entire body was an enormous potential ready to be evoked.

I met the cat's gaze. Lifeless eyes reflected the traffic light changing from green to red. I discharged.

A smell like charred meat, like sparks from metal screeching against metal, rust on old bicycle wheels. The creature arched its spine, its four legs locking together, so much tension in its muscles they thrummed like electric wires. Creaking, making a frothing sound, the alley cat flopped over to its paws and tried to stand.

It lives, I thought and felt no joy or satisfaction.

Blood trickled from the creature's right eye. It tried to blink and the left eye wouldn't open. It was glued shut with postmortem secretions.

My hand was hurting. I shook it, brought it before my eyes, looked at it. A large bulla had formed in the middle of the palm, blue-red and warm. Rubbing it gently, I got up and left, leaving the newly risen feline tottering around the traffic median, strange sounds emitting from its throat as if it were trying to remember how to mewl.

Deep inside the Christian muhallah I waded through rubble, piles of blackened bricks, and charred wood. I stood atop the destruction and imagined the fire consuming rows upon rows of these tiny shacks. Teetering chairs, plywood tables, meal mats, dung stoves, patchworked clothes—all set ablaze. Bricks fell, embers popped, and shadow fingers danced in the flames.

I shivered and turned to leave. Moonlight dappled the debris, shadows twisted, and as I made my way through the wreckage I nearly tripped over something poking from beneath a corrugated tin sheet.

I stooped to examine the object. It was a heavy, callused human hand, knuckles bruised and hairy like my father's. Blood had clotted at the wrist and formed a puddle below the sharp edge of the tin.

A darkness turned inside my chest; rivers of blood pounded in the veins of my neck and forehead. I don't know how long I sat in the gloom, in that sacred silence. Head bowed, fingers curled around the crushed man's, I crouched with my eyes closed and groped for the meat of the city with my other hand's fingertips. I felt for its faint pulse, I looked for its resurrection point; and when the dirt shivered and a sound like ocean surf surged into my ears, I thought I had found it.

I stiffened my shoulders, touched the dead man's palm, and let the current flow.

The hand jerked, the fingers splayed. A sigh went through the shantytown. Somewhere in the dark bricks shifted. The ruins were stirring.

Something plopped on the tin sheet. I looked down. Fat drops of blood bulged from between my clenched knuckles. I let the dead hand go (it skittered to a side and began to thrash). I opened both of my fists and raised them to the sky.

A crop of raised, engorged bullas on my palms. One amidst the right cluster had popped and was bleeding. The pain was a steady ache, almost pleasant in its tingling. As I watched, blisters on the left palm burst as well and began to gush. Dark red pulsed and quivered its way down my wrists.

Trembling, I crouched on my haunches and grasped the dead man's convulsing limb with both hands. I closed my eyes and jolted the Christian muhallah back to life. Then I sat back, rocking on my heels, and waited.

They came. Dragging their limbs off sparkling morgue tables, slicing through mounds of blessed dirt, wrenching free of rain-soaked grass, my derelict innocents seized and twitched their way across the city. I rose to my feet when they arrived, trailing a metallic tang behind them that drowned the smell of the jasmine. Metal rattled and clanged as my last finally managed to crawl out from under the tin sheet and joined the ranks of the faithful.

I looked at them one last time, my people, faces shining with blood and fervor. Their shredded limbs dangled. Autopsy incisions crisscrossed some's naked flesh. Blackened men, women and children swaying in rows, waiting for me. How unafraid, joyous, and visible they were.

I raised my chin high and led my living thus on their final pilgrimage through this land of the dead.

NICK MAMATAS

Exit Through the Gift Shop

WHAT HAPPENED TO THE DRIVERS SO FOOLISH AS TO
STOP FOR the phantom hitchhiker of Rehoboth? Nothing, really.
He's just an intense red-haired man, eyes wild, musk dripping from his
pores. When he vanishes, he leaves behind a cigarette, though it's been
decades since anyone has lit up in another person's car without asking.
And the laughter, the howling maniacal laughter?

What's so funny, anyway? Anyway, not *anyways*. That's hillbilly talk.
A remnant of Middle English, preserved by the toothless and inbred
lower classes of Scots-Irish extraction. You can always tell that a kid's
some jumped-up bumpkin in town for his college edjumication if she
says "anyways". This is New England. Anyway means one alternative
way. Anyways means that there are so many possibilities out there,
doesn't it?

But there aren't so many, are there?

Rehoboth is from the Bible. Surely the verse is on the tip of your
tongue. "And he removed from thence, and digged another well; and
for that they strove not: and he called the name of it Rehoboth; and he
said, For now the Lord hath made room for us, and we shall be fruitful
in the land." Genesis! Right near the beginning. Rehoboth is a place of
enlargement and flourishing. Back in 1643, when the town was founded,
people were familiar with the Bible. They knew what "rehoboth" meant
way back when. Rehoboth was once much larger, but until recently it
was a dinky little town of ten thousand—

Whoops, almost said "ten thousand souls." That would have been mis-
leading. Ten thousand warm human bodies of various morphologies.

The joke is that in 1993, Rehoboth's local leading citizens got all
dressed up in colonial gear and marched on Attleboro to reclaim their
ancestral lands. That's the kind of town it is. Quirky. Nobody bothered
to ask the local Natives what they thought of all these shenanigans.
Dinky.

Speaking of shenanigans: welcome to the attraction. With the decline of the mills and the recession and all that, the town fathers decided that tourism was the way to spark the local economy. There are hiking trails and a clambake, but this is New England. What about the stretch of time between Halloween and May Day, when it snows once a week, and the only way to stop a running nose is to wait for the snot to freeze?

Stretch of time, stretch of time you can imagine some old woman in a peach leisure suit saying, turning the phrase over in she head. Maybe she's at the one okay restaurant in town, her bubble haircut fresh from her weekly appointment, turning whisky over on her tongue as she concentrates. How can we get some money for the town during that stretch of time? Stretch, stretch, what a funny word that is. What else stretches? Roads! Aha!

And in that old woman's mind, *stretch of road* brings to mind the famous Rehoboth hitchhiker. It's just a local variation on the phantom hitchhiker that any chockful-of-snore town with more cemeteries than gas stations has. Lonely looking girl wants a ride. Lonely looking girl gets a ride. Lonely looking girl vanishes right outside the cemetery gates. Had things gone rather more poorly for the old woman back in her college days, she might be the lonely looking girl, forever young and bored with her own tomb.

The Rehoboth hitcher variation is a darker one. A man, a redhead, not a conscientious passenger. He glares, he starts laughing, then shrieking. He'd kill you if he could, with an axe. He'd do much worse, if he could. It occurs to the old woman to check out the local newspaper's morgue, to have her secretary examine the death records. Rehoboth is a small town; if there are any red-haired men who died in their twenties, and on the side of the road, it would be in the town's records. The secretary turns up nothing. *It's not a phantom hitchhiker, after all,* the old woman, decides. *It's the* demon *hitchhiker.*

Plans are put into motion. Letters are sent to particular individuals who have, in a fit of irony and pique, taken to living in Salem, sixty whole miles away. In-person inquiries are made in nearby Providence, because that's just a twenty-minute drive or so down the road.

Certainly we can help, was the general response. Nobody had ever thought to have the witchy Salemites work with the fine upstanding Christians of Providence before, but the old woman believes in covering all the bases. In *enlarging* the possibilities. There is more than one alternative. Anyways, not just anyway. She's on the Cemetery Commission; her husband is on the Zoning Board of Appeals. Paperwork is signed, then shredded. Wheels are set into motion. She puts her shoulder to the task.

By Halloween it's done. The Haunted Stretch. No promises save one—you can drive as quickly as you want on the Haunted Stretch, and if you get into trouble, you can always make a hard right into one of the gravel-filled runaway car ramps.

Forty thousand dollars, for two miles. Your tags and insurance had better be up to date. Leave the Garmin in the glove box. GPS doesn't work on the Haunted Stretch, not anymore, and you won't need it anyway. It's a straight shot. The Commonwealth of Massachusetts knows nothing of it, nor does Bristol County. *It's our little secret* is the sort of thing the old woman would whisper in your ear, if she were here, and interested in whispering anything in your ear, which she is not.

You meet the crew in the parking lot of Uncle Ed's Front Porch, a small ice cream joint on Winthrop Street. It closes early, so nobody's there but the crew, and their flatbed. Two guys, both heavy set and swarthy, eating ice cream. Your breath fogs before you.

"Isn't it a little chilly to eat ice cream?" you say. You regret it a moment later, then decide not to regret anything. *Forty thousand dollars.* You should be able to eat ice cream out of the high school quarterback's jock strap for forty grand, not stand here in the frigid night making conversation with a pair of townies.

The one guy stabs his ice cream with his plastic spoon and says, "Naah." He's got a thick local accent. "Everyone here eats ice cream in the winter time."

"More ice cream is eaten per capita in the Boston metroplex than anywhere else in the United States," the other guy says. He's younger. No accent. They could be father and son. "It's the high fat content; keeps you warm."

"And in the summertime," the father guy says. "You'd better eat ice cream."

"Yeah, you'd better eat ice cream around here, come summertime."

"Why?" you say without thinking, and then they both smile and shout, "Or it'll melt!" and have a good laugh. The older guys gestures for your keys, and you hand them over. You glance at his work jeans—the ass is clean, at least. The son tilts the bed and invites you into the truck's warm cab.

You climb in, belt up, smile at the kid. He's probably a good kid, just working with his dad and trying to find a place in a small town that he's already a little too big for. He should be in school, in Boston, mackin' chicks or suckin' dicks depending on his preference. You'll tell him that afterwards, you decide. Maybe slip him a few bucks if he has any weed, to take the edge off the experience with the night.

"So, is this where you dose me with—" you don't get to say *with the chloroform* before he hits you with the stun gun.

You wake up in your car, a cherry taste in your mouth. You feel very *good*, like the jolt you took from the kid charged the juice in your spine. It was all in the watermarked, password-protected, DRMed and self-destructing PDF you received when you sent your money in. Skeptics used to think that the enhancement drug was the core of the attraction—mild hallucinogens and the power of suggestion was enough to give most rubes the experience they deserve, if not exactly want.

The skeptics shut the fuck up after someone wearing Google Glass took a ride down the Haunted Stretch of Rehoboth. That's when you took out a loan, using your shitty Union City, New Jersey condo as collateral, and got to filling out the proper forms.

You were never even all that much interested in ghosts, or religion, or the supernatural. You just wanted to experience something that most people won't ever be able to. Everything from cage fighting to summers among the Antarctic penguins are available for anyone with the money and spare time. But to keep out the losers, weirdoes, and journalists, the old woman added a wrinkle to her dark ride—the application came with a text box, and no instructions.

In it you wrote:

> Honestly, whenever I think about my past, about stupid things I've said or done, I mutter aloud, "I just want to kill myself." Sometimes I actually sing it to myself, and add "doo-dah doo-dah" to the end. But I don't really want to kill myself. I just think about it for a few seconds every day, several times a day. Hopefully the experience will help me deal with whatever it is that I'm dealing with.

You were surprised at your own admission. Like how you drop a hot potato before you get burned, your fingers typed it in without you even having to think about it. Anyway, it worked. Either that, or they just have a lottery and you happened to win. *Anyways*, something happened and you're here now, behind the wheel of your car, your heart pumping liquid joy to your limbs. You don't want to kill yourself. You want to dig a hole in the asphalt and fuck the world till she comes. You want to drive so fast you'll zip past the patch of light made by your headlamps and into the swirling dark of Rehoboth's winter.

You move to turn the key in the ignition, and only then do realize that the engine is already running. The lights are on, after all. It's warm in the cab, of course. You're so fucking stupid. But you don't think *I want to kill myself*. You smile; you lick your own teeth to taste more of the cherry gunk; you love being alive. Sing that!

I love being alive!

But you ease on the accelerator. You've got two miles for something to happen, and that ain't a lot. Oh, how you want something to happen. You don't even care if it's just an actor, or a hallucination, or both. You don't even care if the redhead opens a mouth full of yellow tombstone teeth and bites your fucking nose off, like what happened to the guy on the other end of the Google Glass.

The car rolls forward, and you start to sweat ice water. Whatever the cherry stuff it, it's pretty crazy. Rehoboth should have just packaged the cherry stuff as an energy drink rather than going through all this trouble to balance the town's accounts. Eh, *it's probably extremely illegal,* you decide. Not like charging people forty thousand dollars to drive down a stretch of decommissioned town road.

Do I step out from behind a tree, thumb out? Should I materialize in the passenger seat, and put my hand on your knee and wink and call you boyfriend? Or just rise up before the car, eyes and mouth wide, palm outstretched.

Fuck it, I take the roof. I don't feel a thing, but you sure do, when two-hundred-twenty pounds of mostly muscle slams into the slope of your PT Cruiser. I crack the windshield with my forehead, and scream and laugh and howl as you jerk the wheel hard to the left, then hard to the right.

I love.

The screech of the tires.

How they smell as they melt by millimeters.

Tree branches snapping against the windows.

Gravel like hail.

My fist through the window, spiderwebbing it.

Glass everywhere, like thousands of shattered teeth.

You're a toughie, man. A cookie what won't crumble easy. You actually throw a punch at me. Right at me. I feel it and everything.

I start laughing and laughing. Oh ho ho ho. That ain't blood pouring out my nose.

It's the cherry stuff.

Anyways.

No, as a matter of fact, I'm *not* from around here.

Hey, sailor? New in town?

Come here often?

I cut your legs out from under you and take a seat on your belly.

You fuck, you *fuck!*

What I am going to do, with my awesome magic powers, is remove your central nervous system, starting from this little slice at the bottom of your pinky toe.

Forty-five miles of string.

Don't worry. I work fast. I have all the time in the world. I'm well practiced. I can do three hundred yards with a tug. Leaves me all night to floss my teeth with the stuff, tie little knots where I want them, and to untie the ones you've tied yourself.

Fucking amateurs.

In the old days, I used to construct harps out of this shit, and human spines.

A phantom hitchhiker ain't nothin'. It's a fingerprint. A cosmic smudge on the night. Me, I'm the real deal, the genuine article. The thing what left the smudge. *Unleashed!* Thanks to the spirit of inter-municipal cooperation.

And you got me for forty grand! Not too shabby, ace.

So what I am going to do now is tie one end of your nervous system to your brain stem, and another to this bright little star I have in my pocket, and then I'm going to let go of it, see, and it's going fly up up up into the firmament, stretching the tissue till it licks the edge of space.

Move over.

Hahaha, I kid, I kid.

Forgive the nudge, I know you can't move over.

Let me just nestle down here, and cuddle on up next to you.

The asphalt's nice and warm, thanks to the skidding. Good job with that.

Doesn't it look cool up there, my little star? It's like an awesome little kite, the string leading down to your nose.

You have a very distinguished looking nose. The nose of kings, friend!

It's nice out here in Rehoboth. Not a lot of streetlamps, or tall build-ings, so you can really see the stars.

One more nudge. See, look at that? Doesn't all the glass on the street look a lot like the stars? And the little snowflakes that are starting to fall? They look like the stars too, the teensy ones we can only see if we live out in the country and eat our carrots, like mama said.

That's some cool shit right there, ace.

Okay. Now what you need to do, and I'll hold your hand and squeeze it until you do, is inhale.

That's right, suck it all back in.

We've got all night. Hell, we've got all night, every night. I hitchhike through space, not through time. I'm already all over this whole stretch of *time*.

Aw, do your fingers hurt? Well, inhale more, you dirty little *fuck*!

Like you're eating spaghetti with your nose. Slurp it all back in to your body.

And no, had you shown up wearing one of those streaming Internet glasses, I just would have ripped your face off. Fuck you apes, and your YouTube.

Keep it up. *Snort snort.* Oink for me, baby.

There is no alternative. Any way you slice it, and I can slice it any which way, you need to get all this stuff back into you, and I need my little star back.

It's a good luck charm.

You're doing real good. Real good. See, you can feel your face again. Yeah, it fucking hurts.

Don't cry.

I'll give you some more cherry stuff. Let me just—

There we go. Keep your head on my lap, just like a little baby, and drink all you like. I'm gonna let it pour right down my chin.

And keep snuffling your nerve tissues back into your body.

Let me tell you a bit more about the old woman. She picked me up once, even though women in those days didn't often drive on their own, and didn't ever stop for strangers.

She liked anonymous dick. There's nothing wrong with it. Lots of people do. *You do*, don't you?

People just don't like to think of civic-minded ladies as horny little nymphs wearing nothing but bush beneath their sundresses. She was a smart girl too. Went to Radcliffe, back when girls went to Radcliffe instead of Harvard proper. And when she picked me up, she sang:

> But if I should leave my husband dear,
> Likewise my little son also,
> What have you to maintain me withal,
> If I along with you should go?

She'd spotted me right off. James Harris, the Daemon Lover. I'm a goddamn English ballad, sport. But I had no ships upon the sea, no mariners to wait upon thee, anymore. They're all at the bottom of the Atlantic. Especially those fucking mariners. They got me here, to America, but they had to die.

So I have to hitchhike.

She picked me up. We had a wild time, a good one. I buried myself deep inside her. So deep she could never stop thinking of me, no matter how many husbands she burned through—and she's had four—nor how many other anonymous lovers she's had.

How many? Count the stars, son. How many can you see, on a clear night like this, through blurred and stinging eyes? And keep *sucking!*

She tried to forget me, but she couldn't.

She's watching right now.

Don't look around.

Anyway, this is how she likes it. It's how I like it too.

Anyways, there are so many things I like to do. And little old ladies are one of them. And my little old lady likes selling kitsch. There's a T-shirt in your goodie bag, back at the hotel.

I SURVIVED THE HAUNTED STRETCH OF REHOBOTH.

It says that, for real. It was blank before, but you're doing such a good job. Tell your friends about us.

There. You're almost done. It's almost dawn.

Don't look around. Not at that hill on the right, that shines so clear to see. Not on the hill to the left, that looks so dark to thee. You look straight fucking ahead. Don't make me break your neck. Eyes ahead, you little shitsack. Anyway, any*ways*, you can.

SUNNY MORAINE

So Sharp That Blood Must Flow

IN THE END, THE WATER GOES BLACK WITH THE WITCH'S blood.

Before this happens, the little mermaid understands that a deal is a deal, a bargain a bargain, and there can't be reneging. But this isn't reneging, she tells herself as she sinks down, down, down into water so black that in truth it would be difficult to discern witch's blood within it even had a hundred witches been slaughtered in its depths.

She is not sea foam. That was the first lie.

She is also not alive. That was truth.

Being not alive, she has no need to breathe. This is terribly convenient, given what she needs to do next.

Surrounded by a hundred crystal lanterns, a prince dances with his princess. This is iconic, archetypal; many of the people in the assembly sense this on some level and take pleasure in its even perfection. This is the ending of all the stories they have ever been told as children, all the stories they have ever told *their* children, all the stories their children will tell. The prince marries his princess and they dance and are blissfully happy.

She watches them from the parapet, her eyes burning and her feet cut to ribbons by invisible knives.

This was not her ending. And she sees no reason why she should take it gracefully.

The water is dark and deep below her and she arcs down into it, her gown fluttering around her. She takes particular care to hit the water at such an angle as to break her neck, and so she sinks before she can dissolve on the little waves.

She dies with purpose. This is a truth she makes.

If she were sea foam, she thinks—and perhaps this is after and perhaps it is before or perhaps it is both things simultaneously—she could become the rain and patter down onto his windowpanes, trickle down the glass and watch him inside in his bright warmth. Or in a storm she could come to him riding, or walking, or anywhere unsheltered, and cut down through the air to strike his cheeks. She could fling herself at him and run down his body like sweat, down his face like tears.

She aches with it. It's worse than the knives ever were. The witch never told her that the knives on which she danced would be the lesser pain.

Did she know? She must have. Witches know all the secrets of love; it's what gives them the power to bargain with all its points and angles and gemstone facets.

If she were sea foam. But she is not. Before, she wants it. After, she wonders at what possessed her, but even in the cold heart of the water she still knows.

It takes her a long time to sink, a long time for the deep currents to carry her. Sometimes she thinks she can still hear the music. It works its way into her ears like droppers of poison, and though the cold water denies her rictus she feels her teeth clench and grind.

As tiny fish nibble on her legs and toes—she still has them, even now, and hates them more every passing second though the knives have at least allowed her a reprieve—she wonders about death, turns the fact of it over in her mind. She is dead, she's sure of that much, but either the witch lied, and that is why she is not foam on the waves—or something else has happened.

Her spirit is not free. And has not passed away.

Perhaps this is what rage does.

She has never felt rage like this, all-consuming, like the coals of deep-sea volcanoes in the core of her breast. She wanted. She reached for. She did everything she should have done. And him.

Him.

But if she's still here, there are other options.

She whispers to the current. It still knows her, and carries her corpse to where she wants to be.

It sets her gently down at the mouth of the sea witch's cavern and there she comes to rest against the rocks, the waving fronds of poseidonia caressing her limbs. She waits.

"Why have you come back to me?" All at once, without any stirring of the water at her coming, the witch is looming over her, the rags of her twelve tails like surf-beaten kelp, the thin strands of her hair like ancient seaweed. Her eyes are like the coals that burn in the mermaid's heart. "You should be foam on the waves, daughter."

By the witch's magic, the mermaid knows she'll be heard, the voice of that coal as it burns higher and more violent. *I'm no daughter of yours.*

"No. At that, not. So, then." The witch reaches down and lifts the mermaid under the arms, clasps her cold body close to hers, which is hot for a host of dark and unnatural reasons. "This tale has ended badly for you."

You meant it to.

"I meant to exact a price. I would in any case. You must know how these things work. I don't make the rules."

The witch glides backward through the water, back into her cavern, carrying the little mermaid with her. It is an embrace, close and dangerous, not intending comfort, not intending any good, but the mermaid has suffered and is dead and is now not afraid of anything. She has spent some of her time of sinking in wondering what might happen to her now, whether the witch might cut her into pieces and use her disparate parts for her magics, whether she might be skinned and used as a bag or a drifting blanket, whether her muscles and fat might be peeled away and eaten raw, her blood spilling down the witch's chin and floating like red gauze in the little currents.

But now she doesn't think those things will happen. Pressed to the witch's bare sagging breasts, she can sense the direction of movements. She can see ways ahead with her blank, dead eyes.

The witch lays her down in a bed of kelp. The bones of whales hang from the cavern's ceiling and make a soft *clunk* sound when the shifting water brings them into contact with each other. The water itself smells of blood, crushed plants, decay, dark things. The blood might draw sharks but the rest keeps them away. Keeps everything away but the desperate.

And the dead.

The witch floats above her, arms loose at her sides.

I want to make a deal.

The witch cocks her head on one side. This close, the mermaid sees that tiny, pale shrimp are crawling through the strands of her hair, picking over her scalp. "Another? The way this one has ended? Be serious with me, girl. What could you offer me? And what would you want?"

You know.

The witch is silent for a time. Her fingers wander over the mermaid's body. Perhaps she is learning humanity. Perhaps she has never touched a human woman.

"It would be difficult," she says at last. "It would require much. Heavy magic. Dense and drawn from the core of the world, through the fire towers in the deepest of deeps. And that still leaves open the question of what you could give me in trade. What would be worth so much effort and such a cost to me."

The little mermaid has had an answer for this ready since her body hit the water. She wishes she could smile.

There is one thing. And against all possibility, the corners of her mouth twitch.

Life and strength flow back into the mermaid both together, a great rush like a wave crashing on the shore of her heart.

Her body wrenches itself upward, a great heave, her chest twisting in on itself with the lungs she no longer has. Her legs are bound and blended, her feet splay and stretch into fins. She opens her mouth wide in a scream with no voice to make it heard.

The witch watches her in silence. She was pale before; now her skin is almost translucent. She is exactly the color of the shrimp that infest her hair. She looks as if she's trying to smile but can't, as if she's taken a little of the mermaid's death into herself, because of course she has.

Death always has to go somewhere.

But that leaves the rest of it. The death the mermaid has promised.

The witch places the silver blade into the mermaid's hand. Two seconds later its point is buried in the witch's breast.

This was not part of the deal, not the promised death in trade. But the witch doesn't look particularly shocked as she dies.

The little mermaid sits in the center of the black-gauze witch's blood. It flows into her gills. She opens her mouth and tastes its old metal and rotten wood. What she promised the witch, what she's offered in exchange—she's done offering. Done exchanging.

This is all for her.

She can hear the music of the prince's ship as she nears the surface.

It's music to dance to, and for a moment she stops just beneath the surface, head cocked, listening. She danced once, danced on the blades of knives and never bled, never screamed, and it had not just been that she had no voice. Love silenced her, terrible love, and she only had eyes for him as he laid his hands on her and spun her across the floor. Alone she had danced for his delight, her eyes beseeching him. She had believed he saw and answered her in the same kind. She had believed that he had entered the cloak of silence that covered her. That when his lips touched hers he had shared in it all.

Now she listens, cold as the water around her.

She breaks the surface. The knife is very heavy in her hand.

The ship is strung with fairylights, bathed in starlight. On the deck she can see bodies turning, turning. She can't see the prince or his precious princess, but she can feel him there. Whether or not he meant to, he *did* share himself with her—if, as she now knows, not his better part. Not the part he's given now.

She stabs the blade into the wood of the ship's side and begins to climb.

She knows they won't see her, not at first. They had never seen her, not even *him*, and now will be no different, though she's a thing of legend, of fairytale, as much as the prince and his princess. She's not a thing of *this* fairytale, has no place here, and so will be unseen. She is supposed to be dead. To them, she is.

She can make use of this.

She pulls herself onto the deck behind a table laden with food. Her gills should make this difficult but some part of her remembers, some part of her unable to shed that form just as she can't yet shed all of her death, so the air she pulls into her is harsh, sharp, a little like the knives that used to torment her. Her tail is strong and she uses it to push herself across the deck, behind the guests, behind the men in their fine suits of clothing and the ladies in their rich gowns. Behind the musicians with their strings and pipes and delicate drums.

And there, in the center of the gathering, *him* and *her*.

The mermaid closes her hand on the edge of the shear's blade and bleeds. Because what's a little more blood?

The prince and his princess turn around each other, spinning and laughing, voices high and clear over the music. The mermaid, in spite of herself, briefly loses herself in watching them. They are so lovely in light that dances as they do, fire and stars, and for an instant—a traitorous instant—she wants this again. Wishes. Dreams. Because it might, it *might*, have been worth the pain.

She lets out a sharp hiss.

All at once, the prince and his princess stop, standing in the center of the circle, gaze to gaze, hand in hand, breathless and flushed and so clearly happy.

This is the last scene of the fairytale, the point at which it ends, the book closes, the light goes out and all the good little children snuggle into their covers and drift to sleep on waves of sea foam.

The little mermaid slaps her tail against the deck and *leaps*.

There's silence. She can hear it. The world itself gone frozen and still, and all eyes on her. Her hands hit the prince squarely in the chest, one hand over his heart, and the shock on his face gives her pleasure as keen as any blade that has ever touched her.

From somewhere in the crowd, a scream. The prince himself is opening his mouth to do the same. The little mermaid opens her own in mimicry of him, and before he can utter a sound she plunges her head down and sinks her teeth into his throat.

He convulses under her. His choked-off scream comes out as a gurgle as her teeth dig in and in; hot blood floods her mouth, flesh giving under the force of her bite, and the prince twists, trying to get away, and this is all the help she needs as she whips her head to the side and tears out his throat, meat and voice sweet together on her tongue.

She swallows. The prince lies there, twitching, drowning in his own blood.

Voiceless.

Now the screams, a chorus of them, women and men alike, and the sweetest scream of his princess, but the little mermaid barely hears any of this over the sound of her own laughter, hard and high and like all the songs she used to sing to him unheard beneath the waves. She eats his scream, the blood running down her chin, and as her death flows into the gaping hole in him, his life burns hot in her belly.

Why, he's mouthing. Silent and already half dead. *Why.*

She lowers herself against him and kisses him once, painting his mouth with his own blood, smiling against him, and now understanding that this is a kind of joy he would have never given her willingly. Now there are running feet on the deck, the pounding of fleeing and pan-icked people, the shouts of the few guards he's brought with him on what should have been a voyage to celebrate life and love. Over the din of all of these things she opens her mouth and speaks to him for the first time.

"Fair's fair," she crows. "Fair is so very fair, and I'll spare you the knives you'd dance on, my love, my love."

She's singing as she begins to cut off his legs with the blade. It is very sharp. The witch gave it magic. He can't scream, of course, as his blood pools on the deck and drips through the slats, but she can feel his cries echoing in her own throat and she turns them into music. To this music, she thinks, she'd dance on knives.

She'd dance and she'd laugh, her teeth glistening like rubies in her mouth.

No one touches her. No one comes near her. She takes the prince's legs in each hand and leaves the knife buried in his heart. She moves to the railing, and before she leaps into the dark she glances back at his princess, still standing at the edge of the crowd, pale as the witch with tears streaming down her face.

Her story has not ended well.

The little mermaid regards her dispassionately, though really, she bears her no malice—the princess has, of course, been allowed to live. In another story the little mermaid knows that it might have been herself. It might have been anyone.

She gives her chin an imperious tilt. The one thing she would never have cared about being was royalty.

"Make your own deals," she says. And lets herself fall.

She slices into the water, a limb in each hand. She lifts the legs to her mouth and kisses each, on the sole of the foot, where the knives had always hurt her most.

And she lets them go.

As she plunges down into the fathoms below, she doesn't look back. The prince's legs float to the surface and bubble, dissolve into sea foam on the waves, and are soon lost and nothing at all.

She allows herself a second to float, light above her and deepest darkness below.

This is a crossroads, a turning-away-forever. But there isn't any going back; that was the deal she made, and she can make her own deals and her own truths, make them solid and real as her flesh will now always be.

JEAN MUNO

The Ghoul

Translated by Edward Gauvin

HE STOPS.

Turns around.

A man of middle age, graying, in a hunting vest and fishing boots. Watchful, no doubt worried. He's alone, and sees no one. No one behind him.

And yet there'd been a cry. A wail, a call, something human.

I have been following this man for a long time. Step by step, keeping my distance, as a hunter does its prey. Because I am wary. Whatever happens, I don't want to be involved, just a witness, as a dreamer is of his dream.

Sometimes the man stops, turns around, but because of the fog, ever denser as the tide rises, he sees less and less. Neither the dunes nor the sea, neither his where he is going nor where he began. Perhaps he has crossed the border, perhaps not—how to tell? He is alone on a meager stretch of beach without landmarks. The cry could have come from anywhere at all.

Leapt from the ground, fallen from the sky, surged from the waves. *A cry from anywhere at all.*

To his right, the ocean, to his left, the line of dunes. Between these barriers, however invisible, you can't completely lose your way. The beach tilts imperceptibly toward the great moist murmur. It is littered with debris, black tresses of seaweed, broken by fat violet jellyfish. Dead, undone, shipwrecked splatters, they smell of kelp. Pale and swollen, a lamb's cadaver stiffens its long legs in desperation.

Where does it run, this invisible line that frees and confines? Never has the man crossed the border, not even a brief foray, without a feeling of something irreparable. *The rapture of borders,* he thinks. Behind him, his patchwork life, worm-riddled, left to the scavengers' feverish devouring. Behind him. As if, in an instant, everything had become possible once more, his dreams of a clean break, starting over! But today is enough to drive him to despair. The same gray everywhere. Gray the fog, gray the sand in which the lamb's remains have softly burrowed, as if the beginning of a grave.

Gray the cry.

This time he's sure of it—the cry is coming from the sea. Before him. The sea is slow, heavy. Reeling under the weight of the fog, it spreads out in short waves, leaving a thin, sinuous fringe of froth. A stupor, the edges of exhaustion, and suddenly that cry, that tearing—the brutal, awaited return of pain.

Help!

Save me!

He recognized the voice; it hadn't changed in what would soon be twenty years. An ageless cry. The first time it was in Provence, in the depths of a narrow, almost impassable canyon. *Help! Save me! Help!* In the rocky wall opened a shadowy maw. The cold hardness of metal, the hand that greedily seized his own, for the first time.

That cry, the feel of metal barely colder than that hand. No matter where he'd gone since then. One day in Flanders, in a village empty as a necropolis; another time, at the edge of a pine wood, before a massive lightning-streaked sky. And that rainy night when, unable to find his way, he'd paced the strangely uneven pavement of a foreign city…It wasn't tied to a single place, but a state of mind. A feeling of failure, loneliness, as if the call came from inner breach. He had answered each time, unable to resist. The idea of what had to follow held him terrified and spellbound, like an abyss.

He has stopped, facing the direction from which the wail came. It seems to be drawing nearer, making its way through the fog, eating it away like an acid, carving vague contours into it. And suddenly the image is there, ever clearer. He recognizes the shape of the back of the chair, the glint of its metallic frame, the underside of a half-submerged wheel. And the hand that reaches out, opens, calls.

How to tear his gaze from that lovely skeleton's hand, elegantly gloved in flesh, that calls him, compels him?

He steps into the water. The tide rises, the crippled woman is a prisoner of the steel chair, he must rescue her from danger. Once more, she has been abandoned. But he feels strong, heroic, and pure, invincible in his dream as if in armor. His dream! To see her again, lift her up in his arms, carry her over the waves, experience once more the incomparable exhilaration of having saved her.

The water is up to his belly now. Like the lamb's corpse, the wheelchair has burrowed into the sand. He seizes the woman's hand, and she turns her unchanging face toward him—the face of a doll, with its great made-up eyes and strange gaze, intense and cold. Her pitiful legs have drowned. She puts an arm around his neck, and for a moment they stay that way, unmoving, as if embracing in a dream. Then he lifts her up and, tottering a bit, carries her toward shore. Jettisoned, the wheelchair lists, topples, slowly disappears.

Strange: she's exactly same as she was in that village crouched at the foot of a cliff that rose, a gigantic mausoleum, in the middle of an unremittingly flat landscape. Seated before the doorstep of that stone house, just as well-dressed, hair as perfect, hands with their red nails resting on the sheepskin that hid her atrophied legs. With night nigh and the air full of crows' panicked cawing, a small circle of youths, girls and boys, formed around her. Backed by the cliff, the voices took on a singular resonance, and the silence of the heights, where a few raptors wheeled, became unfamthomable. Then suddenly a tall sad woman appeared, her older sister. She pushed the wheelchair through the town square to the old church with the lowered parvis, and then, lifting the crippled woman to her chest, carries her inside, like an idol.

She pressed herself against her sister's chest—so frail, so light. A bird, a loving child. What a joy to bring her back alive, maimed but alive, to cross that invisible threshold, to place her at the foot of the altar in a cradle of soft sand. He leans over her; he could stay here all his life, just looking at her. The curve of her shoulders, her breasts, the fine lawn cloth swelling like a sail....Skin of incorporeal delicacy....A face whose harmony no expression troubled, in contrast with the thick, living, wild tangle of her jet-black tresses....Why did he never stop meeting the mysterious creature? Beautiful as a mummy's golden mask, ambiguous as the perfect mortal coil of the departed. Perfect—unfinished.

You saved me, she utters. *You saved me once more.*

They are lying side by side somewhere, under the fog. She whispers right into his ear, repeating like an incantation *You saved me... you saved me...* and then, just as before in the shadow of the cliff in that sleepy town, in the gorges of Provence, the obscure story, the spectral story, in insistent snatches. She called her *witch... melancholy witch....* She who pushed the wheelchair not out of love but interest, with the ignoble hope that one day.... For years, her suffering was hitched to hatred, hatred that would push her to the very edge of sheer cliffs and stop, ecstatic at her terror, standing silently behind her.... Hatred that would drag her with great strides, almost naked, through icy autumn rains.... Hatred that that for no other reason than to make its own omnipotence known, would abandon her in the middle of nowhere, laughing at her pleas and cries...

A madwoman, a demon. Her own death had taken her in hand, was now in charge. Every outing could be her last.

And now, right beside his ear: *I am just like you. Each of us moves forward with our own death for a shadow. Each of us, sooner or later, abandoned...*

How to tell her she was his child, saved once more, that he loved her more than anything in the world—how to tell her?

He carried her along the path she had traveled earlier, before being abandoned. The sea had not yet erased her tracks from before, the wheels' parallel lines and, between them, the firm steps of the other woman, the Melancholy one, wide mannish soles marked by a kind of Maltese cross. At the end, the two tracks went their separate ways, toward the cliff and the fisherman's hut, where the murderer had taken refuge, praying for the tragedy to come to an end at last.

The world is filled with incomplete crimes, begun over and over time and again, ghosts that know no rest and err in the recesses of loneliness, in the embittered memories of the aged, among ruins, the ghastly cawing of crows, deep in gorges where raptors wheel silently overhead. Stories clawed and fanged, stories that feed on blood. Some vague apprehension signals your presence, and I am careful to draw no closer. Woe be unto him who takes no heed, for he who seeks such tales shall find them.

You saved me. I owe you my life.... You saved me. I love you.... My beloved, I love you...

With each step she grows heavier, harder, crueler. Already he can feel the bite of her nails in his neck.

Once more, the terrible metamorphosis is underway. Ineluctable. The moment is nearing when she will be stronger, with all her claws, all her fangs, and she will never let go again. He will fall to his knees, torn to pieces, crawl his way through the sand, bleeding out. It will be the end. His death, begun time and again in the nightmare that feeds on him.

She is lying on the sand, eyes closed, and he is beside her, out of breath. Ever less human and ever more beautiful. That is the horrific part: seeing her draw away, grow ever stranger, and having to suffer this mystery.

Keep me warm, she utters, *hold me...hold me tight.*

He gets back on his feet. The border has been crossed, everything is possible now. She opens her eyes just a slit. A blue, icy stare. Different. Like a chrysalis accomplishing its fearsome birth. The child is no more, neither child nor woman—all that was a trap. When this strange icy blue unfurls its wings, it....He steps back, retreating step by step. But no—it's no trap, because he knew in advance. He never saved her, he will never be able to leave her: he is victim.

He hadn't gone far, he never even took his eyes off her. Leaning on his arm, she thrusts out her chest and, for the first time, smiles. Hieratic and smiling in the serpentine waves of her hair. He kneels before her. Do ghouls, empuses, have such blue eyes?

He will never reach the fisherman's hut now; his strength will leave him long before. He will collapse in sight of his goal, at the foot of the cliff, before the invincible fortress. The crime will remain unfinished, the sea will efface all evidence. Neither victim nor perpetrator. The tragedy without end will return to the limbo haunted by spectral stories.

Hours now he has been walking. Hours, days, following the tracks of wheels toward the nightmare's source. He stoops, back bent, his feet sink ankle deep in the damp sand, each step demands effort from his entire being. Ever since, unable to stand it anymore, he took her astride his back, he has felt lost, demeaned, guilty. Hours, days…perhaps all his life. Who knows? What he carries has no face, is a mute embrace, lethal, from the depths of time—is the Creature, the Creature without a name that sits astride man.

Suddenly the fog is torn to pieces, and the cliff appears, chalk-white, dizzying. As if in a dream, bedazzled, enthralled, he recognizes its unchanging profile. It seems a gigantic altar cracked down the middle by a titan's fist. There, in the depths of the fissure, lies the path that leads to inner lands, toward which the tracks now lead. But the two parallel lines deepen, grow farther apart, become ruts of sand and gravel, as if a wagon launched at a mad speed had riven the beach.

Here and there, perched at varying heights, still as statues, their great black wings folded, the Furies are waiting.

He will go no farther, for this is where it all ends. He has known it ever since the cry, the first cry, long ago, in a canyon in Provence. Now it is too late. Once more, he is in the middle of a fatal arena, in the blinding light.

Light like a blade. The Furies are waiting, draped in their jet-black tresses.

Slowly, with neither haste nor cruelty, with a kind of melancholy ardor, despairing, the talons shred his cheeks, the spurs pierce his sides, a beak tears open the nape of his neck, delves down to the very vertebrae….His back buckles, his knees give….He surrenders to the inexorable embrace, the sweet and monstrous devouring. To torture, to violation.

His face against the earth. He falls, falls again, several times, rushing, held back, as if something immense above him, with him, sought to take flight.

A sudden wind rises, a strange breath, panting, a dying breath. Everything darkens. The sky is no longer anything but a slow, profound beating of black wings.

Then once more the blinding, triumphant light, this time bursting into the very sky.

The eagle flew over the sea, straight toward the setting sun. Its wingspan was not of this world. Between claws stiff as crutches, it held an unmoving body that sowed the sand with a few drops of blood.

SARAH PINSKER

A Stretch of Highway
Two Lanes Wide

ANDY TATTOOED HIS LEFT FOREARM WITH LORI'S NAME
on a drunken night in his seventeenth year. "Lori & Andy Forever and
Ever" was the full text, all in capital letters, done by his best friend
Susan with her homemade tattoo rig. Susan was proud as anything of
that machine. She'd made it out of nine-volt batteries and some parts
pulled from an old DVD player and a ballpoint pen. The tattoo was
ugly and hurt like hell, and it turned out Lori didn't appreciate it at
all. She dumped him two weeks later, just before she headed off to
university.

Four years later, Andy's other arm was the one that got mangled
in the combine. The entire arm, up to and including his shoulder and
right collarbone and everything attached. His parents made the decision while he was still unconscious. He woke in a hospital room in
Saskatoon with a robot arm and an implant in his head.

"Brain-Computer Interface," his mother said, as if that explained
everything. She used the same voice she had used when he was five to
tell him where the cattle went when they were loaded onto trucks. She
stood at the side of his hospital bed, her arms crossed and her fingers
tapping her strong biceps as if she were impatient to get back to the
farm. The lines in her forehead and the set of her jaw told Andy she was
concerned, even if her words hid it.

"They put electrodes and a chip in your motor cortex," she continued.
"You're bionic."

"What does that mean?" he asked. He tried to move his right hand
to touch his head, but the hand didn't respond. He used his left and
encountered bandages.

His father spoke from a chair by the window, flat-brimmed John
Deere cap obscuring his eyes. "It means you've got a prototype arm and

a whole lot of people interested in how it turns out. Could help a lot of folks."

Andy looked down at where his arm had been. Bandages obscured the points where flesh met prosthetic; beyond the bandages, the shine of new metal and matte-black wire. The new arm looked like their big irrigation rig, all spines and ridges and hoses. It ended in a pincer, fused fingers and a thumb. He tried to remember the details of his right hand: the freckles on the back, the rope-burn scar around his knuckles, the calluses on the palm. What had they done with it? Was it in a garbage can somewhere, marked as medical waste? It must have been pretty chewed up or they would have tried to reattach it.

He looked at the other arm. An IV was stuck in the "Forever" of his tattoo. He thought something far away was hurting, but he didn't feel much. Maybe the IV explained that. He tried again to lift his right arm. It still didn't budge, but this time it did hurt, deep in his chest.

"Can't prosthetics look like arms these days?" he asked.

His practical mother spoke again. "Those ones aren't half as useful. You can replace this hand with a more realistic one later if you want, but to get full use of the arm they said to go with the brain interface. No nerves left to send the impulses to a hand otherwise, no matter how fancy."

He understood. "How do I use it?"

"You don't, not for a while. But they were able to attach it right away. Used to be they'd wait for the stump to heal before fitting you, but this they said they had to go ahead and put in."

"You don't have a stump, anyway." His father chopped at his own shoulder as an indicator. "You're lucky you still have a head."

He wondered what the other options had been, if there had been any. It made sense that his parents would choose this. Theirs had always been the first farm in Saskatchewan for every new technology. His parents believed in automation. They liked working the land with machines, gridding it with spreadsheets and databases, tilling the fields from the comfort of the office.

He was the throwback. He liked the sun on his face. He kept a team of Shires for plowing and used their manure for fertilizer. He had his father's old diesel combine for harvest time, his biggest concession to speed and efficiency. And now it had taken his arm. He didn't know if that was an argument for his horses and tractors or his parents' self-guided machines. The machines would take out your fence if you programmed the coordinates wrong, but unless your math was really off they probably wouldn't make it into your office. On the other hand—now a pincer—it had been his own stupid fault he had reached into the stuck header.

Andy's world shrank to the size of the hospital room. He stood by the window and read the weather and fought the urge to call his parents, who were taking care of his small farm next to theirs in his absence. Had they finished harvesting before the frost? Had they moved the chicken run closer to the house? He had to trust them.

The doctor weaned him off the pain medications quickly. "You're a healthy guy," she said. "Better to cope than get hooked on opiates." Andy nodded, figuring he could handle it. He knew the aches of physical labor, of days when you worked until you were barely standing, and then a Shire shifted his weight and broke your foot, and you still had to get up and work again the next day.

Now his body communicated a whole new dialect of pain: aches wrapped in aches, throbbing in parts that didn't exist anymore. He learned to articulate the difference between stinging and stabbing pains, between soreness and tenderness. When the worst of it had broken over him, an endless prairie storm, the doctor gave the go-ahead for him to start using his arm.

"You're a fast learner, buddy," his occupational therapist told him when he had mastered closing the hand around a toothbrush. Brad was a big Assiniboine guy, only a couple of years older than Andy and relentlessly enthusiastic. "Tomorrow you can try dressing yourself."

"Fast is relative." Andy put the toothbrush down, then tried to pick it up again. He knocked it off the table.

Brad smiled but didn't make a move for the fallen toothbrush. "It's a process, eh? Your muscles have new roles to learn. Besides, once you get through these things, the real fun begins with that rig."

The real fun would be interesting, if he ever got there. The special features. He would have to learn to interpret the signal from the camera on the wrist, feeding straight to his head. There were flashlights and body telemetry readings to turn off and on. He looked forward to the real tests for those features: seeing into the dark corners of an engine, turning a breach calf. Those were lessons worth sticking around for. Andy bent down and concentrated on closing his hand on the tooth-brush handle.

Just before he was due to go home, an infection sank its teeth in under his armpit. The doctor gave him antibiotics and drained the fluid. That night, awash in fever, he dreamed his arm was a highway. The feeling stuck with him when he woke.

Andy had never wanted much. He had wanted Lori to love him, forever and ever, but she didn't and that was that. As a child, he'd asked for the calf with the blue eyes, Maisie, and he kept her until she was big enough to be sold, and that was that. He'd never considered doing any-thing except working his own land next to his parents' and taking over theirs when they retired. There was no point in wanting much else.

Now he wanted to be a road, or his right arm did. It wanted with a fierceness that left him baffled, a wordless yearning that came from inside him and outside him at once. No, more than that. It didn't just want to be a road. It knew it was one. Specifically, a stretch of asphalt two lanes wide, ninety-seven kilometers long, in eastern Colorado. A stretch that could see all the way to the mountains, but was content not to reach them. Cattleguards on either side, barbed wire, grassland.

Andy had never been to Colorado. He'd never been out of Saskatch-ewan, not even to Calgary or Winnipeg. He'd never seen a mountain. The fact that he was able to describe the contours of the mountains in the distance, and the tag numbers in the ears of the bald-faced cows, told him he wasn't imagining things. He was himself and he was also a road.

"Ready to get back to work, buddy? How's it feeling?" Brad asked him.

Andy shrugged. He knew he should tell Brad about the road, but he didn't want to stay in the hospital any longer. Bad enough that his parents had been forced to finish his harvest, grumbling the whole time about his archaic machinery. There was no way he would risk a delay.

"Infection's gone, but it's talking a lot. Still takes some getting used to," he said, which was true. It fed him the temperature, the levels of different pollutants in the air. It warned him when he was pushing himself too hard on the treadmill. And then there was the road thing.

Brad tapped his own forehead. "You remember how to dial back the input if it gets too much?"

"Yeah. I'm good."

Brad smiled and reached for a cooler he had brought with him. "Great, man. In that case, today you're going to work on eggs."

"Eggs?"

"You're a farmer, right? You have to pick up eggs without cracking them. And then you have to make lunch. Believe me, this is expert level. Harder than any of that fancy stuff. You master eggs with that hand, you graduate."

Brad and the doctors finally gave him permission to leave a week later.

"You want to drive?" asked his father, holding out the keys to Andy's truck.

Andy shook his head and walked around to the passenger side. "I'm not sure I could shove into second gear. Might need to trade this in for an automatic."

His father gave him a once-over. "Maybe so. Or just practice a bit around the farm?"

"I'm not scared. Just careful."

"Fair enough, fair enough." His father started the truck.

He wasn't scared, but it was more than being careful. At first, the joy of being in his own house eclipsed the weird feeling. The road feeling. He kept up the exercises he had learned in physical therapy. They had retaught him how to shave and cook and bathe, and he retaught himself how to groom and tack the horses. He met up with his buddies from his old hockey team at the bar in town, to try to prove that everything was normal.

Gradually, the aches grew wider. How could you be a road, in a particular place, and yet not be in that place? Nothing felt right. He had always loved to eat, but now food was tasteless. He forced himself to cook, to chew, to swallow. He set goals for the number of bites he had to take before stopping.

He had lost muscle in the hospital, but now he grew thinner. His new body was wiry instead of solid. Never much of a mirror person, he started making himself look. Motivation, maybe. A way to try to communicate with his own brain. He counted his ribs. The synthetic sleeving that smoothed the transition from pectorals to artificial arm gapped a little because of his lost mass. If anything was worth notifying the doctors about, it was that. Gaps led to chafing, they had said, then down the slippery slope to irritation and abrasion and infection. You don't work a horse with a harness sore.

In the mirror, he saw his gaunt face, his narrowed shoulder, the sleeve. His left arm, with its jagged love letter. On the right side, he saw road. A trick of the mind. A glitch in the software. Shoulder, road. He knew it was all there: the pincer hand, the metal bones, the wire sinew. He opened and closed the hand. It was still there, but it was gone at the same time.

He scooped grain for the horses with his road hand, ran his left over their shaggy winter coats. He oiled machinery with his road hand. Tossed hay bales and bags of grain with both arms working together. Worked on his truck in the garage. Other trucks made their slow way down a snowy highway in Colorado that was attached to him by wire, by electrode, by artificial pathways that had somehow found their way from his brain to his heart. He lay down on his frozen driveway, arms at his sides, and felt the trucks rumble through.

The thaw came late to both of Andy's places, the farm and the highway.

He had hoped the bustle of spring might bring relief, but instead he felt even more divided.

He tried to explain the feeling to Susan over a beer on her tiny screen porch. She had moved back to town while he was in the hospital, rented a tiny apartment on top of the tattoo parlor. A big-bellied stove took up most of the porch, letting her wear tank tops even this early in the season. Her arms were timelines, a progression of someone else's skill; her own progression must be on other arms, back in Vancouver. She had gone right after high school, to apprentice herself to some tattoo bigshot. Andy couldn't figure out why she had returned, but here she was, back again.

The sleeves of his jacket hid his own arms. Not that he was hiding anything. He held the beer in his left hand now only because his right hand dreamed of asphalt and tumbleweeds. He didn't want to bother it.

"Maybe it's recycled," Susan said. "Maybe it used to belong to some Colorado rancher."

Andy shook his head. "It isn't in the past, and it isn't a person on the road."

"The software, then? Maybe that's the recycled part, and the chip was meant for one of those new smart roads near Toronto, the ones that drive your car for you."

"Maybe." He drained the beer, then dropped the can to the porch and crushed it with the heel of his workboot. He traced his scars with his fingertips: first the scalp, then across and down his chest, where metal joined to flesh.

"Are you going to tell anybody else?" Susan asked.

He listened to the crickets, the undertones of frog. He knew Susan was hearing those, too. He didn't think she heard the road thrumming in his arm. "Nah. Not for now."

Andy's arm was more in Colorado every day. He struggled to communicate with it. It worked fine; it was just elsewhere. Being a road wasn't so bad, once he got used to it. People say a road goes to and from places, but it doesn't. A road is where it is every moment of the day.

He thought about driving south, riding around until he could prove whether or not the place actually existed, but he couldn't justify leaving after all that time in the hospital. Fields needed to be tilled and turned and seeded. Animals needed to be fed and watered. He had no time for road trips, no matter how important the trip or the road.

Susan dragged him to a bonfire out at the Oakley farm. He didn't want to go, hadn't been to a party since he had bought his own land, but she was persuasive. "I need to reconnect with my client base and I don't feel like getting hit on the whole time," she said. He hung his robot arm out the window to catch the wind as she drove. Wind twenty-one kilometers per hour, it told him. Twelve degrees Celsius. In the other place, five centimeters of rain had fallen in the last two hours, and three vehicles had driven through.

The bonfire was already going in a clearing by the barn, a crowd around it, shivering. Doug Oakley was a year older than Andy, Hugh still in high school. They both lived with their parents, which meant this was a parents-out-of-town party. Most of the parties Andy had ever been to were like this, except he had been on the younger side of the group then instead of the older side. There's a point at which you're the cool older guy, and then after that you're the weird older guy who shouldn't be hanging with high school kids anymore. He was pretty sure he had crossed that line.

Susan had bought a case of Molson to make friends and influence people. She hoisted it out of the backseat now and emptied the beers into a cooler in the grass. She took one for herself and tossed one to him, but it bounced off his new hand. He glanced around to see if anybody had noticed. He shoved that can deep into the ice and freed another one from the cooler. He held it in the pincer and popped the top with his left, then drained half of it in one chug. The beer was cold and the air was cold and he wished he had brought a heavier jacket. At least he could hold the drink in his metal hand. His own insulator.

The high school girls all congregated by the porch. Most of them had plastic cups instead of cans, for mixing Clamato with their beer.

Susan looked at them and snorted. "If I live to be two hundred, I will never understand that combination."

They walked toward the fire. It blazed high, but its heat didn't reach far beyond the first circle of people knotted around it. Andy shifted from foot to foot, trying to get warm, breathing in woodsmoke. He looked at the faces, recognizing most of them. The Oakley boys, of course, and their girlfriends. They always had girlfriends. Doug had been engaged at one point and now he wasn't. Andy tried to remember details. His mother would know.

He realized that the girl on Doug's arm now was Lori. Nothing wrong with that—Doug was a nice guy—but Lori had always talked about university. Andy had soothed his broken heart by saying she deserved more than a farmer's life. It hurt him a little to see her standing in the glow of the flame, her hands in her armpits. He didn't mind that he was still here, but he didn't think she ought to be. Or maybe she was just leaning against Doug for warmth? It wasn't his business anymore, he supposed.

Lori slipped from under Doug's arm and into the crowd. She appeared next to Susan a moment later.

"Hey," she said, raising a hand in greeting, then slipping it back under her armpit, either out of awkwardness or cold. She looked embarrassed.

"Hey," he replied, nodding his beer toward her with the robot hand. He tried to make it a casual movement. Only a little beer sloshed out of the can.

"I heard about your arm, Andy. I felt terrible. Sorry I didn't call, but the semester got busy..." she trailed off.

It was a lousy excuse, but his smile was genuine. "It's cool. I understand. You're still in university?"

"Yeah. Winnipeg. I've got one more semester."

"What are you majoring in?" Susan asked.

"Physics, but I'll be going to grad school for meteorology. Climate science."

"Awesome. You know what would make a cool tattoo for a climate scientist?"

Andy excused himself to get another beer. When he came back, Susan was drawing a barometer on the back of Lori's hand. She and Lori had never been close, but they had gotten on okay. Susan had liked that Lori had ambition, and Lori had liked dating a guy whose best friend was a girl, which she said was pretty unusual. If they had moved to the same city, CTV could have made some cheesy buddy comedy about them, the small town valedictorian and the small town lesbian punk in the big city. He would make a one-time appearance as the guy who had stayed behind.

After his fifth beer he couldn't feel anything but the road in his sleeve. The air in Colorado smelled like ozone, like maybe a storm was about to hit. That night, after Susan had drawn marker tattoos onto several of their former classmates and invited them to stop at her shop, after promises of email were exchanged with Lori, after the hazy drive home, he dreamed the highway had taken him over entirely. In the nightmare, the road crept up past his arm, past his shoulder. It paved his heart, flattened his limbs, tarred his mouth and eyes, so that he woke gasping before dawn.

He set up an appointment with a therapist. Dr. Bird's broad face was young, but her hair was completely silver-white. She nodded sympathetically as she listened.

"I'm not really here to give my opinion, but I think maybe you were rushed into this BCI thing. You didn't have a part in the decision. You didn't have any time to get used to the idea of having no arm."

"Did I need to get used to that?"

"Some people do. Some people don't have a choice, because their bodies need to heal before regular prosthetics can be fitted."

What she said made sense, but it didn't explain anything. It would have explained phantom pains, or dreams that his arm was choking him. He had read about those things. But a road? None of her theories jibed. He drove home on flat prairie highway, then flat prairie two-lane, between fallow fields and grazing land. The road to his parents' farm, and his own parcel of land in back of theirs, was dirt. His new truck had lousy shock absorbers, and every rut jolted him on the bench.

He had lived here his whole life, but his arm was convinced it belonged someplace else. On the way home it spoke to him without words. It pulled him. Turn around, it said. South, south, west. I am here and I am not here, he thought, or maybe it thought. I love my home, he tried to tell it. Even as he said it, he longed for the completion of being where he was, both Saskatchewan and Colorado. This was not a safe way to be. Nobody could live in two places at once. It was a dilemma. He couldn't leave his farm, not unless he sold it, and the only part of him that agreed with that plan was not really part of him at all.

That night he dreamed he was driving the combine through his canola field when it jammed. He climbed down to fix it, and this time it took his prosthetic. It chewed the metal and the wire and he found himself hoping it would just rip the whole thing from his body, clear up to his brain, so he could start afresh. But then it did keep going. It didn't stop with the arm. It tore and ripped, and he felt a tug in his head that turned into throbbing, then a sharp and sharp and sharper pain.

The pain didn't go away when he woke. He thought it was a hangover, but no hangover had ever felt like that. He made it to the bathroom to throw up, then crawled back to his cellphone by the bed to call his mother. The last thing he thought of before he passed out was that Brad had never taught him how to crawl on the prosthetic. It worked pretty well.

He woke in the hospital again. He checked his hands first. Left still there, right still robot. With the left, he felt along the familiar edges of the prosthetic and the sleeve. Everything was still there. His hand went up to his head, where it encountered bandages. He tried to lift the prosthetic, but it didn't move.

A nurse entered the room. "You're awake!" she said with a West Indian lilt. "Your parents went home but they'll be back after feeding time, they said."

"What happened?" he asked.

"Pretty bad infection around the chip in your head, so they took it out. The good news is that the electrodes all scanned fine. They'll give you a new chip when the swelling goes down, and you'll be using that fine bit of machinery again in no time."

She opened the window shade. From the bed, all Andy saw was sky, blue and serene. The best sky to work under. He looked down at the metal arm again, and realized that for the first time in months, he saw the arm, and not Colorado. He could still bring the road—his road—to mind, but he was no longer there. He felt a pang of loss. That was that, then.

When the swelling went down, a new chip was installed in his head. He waited for this one to assert itself, to tell him his arm was a speedboat or a satellite or an elephant's trunk, but he was alone in his head again. His hand followed his directions, hand-like. Open, close. No cows, no dust, no road.

He asked Susan to get him from the hospital. Partly so his parents wouldn't have to disrupt their schedules again, and partly because he had something to ask her.

In her car, driving home, he rolled up his left sleeve. "Remember this?" he asked.

She glanced at it and flushed. "How could I forget? I'm sorry, Andy. Nobody should go through life with a tattoo that awful."

"It's okay. I was just wondering, well, if you'd maybe fix it. Change it."

"God, I'd love to! You're the worst advertisement my business could have. Do you have anything in mind?"

He did. He looked at the jagged letters. The "I" of "LORI" could easily be turned into an A, the whole name disappeared into COLORADO. It was up to him to remember. Somewhere, in some medical waste bin back in Saskatoon, there was a computer chip that knew it was a road. A chip that was an arm that was Andy who was a stretch of asphalt two lanes wide, ninety-seven kilometers long, in eastern Colorado. A stretch that could see all the way to the mountains, but was content not to reach them. Forever and ever.

KARIN TIDBECK

Migration

EDITH THINKS ABOUT WHAT WAS UP TOP, AS SHE SITS ON the edge of her bed waiting for worktime.

It was a desert, dunes shaded in sepia. They lived in little houses on a wooden platform. Edith would dive for spiny shells in the sand and give them to the bowl-maker.

Sometimes, though, she dreams of an ocean, of crawling out of a little cave to stand in the surf. The water is warm like blood. The ocean feels as real as a memory. She once mentioned these things to Irma, who merely shook her head. *I don't know what you're talking about*, she said. *This is our home, you silly thing*. Edith asked, *Then where did we come from?* Irma's face went blank, and then she shrugged.

Gregor's voice rings out on the other side of the door, "Wash your clothes, wash your clothes!"

Edith slips into her cardigan and gently shakes the worn bedsheets out. A seam has split along the cardigan's right shoulder. She'll have to take it to Irma for mending. Maybe after delivery, because today is delivery day.

The downstairs flight yawns at her, darkness seeming to seep up from below, and she has to look away briefly. When she turns back, it's just a set of concrete stairs. Gregor lives down there, after all, and more neighbors below him, and below them, all the way to the bottom, so it's said. Edith starts her upstairs climb.

Most of the doors in the stairwell are propped open, and people are sitting and standing in doorways and on landings, already at their tasks.

Edith greets her neighbors, chanting as she goes, "Mend your things, mend your things?"

"Wash your clothes?" comes the response from above, and she catches up with Gregor, laundry basket in his thin arms.

He nods at Edith, who waves back. A neighbor hands him a frock for washing. Edith and the neighbor look on as Gregor drops the garment into the empty basket. He stirs it around with his stick, picks the garment up again, shakes it out and folds it neatly.

"All done," he says, and the neighbor thanks him kindly.

Only Otto needs something fixed today: his shelf has chipped, and Edith taps her hammer on it to fix it. She gets all the way to the janitor's room at the top landing without another customer. The janitor's door is closed, and Edith's first in line. She sits down at the top of the stairs, gazing idly at the painting on the flat wall where the next flight of stairs should have been. It almost looks like a real set of stairs, gray and crumbling slightly at the edges. It's easy to imagine them switchbacking all the way up to the surface. On the wall between the stairs and the janitor's door, the elevator is still inert. It could ding at any moment now. The janitor will come out of her room and open the elevator door in a gust of fragrant air. Inside will be stacks of brown boxes, one for each of the neighbors. Edith's mouth waters at the thought of fresh mushrooms, crispy little insects, chewy lichen.

It finally happens when the line of neighbors snakes down the stairs as far as Edith can see, and Irma who is right behind her in the queue has just fixed the seam on Edith's cardigan. The janitor steps outside, tall and magnificent in her blue dungarees. She greets the neighbors with a raised hand and a smile. As if on a signal, the elevator dings. The stairwell falls quiet. With a flourish, the janitor reaches for the handle and pulls the heavy door open.

The elevator is empty.

Mealtime consists of the last mushrooms. They've gone soggy and smell rank, but Edith forces them down. She sits down on her bed to wait for bedtime. The window-painting on the far wall needs touching up; the blue part of the ocean is flaking. Edith ran out of the blue color halfway through, and painted the rest green. It's a place where two oceans meet. It'll be all green when she's done it over, as if the window has shifted.

All the janitor had said was *the elevator is empty*, and the words had traveled down the stairs. The neighbors had looked at each other in confusion, then meekly returned to their rooms. Edith had lingered for a moment. The janitor had merely closed the elevator door and gone back to her room. Edith tried the door handle to the elevator. It was locked.

Edith finds herself walking around the room, picking things up and putting them in their place, wiping the table and the shelves, folding her clothes, shaking out the bed sheets. She puts the rubbish in the small bucket and sets it down outside the door, where it'll be empty before morning comes. The stairwell is quiet now. Everyone is waiting for bedtime. There's a strange acidic tickle in her stomach. It shoots tendrils into her legs.

Edith sits back down on the bed, but her stomach is churning. Something is about to happen. It's never good when things happen.

It began in the colonnades under the town on the platform in the desert. Someone saw a pale and unfamiliar figure leaping from shadow to shadow.

Then came the horde.

As the invaders caught the villagers and tore into them, they made soothing, crooning noises that somehow drowned out the shrieking. They strangled the villagers, tore their eyes out, opened their throats with sharp teeth. They rolled the bodies over the edge of the platform, into the sand. When they couldn't find any more victims, they went into the little houses and closed the doors.

Edith wakes up in the middle of the night and retches over the side of the bed. She manages to crawl out and find the chamber pot before her bowels empty themselves in a long, excruciating spasm. When it finally subsides, she slides off the pot and onto the floor. The stink of her own waste makes her retch again, dribbling bile on her shoulder.

Then someone is banging on the door, and she must have blanked out, because the vomit on her shoulder is cold. Three bangs, then silence, then three more bangs. Voices outside, many footsteps marching down the stairs. They're going somewhere, and she should be going with them. They're going to leave her all alone. But every joint in her body hurts, and her bowels empty again before she manages to find the pot, and then she's standing at the edge of the platform, gazing out across the desert.

Some of them managed to escape. Edith persuaded them to hide in the silo. They watched the massacre from a little window on the loft. When the light faded and the invaders hadn't moved for a while, Edith led the refugees out and away from the village. They walked for hours across the hot sand, until they came upon a structure in the middle of nowhere. It was a little concrete shed, perhaps three meters on each side. The heavy door stood ajar. The villagers went inside after very little hesitation, into the cool gloom of a stairwell. The door swung closed behind them. Inside, neatly ordered rooms, as if they had been waiting just for them. They took a room each and sat down to wait for bedtime. When the lights went out, Edith thought she heard a stranger's voice complaining in the stairwell, *They're much too early. It's not right.*

When the ceiling lamp comes on, it's weak and flickering. Edith sits in a puddle of shit and vomit next to the bed. The stink is thick like a fog. Her joints still hurt, but not as badly as in the night, and she manages to stand up on shaky legs. She dries herself off with an almost-clean towel and puts on her dress, thick stockings, cardigan, slippers. There's still a little water in the jug on the table. It eases the burn in her throat.

The slight groan of the door hinges is very loud in the quiet stairwell. It seems somehow larger than it used to. The downward stairs gape at her.

"Hello?" Edith calls weakly.

No reply, save for a faint rustle below. She hobbles across the landing to Irma's door and knocks. Nothing happens. She pushes the handle down: it's unlocked. Inside, Irma's room is tidy and unoccupied: the bed is made, the table empty, her sewing tools sit in a neat row on the shelf.

Edith starts to climb the stairs but her legs refuse to carry her upward. She sits down on the lowest step, heart pounding in her throat.

"Hello," comes a faint reply from upstairs.

Gregor comes shuffling downstairs behind her. His face is very pale and his eyes wide. He gasps as he sees Edith.

"I'm so glad to see you. I thought I was alone." He sits down on the step next to Edith; his nostrils flare briefly but he doesn't comment on her smell.

"What's going on?" Edith says weakly.

"They're all gone, Edith." Gregor gestures upward. "I was just upstairs. No one's here. Not even the janitor."

"Someone was at the door last night," Edith says. "I wanted to go outside, but I was so sick."

Gregor runs his hand over the wall with a rasping noise. "I was afraid," he mumbles. "I wanted to go too, but it was pitch dark and the noise outside. It scared me. And now...they're all gone."

"Everyone?"

"Everyone. We shouldn't be here. Can't you feel it?"

Edith swallows. Gregor's right. It feels like when she once overstayed her welcome at Irma's, and Irma left so that Edith would take the hint and go home.

"We have to go find them," she says.

Gregor looks nauseated. "I'm still afraid."

Edith reaches for his hand and squeezes it.

The first flight of stairs down to Gregor's flat is easy enough, especially for Gregor, of course—he lives there. Gregor finds Edith some water and a handful of dried beetles, and her legs become slightly more steady. The next flight of stairs feels slightly more ominous, but still, it's where Gregor's under-neighbors live, and he knows them well. They knock on one door each, but no reply. The rooms beyond are tidied and empty. No one seems to have brought anything with them. They have left their tools behind.

They both stop short at the next flight of stairs. The light is distinctly dimmer. For a second, Edith thinks she sees shadows rushing up at them, but then she blinks, and they're gone. Gregor grabs her hand.

"I've never been this far," he says.

"Neither have I." Edith pauses. "Do you know how far down the stairwell goes?"

Gregor shakes his head.

The doors on the next landing are identical, and the next. Even though she's counting them, it feels as if Edith and Gregor aren't actually going anywhere, just arriving in the same place again and again. The fear that spreads cold tendrils through Edith's face and ears makes her light-headed, almost giggly. They stop knocking on doors, instead just opening them gingerly. On the ninth landing down, the rooms are no longer furnished, just gray-walled cells. The walls become first damp and then wet to the touch, and the air slowly warms up. Gregor's breathing has a slight squeak. Edith's knees ache. The smell of wet earth creeps up from below.

On the seventeenth landing, water seeps out from a crack in the wall and trickles across the floor. A shadow around the little stream tells of an ebb and flow, like in that dream, by the ocean: the water would draw back to reveal a beach pierced with thousands of little holes, each holding a pale and tiny crab. The trickle runs down to the next landing, where the concrete bleeds more water. When water starts seeping into Edith's slippers, it's warm, like blood.

On the twenty-second landing, the stairs abruptly end. Where the next flight of stairs should have started is a blank wall. One single door stands next to a broken wall sconce. The handle glints in the faint light from upstairs. The floor here is dark and soft and squelches with runoff. Edith takes a deep breath and pulls at the door handle.

A bulb in the ceiling bathes the room in yellow light. It's furnished and cluttered with tools of all sorts. The bed is rumpled, the sheets smell heavily of sour musk. At the far end of the room is another door. Edith's knees are throbbing. She sits down on the bed. Gregor closes the door behind him and crosses the room to try the other one. It's locked.

Warm fatigue creeps up along Edith's legs. "I need to rest," she says.

Gregor's fingers drum an uneven rhythm on the tabletop. "What do you think about, when you think about where we came from?"

Edith blinks. "I thought no one did but me."

"Of course not," Gregor says. "I talked to Adela about it every now and then. We could never agree. She says it was a desert."

"It was," Edith replies.

"No, it wasn't, and I don't understand where you got that from. It was a forest. Tall trees with dark trunks like pillars, and high up there, straight branches covered in little needles. The canopy was so dense that nothing grew on the ground. We lived in spheres hanging from the branches. They were pretty, all coppery metal and with big round windows. We didn't like touching the ground. We ate needles and bark, and we were happy like that."

Edith considers. Then she starts telling Gregor of her own memory, but the light goes out, and sleep takes her.

It is dark and Edith is in bed, under blankets, Gregor curled up next to her. She has woken up because someone just gently pulled the blanket from her shoulder. A presence is looming over the bed.

"Who are you?" Edith whispers.

The sound of lips parting and a dry tongue unfastening from the palate. The words are laden with clicks and smacks. "I am the caretaker. And you're late for your migration."

"Where did the others go?"

"Downstairs."

"Why?"

"It was time."

"I don't understand," Edith says. "Are you the one who makes the boxes?"

"No more questions," the caretaker replies. "All you have to do is move on."

"But where are we supposed to go?"

A brief pause. "You should know that. Haven't you had dreams?"

"I dream of an ocean sometimes."

The caretaker smacks its dry tongue. "That won't do. No. You're heading for houses. Remember that. Houses in a circle, with lanterns over the doors."

The caretaker pulls the blanket off the bed and drops it on the floor. "You'll know where you're going. It'll feel right. Now go. You'll be late. It's the other door."

It moves away. The door to the stairwell opens with a groan. The caretaker's silhouette against the faint light of the stairwell doesn't look quite right.

"First too early and now too late," the caretaker mumbles. "Something's not right."

Next to Edith, Gregor stirs and sighs. "What was that?"

"We have to go," Edith says.

The other door opens onto a tunnel through raw rock, walls glowing faintly with blue-white larvae. The echoes of Edith's and Gregor's footsteps are very faint. Edith's heartbeat is slow and heavy. Their breath and the shuffle of their feet on the rough ground count out a rhythm that sucks her in. She almost doesn't notice when the tunnel widens into a cave, not until whatever is crouching by the little pool moves slightly and Gregor lets out a little squeak. Backlit by the luminous water, the pale figure looks almost like a neighbor. It suddenly turns around and looks up at them. Small eyes glitter in the waterlight. It lets out a small whimper. Edith leans on the wall, because her heart is rushing and her knees are buckling. They stare at each other. The other bounds away into the dark with a rasp of naked feet on stone.

Gregor sits down with a thud. Edith rests against the wall until she can feel her legs again. Then she pushes herself to her feet and walks over to the little pool. The water is full of little glowing specks that tastes strongly of minerals. Edith splashes the water a little, to break the silence.

"It seemed to be afraid of us."

"It was alone," Edith replies. "Maybe next time it won't be."

Stalactites extend from the tunnel's ceiling, leaving just enough room to crawl through. After a while, they can't see the tunnel walls anymore, just irregular pillars stretching in every direction. Winged insects with glowing abdomens crawl over the pillars. They're easy to catch. Bitter and sour juice bursts over her tongue when Edith bites down on them.

Gregor slips on a loose stone and twists his ankle so badly that his foot hangs limp at the end of his leg with a fist-sized lump on the ankle bone. Edith wraps it with her stockings as well as she can, and helps him climb onto her back. They continue in silence, Gregor occasionally wheezing in pain.

"There was a storm, a firestorm," he says after a while.

"I woke up because my house was rocking back and forth. I opened a hatch and looked outside and there it was, a glow between the trees, and all the air was rushing toward it. People were climbing out of their homes, screaming. Someone banged on the walls and made them ring. We threw out ropes and climbed down to the ground. Some people panicked and just jumped. I'll never forget that noise.

"We picked up the children and the frail and ran, but we couldn't run fast enough. The fire was catching up with us, eating everything in its way. We heard the pops and bangs as houses exploded or fell to the ground. A woman shouted, *Save us! Save us!* Soon we were all chanting, *Save us! Save us!*

And there it was: a tree, the biggest tree I had ever seen. The same woman who had led us here banged on the bark and screamed, *Let us in! Hide us from the fire!* We all echoed her: *Hide us! Hide us!*

"A door swung open in the tree. We crowded inside. Inside was a stairwell. And the reason the stairs are blocked is that either the danger hasn't passed, or…because we asked the tree to hide us, but we forgot the rest. We forgot to tell the tree that it should let us out again once it was safe. It's just doing what we asked."

Gregor pauses.

"We should be going in that direction." He points into the murk.

"How do you know?"

"I just know."

Edith doesn't feel any such thing, but does as he says.

Her back is hurting badly when she realizes that the stalactites are trees, and that grey light is filtering down from above. The floor is a carpet of brown needles.

"Gregor," she whispers.

From where he clings to her back, Gregor lets out a small sob. "I know these trees."

He slides down from Edith's back and hobbles over to a tree, resting his cheek on the bark. He turns to Edith, and tears are running down his face. "We're home."

He points upward, and there they are, spheres hanging in branches. Rope ladders trail down from their hatches. The spheres look pristine, waiting for new occupants. Silence is complete.

"We're home!" Gregor shouts.

Edith frowns. "You said this place burned."

"Obviously it's here now," Gregor says acidly.

Gregor waves at the spheres. He hobbles over to the nearest rope ladder.

"Hello? Hello?"

The soft silence eats the sound of Gregor's voice. He tries to tug at the ladder, but the rope somehow slips out of his fingers. He grabs futilely at it.

The silence makes Edith's ears ring. The spheres have no dust on them, no dirt. There's no trace of the firestorm Gregor talked about.

"I'm not sure we should be here," Edith says.

"I don't understand why I can't get the..."

Gregor throws himself at the rope ladder. He somehow manages to miss it by an arm's length. He lands on the ground with a huff.

Edith scoops up a handful of soil and pine needles and sniffs it. Her hand might as well be empty. "Gregor. Shouldn't the trees smell like trees?"

"Of course they do," Gregor replies absently, staring at the ladder. "Look, I'm staying. The others are here, we just have to wait for them to come out."

Edith shakes her head. "I don't want to be here. It's all wrong. And it's not home."

The look Gregor gives her is full of pity. He's never looked at her like that before. "I'm sorry." His right hand is still grabbing for the rope ladder. He doesn't seem to notice.

"I'm sorry too, Gregor. I'm leaving."

"I'll be here," Gregor replies. "I'm climbing up and I'm going to find out what to do. A weaver, maybe. A singer. It depends on what the others are."

Edith turns around. She doesn't look back. The forest seems to push at her back as she leaves.

There's no way to tell whether she's walking in the right direction. The stalactites spread out in an irregular grid. She should have a feeling of where to go, like Gregor did, but she doesn't. Occasionally, she finds traces of others passing through: a scarf, some chewed insect carapaces, dried excrement. She follows them like a trail at first, only to end up where she started. Eventually she just pushes forward without thinking much.

At last, the rushing in her ears is more than her own blood. It rises and falls, rises and falls, and in the distance shines the warm yellow circle of a cave mouth.

It's an ocean, far below, and Edith is standing on a ledge high up on a cliff wall. The sky is bright blue, fading into white; somewhere behind the cliff is a sun. A path snakes down toward the water. The ocean is green. Edith knows it must be warm, like blood. She steps out onto the ledge and follows the little path down. The path ends in a beach, dotted with thousands of tiny holes. She crouches down next to a cluster of them just in time to see a little crab run for shelter. Dark recesses sit in the cliffside. Edith looks into the nearest one; inside is a narrow bed, a little table and two chairs. No dust, no sign that anyone lives there. The only sound is that of waves. Just like Gregor's rope ladder, it proves impossible to climb into the caves. Somehow her foot falls short of the threshold again and again. She's not supposed to be in this place, or the place isn't ready for her. She climbs back up the path.

The glow of a lamp lures her out from between the stone pillars. It's a lantern with glass walls, suspended from the cave ceiling. It lights up a wall of grass that grows higher than her head. It parts before her easily enough, giving off a sharp and herbal scent as she touches the blades. It eventually parts onto a circular clearing. The sky is dark; the only light comes from the lanterns suspended on curved poles over the doors of little houses standing in a tight circle around a high central lamppost. Someone is scuttling between the houses, their movement pattern human but somehow not quite. The caretaker is setting down little brown boxes in front of the door of each house.

It's delivery day.

Edith watches as the caretaker scurries into the high grass, and the sky brightens into a uniform blue, brighter at the edges. People come out of the houses and wave at each other across the lawn. They pick up the boxes, tearing them open with delight. Edith recognizes none of them. They're dressed just like her but they're tall and gangly, their skin slightly darker than her own, and with large, shining eyes. She backs away into the grass before any of them can see her.

Edith finds her neighbors in a huddle among the stalactites, holding each other and whimpering. Everyone is there. They look at Edith in astonishment as she approaches. The janitor, who no longer has a janitor's bearing, slowly gets up on her feet.

"We tried to go home," she says weakly. "Someone was already there. Are you here to help us?"

Irma is leaning on the stalactite closest to Edith and hugging her legs. She doesn't seem to recognize Edith at all.

"Irma," Edith says, but Irma doesn't react to her own name.

Edith looks at the others. "What happened to you all?"

They merely gaze at her.

"We need to go home," the person who once was Irma whispers.

"Then why aren't you walking?"

No reply, just uncomprehending stares.

"Come," Edith says. "We have to go."

They meekly get up and follow, shuffling blindly forward. The janitor, if it still is the janitor, takes her hand and holds it so tightly it hurts.

And finally, a slight tug in Edith's chest. A direction: this way.

The stalagmites become thick and rough and stand on upturned blocks with carved faces, and this is a familiar place at last: a colonnade, and the metallic scent of granite and sun-warmed wood, and the sound of voices. Home.

"This is it," Edith says. "We're here."

"But there are people here," the janitor whispers, and points at a person walking further ahead.

Edith recognizes the gait, that strange grace. They walked just like that when they came to invade and take over. Here they are, usurpers, living in a place that doesn't belong to them. Someone is living in her house, sleeping in her bed, playing at her profession.

She looks at the others. Their faces are blank. They have no memory of this. But they do have hunger. It shines out of their eyes.

"It's our turn," Edith says. "This is our place. Let's take it."

And she starts toward the usurper at a walk, and it turns around and sees her, and when it breaks into a run, her heart floods with a wild joy.

———

The bed is very soft. The hut has just enough room for a bed and a table with chairs. There is also a shelf with some interesting objects. One in particular is very smooth and comfortable to the touch: a bowl edged with soft thorns.

Outside, the sun has risen almost all the way to zenith. The others are already up, wandering among the houses, picking up objects and talking about them. Their faces are different, and so are their gaits; they have already started. By the platform's edge, gazing out across the desert, stands a man.

"Hello."

The man turns around. "Hello." He smiles. "I'm not quite awake yet. You know how you wake up some mornings, and you have to tell yourself, 'Here I am, Urru-Anneh is my name, and I dive in the sand for shells'. It's one of those."

"Exactly one of those. I woke up, and I had to remind myself, 'I'm…'"

Urru-Anneh waits patiently.

"Arbe-Unna," she finishes.

"And where are you going this fine morning, Arbe-Unna?"

Arbe-Unna hesitates. "I'm on … an errand."

"Good luck with your errand then." Urru-Anneh smiles and turns back to gaze at the desert.

Arbe-Unna wanders off into the village, where the others are greeting each other and helping each other remember who they are and what they do. A silo stands at the edge of the platform. Inside, it's very quiet. In the middle of the floor sits a crate on wheels. The crate is filled with little brown parcels. An enticing smell rises from them. Arbe-Unna catches a glimpse of something moving on the loft—a head, an arm?— but when it doesn't happen again, decides it must have been nothing.

Arbe-Unna grabs the edge of the crate and pushes it outside. The other villagers throw their hands up in joy when they see the crate and the parcels.

"Good morning!" cries Arbe-Unna. "It's me, Arbe-Unna, your janitor."

The others cheer, and form an orderly line as the janitor hands them each a parcel. Arbe-Unna chats with each of them, finding out their names and professions. They are more than happy to talk about themselves, sometimes helping each other to remember details. At the end of the ceremony, they're all good neighbors, although they don't all agree on how old the village is or who's related to whom. But that's how people are.

It does feel as if someone's missing, but that might also be because of the dream she had last night. A cave, a forest, a friend who stayed behind. Something had gone wrong. It was a relief to wake up and find everything alright with the world, everyone in their right place.

CHARLES WILKINSON

Hidden in the Alphabet

THE AUTEUR HAS BEEN TRIPPED UP ON THE PAVEMENT outside the Acme Hotel. He's just come through the revolving doors, down the marble steps and turned in the direction of the main thoroughfare. It was not the tip of the sole of his right shoe (chestnut gleam of leather on the upper) catching an uneven paving-stone. And no, it has nothing to do with an occasional weakness of the knees, allowable in a man of seventy years, or even a failure to adjust to his new bifocal spectacles, which lie broken (spider-cracks in both lenses, the frames askew) six inches away from his outstretched right arm (hand marked with chalky grazes, a droplet-chain of blood). It is as if someone's curled a foot, or the curved handle of an umbrella, around his ankle and jerked his leg violently upwards.

Later, he will tell himself that he lost consciousness for several seconds, although now as he levers himself upright, blood dripping from the side of his chin, he is not aware of having done so. But this will be his only explanation for the fact no one is anywhere near him on the street.

The pigeon (iridescence of wing-glaze, white mark on the throat) perched on the roof of a derelict warehouse is not an adequate witness to what happened, though it knows the south side well: has flown many times through the open windows of buildings that glass has forgotten; alighted on chimney tops tufted with wild grass; hopped under bus shelters to inspect abandoned Chinese takeaways; examined crisps wrappers with a critical eye. It has an excellent view of the Acme Hotel: the marble steps, washed every day; the brass glint of the revolving doors; the shafts and arrowheads of black railings; the orange-red brick of the façade; the Gothic windows in all storeys but the sixth, from which you can see the gleaming towers of the second city's centre, though not the ring road that ropes them in.

The pigeon may have noticed the auteur, his silver hair and white linen jacket bright in the sunshine of a waning summer, when he pushed the revolving door, walked down the marble steps and into the street (just as a blue van was passing, too quickly for the driver to witness what happened next) and he could have observed a man or the shadow of a man or a shadow from a nest of English shadows, slipping out from an abandoned factory, or a shop with shuttered windows, where no one has been served for thirty years, and coming up swiftly behind a man leaving a hotel on his way to a meeting with the son, his only child, that he has not seen for a quarter of a century.

As the man brushes himself down (an action he immediately regrets as a streak of blood appears on the right pocket of his linen jacket) and hobbles back to the Acme Hotel, the pigeon flies off in the direction of a café, where there will be the crumbs of croissants and sesame seeds, left over from *de luxe* burger buns.

Cotton wool, commiserations, antiseptic cream and directions to the nearest optician have been provided by the staff at the Acme Hotel. The auteur has phoned his niece and asked her to postpone the meeting. He must not appear in the restaurant (expensive, central, overlooking a canal) with sticking plaster on his hands and chin. As he will be unable to see further than his own table, the other diners will be indistinct blobs of colour, the details on the menu squashed insects on a white background. It is most important that he should meet with his son. There are questions he must ask. He will need to observe his reactions closely.

It is a hot day. The domed mosque with a minaret, the greengrocers selling unfamiliar fruit, the women in *niqabs*, the men with their long beards and traditional dress—all surprise him. Only the red brick of the shop frontages and the scarlet pillar boxes are familiar. He has not visited his native city for many years; it pains him that on his return he is no longer a wealthy man.

The optician's shop is in a side street and as he walks past a row of semi-detached Victorian villas (bow-windows, trimmed box hedges, neat front gardens) he feels a faint longing for his childhood. Opposite is a low white building with a flat roof that consists of three shops. There is a florist and the optician, but the middle unit is empty. A yellow skip sits next to a pile of salmon-pink bricks. The auteur is slightly early for his appointment. He peers through the window. The reception area is not welcoming. No one is behind the desk, and only one rack, which is attached to the wall, has any frames for sale. A free-standing display unit is just shining skeletal bars, somehow sinister, as if it has been expertly boned. In one corner, there are two uncomfortably upright chairs and a low table. Just as he takes the decision to kill time in the florist's, a door at the back opens and a man in an open-necked white shirt steps out. As he is standing in front of an oblong of yellow light from the treatment room, the auteur cannot see his face, but there is no mistaking the gesture signalling him to come in. A bell rings, a tiny ecclesiastical note; for a second, the auteur thinks he can smell incense. Then the dust coats the back of his throat and he coughs.

Instead of waiting for him, the optician has gone back into his room, but the door is open. The auteur knocks once and then enters without waiting for an answer.

The optician, who has his back to him, is bowed over a work space. His elbows are moving very slightly as if he is carrying out some delicate operation.

"Please sit down. I won't be long."

"I'm sorry to be slightly early."

"Don't worry. I assure you that will not be a problem."

The treatment chair reminds him of the dentist (a sharp psychosomatic stab in a back molar) but he takes his seat. As the optician materializes behind him and swiftly positions the chin and head rests, the auteur thinks of a film he once made: the head of a knight encased in a helmet.

"I just need you to sit very still, eyes wide open, look this way."

He grasps the horizontal bars. A puff of air in each eye. The beam of a torch and then the test card appears in the wall mirror. One lens is

exchanged for another until the letters start to clarify. He reads the top
two lines only. A change, much sharper now, AXO TVH and then—
quite clearly—SEX.

The woman who gets off the bus dresses with an eloquent simplicity
unusual for the area. Her skirt and blouse are a vibrant blue. In the
midst of shoppers in shades of milk chocolate, grey and mouse-brown
she has the electric plumage of an American jay in a garden of house
sparrows. She was seen in the lobbies of Parisian hotels. If it were not
for her tinted glasses, we might recognize the eyes that once stared at
us from the back covers of magazines (*Vogue, Tatler*). Her blonde hair
touches her shoulders and is cut straight across her forehead. And she
wears a loose silk scarf (perhaps Jaeger or Hermes) with a blue and
yellow pattern. Her shoulder bag has the sheen of soft Italian leather
bought in Milan.

She walks quickly, ignoring the outstretched hand of the beggar in
khaki trousers (army surplus) squatting on a rug outside the supermarket. At first she appears to be heading past the pawnbrokers, the
snooker hall and the curry house towards the *patisserie* on the corner,
with its display of baked bread in the window, its coffee shop and
small courtyard garden: the one place redolent of France in a suburb
of chain shops, *halal* butchers, convenience stores, moneylenders,
estate agents and one laundrette that smells of hot metal, washing
powder and Saharan-dry heat. But without pausing to look at the
baskets filled with almond croissants and *pain-au-chocolat*, she makes
her way past the chairs on the pavement. One man looks up from his
newspaper and knows in an instant the damage done to the perfectly
symmetrical features: the hairline cracks beneath the repaired porce-
lain skin, the brittle lips that threaten breakdown and grief. And then
she turns down a side street.

Now that she is away from the crowds, her pace slows, and once she
halts and rummages in her shoulder bag. Beneath her dress is a slim
white body that appeared naked in a film made in Paris. An art house
movie directed by her uncle. Every night and every morning when she

steps into the shower, she returns to a scene in the film when she showered with a camera on her side of the curtain. But now she is thinking of a building with a flat roof and three shops, a florist's that sells red flowers only on Tuesdays, an empty room that was formerly filled with brochures for holidays abroad, and an optician's. She knows that if she maintains her pace she will reach her destination in under two minutes. As she is moving more slowly, it is easier to see the streaks of silver in her blonde hair. But there is no one else in the street to observe this. In spite of the heat, the thick green foliage of the trees lining the pavement suggests the dampness of the winter months has yet to be entirely dissipated. The refuse is to be collected today and the front gate of every house has at least one squat black sentry with a topknot on guard next to a wheelie-bin.

She catches sight of the yellow skip and the pile of pink bricks ahead of her and knows there's not much further to go; and indeed it is not long before she opens the door of the optician's (the bell gives its priestly tinkle) and walks over to the reception desk. Although there is no one there, a spectacle case, with a rubber band wrapped around it, is waiting for her. This she slips into her shoulder bag and turns to leave. But before she reaches the front door she hears the sound of someone moving around heavily in the treatment room. She looks at the skeletal frames on display in the racks, the uncomfortable straight-backed chair and the side-table that has no magazines on it. Perhaps she should tell someone that she has collected the glasses. The noise in the treatment room stops. Which would be worse, she wonders: opening the door and seeing no one or finding somebody there?

Even objects he knows to be hard-edged are indistinct. The hotel staff, from Poland, Lithuania and the Tamil-speaking tip of southern India, hover as they walk, their white-sleeved arms blurred like the wings of hummingbirds. The auteur can't read his newspaper, which lies folded on his lap. He is waiting in a fudge-coloured leather armchair in the residents' lounge. His niece has agreed to fetch his glasses (he is shaky, a delayed reaction to his fall) from the optician's and then meet him for lunch. What troubles him most is that he remembers neither the second half of his eye examination nor choosing his frames—or his return to the Acme Hotel. His first recollection is waking in the middle of the night and knowing he has been dreaming about the alphabet: black letters, like those on the treatment chart, swirling in a space as white as snow.

At first light, he wakes up, with a sentence half-formed on his tongue.

A message has been left at the reception desk. His new glasses are ready for collection. Has he already paid the optician? He cannot remember having done so. But now the swing doors of the residents' lounge open and a figure in a blue dress advances (even in the soft world there is a familiarity about her flowing movements) towards him.

He rises and they kiss. (A perfume he doesn't recognize).

"Have you got my…"

"Yes, they are here."

He takes his spectacles and puts them on. The residents' lounge takes a pace sideways. He sees the silvery wires in his niece's blonde hair, scuffed leather on the arms of the sofa; the pattern on the carpet sets in sharply delineated surroundings.

"Do I owe you anything?"

"I don't think so. There was no one there to pay, but since there wasn't a bill I assume you must have paid already. Can't you remember?"

"I've told you—it's all a bit hazy."

As they walk towards the dining room, he remembers the scene in the waterfall: his eighteen-year-old son naked with his niece, the patches of glistening light on their slippery flesh, the sun picking out streaks of lemon and ash in their hair. Their dancing steps in the brilliant white water foaming about their feet. That was the first of his films to be shot in colour. It had something of the freedom of the times, he thought. But later, when his reputation declined, the critics claimed there were scenes that marked his transition from film-maker to pornographer. Such snobs! Why was it that black-and-white had this curious kudos? And as for those people who couldn't distinguish simplicity of vision and candour from pornography…

The *maitre d'* fussing with the chairs. Two enormous menus and a wine list. Would they like a bread and jug of iced water? Olives, perhaps?

"And so he's refusing to meet up tomorrow?" the auteur asks.

"I wouldn't put like that. It's simply not possible. He has other engagements."

"Ah, I see he's punishing me for not turning up yesterday. Didn't you explain to him how badly I was shaken? Since I've come all the way from Paris to meet him, I want to be on reasonable form."

"He's not trying to punish anyone. And he's had to fly from America."

The auteur remembers the ten-year-old who lurked outside his study when he was trying write. Always a creak of the floorboards or a tentative knock at the door just when the words had begun to flow. Of course, it was understandable . So much time had to be spent away, on location or talking to potential backers. And of course, the boy loathed his boarding school.

"Well, tell him it's absolutely necessary that we meet as soon as possible. I've urgent business in France, but it's unthinkable that I should leave without seeing him. Especially as he won't even agree to speak on the phone."

"He's every bit as keen to meet up as you are. He wants an explanation."

A summer afternoon years ago. And a creeping about on the landing outside the study. A deadline for a script and no ideas. What did the child want now? He was good-looking boy in a slightly pale way. Delicate features and enormous blue eyes, but with a sort of shivery sensitivity that was irritating, like a pedigree dog that had been badly inbred. The auteur gave up and they went to the shops and bought comics (*Beano, The Dandy*) and ice creams.

They were in the garage when it happened. The boy had both feet on the floor and one arm trailing slightly behind him when the auteur slammed the door shut. A scream, the fine lines of a face crumpling, jets of tears. The auteur opened the door, took the boy's hand in his: a half moon of hanging flesh, the beginning of the blood grin on a middle finger that would have to be ice-packed and bandaged.

Even now the auteur is not sure whether he did it deliberately.

"An explanation for what? In the circumstances, I'd say that we are the ones who are owed explanations, don't you think?"

"Have you chosen?"

He lifts up the menu, but it's a blur. The glasses aren't bifocals.

The lunch and the wine have made her drowsy. She is not used to being the object of hospitality in the middle of the day. And now it is well past four o'clock and none of the small tasks (the payment of a bill, the visit to the dry cleaners) she set herself have been accomplished. She knows that if she were to change out of her blue dress and shower, or even make herself a cup of tea (fragrant, lemony), she would revive, but she is listless, heavy with the inertia of late afternoon. There are four more days left before she is due to return to the office. Although spending her holiday in the city where she works has had the virtue of economy, she regrets the loss of the two weeks on a Greek island that she had planned.

There is a small patio with plants in terracotta pots and garden furniture bleached by the sun. She pours herself a glass of iced water from the fridge and goes outside.

If she takes her shoes off, she knows the warmth of the flagstones will remind her of the summer she was an actress. The year she was in a film written and directed by her uncle. She remembers the scene, shot from behind, in which she and her cousin are standing on the fringe of the beach: dunes and marram grass beside them, and beyond the full length of the bay at low tide. The sugar-sparkle of white sand. The sheen darkest where the tide last reached. They wriggled out of their clothes. Her cousin was naked first and for a moment he stood beside her. The viewer knew from the angle of his head that he was looking down at her. Waiting for the moment when she too was naked and they would run off together, their footprints the first of the day, the dents almost invisible at first, then slowly darkening until the first wave came dazzling across the breadth of the beach.

What the film will never remember was how the fine the sand was, silkily running through her toes. The first shock of the wave, unexpectedly cold on such a hot day. And later the taste of salt on her cousin's skin.

They were often mistaken for brother and sister. To be close seemed natural.

She sips the water. The sunlight falls on the bench opposite her and the dark shadows of the slats paint the flagstones. At the western edge of the city the evening is gathering melancholy light.

She was just that much older than him, and so it was that she went to his room. The moonlight shone through the blinds, striping his blanket with silver. Then she was with him, skin to skin, both loving as if untarnished.

Later they were told, after the anger, shame and embarrassment subsided, that the children of such close unions are frequently, and quite naturally, stillborn.

At dusk there is a hint of pink in the red brick of the Victorian villas. The trees in the front garden darken and hover, as if about to float towards nightfall. There is no traffic and the auteur is conscious of how his every step rings clearly in the street. Yellow-gold light drenches the lace curtains in front windows. A small wooden summer house is mysterious as a shrine. Then, sooner than expected, he is there. At twilight, the white building looks almost nautical. He would not be surprised to see a funnel appear on the flat roof. Although the florist has closed, the shutters have not been drawn. The auteur can see white flowers pressing against the window pane as if they are the trapped ghosts of seabirds longing for flight.

His appointment with the optician is inconvenient, but tomorrow he is due to fly back to Paris for a meeting on *La Rive Gauche* after he has had lunch with his son. Now that he is no longer rich he can't afford to turn down the optician's offer to replace the lenses without further charge. Contacting him to make this arrangement has not been easy. He'd phoned repeatedly from the Acme Hotel and had no answer. It was late afternoon (past 5 o'clock) before he finally managed to speak to the optician's assistant (her voice distant, muffled, possibly foreign) and he'd had to ask her to repeat what she said several times. But when at last he'd explained his predicament in sufficient detail, she told him that since the optician was working late she would find him an appointment, provided he was prepared to come after eight o'clock.

He is one minute early. Although the front of the shop is in darkness, a cord of light is visible, shining from under the door of the treatment room. He presses a button and waits, but there's no sign anyone is prepared to come out to greet him, although he can hear a ringing. He turns the handle and slips inside: the sound of the bell (a memory of kneeling to pray). At once the door of the treatment room swings open, as if its release has been triggered by his action.

An empty chair held in a cone of light.

"Please go in and take a seat. I'll join you in a minute."

The voice comes from right behind him. Yet this is hardly possible since the auteur has taken no more than a couple of steps into the room. Either the man must have been pressing himself against the inside wall or he has followed him in soundlessly. The auteur begins to turns round and then stops. What if there is no one there? The front door shuts with a sharp click.

"Thank you for agreeing to see me at this late hour," says the auteur, making his way towards the chair.

"Not at all, not at all." The voice is soft, difficult to place.

And now he's in the chair, hands from behind him move the head and chin rests into place. Something is being attached to the top of his skull. He can't remember this happening before.

"What's that?"

"Just a metal cap. Something of my own devising. I use it when I want to make absolutely sure that the head stays completely still. Look upwards and left. And now you'll just feel a puff of air…"

"Are we going to go through the whole thing again? Surely you must have most of the information already."

"Unfortunately my colleague did not keep the notes from your last appointment. No doubt he thought that because you live abroad they would not be needed again."

"And so you're not the optician I saw last time?"

The man laughs lightly, as if acknowledging a whimsical remark made by a small child.

"I assure you I will accept no fee for this appointment."

A test card appears in the mirror; the letters are twigs blurred beneath ice. Lenses change in quick succession until the top two rows sharpen. And then quite plainly, on the third line from the bottom…L O V E.

"Love! It said 'sex' the other day. That's not usual, is it? I mean the letters don't normally spell anything?"

"I'll change the card."

Once again, the auteur begins to read from the top. Everything is much clearer now. He is even able to make out the second to last line without too much difficulty:

"D….A….no, E…A…T…*Sex, Love & Death* . That's the title of one of my films! What's going on here?"

The test card vanishes. He can hear a faint rustling as the optician comes round to the front of the chair. The auteur tries to raise his head so he can see the man's face, but even the slightest movement is impossible. A white shirt and the bottom of a tie come into view.

"I hope my glasses will be ready by tomorrow. Half-past eleven at the latest. I have an urgent meeting with my son before I fly back to Paris. At six in the evening."

How pressing is an engagement with a son who has been dead for thirty years? A son, briefly famous as the co-star of *Desir, l'amour et la mort,* who was supposed have taken his life in the state of Illinois nine months after he had made it plain that he would never speak to his father again. The auteur still has the private detective's report in the bottom drawer of an *escritoire* in Paris. But now his niece has been saying that this was all lies: his son had bribed the detective.

"You can be quite sure that everything will be arranged. Now can you see my middle finger?"

"Yes."

"Tell me what you notice as I move it slowly towards you."

"There's no nail facing me and the remaining three fingers and the thumb have been tucked into the palm of…"

A silver crescent in the flesh, an old wound's emblem.

"I think I'll leave now, if you don't mind."

"If you could stay for a little longer, I'd be grateful. There are a few things I may need to attend to."

The man has moved round to the back of the chair. A cabinet rolling open followed by the reassuringly professional rustle of paper. The auteur sighs and tries to relax. To panic would be unbecoming. Even at the most difficult times on set, he always remained utterly unruffled. The scar could be anybody's scar. As a writer he should know how the alert mind is always ready to find hidden words, however the alphabet is presented. And anyway his film had a French title.

But now there is no sound from behind him. Although he has not heard the creak of the door, he knows the man is no longer in the room. Indeed, he can hear noises coming from the reception area. Furniture is being shifted. He is quite sure the display stands and the uncomfortable chairs are being manoeuvred onto the street. Voices; bottles are being opened. The murmur sounds civilized. Like the opening of an exhibition or a book launch. Then, very faintly, there's a series of gentle chinks. At first he thinks it's merely celebratory: glass glancing convivial glass. But soon the chink changes to a clink and a scrape. Then another clink and scrape. Something is being built. He remembers the bricks and the skip outside. He begins to struggle, and shout and scream, but he is being held fast in the treatment chair. He has never heard himself beg before.

A bright light in the mirror; the test card reappears. For a moment, every vowel and consonant is quite still and he half expects a voice from behind asking him to read, but then the letters whirl and swirl around before finally reassembling themselves: *Desir, l'amour et la mort.* The screen is too narrow for his film, his greatest attempt to fix the permanence of his longings. There will be no images: it is his script. The opening scene is scrolling down. He can no longer see anything in the room except the mirror and its message. Only language moves in the dark. He will fade, walled in with his words.

ISABEL YAP

A Cup of Salt Tears

SOMEONE ONCE TOLD MAKINO THAT WOMEN IN GRIEF are more beautiful. *So I must be the most beautiful woman in the world right now,* she thinks, as she shucks off her boots and leaves them by the door. The warm air of the onsen's changing room makes her skin tingle. She slips off her stockings, skirt, and blouse; folds her underwear and tucks her glasses into her clean clothes; picks up her bucket of toiletries, and enters the washing area. The thick, hot air is difficult to breathe. She lifts a stool from the stack by the door, walks to her favorite spot, and squats down, resting for a few beats.

Kappa kapparatta.

Kappa rappa kapparatta.

She holds the shower nozzle and douses herself in warm water, trying to get the smell of sickness off her skin.

Tottechitteta.

She soaps and shampoos with great deliberation, repeating the rhyme in her head: *kappa snatched; kappa snatched a trumpet. The trumpet blares.* It is welcome nonsense, an empty refrain to keep her mind clear. She rinses off, running her fingers through her sopping hair, before standing and padding over to the edge of the hot bath. It is a blessing this onsen keeps late hours; she can only come once she knows Tetsuya's doctors won't call her. She tests the water with one foot, shuddering at the heat, then slips in completely.

No one else ever comes to witness her grief, her pale lips and sallow skin. Once upon a time, looking at her might have been a privilege; she spent some years smiling within the pages of *Cancam* and *Vivi*, touting crystal-encrusted fingernails and perfectly glossed lips. She never graced a cover, but she did spend a few weeks on the posters for *Liz Lisa* in Shibuya 109. It was different after she got married and left Tokyo, of course. She and Tetsuya decided to move back to her hometown. Rent was cheaper, and there were good jobs for doctors like him. She quickly found work at the bakery, selling melon pan and croissants. Occasionally they visited her mother, who, wanting little else from life, had grown sweet and mellow with age. Makino thought she understood that well; she had been quite content, until Tetsuya fell ill.

She wades to her favorite corner of the bath and sinks down until only her head is above the water. She squeezes her eyes shut. *How long will he live*, she thinks, *how long will we live together?*

She hears a soft splash and opens her eyes. Someone has entered the tub, and seems to be approaching her. She sinks deeper, letting the water cover her upper lip. As the figure nears, she sees its features through the mist: the green flesh, the webbed hands, the sara—the little bowl that forms the top of its head—filled with water that wobbles as it moves. It does not smell of rotting fish at all. Instead, it smells like a river, wet and earthy. Alive. Some things are different: it is more man-sized than child-sized, it has flesh over its ribs; but otherwise it looks just as she always imagined.

"Good evening," the kappa says. The words spill out of its beak, smoothly liquid.

Makino does not scream. She does not move. Instead she looks at the closest edge of the bath, measuring how long her backside will be exposed if she runs. She won't make it. She presses against the cold tile and thinks, *Tetsuya needs me*, thinks, *no, that's a lie, I can't even help him.* Her fear dissipates, replaced by helplessness, a brittle calm.

"This is the women's bath," she says. "The men's bath is on the other side."

"Am I a man?"

She hears the ripples of laughter in its voice, and feels indignant, feels ashamed.

"No. Are you going to eat me?"

"Why should I eat you, when you are dear to me?" Its round black eyes glimmer at her in earnest.

The water seems to turn from hot to scalding, and she stands upright, flushed and dizzy. "I don't know who you are!" she shouts. "Go away!"

"But you do know me. You fell into the river and I buoyed you to safety. You fell into the river and I kissed your hair."

"That wasn't you," she says, but she never did find out who it was. She thinks about certain death; thinks, *is it any different from how I live now?* It can't possibly know this about her, can't see the holes that Tetsuya's illness has pierced through her; but then, what *does* it know?

"I would not lie to you," it says, shaking its head. The water in its *sara* sloshes gently. "Don't be afraid. I won't touch you if you don't wish me to."

"And why not?" She lifts her chin.

"Because I love you, Makino."

She reads to Tetsuya from the book on her lap, even when she knows he isn't listening. He stares out the window with glassy eyes, tracing the movements of invisible birds. The falling snow is delicate, not white so much as the ghost of white, the color of his skin. Tetsuya never liked fairytales much, but she indulges herself, because the days are long, and she hates hospitals. The only things she can bear to read are the stories of her childhood, walls of words that keep back the tide of desperation when Tetsuya turns to her and says, "Excuse me, but I would like to rest now."

It's still better than the times when he jerks and lifts his head, eyes crowding with tears, and says, "I'm so sorry, Makino." Then he attempts to stand, to raise himself from the bed, but of course he can't, and she must rush over and put her hand on his knee to keep him from moving, she must kiss his forehead and each of his wet eyes and tell him, "No, it's all right, it's all right." There is a cadence to the words that makes her almost believe them.

Tetsuya is twelve years her senior. They met just before she started her modeling career. He was not handsome. There was something monkeylike about his features, and his upper lip formed a strange peak over his lower lip. But he was gentle, careful; a doctor-in-training with the longest, most beautiful fingers she has ever seen. He was a guest at the home of her tea ceremony sensei. When she handed the cup to him, he cradled her fingers in his for a moment, so that her skin was trapped between his hands and the hot ceramic. When he raised the drink to his lips, his eyes kept darting to her face, though she pretended not to notice by busying herself with the next cup.

He thanked her then as he does now, shyly, one stranger to another.

She has barely settled in the bath when it appears.

"You've come back," it says.

She shrugs. Her shoulders bob out of the water. As a girl Makino was often chided for her precociousness by all except her mother, who held her own odd beliefs. Whenever they visited a temple, Makino would whisper to the statues, hoping they would give her some sign they existed—a wink, maybe, or a small utterance. Some kind of blessing. She did this even in Tokyo DisneySea, to the statue of Rajah the Tiger, the pet of her beloved Princess Jasmine. There was a period in her life when she wanted nothing more than to be a Disney Princess.

It figures, of course, that the only yōkai that ever speaks to her is a kappa. The tips of its dark hair trail in the water, and its beaklike mouth is half-open in an expression she cannot name. The ceiling lights float gently in the water of its sara.

She does not speak, but it does not go away. It seems content to watch her. *Can't you leave me here, with my grief?*

"Why do you love me?" she asks at last.

It blinks slowly at her, pale green lids sliding over its eyes. She tries not to shudder, and fails.

"Your hips are pale like the moon, yet move like the curves of ink on parchment. Your eyes are broken and delicate and your hands are empty." It drifts closer. "Your hair is hair I've kissed before; I do not forget the hair of women I love."

I am an ugly woman now, she thinks, but looking at its gaze, she doesn't believe that. Instead she says, "Kappa don't save people. They drown them."

"Not I," it says.

Makino does not remember drowning in the river. She does not remember any of those days spent in bed. Her mother told her afterward that a policeman saved her, or it might have been the grocer's son, or a teacher from the nearby elementary school. It was a different story each time. It was only after she was rescued that they finally patched the broken portion of the bridge. But that was so many years ago, a legend of her childhood that was smeared clear by time, whitewashed by age. She told Tetsuya about it once, arms wrapped around his back, one leg between his thighs. He kissed her knuckles and told her she was lucky, it was a good thing she didn't die then, so that he could meet her and marry her and make love to her, the most beautiful girl in the world.

She blinks back tears and holds her tongue.

"I will tell you a fairytale," the kappa says, "Because I know you love fairytales. A girl falls into a river—"

"Stop," she says, "I don't want to hear it." She holds out her hands, to keep it from moving closer. "My husband is dying."

Tetsuya is asleep during her next visit. She cradles his hand in hers, running her thumb over his bony fingers—so wizened now, unable to heal anyone. She recalls the first time she noticed her love for him. She was making koicha, tea to be shared among close companions, under her teacher's watchful gaze. Tetsuya wasn't even present, but she found herself thinking of his teeth, his strange nervous laughter, the last time he took her out for dinner. The rainbow lights of Roppongi made zebra stripes across his skin, but he never dared kiss her, not even when she turned as the train was coming, looking at him expectantly. He never dared look her in the eye, not until she told him she would like to see him again, fingers resting on his sleeve.

She looked down at the tea she was whisking and thought, *this tastes like earth, like the bone marrow of beautiful spirits, like the first love I've yet to have. It is green like the color of spring leaves and my mother's favorite skirt and the skin of a kappa. I'm in love with him.* She whisked the tea too forcefully, some of it splashing over the edge of the cup.

"Makino!" her sensei cried.

She stood, heart drumming in her chest, bowed, apologized, bowed again. The tea had formed a butterfly-shaped splotch on the tatami mats.

Tetsuya's sudden moan jolts her from her thoughts—a broken sound that sets her heart beating as it did that moment, long ago. She spreads her palm over his brow.

Does a kappa grant wishes? Is it a water god? Will it grant my wish, if I let it touch me? Will I let it touch me?

She gives Tetusya's forehead a kiss. "Don't leave me before the New Year," she says. She really means *don't leave me.*

This time, it appears while she's soaping her body.

It asks if it can wash her hair.

She remains crouched on her stool. The suggestion of touch makes her tremble, but she keeps her voice even. "Why should I let you?"

"Because you are dear to me."

"That isn't true," she says. "I do know about you. You rape women and eat organs and trick people to get their shirikodama, and I'm not giving you that, I'm not going to let you stick your hand up my ass. I don't want to die. And Tetsuya needs me."

"What if I tell you I need you? What if I could give you what you want? What if I," it looks down at the water, and for a moment, in the rising mist, it looks like Tetsuya, when she first met him. Hesitant and wondering and clearly thinking of her. Monkeylike, but somehow pleasing to her eyes. "What if I could love you like him?"

"You're not him," she says. Yet when it reaches out to touch her, she does not flinch. Its fingers in her hair are long and slim and make her stomach curl, and she only stops holding her breath when it pulls away.

The grocery is full of winter specials: Christmas cakes, discounted vegetables for nabe hotpot, imported hot chocolate mixes. After Christmas is over, these shelves will be rapidly cleared and filled with New Year specials instead, different foods for osechi-ryori. Her mother was always meticulous about a good New Year's meal: herring roe for prosperity, sweet potatoes for wealth, black soybeans for health, giant shrimp for longevity. They're only food, however; not spells, not magic. She ignores the bright display and walks to the fresh vegetables, looking for things to add to her curry.

She's almost finished when she sees the pile of cucumbers, and ghostlike, over it, the kitchen of her childhood. Mother stands next to her, back curved in concentration. She is carving Makino's name into a cucumber's skin with a toothpick. "We'll throw this in the river," Mother says, "so that the kappa won't eat you."

"Does the kappa only appear in the river, mother? And why would the kappa want to eat me?"

"Because it likes the flesh of young children, it likes the flesh of beautiful girls. You must do this every year, and every time you move. And don't let them touch you, darling. I am telling you this for you are often silly, and they are cruel; do not let them touch you."

"But what if it does touch me, mother?"

"Then you are a foolish girl, and you cannot blame me if it eats up everything inside you."

Young Makino rubs the end of the cucumber.

Is there no way to befriend them, mother? But she doesn't say those words, she merely thinks them, as her mother digs out the last stroke, the tail end of *no* in *Ma-ki-no.*

She frowns at the display, or perhaps at the memory. *If I throw a cucumber in the hot spring it will merely be cooked,* she thinks. She buys a few anyway. At home, she hesitates, and then picks one up and scratches in Tetsuya's name with a knife. She drops it into the river while biking to work the following morning. The rest of them she slices and eats with chilled yogurt.

When it appears next it is close enough that if it reached out it could touch her, but it stays in place.

"Shall I recite some poetry for you?"

She shakes her head. She thinks, *the skins we inhabit and the things we long to do inside them, why are they so different?*

"I don't even know your name," she says.

The way its beak cracks open looks almost like a smile. "I have many. Which would please you?"

"The true one."

It is quiet for a moment, then it says, "I will give you the name I gave the rice farmer's wife, and the shogun's daughter, and the lady that died on the eve of the firebombs."

"Women you have loved?" Her own voice irritates her, thin and breathless in the steam-filled air.

"Women who have called me Kawataro," it says. "Women who would have drowned, had I not saved them and brought them back to life."

"Kawataro," she says, tears prickling at the corner of her eyes. "Kawataro, why did you save me?"

"Kindness is always worth saving."

"Why do you say I am kind?"

It tips its head, the water inside sloshing precariously. It seems to be saying, will you prove me wrong?

She swallows, lightheaded, full of nothing. Her pulse simmers in her ears. She crosses the distance between them and presses herself against its hard body, kisses its hard little mouth. Its hands, when they come up to stroke her back, are like ice in the boiling water.

Kawataro does not appear in the onsen the next time she visits. There are two foreigners sitting in the bath, smiling at her nervously, aware of their own intrusion. The blonde woman, who is quite lovely, chats with Makino in halting Japanese about how cold it is in winter, how there is nothing more delightful than a warm soak, or at least that's what Makino thinks she is saying. Makino smiles back politely, and does not think about the feeling rising in her stomach—a strange hunger, a low ache, a sharp and painful relief.

———

This is not a fairytale, Makino knows, and she is no princess, and the moon hanging in the sky is only a moon, not a jewel hanging on a queen's neck, not the spun silk on a weaver's loom. The man she loves is dying, snowfall is filling her ears, and she is going to come apart unless somebody saves him.

The bakery closes for the winter holiday, the last set of customers buying all the cakes on Christmas Eve. Rui comes over as Makino is removing her apron. "Mizuki-san. Thank you for working hard today." She bows. "I'll be leaving now."

"Thank you for working hard today," Makino echoes. She's not the owner, but she is the eldest of the staff, the one who looks least attractive in their puffy, fluffy uniforms. Rui and Ayaka are college students; Yurina and Kaori are young wives, working while they decide whether they want children. Makino gets along with them well enough, but recently their nubile bodies make her tired and restless.

She never had her own children—a fact that Tetsuya mourned, then forgave, because he had a kind heart, because he knew her own was broken. She used to console herself by thinking it was a blessing, that she could keep her slim figure, but even that turned out to be a lie.

Rui twists her fingers in her pleated skirt, hesitating. Makino braces herself for the question, but it never comes, because the bell over the door rings and a skinny, well-dressed boy steps in. Rui's face breaks into a smile, the smile of someone deeply in love. "Just a minute," she calls to the boy. He nods and brings out his phone, tapping away. She turns back to Makino, and dips her head again.

"Enjoy yourself," Makino says, with a smile.

"Thank you very much. Merry Christmas," Rui answers. Makino envies her; hates her, briefly, without any real heat. Rui whips off her apron, picks up her bag, and runs to the boy. They stride together into the snowy evening.

That night, the foreigners are gone, and Kawataro is back. It tells her about the shogun's daughter. How she would stand in the river and wait for him, her robes gathered around one fist. How her child, when it was born, was green, and how she drowned it in the river, sobbing, before anyone else could find it. How Kawataro had stroked her hair and kissed her cheeks and—Makino doesn't believe this part—how it had grieved for its child, their child, floating down the river.

"And what happened?" Makino says, trailing one finger idly along Kawataro's shoulders. They are sitting together on the edge of the tub, their knees barely visible in the water.

Kawataro's tongue darts over its beak. Makino thinks about having that tongue in her mouth, tasting the minerals of the bathwater in her throat. She thinks about what it means to be held in a monster's arms, what it means to hold a monster. Kappa nappa katta, kappa nappa ippa katta.

Am I the leaf he has bought with sweet words, one leaf of many?

Kawataro turns to her, face solemn as it says, "She drowned herself."

It could not save her, perhaps; or didn't care to, by then? Makino thinks about the shogun's daughter: her bloated body sailing through the water, her face blank in the moonlight, the edges of her skin torn by river dwellers. She thinks of Kawataro watching her float away, head bent, the water in its sara shimmering under the stars.

Katte kitte kutta.

Will I be bought, cut, consumed?

She presses her damp forehead against Kawataro's sleek green shoulder. *Have I already been?*

"How will this story end?" she asks.

It squeezes her knee with its webbed hand, then slips off the ledge into the water, waiting for her to follow. She does.

She spends Christmas Day in the hospital, alternately napping, reading to Tetsuya, and exchanging pleasantries with the doctors and nurses who come to visit. She leans as close as she can to him, as if proximity might leech the pain from his body, everything that makes him ache, makes him forget. It won't work, she knows. She doesn't have that kind of power over him, over anyone. Perhaps the closest she has come to such power is during sex.

The first time she and Tetsuya made love he'd been tender, just as she imagined, his fingers trembling as he undid the hooks of her bra. She cupped his chin and kissed his jaw and ground her hips against his, trying to let him know she wanted this, he didn't need to be afraid. He gripped her hips and she wrapped her legs around him, licking a wet line from his neck to his ear. He carried her to the bed, collapsing so that they landed in a tangled pile, desperately grappling with the remainders of each other's clothing. His breath was ragged as he moved slowly inside her, and she tried not to cry out, afraid of how much she wanted him, how much she wanted him to want her.

On his lips that night her name was a blessing: the chant of monks, the magic spells all fairytales rest on.

Now he stirs, and his eyes open. He says her name with a strange grace, a searching wonder, as if how they came to know each other is a mystery. "Makino?"

"Yes, my darling?"

His breath, rising up to her, is the stale breath of the dying.

"So that's where you are," he says at last. He gropes for her hand and holds it. "You're there, after all. That's good." He pauses, for too long, and when she looks at him she sees he has fallen asleep once more.

The next time they meet, they spend several minutes soaking together in silence.

She breaks it without preamble. "Kawataro, why do you love me?" Her words are spoken without coyness or fear or fury.

"A woman in grief is a beautiful one," it answers.

"That's not enough."

Kawataro's eyes are two black stones in a waterfall of mist. It is a long time before it finally speaks.

"Four girls," it says. "Four girls drowned in three villages, before they fixed the broken parts in the bridges over the river. My river." It extends its hand and touches the space between her breasts, exerting the barest hint of pressure. Her body tenses, but she keeps silent, immobile. "You were the fifth. You were the only one who accepted my hand when I stretched it out. You," it says, "were the only one who let me lay my hands upon you."

The memory breaks over her, unreal, so that she almost feels like Kawataro has cast a spell on her—forged it out of dreams and warped imaginings. The terrible rain. The realization that she couldn't swim. The way the riverbank swelled, impenetrable as death. How she sliced her hand open on a tree root, trying desperately to grab onto something. How she had seen the webbed hand stretched towards her, looked at the gnarled monkey face, sobbed as she clung for her life, river water and tears and rain mingled on her cheeks. How it tipped its head down and let something fall into her gaping, gurgling mouth, to save her.

"I was a stupid little girl," she says. "I could have drowned then, to spare myself this." She laughs, shocking herself; the sound bounces limply against the tiles.

Kawataro looks away.

"You are breaking my heart, Makino."

"You have no heart to break," she says, in order to hurt it; yet she also wants to be near it, wants it to tell her stories, wants its cold body to temper the heat of the water.

It looks to the left, to the right, and it takes a moment for her to realize that it is shaking its head. Then in one swift motion it wraps its arms around her and squeezes, hard, and Makino remembers how kappa like to wrestle, how they can force the life out of horses and cattle by sheer strength. "I could drain you," it says, hissing into her ear. "I could take you apart, if that would help. I could take everything inside you and leave nothing but a hollow shell of your skin. I do not forget kindness, but I will let you forget yours, if it will please you."

Yes, she thinks, and in the same heartbeat, *but no, not like this.*

She pushes against it, and it releases her. She takes several steps back and lifts her head, appraising.

"Will you heal my husband?" she asks.

"Will you love me?" it asks.

The first time she fell in love with Tetsuya, she was making tea. The first time she fell in love, she was drowning in a river.

"I already do."

Kawataro looks at her with its eyes narrowed in something like sadness, if a monster's face could be sad. It bows its head slightly, and she sees the water inside it—everything that gives it strength—sparkling, reflecting nothing but the misted air.

"Come here," it says, quiet and tender. "Come, my darling Makino, and let me wash your back."

Tetsuya drinks the water from Kawataro's sara.

Tetsuya lives.

The doctors cannot stop saying what a miracle it is. They spend New Year's Eve together, eating the osechi-ryori Makino prepared. They wear their traditional attire and visit the temple at midnight, and afterward they watch the sunrise, holding each other's cold hands.

It is still winter, but some stores have already cleared space for their special spring bargains. Makino mouths a rhyme as she sets aside ingredients for dinner. Tetsuya passes her and kisses her cheek, thoughtlessly. He is on his way to the park for his afternoon walk.

"I'm leaving now," he says.

"Come back safely," she answers. She feels just as much affection for Tetsuya as she did before, but nothing else. Some days her hollowness frightens her. Most days she has learned to live with it.

When the door shuts behind him, she spends some moments in the kitchen, silently folding one hand over the other. She decides to take a walk. Perhaps after the walk she will visit her mother. She puts a cucumber and a paring knife into her bag and heads out. By now the cold has become bearable, like the empty feeling in her chest. She follows the river towards the bridge where she once nearly lost her life.

In the middle of the bridge she stands and looks down at the water. She has been saved twice now by the same monster. Twice is more than enough. With a delicate hand, she carves the character for love on the cucumber, her eyes blurring, clearing. She leans over the bridge and lets the cucumber fall.

CONTRIBUTORS

Kathe Koja's 16 novels include *The Cipher, Skin Buddha Boy, Talk,* and the Under the Poppy trilogy (*Under the Poppy, The Mercury Waltz,* and *The Bastards' Paradise*). Her work has been multiply translated and optioned for film. She creates immersive events with her performance ensemble, *nerve.*

Michael Kelly is the Series Editor for the *Year's Best Weird Fiction.* He's been a finalist for the World Fantasy Award, the Shirley Jackson Award, and the British Fantasy Society Award. His fiction has appeared in a number of journals and anthologies, including Black Static, Best New Horror, Postscripts, and Supernatural Tales. He is the proprietor of Undertow Publications.

Nathan Ballingrud is the author of *North American Lake Monsters: Stories,* from Small Beer Press; and *The Visible Filth,* a novella from This Is Horror. His work has appeared in numerous Year's Best anthologies, and he has twice won the Shirley Jackson Award. He lives with his daughter in Asheville, NC.

Siobhan Carroll's research has required many tea sessions at the Scott

Polar Research Institute and much time spent squinting at explorers' handwriting. However, 'Wendigo Nights' represents the first time the Arctic appears in her fiction. She suspects this development triggered the 2014 discovery of the HMS Erebus through some mysterious entanglement of the universe. When not globetrotting in search of dusty tomes, she lives and lurks in Delaware. Her other fiction can be found in magazines like *Beneath Ceaseless Skies* and *Lightspeed*. For more, visit http://voncarr-siobhan-carroll.blogspot.com/

Michael Cisco is the author of novels *The Divinity Student* (Buzzcity Press, 1999, winner of the International Horror Writers Guild award for best first novel of 1999), *The Tyrant* (Prime, 2004), *The San Veneficio Canon* (Prime, 2005), *The Traitor* (Prime, 2007), *The Narrator* (Civil Coping Mechanisms, 2010), *The Great Lover* (Chomu Press, 2011), *Celebrant* (Chomu Press, 2012), and *Member* (Chomu Press 2013). His short story collection, *Secret Hours*, was published by Mythos Press in 2007. His scholarly work has appeared in *Lovecraft Studies*, *The Weird Fiction Review*, *Iranian Studies*, and *Lovecraft and Influence*.

Considered a modern master of the short story, and one of the founders of the Latin American Boom, Julio Cortázar was an Argentine novelist, short story writer, poet, translator, and essayist. Born in 1914, Cortázar died in 1984.

Amanda C. Davis has an engineering degree and a fondness for baking, gardening, and low-budget horror films. Her work has appeared in *Crossed Genres*, *Shock Totem*, *Goblin Fruit*, and others. She tweets enthusiastically as @davisac1. You can find out more about her and read more of her work at http://www.amandacdavis.com.

K.M. Ferebee's work has appeared or is forthcoming in *Lady Churchill's Rosebud Wristlet*, *Strange Horizons*, *Shimmer*, and *Tor.com*. Formerly a musician with the band Beirut, she holds an MFA in Creative Writing from The Ohio State University, where she is currently pursuing a PhD in Rhetoric. She can usually be found on the Internet.

Karen Joy Fowler has written literary, contemporary, historical, and science fiction. She's published three collections of short stories, most recently *What I Didn't See*. Her novels include *Sarah Canary* and *The Jane Austen Book Club*. Her last novel to date, *We Are All Completely Besie Ourselves*, won the 2013 PEN/Faulkner, the California Book Award, and was shortlisted for the Man Booker in 2014. She lives in Santa Cruz, California.

Two-time winner of the John Dryden Translation prize, Clarion alum Edward Gauvin has received fellowships from the NEA, PEN America, the CNL, ALTA, and the French Embassy. His books include Georges-Olivier Châteaureynaud's selected stories, *A Life on Paper* (Small Beer, 2010), winner of the Science Fiction & Fantasy Translation Award, and Jean Ferry's *The Conductor and Other Tales* (Wakefield, 2013). His work has been nominated for the French-American Foundation Translation Prize, the Oxford-Weidenfeld Translation Prize, and the Best Translated Book Award.

Vince Haig does design, layout, and illustrative work. Find out more at barquing.com

Cat Hellisen lives near the sea in Cape Town, South Africa. She is the author of the fantasy novels *When the Sea is Rising Red, House of Sand and Secrets*, and *Beastkeeper*. She likes Bloody Marys, miserable folk songs, and long walks in nuclear fallout.

Kima Jones has received fellowships from PEN Center USA Emerging Voices, Kimbilio Fiction and The MacDowell Colony. She has been published at *Guernica*, NPR, *PANK* and *The Rumpus* among others. Kima lives in Los Angeles and is writing her first poetry collection, *The Anatomy of Forgiveness*.

Caitlín R. Kiernan is a two-time recipient of both the World Fantasy and Bram Stoker awards, and the *New York Times* has declared her "one of our essential writers of dark fiction." Her recent novels include *The Red Tree* and *The Drowning Girl: A Memoir*, and, to date, her short stories have been collected in twelve volumes, including *Tales of Pain and Wonder, A is for Alien, The Ammonite Violin & Others,* and the World Fantasy Award winning *The Ape's Wife and Other Stories.* Currently she's editing her thirteenth, fourteenth, and fifteenth collections—*Beneath an Oil Dark Sea: The Best of Caitlín R. Kiernan (Volume 2)* and *Cambrian Tales* (Subterranean Press) and *Houses Under the Sea: Mythos Tales* (Centipede Press). She has recently concluded *Alabaster,* her award-winning, three-volume graphic novel for Dark Horse Comics. She is working on a screenplay and will soon begin work on her next novel, *Interstate Love Song.* She lives in Providence, Rhode Island.

Born in Poland and educated at the Polytechnic Institute in Wroclaw, Tomasz Alen Kopera now lives and works in Northern Ireland. His work is inspired mainly by surrealism and symbolism. He is fascinated with the work of famous painters such as Z.Beksinski, J.Malczewski and H.R.Giger. He is a talented and skilled artist, whose already developed artistic workshop convinces about high susceptibility; what is more, accuracy of drawing and his unique perception of colours are of the highest artistic level. "Throughout my works I try to reach and influence human sub-consciousness. I always wish to embrace the viewer's attention for a while; to evoke necessity for contemplation, thinking and considering.I hope to have created some specific climate of anxiety and mystery at the same time. The subjects of my paintings are connected with visualisation of reality, with variety of emotions and sometimes with fears I experience in every day life. It happens that my works awake negative feelings and, to some extent that is intended; but what really matters is the rule to affect senses by contrasts. Eventually I would like the viewer to find positive aspects of life." His new paintings are eagerly sought by a growing body of fine art collectors both in his native Poland, Ireland and Great Britain. His work was also recently accepted for inclusion in the 124th Royal Ulster Academy of Arts Annual Exhibition in Belfast.

Rich Larson was born in West Africa, has studied in Rhode Island and Edmonton, Alberta, and at 23 now works in a small Spanish town outside Seville. His short work has been nominated for the Theodore Sturgeon and appears in multiple Year's Best anthologies, as well as in magazines such as *Asimov's, Clarkesworld, F&SF, Interzone, Strange Horizons, Lightspeed, BCS* and *Apex.* Find him at richwlarson.tumblr.com

Carmen Maria Machado is a fiction writer, critic, and essayist whose work has appeared in *The New Yorker, Granta, The Paris Review, AGNI,* NPR, *The American Reader, Los Angeles Review of Books, VICE,* and elsewhere. Her stories have been reprinted in several anthologies, including *Best American Science Fiction & Fantasy 2015* and *Best Women's Erotica.* She has been the recipient of the Richard Yates Short Story Prize, a Millay Colony for the Arts residency, the CINTAS Foundation Fellowship in Creative Writing, and a Michener-Copernicus Fellowship, and has been nominated for a Nebula Award and the Shirley Jackson Award. She is a graduate of the Iowa Writers' Workshop and the Clarion Science Fiction & Fantasy Writers' Workshop, and lives in Philadelphia with her partner.

Usman T. Malik is a Pakistani writer resident in Florida. His fiction has won the Bram Stoker Award and been nominated for the Nebula. His novella *The Pauper Prince and the Eucalyptus Jinn* is out at Tor.com. In 2013, he led Pakistan's first speculative fiction workshop in Lahore in conjunction with Desi Writers Lounge. He can be found on Twitter @usmantm

Nick Mamatas is the author of several novels, including *Love is the Law* and *The Last Weekend,* and over one hundred pieces of short fiction. His stories have appeared in *Weird Tales, Asimov's Science Fiction, Best American Mystery Stories* and many other magazines and anthologies. Nick works as an editor for VIZ Media, and recently co-edited the anthology of Japanese SF/fantasy crime fiction, *Hanzai Japan.* His fiction, non-fiction, and editorial work has been nominated for the Hugo, World Fantasy, Shirley Jackson, and Bram Stoker Awards.

Sunny Moraine's short fiction has appeared in *Clarkesworld, Strange Horizons, Nightmare, Shimmer,* and *Long Hidden: Speculative Fiction from the Margins of History,* among many other places. They are also responsible for the novel trilogies *Casting the Bones* and *Root Code.* Her first collection of short fiction, *Singing With All My Skin and Bone*, is due out in 2016. They unfortunately live just outside Washington DC in a creepy house with two cats and a very long-suffering husband.

Heir to Jean Ray and Thomas Owen, Jean Muno, born in 1924, is considered the greatest of Belgium's Silver Age fabulists. A member of Belgium's Royal Academy of Language and Literature, Muno is the author of nine novels and four short story collections. In 1979 he received the Prix Rossel. He died in 1988.

Sarah Pinsker's fiction has appeared in *Asimov's, Strange Horizons, Fantasy & Science Fiction, Uncanny,* and *Lightspeed,* and in anthologies including *Long Hidden* and *Accessing the Future.* Her novelette, "In Joy, Knowing the Abyss Behind," won the 2014 Sturgeon Award and was a Nebula finalist. She is also a singer/songwriter and toured nationally behind three albums on various independent labels. A fourth is forthcoming. She lives in Baltimore, Maryland and can be found online at sarahpinsker.com and twitter.com/sarahpinsker

Karin Tidbeck is the award-winning author of *Jagannath: Stories* and the novel *Amatka.* She lives and works in Malmö, Sweden, where she makes a living as a freelance writer. She writes in Swedish and English, and has published work in *Weird Tales, Tor.com, Words Without Borders* and anthologies like *Fearsome Magics* and *The Time-Traveler's Almanac.*

Charles Wilkinson's publications include *The Pain Tree and Other Stories* (London Magazine Editions, 2000). His stories have appeared in *Best Short Stories 1990* (Heinemann), *Best English Short Stories 2* (W.W. Norton, USA), *Unthology* (Unthank Books), *Best British Short Stories 2015* (Salt), *London Magazine, Under the Radar, Able Muse Review* (USA), *Ninth Letter* (USA) *The Sea in Birmingham* (TSFG) and in genre magazines/ anthologies such as *Supernatural Tales, Horror Without Victims* (Megazanthus Press), *Rustblind and Silverbright* (Eibonvale Press), *Theaker's Quarterly Fiction, Phantom Drift* (USA), *Bourbon Penn* (USA) and *Shadows & Tall Trees* (Canada). *Ag & Au,* a pamphlet of his poems, has come out from

Flarestack and his new short stories are forthcoming in *Prole* and *Night-script* (USA). He lives in Powys, Wales, where he is heavily outnumbered by member of the ovine community.

Isabel Yap writes fiction and poetry, works in the tech industry, and drinks tea. Born and raised in Manila, she has also lived in California, Tokyo (for 96 days!), and London. In 2013 she attended the Clarion Writers Workshop. Her stories have appeared in *Tor.com*, *Shimmer*, *Interfictions Online*, *Nightmare*, and *The Best of Philippine Speculative Fiction 2005-2010*. She has a short fiction series forthcoming from Book Smugglers Publishing. She is @visyap on Twitter and her website is isalikeswords.wordpress.com.

Copyright Acknowledgements

YEAR'S BEST
WEIRD FICTION
VOLUME ONE

EDITED BY
LAIRD BARRON
AND MICHAEL KELLY

Year's Best Weird Fiction, Volume One

"Well, it's a triumph. A really well-assembled collection,
which succeeds in distinguishing itself from the best horror and
best fantasy anthologies with an eclectic table of contents."

—Nathan Ballingrud, author of North American Lake Monsters

Oct. 2014   www.undertowbooks.com

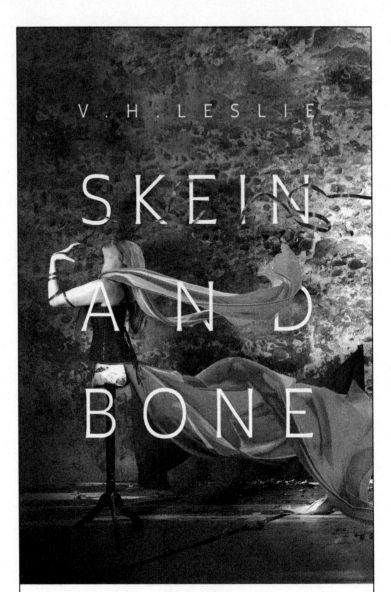

V . H . L E S L I E

SKEIN
AND
BONE

Skein and Bone

"An absorbing and gorgeously unsettling collection."

—Alison Moore, The Lighthouse, (Short-Listed for the Man-Booker)

August 2015   www.undertowbooks.com

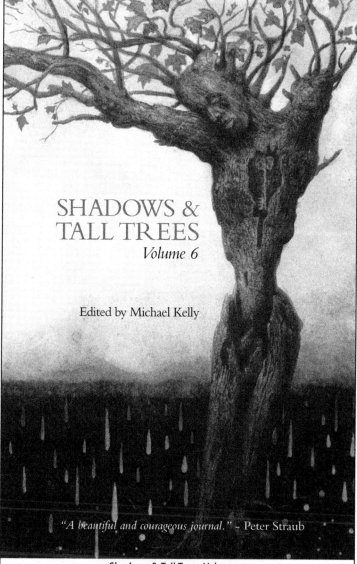

SHADOWS &
TALL TREES
Volume 6

Edited by Michael Kelly

"A beautiful and courageous journal." - Peter Straub

Shadows & Tall Trees, Volume 6

(Shirley Jackson Award Nominee, Edited Anthology)

"A beautiful and courageous volume."

—Peter Straub, author of Ghost Story

March 2014   www.undertowbooks.com

CPSIA information can be obtained at www.ICGtesting.com
Printed in the USA
BVOW08s1605310716

457186BV00026B/25/P